THE BOOK
OF RECORDS

THE BOOK
OF RECORDS

A NOVEL

MADELEINE
THIEN

W. W. NORTON & COMPANY

Independent Publishers Since 1923

Copyright © 2025 by Madeleine Thien

All rights reserved
Printed in the United States of America
First Edition

For information about permission to reproduce selections from this book, write to Permissions, W. W. Norton & Company, Inc., 500 Fifth Avenue, New York, NY 10110

For information about special discounts for bulk purchases, please contact W. W. Norton Special Sales at specialsales@wwnorton.com or 800-233-4830

Manufacturing by Lakeside Book Company

ISBN 978-1-324-07865-4

W. W. Norton & Company, Inc., 500 Fifth Avenue, New York, NY 10110
www.wwnorton.com

W. W. Norton & Company Ltd., 15 Carlisle Street, London W1D 3BS

1 0 9 8 7 6 5 4 3 2 1

In memory of Y-Dang Troeung, 1980–2022

⚬⚬⚬⚬⚬

I require a Thou to become; becoming I, I say Thou.
All actual life is encounter.
—MARTIN BUBER, *I and Thou*

CONTENTS

∞∞∞∞

LINA

1.

Half a century ago, during the rainy season, when I was seven years old, my father and I reached the Sea. It was evening and the buildings were coloured glass against the night. I remember that we disembarked into water, we crossed the sand, we entered a pale door of the Sea. Inside, the hallways were noisy and hot, there were people everywhere, and I wanted to escape to the open air. But my father found a room in which we and others could shelter. For a day, perhaps even two, I slept.

When I awoke, I saw my father standing at the window, mesmerized by something I couldn't see or hear. His yellow sweater glowed in the blue light.

Within days, the people we had met on our voyage began to depart. They crowded onto small boats which carried them out to cargo ships which, little by little, slid behind the horizon. But we remained. My father had been ill and needed time to recover. Next week, he said, or the week after, we would set off again, and rejoin those who had gone ahead.

Near the beach, by an entrance known as West Gate, the rooms were full, but further away we discovered abandoned buildings. Every night, we moved deeper into the enclave. According to rumours, this place had started as a military outpost. The empire to which it belonged had crumbled and the outpost, over centuries, had fallen outside the control of nearby countries, becoming a no man's land. People who needed to disappear, or who had no other nation, began to take refuge here; they constructed dwellings atop dwellings, until hundreds of buildings appeared to wrap around, and even through, one another. These people named their home the Sea. But that was long ago and the former inhabitants, as many as sixty thousand, had scattered to places unknown.

Whole buildings now stood deserted, their roofs collapsed by storms. Some had a feeling of permanent night; some became lively neighbourhoods, brought momentarily to life by families who arrived and departed together. Several times, my father and I walked for hours, never turning or doubling back, but somehow found ourselves standing back at West Gate. It was impossible. We learned that the simplest way to navigate the enclave was over the rooftops, which made a kind of patchwork road across the Sea.

One afternoon, we explored a staircase that seemed to branch into itself. I had the sensation that if I turned around, I would be behind or even above us, as if I were falling at different speeds. Full of wonder, I asked my father, "Where are we now?"

He looked out a round window. "The northern perimeter, I think . . . but I'm not sure."

"Why does it look like this?" The staircase, despite being solid, felt like air or emptiness.

My father examined the green-tiled walls. "It's another time."

"Like another time zone?"

"Something like that. The body of water outside, Lina, what is it?"

"The South China Sea."

My father nodded. "That's what I think, too. But others might tell you something different."

That night, I met a couple who were selling lengths of cotton cloth. When I asked about the view from their window, the man said, "The Baltic Sea. I would know that blue anywhere." The woman eyed me warily and wouldn't answer.

Undeterred, I struck up conversations with everyone I met, always steering us towards this question. Most gave me a pitying smile, as if this were the kind of thing only a young girl, severed from reality, could ask. But others hesitated, as if I were daring them to tell an outright lie or to cup a river in their hands. One woman thumped her cane on the floor and huffed, "It's the Atrai River where the water reaches the Dhepa valley. Don't they teach you kids geography?"

Another, bored, said, "The Atlantic, what else!"

No one I met intended to stay longer than necessary. The Sea was just one stop on the way to a better place.

Around us, the water was rarely at peace. Waves became mountains became valleys; it was the back of a giant creature whose scales rippled the sky. A blue shadow floated on the horizon, and I believed it must be the country we'd left behind. Already, my memories of the city of Foshan were fading. When I tried to picture the faces of my mother, aunt and older brother, it felt as if someone were pressing my eyes closed.

I spent hours contemplating the horizon, looking for an answer. Finally I asked my father, "Where does this water belong? If it isn't the South China Sea, what is it?"

"I already told you. The buildings of the Sea are made of time."

I was seven years old. I knew that he was pulling my leg and also that he was being truthful.

He tried to explain. He told me that everything would be obvious if I took a piece of string and folded it over and through itself to form a double coin knot. I studied his haggard face, his black-rimmed glasses stained by dust, his ruffling hair which, in a matter of months, had gone completely grey. "The string is time and the knot is space," he concluded. "But they're the same. See?"

A knock rattled our door. A man appeared, dressed head to foot in beige. He was accompanied by four small children, who clung like wings to every part of him. The man said he needed help repairing the cistern on an adjoining roof. He disappeared down the stairs, his voice echoing up. "It's a catastrophe for people like you and me. An ending. But children adapt more easily. These days, not knowing is their fortune."

We'd been in the Sea a month when we discovered an area that seemed better maintained than others. Up on the highest floor, at the top of twelve narrow staircases, was a furnished room that had two windows. Sunlight entered from the north and west, and met like two rivers in the middle of the floor.

"What do you think?"

I stood in a burst of sunshine. "The red curtains are pretty."

My father told me to stay put while he went to collect our things.

The room had a table, bed, chesterfield, and a squat bookshelf. I climbed onto the table and lost myself to the view. Outside, it stormed, but people waited stubbornly in the open, unwilling to lose their places on the sand. When the boats arrived, families had to fight for passage; their greatest fear was to be divided. Time passed and the world softened like a smudge in the rain. All the boats filled and departed, scavengers emerged to find abandoned treasure, and the shore was soon swept clean. The sky brightened. Finally my father returned, carrying our belongings. He told me that he had taken the most direct path over the rooftops, but it was still more than an hour's walk from here to West Gate.

I pointed at the horizon. "There," I said, unable to contain my relief. "Look how close Foshan is. Just beyond that ship."

My father peered out.

All we had to do was stand perfectly still and let the past catch up to us. This was what I wanted to say even though I didn't have the words.

"That isn't Foshan," he said. "That isn't even land." Exhausted, he lowered himself into one of the chairs. "Lina, don't upset yourself. You'll never be content if you can't separate what you want from *what really is*. This world isn't what you wish it to be, this world is more than we can begin to imagine, and sometimes I think it's more than we deserve." He flushed. His illness, when it flared, caused stabbing pains in his chest. His whole body hunched forward as if to protect itself.

Ashamed, I ran to fetch him water.

That night, we unpacked; it took just a few minutes. Dad put our three books on the shelf beside the vegetable peeler and the cleaver, next to our family photo. Nearly fifty years stand between then and now, but his words approach me like a warning. *The world we deserve. The world we can imagine.* They are a map and a caution as I try, once more, to find the Sea.

In Foshan, my father had been a systems engineer managing the structures of cyberspace. He had worked for the government and, later, against it. He wouldn't talk about my mother or aunt or brother. Instead he repeatedly told me that exile was a blessing because we had freed ourselves from an empire in ruins, a hall of mirrors in which good people could betray themselves and never even know it.

"From now on," he liked to say, "not a single hour will go to waste. We belong to a new world."

Dad would follow this speech by tending to everything in our room, a mix of precious things from Foshan and practical items we'd collected along the way: the green tablecloth sewn by Aunt Oh; the bedspread with its pattern of southern constellations; a bag of clothing; four plates, two cups, and so on.

I hope that, even now, the beautiful tablecloth and bedspread enrich some other family's life. When I left the Sea, I carried only what I couldn't leave behind. My father's notebooks, for instance, with their equations and writings, their covers emblazoned with the purple logo of Tsinghua University and its motto, *Self-Discipline and Social Commitment*. I also kept our surviving family photo. In it, my brother Wei is pretending to be a robot; my father has an arm around Aunt Oh, who leans on her cane; and Mom is holding a potted plant in one arm and me in the other. Wei is nine and I am six. Studying the photo, I can feel the ghostly warmth of my mother's touch, and the way her thumb absent-mindedly strokes my shoulder. In the sky above us, the white dome of the People's Hall of the Greater Bay Area curves like a shell.

On the twelfth floor of the Sea, this photo had stood on our shelf, next to the only three books we'd packed. The books had been part of a collection of ninety books, *The Great Lives of Voyagers*, which had obsessed my brother. The two of us had spent hours re-enacting its adventures. Wei cast me in challenging roles—warlord, councillor, tiger—and we would wrestle one another to the ground, shout curses, eat banquets, and engage in death-defying tests of courage. My brother read me to sleep each night, even describing the pictures if my eyes started to close. Beneath his voice, I'd drift in and out of dreams. Each book in the series opened with the same epigraph,

Being forbidden to show gratitude for your services, I leave you my one remaining possession and my best: the pattern of my life.

When we left Foshan, Dad had packed Volumes 3, 70 and 84. I wished he'd taken number 1, about the Ming dynasty sailor Zheng He. Or 23, on the tireless wanderer Ibn Battuta. The illustrations in those volumes still blaze in my memory. And, given his own scientific passions, why hadn't he chosen number 6, Albert Einstein, or 11, about the invention of algebra? Even now, I can hear my brother reading the first line: "Few details of the Persian al-Khwarizmi's life are known with certainty." My father protested that, in the chaos of flight, he hadn't even looked at the titles. He'd passed over the most battered volumes, grabbing ones that looked untouched or barely read; otherwise the choice was pure accident.

In the weeks after we left Foshan, my father read these books to me in order. Number 3 was about Du Fu, the poet. Number 70 was Baruch Spinoza, a philosopher. Number 84 was Hannah Arendt, a writer. Dad said these people had each, at different times, been figures of fascination in the People's Republic of China. *The Great Lives of Voyagers* had foot-long maps you could unfold. The chapters kept you on the edge of your seat by describing narrow escapes, crushing heartaches, assassination attempts, and horrible betrayals. Sometimes my father would interrupt his reading and say, "That can't be right." Or he'd burst out laughing, slap his knee and say, "Who makes this stuff up?" When I complained that number 70 barely left his hometown, my father said that voyages were not just about sea crossings and interstellar exploration, but journeys of the mind.

On the back cover, the series promised that if you read every volume, you would become an educated person. I longed for the other books with a kind of furious, greedy hunger.

But what my father had said was true: departing Foshan had been chaotic. We had fled first by car and then by boat, arriving in one besieged place after another. I saw things that time has not erased. The old man who lost everyone except a white bird who knew hundreds of words, and who reminisced with him about his family. I never knew the man's name but I remember the bird was called Bohu. One morning, the man woke to find that someone had opened the cage, tried to steal the creature, and left it nearly dead. The old man raged and wept as if calling out for his only child among the ruins. Or the boy, Reza, who played the santur, a type of zither which was like a guzheng, but with a completely different spirit. He could strike the strings with such speed and beauty, the music created worlds more real than the ground itself. He disappeared and was presumed drowned. People took the musical instrument apart. They fought over the wood and strings, and all the decorative pieces in the shape of roses. A few weeks later, the boy returned with a completely different name, and he didn't seem to remember that he'd ever been a musician. But one day he saw one of the santur's roses on a necklace worn by a young girl. He snatched it from her neck so violently she cried out in pain. When the girl fought to get the necklace back, he fell to his knees and began to weep, but wouldn't relinquish it, no matter what anyone said or did. The truth was, almost everyone was more forsaken than us. To stop my questions—"Is Mom coming to meet us?" "Where is Wei?" "Is someone after us?"—Dad read to me. He pretended that, along with *The Great Lives of Voyagers*, we were participants in the most consequential adventures of our times. These blue-covered books were a net that would suspend us outside the present. Later on, when I was capable of reading them for myself, I discovered that my father had added episodes that were not in the books. He had made things up and thereby slowed time down, ensuring that no matter how long our journey lasted, we'd never run out of history, no matter how true or inaccurate it was.

During our first year in the Sea, the buildings around West Gate filled and emptied. Initially, there was a makeshift school, run by the Foshan Benevolent Association before it eventually dissolved and was replaced by another, also temporary, group. The kids and I invented games and told each other epic tales of flight and escape. We said we would certainly meet again: all roads converge and this was just one step on the ladder of departure. Everyone insisted the Sea was a nothing place. Unless someone was too old to continue, or too sick like my father, they left at once, thankful to get away.

In the second year, I started working as an errand runner and helper. Little by little, I stopped frequenting the school. For stretches of time, there were no teachers and no books, and I envied the other children their departures. I consoled myself by loving the Sea. The enclave had hallways made of hallways, and my father and I kept stumbling into new areas. I collected known things—water filters, spare parts for generators, extra clothes and so on—and also unusual things, items mysterious to me until I met someone eager to trade for them: woodblocks for paper and fabric printing, an inclinometer, an egg-poaching pan, a travelling desk, and, once, a tomb guardian. Out on the beaches, along with kelp and sea life, edible and useful things washed in. I was proud to have a function, trading what we gathered for medicine and necessities, and earning money through all kinds of chores. I learned to make paper from scraps and from milkweed. Paper was needed for everything from letters to cigarettes to rags to fuel, and it was rare to find an intact book or even an old magazine.

My father said that, after the next rainy season, we, too, would depart. Year after year he made this promise. He suffered from congestive heart failure, which he assured me could be managed by rest and time. I didn't doubt him. Still, there were days when the palpitations were so strong, and his body so weak, that he didn't rise from bed. My father was an anomaly in the Sea, young enough to move on yet unable to do so.

Lately, a dream that visited me regularly in childhood has returned. The passage of time has not faded it, which I find both troubling and remarkable.

In the dream, my mother and I are in a train that streams beside the river in Foshan. The train is unbearably crowded. For reasons I can never see, the train seems to lift. I am pulled from the ground and hurled forward. My mother grips my arm but I know the crowd is squeezing us into oblivion. My mother holds on to me with superhuman strength but I'm the one who breaks:

my shoulder snaps and I begin to scream. I am looking into her eyes when she lets go. This is the worst moment. And then, somehow, someone plucks me from the air and runs with me. I'm overwhelmed by grief, confusion and also hope, because I'm flying. The train is now the wind and I never see this stranger. During this long escape, the dream collapses and I jolt awake. When I touch my arms and shoulders, expecting to feel bruises or broken bones, there's nothing. But for a few precious moments, and despite the pain, I feel my mother holding me and, simultaneously, the sensation of flight.

Each time, I wake and gaze into the dark, weeping not from fear but from unabated love. Is the dream about an ending or salvation? Is it a memory or a premonition? I hear my brother reading me to sleep, and feel certain we are on the verge of meeting again.

One day, I was studying *The Great Lives of Voyagers*, which I had read so many times I could recite the pages from memory. By then, we had been living in the Sea for three years and I was almost ten years old. A pinkish light fell across the volume in my hand, number 84. On the inside cover my brother Wei had written the word *voyage* over and over:

航海
航海
航海

The characters, tilting and swaying, joined the words háng and hǎi, *vessel* and *ocean*.

I showed it to my father. "Do voyages always involve the ocean?"

He was working on his equations and his proofs zigzagged across the page. "Not always, though human life is only possible thanks to water." He slid his glasses up onto his forehead and pinched the bridge of his nose. "Your brother once told me the earth is three-quarters water, and even a person is mostly water."

"How did he know that?"

"School, I suppose."

"Sounds nice." All I had were these three books, which my father said were filled with exaggerations, errors and outright lies.

Annoyed, he said, "I'm teaching you all the time."

I held up Volume 84 and showed him how the pages were falling out. "Your life has had so many obstacles, you could be a hero in *The Great Lives of Voyagers*." I knew my father would have been an orphan if not for Aunt Oh. She had taken him in when he was nine, sacrificing everything for his education. In Beijing he'd studied systems engineering, completing his Ph.D. at Tsinghua University when he twenty-four. The government recruited him when he was still a student.

"I've lived some dramatic moments but that's not the same as living a great life. What's a good life? A series of exploits? I mean, is a celebrated existence the same as a good one?"

His pencil scratched the smoothness of the page.

"Well," I said finally. "Is it?"

My father looked up, as if surprised to find me still there. Impatiently, he flipped the page and all the numbers disappeared. "What is great? What is good?" The word *good* clattered like a coin on a metal dish. "The truth is, Lina, I'm the last person who could tell you. So what *good* is this father?" Gently, as if against his will, he pulled the page loose from his notebook and set it aside. I knew better than to push him further.

2.

The next day was the one when things began to change. Wandering up from the eleventh floor, I noticed a doorway I hadn't seen before. I turned the handle, but it was stuck and I had to jiggle it for a long time to get it open. Once it did, the click filled my ears like a bell.

I went through. The walls fell away and I was in an atrium. Cracks let in particles of light which seemed to rush along the floor like a river. I stepped into it. The Sea was like this everywhere, turning over on itself like a tangled ribbon.

An old man was watering a row of potted plants. He was wearing a green housecoat over pyjamas and battered cloth slippers on his feet. He set down his watering can and attempted to lift the heaviest pot. Without looking up, he called out, "Aduan, I need help with this."

It was a ficus, identical to the one in our family photo. The grandfather was thin, even gaunt, and had toothpick legs, but together we managed to lift the plant and move it to a sunnier spot. Straightening, he looked at me.

"But where's Aduan?" he said, startled. "Isn't he back yet?"

I'd never met anyone with that name. "Does he live on this floor?"

"He's checking the cistern. It must be more damaged than we thought."

The old man was winded by our effort so I lent him my arm. His grey beard, long as a plume, was impractical yet beautiful.

Together we made our shuffling way into his room. To our left was a painting of a galloping horse; the opposite wall had a round window. On the lone table, writing brushes stood tall in a yellow pot next to a dish of ink.

He gave me another curious look. "You must be looking for Bento. He gets all the visitors. What's your name again?"

"Lina."

"Lina, Lina . . . in 12/C, right? That's a very good room. Two big windows. Your father, isn't he the shipwright?"

"No, he's a security engineer. He was an expert on cyberspace." The old man didn't recognize the word I'd used, so I offered my father's definition. "Cyberspace is like an ocean you can hold in the palm of your hand."

"Really? You have the face of a southerner. I bet you come from somewhere below the Yangtze."

"That's right! We came from the Pearl River Delta."

"Has the war spread so far?"

"No, it was because of Daybreak." He looked bewildered so I said, "People had to relocate after the borders were redrawn. A hundred thousand kilometres were returned to the water." I didn't feel like talking about this, and fell silent.

"You're alone, no brothers, no sisters?"

"I have a brother but I don't know where he is."

"When the rebellion started," he said, "people were driven this way and that . . . it was a nightmare. My wife and kids disappeared. For two years, I barely slept. The rumours were crushing, it was like they died a hundred times. But our family was reunited. I hope that will happen to you, too."

"Are you—"

"The others call me Jupiter. The fattest planet!" He slapped his skinny belly and laughed at his own joke. But then his face grew discontented, as if he'd eaten food gone cold. "Jupiter is the God of the Year," he said. "Do you know him?"

"Not really."

"He's the only god who has to pack up his house every spring. The almanac tells him where to go."

"Oh . . . I guess you haven't been in the Sea long?"

Instead of replying, the old man picked up a shell from his table and offered it to me. Warm yellow with dots of blue, shining like porcelain, it fit perfectly in my hand. "It's a cowrie shell. Keep it, if you like." I nodded, a little embarrassed by how desperately I wanted it.

He led me to a half-open door and rapped with his cane.

"Bento? Your helper is here."

We passed into a second room which had one tall window. Sunlight flickered like a candle against the walls.

A man my father's age, in his early forties, was engaged by some tools on his desk. "I don't need a helper," he said, after Jupiter introduced me. His curly hair stood on end, like a pine cone. His eyes, passing briefly over me, were dark as night.

"He needs a helper," Jupiter assured me, as the man returned to his tools. "Bento has 'a thousand matters of state' to attend to, as we say. There's no shortage of work."

Through the window the ocean was silvery blue. I followed Jupiter across the room, past sacks as big as me that leaned against the wall. The floors were dusty, and our steps left tracks behind us.

"Is this a food warehouse?"

"I wish! It's not rice. It's not even millet. It's just sand."

Music crept through the door of the next room. I recognized it, and my heart stilled. My mother used to play music at all hours of the night. She had loved Bach. Yet this piece sounded different—it was played by a guitar not a piano, and the melody, slowed down, was made of inward turns. The notes glided around corners, they slid and fell, and piled up like dreams. My shoulder ached and I looked at my left arm and wrist, expecting to find it covered in bruises.

Was she here? Outside the door, Jupiter and I paused. The music surrounded us simultaneously with Foshan and the sea, catching us in a net of overlapping spheres.

I touched the door and opened it.

The net scattered. My father's voice echoed in my ears, warning me to distinguish between the false and the real.

I saw the back of a woman.

There were shelves against every wall but they were entirely empty. Yet the woman, in her sixties maybe, only a little taller than me, with an upright posture like a dancer or a boxer, was gazing fixedly at them. She wore an emerald-green skirt that touched the tops of her shoes, and a pale grey blouse. The woman ran a determined hand through the air, as if along the spines of books. A record turned on the player, and seemed to pull notes out of the air and into itself. As if the woman, the old man and I were the music, and the record player was the listener.

"Blucher? Your helper is here."

"I expected you yesterday. I completely ran out of paper." The woman turned. Her eyes, at first bright with interest, dulled to disappointment. "But you're just a kid."

"I'm almost eleven."

"She's Aduan's little sister," said Jupiter. "Lina."

"No, my brother is Wei—"

"Lina, fine," she sighed. "I've got a million things to do. Let's get started."

At the opposite end of Blucher's room was a door that led into ours. My father and I hadn't noticed it because it was the wall itself. It had no exterior handle, but if you used your foot to push the bottom corner, it popped open. When I stepped out that first time, and into our room, Dad spilled a glass of water on himself. "My child," he said laughing, "appearing like a genie from a teapot."

He went into the atrium with me and through the adjoining rooms, and met our three neighbours. We learned that each was waiting for another person, and was therefore reluctant to leave the Sea. That evening, when we kept the door propped open, the cross-current made everything feel alive. How fortunate, my father said, to have good neighbours. They had been here even longer than us, and didn't seem in a hurry to depart.

Dad speculated that, long ago, the entire floor had been a single dwelling. As the building filled up, inhabitants divided and subdivided it. The strangeness of the buildings, how they grew out of each other, must have been created by necessity. Windows sometimes turned out to be doors, and rooms turned out to be hallways. "I kept hearing Bach," he said, "but thought I was imagining things."

He went to our shelf and pulled down a stack of Tsinghua University notebooks. Flipping through them, he showed me drawings of wobbly geometric shapes, like balloons squashed and folded over themselves.

"See?" he said. "The problem of the Sea is the problem of the Königsberg bridges. Euler solved it. The problem has nothing to do with geometry, it's network theory and connects to Riemann manifolds. Component surfaces might feel like Euclidean planes but globally, when pieced together, they turn out to be a sphere like the earth, or a torus, or a higher-dimension manifold, do you understand?"

I didn't understand. Dad sometimes forgot that I didn't share his brain. He was already off on his own explanations, writing equations that joined letters, numbers and figures, making shapes that rose from the page and became three-dimensional or, as he told me, "4-torus."

I grew bored and went to the window.

Despite wanting to heed my father's words, I believed that Foshan was within reach, and that it drew ever nearer, like a ship carrying my brother towards us. I imagined that the others on the twelfth floor were, like us, mere echoes. Waiting to return, we weren't ready yet to face a new beginning.

And so another three years passed. My childhood felt, at once, endless and momentary. Jupiter, Bento and Blucher became family to us, and our separate rooms were like a single home. Like my father, they were quick to talk about everything except the past. Once, when I was annoying them with my questions, Jupiter said, "Birds and children don't look back."

"Are you birds?"

"Either birds or gods," joked Blucher.

I did laundry, carried water and scavenged, and as I ran from here to there, I conversed with the passageways, which I had come to know as well as my own self.

Around West Gate, the buildings continued as usual, waxing and waning. Voyagers touched land and immediately set off again. Some came from the lost cities of the Pearl River Delta, but many arrived from places that were new to me. Alexandria, Kiribati, Abidjan. I sold paper to a woman who used to be an oceanographer, who told me it wasn't an accident that continuous waves of people landed here.

"The ocean," she explained, "contains many rivers within itself."

I was perplexed. How could water resist disappearing into other water?

"It's simple. Varying temperatures result in different speeds and pathways. This particular inlet is located at a confluence of rivers within the sea. Think of them as roads that travel over the 'hills' and 'valleys' of the ocean. What's the saying here about the future? *To travel by boat...*"

"To wash in by boat and wash away by ship."

"Right," she said. "There's an infrastructure to the water. This place is probably some kind of tangle in the structure." On my arm, she drew a map. "You and your Pa should go south. It's not like it was when your family left Foshan. Six years makes a big difference. Now the routes are patrolled and less dangerous. I heard there's even a huge centre that processes everyone, and resettlement only takes a couple years." According to rumours, which I wasn't sure I believed, it didn't matter where you came from. While you waited for a permanent place, you'd be enrolled in school or given work in one of the new construction zones along the way.

"Tell your father to put you on a ship list. You'll get a voucher. Everyone gets one. If you don't get out soon, you'll be stuck here forever."

The year I turned thirteen was a memorable one: for weeks, which turned into months, my father became determined to leave. He insisted on descending and climbing all twelve flights of stairs every day. What had once seemed fantastical was now real. In preparation for our journey, I sold some of our most precious objects. The neighbours each gave me a parting gift. Then, one evening, Dad became dizzy on the stairs. He lost his footing and tumbled forward. It happened so fast, I only half caught him. When we hit the ground, he broke his arm.

It seemed a minor thing. But afterwards, even when the arm healed, he didn't get stronger.

To pay the itinerant doctors who passed through, I took on more errands and housekeeping work. Dad no longer spoke about leaving.

I remember that I met a ten-year-old whose name was King, and who described famous paintings as if he'd seen them with his own eyes. He studied physics from a full-colour textbook. I tried to persuade King to sell me the book, and in desperation even offered him *The Great Lives of Voyagers*, whichever volume he wanted. But he said the textbook had once belonged to his older sister, and he couldn't trade his sister for a children's book.

"It's too bad," he said apologetically. "I don't even like physics. I want to paint murals. It's an accident I ended up with this text-book, but my mom said accident is fate."

At home, I pressed my father again about leaving. We could go slowly, and make our way little by little. Shouldn't we at least try? In two years, I'd be fifteen and no school would take me in. With each passing day, my future narrowed.

He was sitting at the window. His yellow sweater looked so huge on him, like a folded sun. "If we leave, your mother won't be able to follow us."

The word *mother* confused me. I couldn't remember the last time it had passed his lips. Finally I asked, "What's the difference between here and any other place?"

"Everyone passes through the Sea. After these buildings, his-tories break apart. I already explained it to you. The Sea is a length of string crossing over itself. The Sea is made of time."

"When we leave, our names will be written in the shipping records—"

"I'll never leave this place. That's the truth."

Disbelieving, I laughed. Surely, if my mother had wanted to find us, she would have done so long ago.

He lifted his hand to shield himself, as if my laughter were a blow. "Yes, she knows we're here. I don't blame you for wanting to get away—"

The word *blame* hit me hard. My father's life was a weight I should never have been made to carry. I said as much to him.

"Yes, it's all my fault," he said. "Leave, if that's what you want. As if I could stop you."

The unhappiness inside me was blinding. I went to our shelf of precious things. A bundle of utensils, a chopping board, a wok, and three books for teenagers. Trembling, I picked them up one by one, as if I were already saying goodbye.

"Lina, what more do you want from me? What more can I do?"

I went out, crossed the atrium and stood alone on the stairs. He was so ill he could barely rise from bed. I could hear him repeating, "I'm sorry. I'm sorry, Lina. Don't leave. If you leave, both of us will be alone." When I heard those words, I felt tears rolling down my face but I could not accept that I was crying. I knew he was grieving. I knew he wanted to prepare me for a future which, he feared, he might not live to see.

My mother had kept my brother and left me behind. Maybe she had entrusted me to my father, maybe this was only temporary, maybe she was searching for us this very moment. I wanted to believe that she longed for me as much as I longed for her. But I was not a child anymore, and could not accept that acts of cruelty could also be acts of love.

I could rush out to the boats, I thought. It was within my power to cut the last thread that connected me to my father. This could happen in an instant, it could happen at any moment I chose, it could happen today. I imagined doing this: I saw nothing and everything at once, as if I were staring straight up into the night sky, which I imagined as the future itself. The facts that shaped my life were hidden from me, but even so these facts existed. Even if invisible, surely they remained within my reach, as patient as roots waiting within the earth.

All afternoon, I hid in Blucher's room. I had a game back then which helped to steady me. I imagined I was rain, a porous, transparent element. When I turned into rain, I could escape the Sea. I was back in my brother Wei's room. On the shelf, his books gleamed, unreal, and I felt comforted and even happy. The whole series, *The Great Lives of Voyagers*, was there, beginning with the explorer Zheng He. Philosophers, artists and scientists slipped from one volume to another, Homer (8) next to Amo (9), Çelebi

(50) before Gautama (51). All the rooms I remembered disappeared into one another like a sound inside a sound. Beside me, my mother took a book down from the shelf, but it wasn't a book, it was music, Mozart's Sonata No. 10 in C Major.

My favourite part was the second movement. Everything stopped, even my own heartbeat. At last, I could escape time by standing still. Inside the music, I heard the floor creaking. When I opened my eyes, Blucher was beside me. Her dark hair was swept back, as if she'd been out walking in the wind. I had tears in my eyes and couldn't speak, so we stood looking at one another. There was a strictness in her expression that I read as impatience; or perhaps pity. I expected her to reprimand me for crying, but instead she reached up to the shelf and took down the book I had placed there, number 84 in the series. She began to page through it.

"You're always reading these," she said. "Which one is this?"

"That one's about Hannah Arendt. She was a traveller."

"A traveller." Blucher shook her head and laughed. "That's her big accomplishment?"

I said the books had been part of an educational series, and had arrived every month, free of charge, alongside a magazine to which my mother subscribed.

Blucher smiled. "My mother had a similar set of books. *Great Lives from History*. Or maybe *One Hundred Lives*." She was holding the volume upside down. "It had Machiavelli, Hegel and Genghis Khan in a single volume. Even now I still think of them as a combo."

"No hero has to share in *The Great Lives of Voyagers*. Everyone gets their own cover with its own unique number."

"You enjoy this kind of thing, snooping around in people's lives?"

I wasn't sure if she was teasing me or if she was really asking. "They keep me company. They don't have anywhere else to go."

Her expression was bemused and irritated and sad all at once.

"Why don't you read a bit for me? I could use the distraction and maybe you could, too."

I took the book from her, read the familiar epigraph, and started the first chapter. I did my best to interpret the pages, even making up passages that were more exciting, just as my father had done for me. Blucher listened.

When I finished the chapter, she put her hand on the page. "It wasn't like that at all. How old are you again?"

"Almost fourteen."

"Old enough to think about things differently. I can tell you quite a lot about Hannah Arendt. Are you interested?"

"Yes."

She took the book from me and shook it a little. "What would you do with a story like that? Would you even remember it?"

"Yes, I remember everything."

She smiled, skeptical. "Some things you might only understand later. But frankly there are a lot of things adults never understand."

I said nothing.

"Maybe you would write it down. Not all of it. And not now, but later on, when you're older. When you've lived a long life, here or somewhere else."

She was looking at me so intently, I took a half step back. "I could."

"But you'll write it differently?"

"No. I'll remember it exactly the way you tell me. Word for word."

"Impossible," she said, almost angrily. "You won't. The only way to really remember is to forget everything and let time fill the story up. To reach it through a different doorway. Things have to inhabit the living or else disappear from the world and cease to exist. If things survive it's not through abstract thought, but the realities that gave rise to those thoughts."

I saw my mother, Wei and Aunt Oh as if they stood to one side of her, listening intently. *If a million years passed I would never forget them.* How could I? But even as I thought the words, I saw that they were impossible and, therefore, untrue.

She put the book back on the shelf. "Alright," she said. "Let's see."

3.

A lifetime ago, behind that shut but unlocked door, when the Lecturer put his hand on her neck, when she said yes and not no, Hannah Arendt had been eighteen years old. The Lecturer had been holding office hours. It was 1925, the beginning of February. They sat on two chairs facing one another in the centre of a room, away from the books and papers crowding the Lecturer's desk. She was wearing her raincoat and hat. Behind the curtains, the windows were wide open and the room was cold.

"You have my mother's name," he said.

Her birth name, Johanna—the graciousness, *hanan*, of God. It was a common name.

Their knees were only millimetres apart but he didn't touch her there. They had been talking for almost an hour when he lifted his hand and held her neck. Not roughly, not impulsively, but calmly, as if to prevent her from speaking even though she had been quiet for several moments. Schlüsselbein, the belly of the throat. In Latin, she knew it as *clavicula*, the little key. The pressure brought dread but also relief, as if something hidden was beginning to materialize. The Lecturer withdrew, adjusted his chair to move closer, and carried on the conversation as if he had never touched her. Except now there were two existences, the one in which they were speaking and the one in which they kept watch, neither less real than the other. She was trying to convey what she glancingly understood. In this morning's seminar, another of her teachers, Rudolf Bultmann, a professor of theology, had spoken of Saint Augustine's trinity of no longer, not yet, or not at all. The belief that this world is transient, temporary, made of time. Thus love of the world and its temporal objects, love of another person, creates perpetual mourning.

The Lecturer stretched towards her again, grazing the book on her lap, as if he meant to take it from her. Instead his hand softened against her dress, curved against her knee and fell, with a change of intention, around her leg and up along her thigh, so that she froze, tightened and opened in the same moment.

"When Einstein," she said, as if addressing a third presence, someone the Lecturer ignored, "surrounded by the clocks of Bern, formulated his theory of relativity, he couldn't afford to buy a clock for his living room wall. And Kafka," she said, turning to another thought as if towards a sound in the dark, "Kafka's *I have found out* . . . the story about the flower. That line from the story he didn't want destroyed. The line goes—"

"And here you are," the Lecturer said, as if only now becoming aware of what he was doing. As if giving permission to it, because what he felt could not be tolerated yet must be lived nevertheless. He leaned towards her, opening her coat, which was still wet from the rain. A trickle of water slid from her hat down her neck. She could feel all at once the chill of ice and the warmth and care of his hands.

Soon it was April. She had been waiting, that evening, in the park below his office as he had instructed her to do all semester. *Come at nine, if the lamp is lit. If someone is with me, come at the same time tomorrow night.* When she knocked, the door opened to reveal the Lecturer alone, standing at the window. His evident happiness when he saw her. She stepped into his office, he closed the door.

He kissed her for a long time. The door fell open. There was no one there, or did she imagine it—the shadow of a child in a coat blue as the ocean? He reached out to shut the door. The air smelled of wood or pine. He was satisfied, even euphoric, as he often was after being surrounded by students. "Let's leave," he said, and they went out. The sky was a shimmering blue-black, the thinnest paper.

They walked side by side through a corridor of trees, without touching.

They talked. She wore a medium-weight coat, a heavy scarf. Occasionally, hidden by trees or a bend in the path, he reached for her, wanting to be reassured, impatient. Yet when he undid her coat buttons, insisting his way between the fabric and her skin, the pleasure had an aftertaste of pain. Again and again they stopped to kiss, for his hands to reach her, and each time they had to rouse, pull away and continue walking. He was thirty-five, nearly twice her age. She felt like they were walking through a room they knew by heart. Soon they reached the house where she boarded. "Well," she said, "I forgot. I meant to ask you about Professor Bultmann—"

"Of course." He gave a small laugh. "You said so earlier and it slipped my mind. Do you still have time?"

"Yes, would you like to come upstairs?"

"Well . . . it's cold tonight. I'll come in for a moment and then get home."

Their footsteps on the stairs seemed to echo ahead of her.

Tonight she was unprepared for the privacy of her room. She had also been unprepared a few nights ago, and the nights before that. But this was different. They talked through the dark without touching, not even daring to do what little they had done in the woods, even though their coats and scarves were now gone, even though he had already half undone her dress. No one would interrupt them. You could be, in the same instant, with someone and against them, and never appeased. Longing was terrible, but for now it was the most familiar part of love and even the very proof of it. When at last and inevitably they fell silent, the rushing inside her slowed. Longing turned into possession. Possession turned into loss. She was at the mercy of her own desires, his severity and even his cruelty. She could not think how any person could survive such want. Except that he, despite being married with two small sons, was with her, and this shared loneliness turned out to be another belonging.

In class, surrounded by students who revered him, Hannah felt oddly detached. *I am grateful*, the Lecturer wrote to her on a small white notecard. *Your love has made me grateful.* Craving, she realized too late, has a life of its own. Each time it was satisfied in one part of them, it expanded to another. She felt she lived inside a locked box that was more liberating than the open sky. *To suffer and to know*, she wrote to him. *To know every minute and every second with full awareness and cynicism, that one has to be thankful even for the worst of pains, indeed that it is precisely such suffering which is the point of everything and its reward.*

To protect him from rumour, she went away to study in Freiburg. Still, they saw one another. *When you spoke to me last week*, he wrote, *you were transformed. Your confidence and a spontaneous, joyful sense of belonging to me.* The ease with which she kept their love hidden from her friends was a revelation, as if an essential part of her were rising into solitary view. After one semester she moved again, this time to Heidelberg. But the train became their accomplice. She would startle awake and find herself, once more, en route to see him. She felt his hand around hers. She met him in hotels along the railway. So passed three years. He would write her two days in advance. No, just one day in advance. She would drop everything and hurry to meet him. He described his love as an unconditional faith in her. *If I have done you wrong, perhaps it is by understanding you.* Month by month, even though the villages and hills remained constant, now clothed in winter, now in spring, she felt as if the roads were in fact liquefying.

"Did you destroy my note?" he would always ask, even as he hurriedly, roughly undressed her.

"Yes."

His severity, his tenderness. They turned out to be the same thing. "Be sure to destroy it."

On the trains, her fellow passengers read novels and pamphlets whose words she couldn't help but see. Jew Republic. Jewish Bolshevism. A People Without Space.

Impulsively she left Heidelberg and moved to Berlin. Impulsively, she married a fellow student who knew nothing of her affair with the Lecturer. Her husband was destined for great things and she was determined to be loyal. The Lecturer wrote to commend *her radiant goodness. The moments when I am completely happy for you are also my happiest moments.* Her own capacity for deception continuously surprised her. My ability to lie is not an aberration, she thought, it has become a habit.

One evening, she and her husband received an unannounced visit. There he was, the Lecturer, Martin Heidegger, suddenly at the door. It was night, and he appeared immense in his heavy coat. He offered warm congratulations and a wedding present. A bowl for punch. He barely addressed her, and went in to take coffee with her husband. Such acts appeared to her as a sign of the Lecturer's love and even valour. *I know*, he wrote to her afterwards, *that even when I am alone, you are with me. Only trust can preserve our love.*

What year, then, what month? Hannah was twenty-four, and still entangled with him. It was 1930. Every time she went out, she had the feeling that she would be revealed as what she was or never could be. One day she saw a man slap a Jewish shopkeeper across the face. Shocked and in pain, the woman stepped backwards into her store and out of sight. Assaults in broad daylight, even the most revolting episodes, went from unimaginable to ordinary.

Everything seemed possible, nothing seemed attainable. Or this was the feeling she saw around her in the packed bars, on the busy train lines, in the Berlin streets, elegant in spite of the poverty everywhere, and in her own collapsing marriage.

Not long after her twenty-sixth birthday, on her way home from the State Library, she saw a used clock in a tambour-style case, and purchased it from the market seller with money she couldn't spare. At home she placed it on the mantel. A mistake. Its ticking and hourly chime aggravated her husband. His dissertation had come to nothing, he might as well trash the pages, and now, he shouted, now he was stuck with her: she was distant, hardly a woman and incapable of love. "Be honest," he shouted, smacking the clock to the floor. "Be honest about yourself!" Shamed by his own behaviour, he rushed out. She picked up the clock, opened the cracked case, fit the key into its slot but did not wind it. When her husband came home, she gathered him in her arms, took him to bed with a passionate indifference. It wasn't that she didn't love him, but love had sunk so far away she could no longer grasp it.

The following week, after another violent argument, he left for Paris.

New laws came into effect. Henceforth neither she nor her husband would be permitted to work in Germany as teachers, professors or in any government position. She focused her attention on the book she was writing, a biography of Rahel Varnhagen, whose six thousand letters she had read as a teenager. When Hannah's childhood friend, Anne Mendelssohn, told her that a communist group was organizing border operations for people forced to flee, she offered, immediately, to help. It was a relief to do something, to act. Soon after, fugitives began arriving at Hannah's door late at night and vanishing a day or two later.

Jewish lawyers, doctors and musicians were dismissed, in compliance with the new laws. Benno von Wiese, gregarious Benno whom she had known in Heidelberg, visited her in the café where she wrote each morning. He was fit and beaming, and full of awful marital advice. He made her laugh until tears dripped into her coffee cup. How good this glee felt. They wheeled out their old questions. What is a theory, what is science, what is method, what is understanding, sit closer and tell me what it is! But then he began to speak, euphorically, about the situation, concluding, "We are living in great times."

A train went by, making the glass rattle.

"I can hardly agree," was all she allowed herself to say.

"Because you're a God-loving theologian at heart," he said, teasing her in the old way. "You don't have a political mind. You'll never admit this elemental truth: war is a permanent human obligation."

"Is this the staggering insight of your political mind?"

"The fact is, what we *must* suffer can be delayed but not averted. We've got to fight this war now, today, so that future generations won't inherit this war. Don't you see, Hannah? The spirit of our age is one of awakening and unconditional duty. The utter aimlessness, the alienation of the past years, it was meant to sap our strength. But we've discovered an idealism which refuses all limits, and with this resolve, we're coming face to face with our authentic selves."

"We may not like the authentic selves we come to meet."

"The old world is gone and the new one is not yet born," he said as if it were the punchline to a joke. "Marx seduces with clichés. But of course," an appraising look in his eye as if she had defied him, even as he took her hand and kissed it, "how could you understand?"

Perhaps, she thought but did not say, the problem was not only what her enemies were planning, but what her friends were now doing. The café owner came busily to collect their cups, nearly breaking Benno's. Hannah kissed him goodbye. She would never see him again.

At her apartment, more guests arrived and disappeared.

Her husband sent a melodramatic letter. *I have been informed of your activities. You will get us both in trouble, and you will not be able to charm your way out. Don't destroy everything. I beg you, come to Paris. I'm sorry. I am forever sorry. I love you and cannot face the future alone.*

The Editors Law, followed by the Law for the Prevention of Offspring with Hereditary Diseases, was voted in. Indefinite imprisonment became legal. One night her apartment was crowded with a family of six. The father, so battered half his face had ballooned, was on someone's list. The smallest child, a boy with strikingly large ears, refused to speak. Before dawn, Hannah left the apartment and walked to Stadtpark U-bahn. A bench offered respite. The new station was decorated with stone tritons carrying nymphs on their backs, shivering each time a train arrived or left. She watched daylight touch the unfilled pool. The light in its square cup began to overflow. When the sky transmuted into dull pink, she stood up. Life must be attended to. The family needed bread and cheese, chocolate sprinkles for the soundless boy, iodine and bandages for the father.

The family got safely away. In June, a copy of *The Good Soldier Švejk* arrived with an inscription that read, *To Hannah, we hope to meet again in better days.* The father had marked a page halfway in, when feckless soldier Švejk and Vodiçka are bidding each other a roundabout farewell, promising to meet at six or maybe six thirty at the Chalice pub at Na Bojišti. *When the war's over,* they kept repeating, this is where we'll find each other, this is where we'll drink our toast. This is where, this, this . . .

A pub in the future, she thought, where all the past can meet.

Revision of Paragraph 175 passed, criminalizing not just sex but any intimate signals between men. Hannah got in the habit of going about the same streets knowing they were not the same. The unthinkable became regular, the new regular became unthinkable, and on it went. Her friend Hans Jonas told her that the Lecturer, now rector of his university at Freiburg, was the Nazi Party's brightest star, and had supported the removal of his Jewish colleagues, including Edmund Husserl, including his closest friends. The Lecturer had hailed the "nobility" of this national revival. She was not shocked, and this lack of shock was itself disturbing.

Nonetheless, she told Hans it wasn't true. "What's the use," she said, "in spreading ugly rumours?"

He shrugged. "It's obviously true."

That night she wrote to the Lecturer. Scholars, philosophers, scientists, writers, intellectuals: they were lining up to offer cooperation with the Nazi Party. Could he tell her why? How can one claim to *think*—no, how can you of all people make this claim— when you, too, are nothing more than an opportunist?

His reply was a shout: *I have done nothing wrong.*

Do not lie to me and do not deceive yourself, she begged. I want to recognize the one I love.

But he did nothing, said nothing, folded himself away from her.

Near the beginning, when she was eighteen, he had written her, *I know that I will draw you back to me again because you can understand.*

He knew it, and she knew it, too.

But then something happened. He summoned her to Freiburg. She stood at the station as the train arrived, but it pulled away without her. *There is nothing left but to let it happen, and wait, wait, wait.* The train disappeared. All too soon another arrived. She prevented herself from boarding it, as if she were fixed to the ground, the walkway, the platform. Still, the duty of love would not leave her because love was a duty and a reverence, a belief in one's own existence. So she remained in the station.

Passengers crowded together and dissipated. They departed and kept departing.

Three Worker Youths, mere boys, passed her, berets and neckerchiefs neatly fastened. And then came another wave of boys, each carrying their copy of *Der Pimpf*. They looked so confident, even contented. She had a sense of trees moving mutely around her.

She did not allow herself to sit on a bench or put down her overnight bag. She stood on the platform until her body ached, until she could no longer stand it, and even then she remained where she was, watching the trains with the greatest concentration, as if she could somehow shame them into stopping their relentless continuity.

She did not board the train to see him.

At last, without weeping, without regret, she left the platform and walked home. That evening, two women stopped at her door: "We'll drop this laundry off and go have supper, Helga." She opened her door and they stepped inside, talking all the while about the washing. She and they exchanged barely any other words, only bread and coffee, gestures of concern and gratitude. Just before dawn, she woke to find the apartment still. The two women had already departed for the border, leaving only clean plates and cups gleaming on the table and, to her surprise, yet another copy of *The Good Soldier Švejk*. Was the book a talisman because it was heavy, because it was comical, because it was true? She placed it on the shelf beside its sister, and pondered a thousand questions. *Attend to what appears before you*, she thought. *That is what I must teach myself to do.*

Years later, when the war was over, Hannah met the Lecturer again in the city where everything had begun. "There are certain memories," he said to her, his suit crumpling in the summer humidity, "that for years I barely knew I had. It turned out they were lying in wait. Incidents I had set outside my thinking."

She couldn't help but grimace at the word *incidents*. The glass in her hand felt warm, yet so light it hardly existed at all. She wasn't entirely sure where she was. Her eyes flickered over the limestone hills, the people, the sky, the river.

He stared at her hand, at the glass, and again into her eyes. "There are . . . acts I've thought about every single day between the ages of fifty-five and sixty. I was able to bypass those memories for a decade but then, in my seventies, they returned with extreme severity. I look in the mirror and find I'm like everyone else. Not just old, but ordinary."

"Well," she said. "We were fools."

"If I had done right by you, and you had stayed behind in Germany, what would have happened? Can you even imagine? The hideous events, after all."

Her laugh was cruel. Could she *even* imagine?

He shook his head, petulant. "So you see, I was not wrong."

"Let's not argue," she said. "What's that you're reading?"

"Oh this?" He glanced at the paperback in his hand. "Some poetry. And you?"

This bit of theatre between them was absurd. He had carried the same books for centuries and she had spent her youth memorizing them. *Before either of us knew it, we belonged to each other.* A truth that was still a fiction that was yet true. How difficult it was that even though she knew he was cunning, that he was selfish and grasping to the core, she still loved him with a kind of piety.

"Have the poems changed in all this time?"

"Oh yes," he said. "The times have changed them. Words are flimsy, no better than a sieve. Time is unforgiving, but that's obvious from the day we're born."

The word *unforgiving* rattled something in her heart. She remembered another moment. Before the war, she had said to him, "I love you as I did on that first day. Our love has become the blessing of my life." Soon after, her German citizenship was revoked and she became stateless. She knew she would have to flee the country. *Above all,* he wrote, *none of this can touch my relationship to you.* She was arrested by the Gestapo. It turned out that a librarian in the archives had informed on her. People were really unbelievable. She was released. She went home and hurriedly packed her bags, including her husband's unfinished novel which he had bundled in old cheesecloth and hung in the pantry, disguising it as smoked meat. Two days later, she hiked into the Ore Mountains. She took refuge in a house where the front door opened into Germany and the back door into Czechoslovakia. She crossed from the living room to the kitchen, trespassed the border and became an outlaw. As simple and strange as that. She had escaped, yet why was her heart crumbling inside her chest? From Prague, she took the train west and eventually knocked at her husband's door in Paris. He said nothing when he saw her, only pulled her into his arms. The Lecturer did not write to her. Not a single word.

So many other detours had happened between youth and old age. But this is true for everyone who arrives by chance, who grows old in countries not their own. She had the strangest sense of unease, as if this conversation with the Lecturer were occurring out of order. Marburg was in a region filled with salt mines and in such places, people say, time *thickens.* Time does not obey. During the war, books from the university, paintings and treasures from Berlin and from across the annexed territories, were transported there and hidden in the mines.

He must have left without her noticing. She looked up expecting to see a train station, or the passing mountains, but all she saw through the window was the churning ocean.

ooooo

I was standing at the shelf, listening. Wind clattered the windows and ruffled the papers on Blucher's desk. Outside, the sun had slipped beneath the waves.

"This is only the prologue, but I'm thirsty," Blucher said. "Remind me where you're trying to go? Which train are you waiting for?"

For a moment I was confused. Then I said, "I'm trying to get back to Foshan."

She considered this problem but said nothing more. We got up and walked into 12/C, where my father was looking at the twilit night. He appeared at peace, as if reflecting on some happy memory. We crossed the atrium and entered Jupiter's room. A long sleeping cap was pulled over his eyes; he didn't stir as we went through.

When we came to Bento's room, she said, "Show him those books you're always carrying around. *The Great Lives of Voyagers*. Tell him Spinoza's big accomplishment is that he was a 'voyager.'" She laughed. "Give him a chance to undo the story. I think that's how you find your way back to . . . where was it again?"

"Foshan."

"Right," she nodded. "Foshan, of course."

"Tell me again," I persisted. "How did you get to the Sea?"

Blucher thought for a moment. "By train. It was awful. I thought it would never end."

"But there's no train here."

She brushed my words away. "Go on," she said mischievously. "Ask him."

Bento was standing in the centre of his room, thinking. A stray cat who haunted the building was stretched out beside him on the floor. Bento said, "You're whispering but I can still hear you."

"She's trying to get to Foshan. Have you been?"

"No, but these days every trade route comes through here. Isn't Foshan on the way to Brazil?"

I did as Blucher had requested, and told him about the famous voyager, Baruch Spinoza.

Bento's face lit up. "Where did he travel? I hope it was somewhere warm."

"He went all the way to the next town," Blucher joked.

"And what did he find there?"

"God," Blucher said, "or Nature."

Bento smiled. He went to the window and opened it, and now we could hear the tide crashing on the rocks. The stray cat stood tall on his hind legs and boxed the curtains, and all through the room light and shadow swayed. Outside, the water was jade green turning to hazy pink. "Spinoza lived in interesting times." He pointed to a shape on the horizon. "What's that, by the way? I haven't seen it before."

I was reluctant to say China, afraid that he would correct me. So I said, "The old port."

"We've been away so long, I didn't recognize it."

I showed him Volume 70.

Bento took it eagerly. "It's been ages since I had something new to read. Are you selling it?"

"No. Anyway, look how damaged it is."

Number 70 was the most weathered. At some point in our journey, I had accidentally left it out in the rain. While I sobbed my heart out, my father had shown me how to carefully dab off the excess water, and stand it up with all the pages open like a fan. We left it alone for a week. Finally, Dad rigged up a makeshift iron to suck out the remaining moisture and flatten the pages as best we could. After its water damage, number 70, which had always had the fewest pages, became the thickest of the three.

Bento turned the pages with care, studying the Chinese words. Unlike Blucher, he didn't seem fazed. He entered the book as easily as a child climbing through a window and began to tell it back to me. "You can probably get to Foshan by going through Amsterdam," he told me. "That's just how the world is now."

4.

Baruch Spinoza watched rain falling into the dark water. He was twenty-one years old, and seated on a barge pulled through the river by a white horse. It was 11 Nissan 5414, it was the end of March, 1654. Baruch's father, his Pai, Miguel d'Espinoza, had died on the Sabbath, and so they had waited until nightfall to wash and dress him, to prepare the casket, and to arrange transport to the burial grounds. Already it was the afternoon of the second day. A line of mourners, their black cloaks glistening, walked along the shore; the procession had set out from Amsterdam almost three hours ago.

The wind, ever constant, sometimes carried their prayers to the barge, and sometimes covered them.

Fifteen years ago, Baruch had made this journey to Beth Haim for the first time. Then, like now, a pine canopy had sheltered the casket in the barge. He remembered the presence of the pallbearers and the men of the Chevra Kadisha, and how rain had streamed from their wide-brimmed hats. The wind had been so cold. When the moment to disembark had arrived, his feet were blocks of ice. If not for the firm hand of his brother Isaac, who was barely two years older, Baruch would have fallen into the mud.

During that journey, or perhaps on the return, Baruch had watched the cantor of their synagogue hold himself in dignified solemnity, as if the barge did not lurch or wobble, as if the rain did not soak his shoes. The voices of his father and the cantor had circled above his head.

"Your oldest boy, Isaac, has a sharp mind. And your second son . . . how old is he now?"

Baruch said softly, "I am six," and the two men paused before continuing.

"This boy has a pious look," the cantor said. "Why not enrol him in Ets Haim sooner rather than later? It could be easily arranged."

"He's too young, I fear."

"Not by much. And perhaps it could ease some burdens, Miguel, what with their mother gone and five little ones in your care?"

The cantor's suggestion made Baruch feel as if he were a white feather floating above a deep green field. At home, he had often lingered in Pai's study where, through the window, he could see across the canal and straight into the classrooms of Ets Haim. But how could he feel this lightness, this happiness, when Mai was gone and would never speak his name again? Ashamed, Baruch had placed his hand over his heart, as if to weigh it down.

That was long ago. Now Baruch watched the draft horse, draped in mist, trudging along the bank. Sometimes only its hooves were visible, sometimes just its head, and sometimes the horse was only a sound. In five short years, Baruch had made this journey four times. In Beth Haim, the House of Life, most of his family now lay resting.

The streets of their neighbourhood had been the family's universe. Chatter in Portuguese, prayers in Hebrew, poems in Spanish, jokes in Dutch—a never-ending *Atenção! Pas op! Cuidado!* along the Houtgracht as wagons, filled with flowers or sheep or casks, lumbered through. Baruch would stand, awe-struck, until his mother shouted, "Move your feet, avôzinho!" *Hurry up, little grandfather!*

The endearment stuck. *Eat dirt, avôzinho! You stink, Grandpa!*

The children—Miriam, Isaac, Baruch, Gabriel, Rifka—were as close as the five digits of a hand. Mai would stand them in a row and demand answers. "Who cracked the dish?" "Who pulled Rifka's hair?" "Who started throwing mud?"

Isaac always said: "Avôzinho did it."

It wasn't true. Baruch, feelings hurt, would hide in his father's study, lying quiet as the deadest dead. But breathing always betrayed him.

"Come out, child," his father would say, "and tell Pai what saddens you."

"I want . . . I want . . ."

"A telescope? A whirligig?"

Pai would clap his hands and materialize, as if by magic, a tiny envelope of candied ginger, tuck it into Baruch's pocket and send him out the door.

Miriam and Isaac always pounced. "Avôzinho, avôzinho, don't look behind you!" "Avôzinho, when I catch you, I'll kick your head to the moon!" They chased him up and down the stairs and stole his candy.

But at bedtime they came together like the petals of a flower. Isaac read aloud from *Don Quixote*, the book of wonders which fed all their games. Using towels as shields and socks as banners, they played at being knights and windmills, and together pursued great adventures. One by one, Rifka, Gabriel, and Miriam would fall asleep, and Baruch would watch Isaac close the big book, return it to the bookcase, and turn down the lamp. Enclosed by his family, listening to their breathing, Baruch felt himself carried on an infinite current.

After two months of suffering, Mai, unable to breathe, died on 28 Cheshvan 5399. By evening, the family was on a barge, pulled by two horses, which left the Houtgracht and joined the wide river.

Afterwards, their father grew thin and quiet. Long ago, Pai had been born in a village of olive trees and rolling hills, where the light was tinged with gold. It was called Vidigueira. But Pai's grandfather, uncles and aunts were accused, one after the other, of being hidden Jews. They were imprisoned and tortured, humiliated in auto-da-fé ceremonies, and some were burnt at the stake as heretics. Pai was nine years old when he took flight, first to Nantes, and, later on, to Amsterdam. "When I breathed free air for the first time," Pai told them, "it smelled of the sea and tasted of salt."

Two years after their mother died, Pai married Esther. She was newly arrived from the Algarve; she was cheerful and spirited and shaped like a small bear. Esther told them horrifying stories of a ship blown sideways and almost upside down, a ship blown hither and thither until all hope was gone. And then, one morning, Esther said, its desperate passengers, herself included, were saved. That was how she'd come to Amsterdam, and become mother to five motherless children; she, who had never even learned to write her own name! "Our days," Esther said, "are more mysterious than the wind." Before she became Esther, her name was Guiomar de Solis, and she didn't know Hebrew but was Marrano like their lost mother, and sang the same Portuguese and Spanish songs:

Si yo m'empeso a descuvrir	If I begin to discover
secretos de mi vida	secrets of my life
el cielo quero por papel	I want the sky for paper
la mar quero por tinta	I want the sea for ink

If anyone suffered a wrong, Esther consoled them with gentle words: "Estou aqui com você. Don't be sad, your neighbour's chicken is always fatter than your own."

For Baruch, classes were six hours most days followed by evening service. Meanwhile, Isaac spent the mornings at school, and the afternoons with Pai in the family business. The war with Spain was dragging on, there were blockades everywhere, and even a shipment of figs needed naval guards. Export was becoming impossible, but the family was blessed: Isaac, quick-witted and confident, had the knack for trade.

"When know-how was handed out," Pai said one night, "Isaac took it all. He'll be the family's salvation."

"And me, Pai?"

It took his father a moment to locate the voice. "Baruch," he said tenderly. "You have the light of your kind mother."

At the age of fifteen, Baruch completed the fourth and last escuela. To mark this milestone, Pai gave him a fine ledger with gilt-edged paper and a leather cover. Gripping the ledger in his hands, Baruch told his father he wished to continue at the yeshiva, reading Maimonides, Ibn Ezra, and Rashi's commentaries; and wouldn't it be beneficial for him to study Latin and mathematics in the city itself, at the Athenaeum Illustre?

Pai was bewildered. "Whatever for?"

Isaac laughed. "Avôzinho wants to add more school to his school."

"Just one more year."

Isaac cuffed him lightly on the side of the head, smiling complacently, but he took Baruch's side. He convinced Pai that the cost of such lessons would, in the end, be an asset to the business.

Two nights later, Isaac spat blood. Within the week, he died, nearly ten years to the day after their mother. Once more into the barge, this time under a pale sun. Then, Miriam died in childbirth, leaving behind a baby son, and again the river carried them to Beth Haim. Afterwards, Esther began to weaken. Month by month, her bear-like beauty fell away. Baruch realized, too late, that after all these years, none of them had taken the time to teach Esther how to write her name. By summer, she could barely lift her hand. The doctors insisted it wasn't the plague—so what was it? "Our lives rush through us," Esther said, "like the wind." On 3 Cheshvan 5414, unable to swallow, delirious with sadness, she died.

Pai's clothes hung off him. Half his weight evaporated and he looked like a child, his hat looming high. The collapse, when it came, was severe.

"Avôzinho, I have more debt than I can pay. I've left you, Gabriel and Rifka nothing. That's the truth. Forgive me."

"Don't say such things, Pai. Try to rest."

"I failed our family. You are the softest of all my children. Promise me you'll bring the little horse in from the rain."

Baruch wanted to carry out Pai's wishes, but he didn't understand, and his father said no more.

It was true that they were sinking in debt. When Pai died, his stone was by necessity the simplest, without decoration, carrying only his name and the date of his passing. *Michael (Miguel) Espinoza* was entered into the book of records, the Livro de Beth Haim. On the return journey to Amsterdam, the barge passed a giant windmill, and Baruch remembered that, when their mother died, Isaac had told him that the sails of a windmill are called *wieken*, wings, and that the people of this village, Ouderkerk, had named their windmill the Swan, and all day and night the Swan pumped water from the earth, and wasn't that a wondrous, almost unbelievable, thing?

All in a row, Baruch thought now. Nearly his entire family gone.

After seven days had passed, he folded up Pai's three sets of clothes, larger and more threadbare versions of his own. Rivka, soon to be married, was in good hands. Therefore Gabriel, Baruch thought, must be the little horse. Gabriel was clever and fearless; he could excel in the export business if Baruch could give him a clean start.

Day after day, surrounded by unsold goods, going back and forth to the Amsterdam Exchange, he worked to secure the household. The customs paperwork was a nightmare. When the sun went down, he paced for hours along the canals, saddened.

Four years ago, the war with Spain had ended; that year, the plague had taken twenty thousand lives in Amsterdam alone.

Death is routine, Baruch told himself. Mere routine. "What right," he asked, "do I have to pity myself?"

"What right?" echoed an old man, passing by on a barge, his face turned towards the heavens.

Little by little, the family's finances were set right; Gabriel finished his schooling and entered the business.

After long days at the Exchange, drafting contracts and translating papers, Baruch would go to the city taverns to eat a little something and to sit in peace. His favourite refuge was the Papist, which had high carpeted tables, a clientele of young men with time on their hands, and tobacco which came in all varieties. Mixed with belladonna, it induced hallucinations that were, according to its users, sweet and spongy.

It made the Papist a tranquil place, and Baruch could read in peace.

Despite his reserve, the regulars took a shine to him. One night a boy named Quakel whispered in his ear: "Aren't you, Blessed Baruch, despite your Israelite religion which I frankly do not comprehend, like me? Aren't you, too, searching for relief from this city, which kills us slowly and yet so pleasurably? Belladonna is terribly soothing. Have a puff! She relieves our meagre bodies of all their pains and griefs. Even thirst, even hunger! First she makes you happy, she helps you flllllyyyy, and finally she makes you tired, so deliciously tired . . ."

"Yes," Baruch nodded, gazing into Quakel's melancholy eyes, "I *am* looking for relief." He lifted his pint. "I have found it in this ale."

"Touch my gloves," said a voice from the corner. "These cost a thousand guilders, believe it?" The speaker's clothes were very ruffled, especially from the waist down, as if he were being consumed by clouds. The shoes were charming. Square-toed, fastened with ribbons rather than buckles, and decorated with red roses.

THE BOOK OF RECORDS 45

The book Baruch was reading sat on the table, discreetly wrapped, its title hidden. He tried to concentrate. *I attempted to never accept something for true*, he read, *which I did not clearly know to be true. That is to say: I sought to avoid—* His mind drifted. Beside Baruch sat a group of eight; all, like him, austerely clothed in black. The group passed thoughts back and forth like a ball of dough kneaded firmly until, magically, their thoughts took on a light and elastic shape. For two whole hours, he eavesdropped shamelessly.

The man beside Baruch turned to him. "Why don't you join us? If you lean in any further, you'll be in my lap."

Rattled, Baruch knocked over his empty glass.

"Pierke Balling," the man said, deftly catching it. "That's me. Shift over to our table and I'll introduce you to the rest. That big guy is Rieuwertsz. You hang around his bookshop, right? Under the Rose. Don't panic! I can tell by the wrapping of your book. And those two are Simon de Vries and Jos Bouwmeester." He tapped at the pages in Baruch's hand. "René Descartes was an acquaintance of ours. Lived right around the corner from here, did you know? But he was always relocating, liked to change house every season! René's sudden death, it's a blow to us, I still can't quite believe it . . ."

Baruch stared, agog.

"Our group meets on the regular," said Pierke. "This Wednesday, Frans Van den Enden is hosting, so the eatings will be good. Hobbes is our book of the week. I'll jot down the address. You could use some fattening up. What was your name again?"

"Spinoza," he said. "Baruch."

Summer came, and somehow Pai had already been buried a year. Baruch was reading in a different tavern, the Grape, when three familiar faces startled him at his table. The men were a few years older than Baruch, and he recognized them from the classrooms of Ets Haim.

"Espinoza? What are you doing in this part of the city?"

"I take classes at the Athenaeum Illustre."

"With the Remonstrants!" The first man grimaced.

"Whatever for?" asked another.

"I'm studying algebra."

A big orange cat had entered behind them, picking its way daintily over the sawdust.

The three men spilled into the surrounding chairs, debating algebra and the new mathematics of joining and completion. They began talking about . . . someone? And then they were talking about someone else. Baruch downed his glass. Eager to return to his book, al-Khwarizmi's commentary on Euclid, he tapped it impatiently.

The first man glanced at the cover and frowned. "Some books are pure provocation," he said. "Their aim is to unsettle and weaken us, and thereby shatter our peace."

Annoyed, Baruch refilled his glass. "The Holy Books, you mean," he said.

"Well . . . !" exclaimed the third, bewildered. "Unholy books, certainly. I must have misheard you."

Baruch pointed across the room. "Look at that cat!" The three turned and stared. "Isn't that the huge cat from our neighbourhood? He must have followed you across town. Let's invite our orange friend to join us!" This unexpected sighting made him feel suddenly jovial.

"Absolutely not," said the second. "Long-haired cats make me sneeze. And I feel . . . nervous around creatures."

Baruch threw an arm around the man beside him. "But him, him, and me? We blessed animals?" The orange cat stretched out a surprisingly graceful leg. I *do* know you, Baruch thought. Miriam and Rifka named you Brother Orange because of the way you lorded over the street, acknowledging everyone, and in this way kept the peace.

The second man was also a little tipsy. "I can help you distinguish an animal from a man. If I were to go over and kill that cat with my knife, would its soul be released?"

"Soul?"

"A God-given soul, Espinoza. A thread escaping and returning to its creator."

"Oh, *that.*" The word *thread* struck him as hilarious. "I'm afraid that if you were to kill *me* with your knife, my sacred thread would fail to appear!" He giggled and topped up the man's beer.

The first man said, in a whisper, as if there were a sleeping baby on his lap, "But what would we see if we killed you? No soul? Nothing at all?"

"If you were a patient man you would see my skin and organs dissolve and liquefy into nature." He began to describe this process, which Isaac had once detailed to him at some length. The men pushed their drinks away, disgusted. The second swung a paper bag of sweets back and forth, as if shaking a head. "Alright," Baruch conceded. "Enough about rotting bodies! Didn't you say you were curious about algebra? I tell you, it's a relief to study a method of thought which shows the light but doesn't punish you for seeing."

All three gaped at him.

Finally the second cleared his throat. "These new philosophies make a fetish of doubt. They think if they calculate the movement of a star, or calculate the area of a cone, they've burped out a revelation. It's sad, really. This algebra, this $x^2 y^2$ *abcd* answer to everything, can't make a true thing untrue. Algebra is a language like any other, in service to God."

"I don't know what debauched reasoning has fattened your head, and made you so superior," added the first.

"I suppose I've snapped my thread," Baruch laughed. It was a wonderful joke, but the others failed to laugh.

The third, who had said nothing all this time, now sought his gaze. Ever so firmly, in a voice that reminded Baruch of his dead brother, he said, "You mustn't say things like that, Baruch. It's madness."

"Madness?"

"It's against the law."

"Against the law for me, a speck of dust in the universe, to believe I do not have a soul? Is that a crime in this city?"

The Third Man didn't reply because he knew, and knew that Baruch knew, that the Third Man was correct.

Abruptly, they vacated the table and Baruch got to finish the pitcher by himself. When he stood up, the world was soft as cake. He went out and Brother Orange followed, a warden of the peace. Baruch tripped into a church courtyard and climbed onto a stone bench; Brother Orange, too, chose a bench. Baruch remembered, as a child, losing his only ring of keys. Someone had beat him. Pai? Isaac? He must have been very young, because he had still been wearing the dress of childhood and had not yet received a boy's clothes.

After Mai passed away, her name had rarely been spoken. In the years that followed, Baruch had wondered what kind of world could possibly fit the accumulating dead. Also, could you prove someone had existed if no one spoke of them, and if they vanished completely from living memory? People said that in order to return to God, a human being had to forget themselves, give way, and *render themselves unnecessary*. His mother and father had been forced to give up their entire selves, their hearts and hands and the voices inside their heads. Did all those things belong to God alone? Was that better than if they belonged to no one?

In the courtyard, he looked up at the liquid night and detected a pebble in his shoe, and told himself that the pebble and the night must also belong to the will of God. Trembling, he held up his own two hands, knowing that one day they would be no more.

Perhaps he and everyone he loved was insignificant. But he did not think he could spend his life gathering, hoping, loving, learning, only, at the very end, to render all of it unnecessary.

ooooo

The wind around the Sea had grown blustery, and a heavy rain began to drum the roof.

My stomach growled. Bento glanced at me and then out into the growing storm. "I lost track of where I was. It must be almost dinnertime. Where did Blucher go?"

"To smoke a cigarette."

He latched the window shut.

"In the tavern," I said, "did Baruch really meet an orange cat?"

"Definitely."

I knew that he was pulling my leg and also that he was being truthful.

"Anyway," he continued, "I'm not making the story up. It was already in the world, no different from a tablecloth or a name or an old coat."

"What was already in the world?"

"Misunderstanding."

The stray cat came and twined around my leg. When I gathered him in my arms, I breathed in the smell of sawdust and bread.

Bento shuffled some loose pages on his desk. "Is that your stomach or mine making all that noise?"

"It's yours," I said, even though it wasn't.

That evening, we all ate together on the landing. I set out a meal of pears, steamed arrowroot, and a soup of wild greens. The neighbours spun tall tales, passing the time with comical and frankly unbelievable stories that transported my father and me far from the present moment. But I was preoccupied, thinking of the child Baruch floating out on a barge. Would I prefer to be remembered wrongly, I wondered, if it meant that some trace of my life would persist, a barnacle on a raft, into the future? Would everyone want the same?

My mother's face blurred behind my eyelids. Could a person and the memory of that person diverge so far that recollection itself became a kind of betrayal?

After dinner, my father and I slowly climbed the stairs to the rooftop. Here was the place that set his heart at ease. The moon, bobbing on the ocean, was very near, as if it might float into our laps. Music rippled from Blucher's room, the second and final movement of Beethoven's Piano Sonata No. 32. The notes seemed to climb the staircase and dance round and round the passageway.

"Lina," my father said. "You were right. Your mother, Wei and Aunt Oh have gone on with their lives. Each year of waiting hasn't brought them any nearer. But you were still a child when we got here. I told myself that I was getting stronger. I thought it was true. Even if I couldn't stay with you the whole way, at least I could get us both a little further. How could it be otherwise? I should have sent you ahead, found another family to care for you, but I couldn't."

"I'm not leaving," I said, perturbed by his words. "I only want to visit Jupiter."

But Dad didn't laugh at my silly joke. Instead he rambled about the maps and notes he'd gathered for me. "When that day comes, the day when it's time for you to leave, remember to pack lightly. You won't be able to carry everything, and taking too many things will slow you down. Do you understand? In the end, both the present and past have to make the journey out, the mind and heart have to stay together. That's where I went wrong."

I watched the moon etching its reflection in the waves. Because he was upset, I wanted him to stop remembering, to save his strength, and yet to talk to me forever. "If I have to leave one day, I would want . . ."

"What is it?"

"Before that day comes, will you tell me everything?"

He nodded.

When my father made that promise, I had the strangest sensation of the Sea shifting around us. Even though we were up on the roof, we seemed to stand on the shoreline. I could hear stones giving way beneath my feet.

Seeing that I was crying, he tried to make me smile. "Those old books of yours were right. The stories that last are the ones about voyages, about odysseys and escapes. How could it be otherwise? Stories of return are the ones that survive the journey out."

That night, I slept poorly. I dreamed of a future in the shape of a door. At long last I opened it and on the other side was a silent, glowing lake. But the ripples of water were made of paint or perhaps ink. I stayed in the frame of the door hoping a breeze from the past would move from one world to the other. When I woke, I heard shouting. Outside our window I saw people running back and forth along the sand, calling desperately towards a boat that was already disappearing. I sensed the strange calm that had protected me for years was eroding and I didn't know what, if anything, could ever replace it.

In the morning, Jupiter needed help repotting his vegetable garden. Outside, the sea was turbulent, it twisted and leaped against a yellow sky. As we worked, I asked him about the people who had lived in 12/C before Dad and I arrived. What had they been fleeing and where had they gone? Had he ever heard from them again?

Jupiter paused to rest. "Before you, there were twin sisters. They spoke Sogdian and stayed for a year before heading east. They were trying to rejoin their brother, I remember. Your table is the one they left behind. Before them . . . it was a woman, Hamdi, or Hamadi, she was called. Her daughters found the bookshelf in some other building. Those little girls were clever. They took the furniture apart, carried it up in pieces, and built it again. You're still using it, right? And before them . . . I don't know. I've only been here a few years."

No matter how much time passed, for Jupiter it was always *a few years,* and he always said he would leave next spring. When I pointed this out, he changed the subject.

"You left your books on the stairs last night," he said. "The pages are falling out. Find me some glue and I'll try to rebind them. Anyway, Blucher was snoring like an ox, I couldn't sleep and started reading."

"They're really good, aren't they?"

He made a face. "Number 84 is exciting, especially when they run away over the Pyrenees. I can see why you like reading about exotic places. But the writing is terrible. Did some kind of machine write these books?"

I laughed. I guess I knew what he meant.

"We had a series like this when we were kids," Jupiter said. "*The Eighty-Eight Immortals Who Carved the Flying Dragons.* And also a competing series, *The Doubters of Antiquity.*"

"I wish I could find those. Did you read them all?"

"Every volume. My brother had both sets, we called them the Yellow and the Red. The funny thing is, both series had almost exactly the same historical figures."

My three books were stacked on his windowsill, and I went over and retrieved my favourite one. "Did you get a chance to read number 3? It's about Du Fu."

"What about him?"

"He wrote fourteen hundred poems," I said with great confidence. "He lugged them all over China in the middle of a civil war, when he couldn't even afford shoes and had nothing to eat but turnips. My dad says Du Fu is one of the greatest poets who ever lived."

"I skimmed it. But it goes on and on about how Du Fu plummets through the world like a melon tossed out a window." Jupiter stabbed his trowel into a pot of green beans. His bushy eyebrows seemed to tremble in sorrow. "The 'number 3' position in *The Great Lives of Voyagers* is just to trick people into reading it. It upset me all night but I know who wrote it: that know-nothing Bao Yan. He was so rich he never had a bad meal his whole life. He got a job at the imperial library thanks to his uncle, who happened to be the director! The whole series was probably Bao's idea, since discrediting others is the only way he can remind you he exists. He pretends Du Fu's greatest achievement is getting thrown here and there like a bug in the wind, and ending up a homeless person. Some of the poems in the book aren't even written by Du Fu! They must be Bao's poems, so he can sneak himself into history."

"Don't get upset. There's two volumes on Du Fu but my dad only saved the first one."

"Do I look upset? I love living in a room with almost no furniture, wearing threadbare robes, and waiting for someone to give me a job."

I fetched the broom and began sweeping up dirt that was flying everywhere. Jupiter gripped Volume 3 as if to fling it out the window.

"That's my book," I reminded him.

"It's full of mistakes," he cried. "The publishing house didn't even proofread it. What kind of historical record behaves like that?"

I made him red date tea and ordered him to sit while I finished repotting the bittercress and beans. There were dozens and dozens of plants. It was a greenhouse in here and smelled of the warm earth.

In time, Jupiter calmed, and the waves outside approached peacefully across the beach. A ferry arrived and docked, and even though it unrolled a bright yellow cloth along the sand and played upbeat music from its deck, no one boarded. Not a single cargo ship waited on the horizon, so where could this vessel possibly take those wanting to depart? We watched it for a long time until, bit by bit, it was lost to fog.

"Du Fu's father died suddenly. That part is true," Jupiter conceded. "His father *was* disappointed in him, but whose father isn't?"

He fished out a date from his cup, chewed it dejectedly and spat the seed out the window. We watched it shoot into the air and begin to fall. I wanted to tell him that a big melon and a tiny seed, flung into a canyon, would both hit terminal velocity, and once that happened, they would fall at exactly the same speed as if they were holding hands. Maybe an event and its telling met in a similar way, touching on the long descent. Could something ten million years old fall into step with something ten seconds old, if they both hit terminal velocity and aged through space together? But he was still going on about Bao Yan. "He exaggerates everything," Jupiter insisted. "I know I'm just a forgotten person in an empty room. I don't own purple robes and a fancy cicada hat or direct a library with all the great books. But only someone like me can tell you what it was *really* like."

I thought of my father. Then I remembered what Blucher had said, and asked Jupiter the same question: "Do you want me to remember the story word for word and write it down, or do you want me to forget it?"

"What? That's irrelevant. All things vanish. Just be with him, while he's here."

5.

It had taken the death messenger twelve days to reach Du Fu, who set off immediately for his father's house. The road was difficult. By the time he reached Yanzhou, sleepless and exhausted, his father had been dead nearly three weeks.

It was twilight. The front gate overflowed with paper flowers, pyramids of fruit, hundreds of tiny human figures made of dough, and banners which tapped a rapid drumbeat in the wind. The stable boy ran out and led Du Fu's horse away. The gatekeeper shouted, "The eldest son, Du Fu, esteemed scholar serving the emperor at the rank of . . ." His words echoed in quavering notes.

"No rank," Du Fu said. "No service."

The gatekeeper closed his mouth. He began again: "The eldest son, Du Fu . . . arrives!" His words were echoed three times by a voice in the next courtyard.

No one came to escort him. He skirted the formal hall, and carried on through a long portico which eventually funnelled him into the family quarters. The walls seemed to melt before his eyes. His stepmother stood there, panicked and weeping. At first all he could make out was her dark hair collapsing from its tall binding.

"The new magistrate has to move in right away." Her voice came at him like a bright light. "His people want us out. We'll have no roof over our heads! Do something, why don't you?

My husband has been dead twenty days and finally his son shows his face! You're the one in charge now, aren't you?"

Du Fu felt dizzy. He saw an old man scurrying away from them, the four black ribbons of his hat rippling out behind. He disappeared, a complete hallucination, or maybe Du Fu had glimpsed his father's fate, suspended in death, awaiting rebirth, rushing inconsolably from room to room.

His half-siblings were beside him now, three brothers and a baby sister. The little girl flung her arms around his neck and he was drowned immediately in tears.

"*Do* something," his stepmother wept. "Or we'll be on the street. Your suffering father. Your poor dead brother. What will happen to us now? Father died a disappointed man."

It was sorrow that made her say these things. Anyone could understand.

Afterwards, he went to the stables to tend his horse, Big Red. In the dark, he tried to rearrange his emotions, fold them together in a different way, and make them bearable. Death is routine, he told himself, mere routine, and his horse huffed and exhaled in reply, and seemed to shudder in sorrow.

His clearest memory of his father was not a happy one. Du Fu had returned from Chang'an two years earlier without a job. Despite being the highest-ranked candidate in the region, he had failed the civil service examination. Father had said, "It takes ten thousand books and ten thousand miles to become an educated person." A cliché, as if that were all his son could grasp. "There's no need to rely on merit alone," Father had said, without looking up. "When I pass from this life, you'll benefit. As the oldest surviving son, a position in the imperial bureaucracy will become yours. A modest one, of course, at the level of a functionary."

Du Fu had fled into the night. On impulse, he'd climbed Yanzhou's city walls. When dawn came, all that could be seen was a glowing shroud of fog and he knew that if a person journeyed into this mist they would stand inside history, ruined palaces, old empires, desperate hideouts, lost time. *I love the past*, he thought. *I always have.* In the twenty years he'd spent preparing for the examinations, which is to say, shaping himself to his destiny, he had committed the Five Classics and the great works to memory. What did he have to show for it? Ten thousand poems at his fingertips, yet he was utterly lost in the very place he stood.

For the children of the dead, the law required three years of austerity. During that time, Du Fu's cherished Third Aunt, who had raised him like her own boy, fell ill. Du Fu failed to reach her village in time; she left this world with only a long-time servant and her neighbours to see her off.

He paced her library, opening and closing the scrolls she had accumulated for his education. Father had sent Du Fu away, age six, when Mother died. After his failure at the examinations, Third Aunt had loved him as if he'd been victorious. "It is not your fate to be a government official," she said. "Your gifts were not fit for that purpose. Moonlight seeks out the corners of things." She had recited Du Fu's own lines to him, forgetting that he was the poet.

Solitary in the mountains I seek
river ice and snows of spring

This stone gate wide
to silver golden light

Yet if I were to leave
yet remain floating

She'd asked if he knew this poem. "Written in Honour of Zhang's Retreat," she'd named it, attributing it to an older, and more talented, poet. "When I recite these words," she confided, taking a sip of her blackthorn tea, "I feel myself passing through the earth's curtain."

Mute with pride, dust motes floating through his vision, Du Fu hadn't corrected her.

The last time he'd seen her, his aunt's eyes were failing and she had spoken to him as if he were another Du Fu. "For twelve generations," she had said, "our family was blessed. But happiness and fortune give no man the right to impede the wheel of history. I know that entire families will slip from this world. When a high mountain erodes, a jagged stone at the summit will learn the vast distance between heaven and earth. Perhaps only this jagged stone, reshaped by everything it touches, worn down in the end to almost nothing, to a circle as small as a bead, will be remembered."

Du Fu's stepbrother, all agreed, should receive the inherited civil service appointment. In this way, the stepmother's family would have a reliable income. His responsibilities thus fulfilled, what was there to keep Du Fu in his father's town?

He was a devoted man unable to find employment. By then it was the winter of 741, and he was twenty-nine years old.

Du Fu set off, searching for his life. One morning, on the road to Shangqiu, he ascended a crumbling mountain pass. The road was as thin as a needle but still he persisted until the road was suddenly nothing but sky. To left and right, only emptiness. This gorge below his feet was the open throat of the universe. Inside it, stone melting to abyss. Worse, he'd been a fool. He and his horse had destabilized the road. First there was the sound of tearing, followed by pure silence. A chunk of earth spinning mutely down. He couldn't hear. He saw a pink-tinged pebble and then, all at once, boulders leaping at him—but in fact, they were falling. Big Red twisted and reared up, Du Fu holding on for dear life.

They slid backwards, stopped, stuttered back another step. Was this oblivion? He heard a gust from behind his eyes. Was this his last breath?

Or this?

Bit by bit, they found stable ground.

That night, wrapped in a blanket, he had the disturbing sensation that he had swallowed his own life. He spoke aloud to the trees so that he could hear his own voice.

"My future is escaping me," he confided. "Sometimes I feel as if I'm the ghost of a ghost."

Big Red and the stillness listened.

"The old books say that this world contains the 'perfect garden' and the 'perfect wild' but . . . what if neither is adequate for a human being?"

The wind whistled and Du Fu pulled his robe more tightly around himself.

"Thirty years of education have made me what I am, just as a square cup makes the water square. All these years of studying the classic texts have surely made my heart rú."

Rú? the stillness inquired.

"In *The Analects*," he explained, "Confucius says that when a person is instilled with 儒 rú, they know that virtue is synonymous with the good of the whole. A heart that is square, that is rú, is guided by this truth. The perfect square finds its meaning inside the perfect circle. In this 'perfect garden' no life is wasted, and each existence, no matter who or what or when, is able to attain fulfillment."

The stillness made no comment and Big Red only scuffed one hoof. But he knew exactly what they were thinking:

Du Fu! Maybe the surface of your heart is rú, but what about the rest of you? Your square heart wants to smash its square cup! Your legs have been chasing a life far from the perfect garden, distant from the imperial court. Be honest. You suspect the perfect garden is not *the proper aim of a life*. But you're too cowardly to deviate from expectations. You fear the perfect wild.

"My heart is square," he protested. "It is rú."

The next week, he kept wandering. And the week after.

The mountain wilderness was home to painters who destroyed their paintings. Poets who consigned their poems to silence. Talented officials who, exiled from the capital, oversaw nothing but their plants. He slept beside all these on bamboo mats, needling them with his questions.

"But isn't it a waste of your gifts to withdraw so fully from the world? Wouldn't it be better to use your talents to improve the well-being of others, especially those who suffer?"

"How could the wild be wasteful?" mused a painter, pulling back a little more of their shared blanket. "I think it's wasteful to fail to properly perceive this universe into which we have awoken. Doesn't each and every human being have a responsibility to existence? Doesn't existence rely on all living things in order to perceive itself?"

"Those who suffer terrible injustices," said a former minister, in answer to the same query, "are consigned to that fate because of the perfect garden, not despite it."

Du Fu returned to the capital in search of a job. Another fruitless year.

Defeated, he returned to Yanzhou and rented a tiny scrap of a house on a tiny scrap of land, where two sheer cliffs faced one another in a high portico, like a stone gate for the gods. It was affordable, too, the kind of place where humble living should come naturally. He wrote poems. The more formal the poetic constraints, the more ungovernable each word seemed. What if unruliness constituted the hidden form of order?

Any day now, he would wake up a better man. Months passed.

One night, in the city of Luoyang, he met up with boyhood friends. They feasted on wild boar, and toasted one another with impromptu poems. Du Fu's lines were proclaimed the best: his sober poems, everyone teased, had an intoxicating rigour. Six of these friends were government ministers and one a court poet. The minister of propriety, his eyes gleaming like silver pins, remarked, "By the age of thirty, a man's chances are either seized or squandered, and his worth is revealed for all to see."

Du Fu wanted to die on the spot. Instead he smiled, downed his glass, and held it out for more.

Afterwards, tipsy on his horse, he saw that he had failed. Even the most sublime landscapes appeared as dust before his eyes. "Is it really true," he said, "that the perfect garden and the perfect wild can't coexist? Are human beings therefore doomed to live with one eye closed? Does either choice lead to only half a life?"

Big Red slowed, exhausted. Du Fu's inheritance had evaporated. His clothes were thin and worn. Soon it would be hard even to appear in public. The fulfillment he desired could not be attained in the wilderness. Only success could diagnose his problem and make him right.

"I can't abandon my ambitions," Du Fu said. "I must seize my life."

And so, the following spring of 743, he and his horse set off again, tracing the infinities of the Yellow River. Landscapes held him like a series of robes until, like water overflowing its banks, yet another year rose up and ebbed away.

Wave, wave, the trees were waving, emerald green! Du Fu was awestruck. It was the autumn of 744, and here he was, galloping through the woods with friends Gao Shi, a swaggering soldier, and Li Bai, the greatest poet of the age.

Within the forest, an old tower appeared, one face in utter ruin, dignified by a burst of golden light. Li Bai made a swinging dismount, landing in a plume of colour. "Our horses need a rest," he announced. "Come, let's pay our respects to this distinguished ruin!" Off they went, Gao and Li singing at the tops of their voices and greeting the sky as if meeting their own brother. Du Fu, out of breath, tripped and bruised both knees.

At last, contemplating the round moon, all three grew reverent. Du Fu lay flat while Li and Gao sat on either side of him. The tower made a disturbing noise; in such poor repair, it might come crashing down. Pure foolishness to climb so high.

"I've decided to sit the imperial examinations again," Du Fu whispered. "Next spring." What a boring thing to say, but the confession had popped out of him like a burp.

His friends looked down at him, concerned.

"I suspect you have the illness of our age," said Gao finally, his blue gown a ruffling river. "You want to rise up through the world as if rising were in your nature."

"What else can I do? I'm old now."

"Old," Li Bai nodded. "The way the shape of an egg is old." With his eyes half-closed and his grey robe rumpled at his neck, he had the look of an enormous owl. "In any case, it's your turn, Invincible Du. Give us a poem."

He obeyed. Was he really reciting his lines for Li Bai, the most gifted poet in ten generations? Du Fu's poem was four lines, there and gone in an instant.

The silence that followed was excruciating.

"On a technical level," Gao said at last, "the composition is not terrible. But listen to you, *As the sun declines, we hear mallets pounding laundry. Boom ba-da-boom! We sing a song in praise of lemons. Oh ho, sweet lemons! When even the veggie soup is gone, gosh I really miss it!*"

Gao was exaggerating, but not by much.

"You have no sense of occasion. You lack even the whiff of authority." Gao's sleeves were so broad that when he stood up and flung open his arms, he covered even the moon. "Remember your last poem? 'After Being Sick, I Stopped by Wang Yi's House to

Drink.' Holy heavens, what's next? Can't you even pretend to be sophisticated? It can't be that you have no use for money."

"A poem should also be a temptress," Li Bai murmured.

Gao stretched himself even taller. "Seduce the influential, flatter and fawn, put people in your debt, that's basic survival, no? How can you not know something so obvious about how to succeed in literary life?"

The pair reached for their wine flasks. They took long gulps, whales drinking from a hundred rivers. Du Fu rolled gingerly over and sat up.

"But this line sings," Li Bai said. *"Four seas and eight horizons, the whole world all one cloud."*

To hear his words in the poet's voice made Du Fu nearly faint with joy, which ballooned into hope, before evaporating into sadness. Stars pricked the sky.

"The problem is I'm broke," Du Fu confessed. If his two friends hadn't paid for everything, he'd have had to forage herbs for supper.

Li Bai took hold of his hand. "Your poem was a sumptuous passage about rotting vegetables and a nearly homeless man."

"Because he's my friend."

Li Bai gazed at him. The light of the moon was shattering, otherworldly. Du Fu lifted up his own arm, saw the same cold gleaming.

"Idiot," Li Bai chided. "That was a compliment. What I'm saying is that politics is dead. Integrity is dead. Art and ingenuity have been assassinated. Rot festers everywhere, and its source is the imperial capital. We live in an age of total corruption. Haven't you been paying any attention? Don't you see how abundance has created extravagance, which has necessitated scarcity everywhere, and the men in the capital are up to their necks in extortion, and that's just the beginning? What's left for you and me, a bit of poetry? If so, we should wear our learning with a bit more disrespect, do you know what I mean?"

Du Fu didn't know.

"What I'm trying to say is, there's such rigidity in your poems. You're a sincere man, maybe you should try a more boneless style. Make real the shifting space between the words. That's how eight lines risk eternity."

Gao was serenading the stars. "I know your type, Du Fu," he said, pausing his song. "When you finally get some recognition in this world, it will . . . *waaaaaa! Boom ba-da-boom!* The kingdom will collapse. The only thing to eat will be the dirt on the ground! Please warn us if anything good ever happens to you." He laughed, almost bitterly. "It'll mean we're all dead men."

Big Red cantered reluctantly towards the capital, a hesitancy that Du Fu ignored.

They passed salt merchants, milliners and perfume shops. They rode alongside boats plying the Grand Canal, heavy with bronze, sugar, jewels, coffins. From the eastern court, Luoyang, to the western capital, Chang'an, trade never ceased. He saw Bactrian camels walking pensively in the rain, followed by six silent women in northwestern dress, and a boy in a yellow tunic swinging a huge ostrich fan. The most brazen were the government couriers. Beaten for late deliveries, they hurtled past half-crazed, brandishing swords to clear the road.

In Chang'an, the imperial city, he found a room in the Weights and Measures District where steelyard balances dangled from every shop. Du Fu ate his breakfast while little kids filed brass wires to a perfect filament and old-timers carved balance beams from cow bone and even ivory. Counterweights swayed through the air, individually sized for gold ingots and copper cash, or for rose petals, cannonballs or fish. What would happen now that people endeavoured to weigh and compare everything under the sun? Would such exactitude change everything? Perhaps not the reality, only the meaning.

In a laneway, he discovered an entirely different category of scale. Sold in bulk to temples, they claimed to weigh virtue against vice, truth against falsehood, justice against injustice. He hurried past, fearing such scales could also weigh delusion and hope. *Weights and measures!* A cosmic joke. No other dreamer, preparing to sit the examinations, had been fool enough to take a room in this district.

At last it all began. Once more the pomp, once more the boring speeches. Once more he was locked inside a stuffy room.

He opened the first fascicle and read the question. "One man, two men. One with intention, one without. Discuss."

In essay after essay, each more refined than the last, Du Fu celebrated the prime minister, the spirit of the age, and the might of the realm. But his older brother who died too young, and of whom Du Fu had not dreamed in years, stared out at him from the corner of the room. *Little brother, don't collude with lies.* Du Fu ignored him. Flattery, expedience, flattery. His rare criticisms of the government were so nuanced they seemed to melt from the page. Time, mortality, the hubris of the capital, flattery. Hadn't Li Bai warned him? Politics was dead.

Eight days of testing, each longer than the last. Finally, he wrote an ending. His brush, placed on the desk, made a hollow knock of protest. His father, older brother, beloved aunt, Li Bai and Gao Shi all seemed to chase him outside. "Congratulations," they scoffed. "Six years of searching—six years!—and all for what! To write words you don't believe?" Even the fading light seemed to creep away, embarrassed.

It was shameful but what could he do? A man had to seize his portion of life before he could live it.

Three weeks later, Chang'an resounded with a bitter silence. Every single examinee, every last one of them, had failed.

After the results were posted, Du Fu lay motionless on the floor of his room, listening to the clattering of weighing pans and the bartering voices outside. He had squandered his youth, and here he was, aged thirty-three, with no prospects whatsoever.

He got up and tapped his reflection in the mirror but his existence slumbered on. Gathering himself, he went outside to face his horse. Big Red knew everything. His gaze seemed to say: Is it true that rather than choosing a life of inner freedom, you prefer to chase advancement and status in a compromised world?

"No," Du Fu protested. "I want to serve the greater good."

Big Red said nothing.

"Poetry is the distinction of my family." This was something Father had drilled into him. "The sunflower has no choice but to follow the sun." Another cliché. Perhaps clichés were all he had retained. "Fine if you think I'm a hypocrite. Let me confess it to the world! I want to serve the government and by serving gain influence. Is that so wrong-headed?"

His horse looked away.

Du Fu bought a bronze countermeasure, delicate enough to weigh a single hair. Its purpose was to weigh a man's soul. They left Chang'an. Big Red carried him along the city walls until finally the road softened towards the east, into the endless surroundings. What am I becoming? he wondered. Midway through my life, I feel the freezing chill of winter at the height of summer.

ooooo

Outside the ocean had grown calm, glowing like a plate of ice. The pot of red date tea was empty and I got up to add water from the thermos.

Bento, who had come in midway through the story, was lying on Jupiter's bed. He propped his head on an elbow. "Du Fu is ignoring a simple truth. True honour and true disgrace reside in a person's inner life not the outer one."

"No kidding," Jupiter said. "Everyone knows that."

"Du Fu studied for years and years," I said, coming between them. "He wanted to have a purpose in this world."

Jupiter sighed. "And being admired wouldn't be so awful either, would it?"

Bento plucked a hot pepper from a nearby plant and popped it in his mouth. Even though his mouth was clearly on fire, he kept crunching it. "I'm not disparaging Du Fu. I understand his feelings."

I poured water for him and relayed Jupiter's suspicion that Volume 3 of *The Great Lives of Voyagers* had been written by an adversary named Bao Yan. Volume 3, I explained, dwelt on Du Fu's poverty and failures, perhaps distracting readers from his earth-shaking poetry.

Bento sat up in bed. He had wrapped himself in Jupiter's quilt, which had a beautiful pattern of interlaced blue circles. All Bento's curly hair stuck up like a bouquet. "So if this nemesis, Boudewijn—"

"Bao Yan."

"—is trying to diminish Du Fu, shrug it off. Look, everyone has enemies. Inevitably, some will outlive you. Who doesn't have humiliations?" he said with great feeling. "The universe stabs each of us with a million tiny pinpricks. Laugh them off, or else the pins will burrow deeper."

"My heart is soft. If only my heart were a stone that could be rolled. Is that what you're saying?"

Side by side, the two men contemplated humiliation.

I ducked out. Back in our room, Dad was sleeping fitfully. Loose papers were scattered over the bedspread; he had been working incessantly on knot and topology mathematics. A sign, I knew, that his pain had returned and he was seeking distraction. Gently, I lifted off his reading glasses, gathered the pages, and made sure his medicines were within reach.

Facing north and west, our home shone like a boat of light. I sat beside him, listening to the sounds of the building. Dad murmured, "Not to worry," and then, "Don't be sad, Lina. When it happens, it happens quickly," and drifted away again.

Everyone has enemies. Someone had said those words to me long ago, but who? The ocean looked immense, thrilling to my eyes, yet indifferent to our presence. To escape this melancholy, I went up to the roof and began walking. A week ago, near West Gate, I'd met two girls my age. We'd planned to forage on the beach together, and wanted to exchange the information we'd gathered, but now when I got to their building nothing stirred. The whole family was gone. In a drawer, I found a glove, a hammer, five chess pieces, and to my surprise, a bag of starchy flour, three cans of powdered milk, and a small painted box filled with saffron.

They must have left in a hurry. I went to the window and scanned the seas, but all the boats were gone.

At the first sign of a cargo ship, people would head out to sleep on the shore. They were terrified of being separated from loved ones, or worse, left behind. Many nights I had stayed awake, following the light of lanterns weaving through eternity as people were ferried to the larger ships. These ships commonly arrived in groups, but I'd heard that, out on the ocean, they were constantly rerouted as quotas changed and ports shut down. If families were divided they could remain so forever. Until you were on dry land, and a receiving officer had stamped your voucher, you couldn't be certain where on earth you stood.

The saffron box was painted with a picture of silver trees, rolling hills and blue light tinged with gold. It seemed too delicate for a voyage and yet it must have come from far away.

I put everything in my bag, went up the staircase, and made my way across the rooftops, past abandoned furniture, and blowing laundry, and dark solar panels. The saffron, in such quantity, was a gift from the heavens; for just a spoonful of the past, people would be willing to trade necessities and even medicine. Halfway home, I stood still, watching the sky and the ocean, whose deep green colours swept into and through one another.

In Jupiter's room, the neighbours were still talking.

"A name is a guest of the real," Jupiter was saying. "Shall I then play the role of the guest?"

"Sure," replied Bento. "We can eat at my place. I have bread and soup. Oh, and fresh almonds." The top half of his door was already open. Jupiter reached over, unlatched the lower half and we all passed through.

On Bento's desk, the stray cat, which I had started calling Brother Orange, lay snoring. At the tip of one paw was number 70 of *The Great Lives of Voyagers*. When Jupiter pulled the book free, the big cat sneezed, stretched, glared at us, and returned to his dreams.

"Didn't I tell you it was a conspiracy?" Jupiter whispered, waving the volume at us. "Look at this cover. Baruch Spinoza wears a fancy brocade gown and his book is a golden ledger! Is that *a cloud* he's sitting on? But on number 3, Du Fu wears a ratty blue robe and a grass hat, and his poems are bits of paper that fly around in the wind."

I busied myself laying out the bread and fruit. Music from the next room rolled towards us like a question. "Blucher," I called. "We have food!"

"Listen," Bento said. "If you want to destroy someone's reputation, you have to begin by making them powerful. If you want to smash a stone, you have to lift it high above your head. Nobody cares if a feather falls to earth. The fact is, your adversary will always tell the best stories, which is lucky because the best stories become part of time."

"But what about the truth?"

"A true thing doesn't cease to be true even if no one believes it."

Jupiter shook his head. "There you go again, changing the subject. I give up. Fine, it's your turn. I know you're dying to tell us every little thing about Spinoza."

"Wait one second," Blucher said, coming in. "Lina, make a dish for your father. Otherwise those two great minds will gobble up everything."

6.

The sky was a shimmering blue-black, like the thinnest paper. Brother Orange, having returned from a long night of hunting, stared at a bird outside the window. He tapped one paw on the glass as if to test its reality, and ignored Baruch Spinoza, who was sprawled on the floor beside him.

Full of self-pity, Baruch rolled to sitting. A white envelope, pushed beneath the door, caught his eye. *Confidential*, the sender had written on the seal, as if that had ever stopped prying eyes. He pulled it open.

I met you last week at a tavern called the Grape. I was the one who warned you. Shouldn't we meet again?

This was followed by the Third Man's address on the Breestraat, and the proposed hour of the engagement.

The Third Man's room was small, and held only a table, a chest of drawers, a chair and a bed. It was cold, despite the summer heat.

A girl arranged raisins, almonds and bread in a shallow Chinese bowl. When she was done, she slipped out of the room.

The man looked pinched and nervous. "I was also a student at Ets Haim," he began, "back when the classrooms were in the little house attached to Bet Jacob."

"Yes, I remember."

A disbelieving smile. "We used to tease you and call you names. Hedgehog. Stoat, if memory serves."

Baruch had forgotten. He did not answer.

The Third Man poured ale, and in the silence, it made strange small gasps. He handed Baruch a cup, downed his own and hurriedly refilled it.

"I haven't been well," he said. "I'm sick, but not . . . well, perhaps you know." His eyes darted about the room as if to catch an intruder. "My problem is of a spiritual nature."

Baruch waited.

"I feel agitated and scared, as if a drop of . . . contagion has settled in my lungs. I know I'm not alone in these thoughts. The young in our community suffer. There are no moral codes to follow, or at least none we can pretend to believe in."

"In school we practised a moral code and a spiritual life."

The Third Man laughed. An awkward, almost ugly, laugh. A face rose up from the kaleidoscope of Baruch's childhood: a boy's familiar eyes, mocking and sad. "I want something I can trust, Baruch. I do not want to follow a code interpreted for me by another man. I want to *know* what is right. I want to know it in the fibre of my being."

The bells of Zuiderkerk, massive as cannons, sounded the hour. Glancing out the window, Baruch glimpsed a swiftly moving barge and three slender men clothed in white. Their words drifted out behind them—Javanese? Malayan? He didn't realize he was looking for Brother Orange until surprise washed over him: the cat was not there outside, waiting for him. Disoriented, he turned back to the Third Man. "That day when we ran into each other at the Grape, you three were coming out of the Mennonite bookshop. It's an . . . exceptional place."

The Third Man flushed. There was a piece of bread in his hand. Unsteadily, he set it on his knee.

"That bookshop of Jan Rieuwertsz," Baruch began.

"We didn't buy the outlawed books! I swear to you."

"What, then?"

"Del Medigo, Avicenna." The man's gaze shifted to the window. "Galileo. But those aren't the ones that have unsettled me. I keep returning to the *Guide for the Perplexed*. Maimonides wants me to see."

Baruch nodded, touched by the echo he felt.

They talked for a long time. Little by little, the Third Man's agitation subsided.

Each time he felt a kinship with him, Baruch took another bite of bread. The shallow bowl was soon empty, revealing a scene of dragons and clouds.

"This colour," Baruch said, running a finger over it. "It's very beautiful."

"Sumatran blue. A mix of Persian and Chinese colours. It's new in the world. A creation of our time." The Third Man glanced outside and burst out laughing. "Look at us. Night has fallen, the stars are burning, and here we are, talking about blue. Talking piffle."

"Yes," Baruch said, feeling oddly jubilant. "A universe of piffle."

Later, walking home, he had the sensation that the glow of every star brushed his skin. Brother Orange reappeared, walking ahead of him proprietorially.

Baruch teased him. "You don't want me to have other friends."

The cat swayed.

"Men are not like you. Humans rarely survive alone. Loneliness twists them."

In his room, Baruch found his father's copy of Maimonides and turned its pages without seeing, remembering only the depths of emotion he'd felt, huddled in Pai's study, trying not to breathe, a thousand questions rushing through his body, on the day he'd first encountered this book whose words had seemed to coalesce into a path. *Lastly, when I have a difficult subject before me—when I find the road narrow, and can see no other way of teaching a well established truth except by pleasing one intelligent man and displeasing ten thousand fools—I prefer to address myself to the one man, and to take no notice whatever of the condemnation of the multitude; I prefer to extricate that intelligent man from his embarrassment and show him the cause of his perplexity, so that he may attain perfection and be at peace.*

Baruch had accumulated a dozen books, paper stacks bound with string, none of which he could afford to bind. *Objections to Tradition, Geometry, Meditations on First Philosophy*, and so on. Money he could not afford to waste and yet, there he was, wasting it away. He and the Third Man met every evening. They read slowly, shoulder to shoulder, and he had the sensation of walking in the dunes of Brabant, just as he had once in childhood with Isaac and Gabriel, the sand rearranging itself, stirred up again and again into new forms by the wind.

"But I still don't understand what you want to happen exactly," the Third Man said one night. "We agree that an honest man submits to God. The honest man knows he is frail and mortal next to godliness and next to . . ."

"Truth."

"You want us to be free from false teachers. Yet we, who have long submitted to God, would we be able to lose the habit of submitting?"

"Not easily or quickly. But—"

"I know you think that's the gain, Baruch: at last each man will see things for himself. He will use reason to grasp this life, and thereby move towards freedom by degrees. I agree with you: the clerics are hypocrites. They hold far too much power, and some use sin and punishment to terrorize other men. But get rid of the *idea* of Sin and you get rid of the *feeling* of Shame. With Shame goes Remorse. With Remorse goes Forgiveness. Rid a man of the possibility to forgive and be forgiven, and where does that leave him and his relation to divinity? Worst of all, Truth will be replaced by something human and mortal. Imperfect truth, partial truth, subjective truth and finally . . ."

"Untruth," Baruch said.

"For an ordinary man such as myself, is that really a better world?"

"It is better to remove that which prevents us from seeing clearly."

The Third Man dipped his hand into a bowl of macadamias, but it had long been empty. He pushed the bowl away and frowned. "You always speak as if things were simple! A man's heart is not a stone that can be rolled."

That night, Baruch walked along the canal, exhilarated. He looked at the sky and told himself that the sun did not move. The sun *did not* rise and fall. No, it was the earth that spun and travelled, and every revolution around the sun completed the circle and brought them back to a changed beginning. It defied what he saw with his own eyes, and was almost too laughable, too absurd, to be believed. Yet the truth was that every face he ever saw, every single being, would die. Their singular experience would vanish from the world. Human life rose and fell, as momentous and untraceable and unrepeatable as the wind, and yet every single instant could not be disentangled from all that had ever been.

And the most bewildering thing, he thought, as Brother Orange walked ahead of him, is that, even knowing this, I am happy. I know that happiness is within my grasp, just as it must be for every person I encounter.

"Don't you feel as I do, Brother Orange, that joy is not at odds with knowledge? Or is this, too, a naive and unexamined hope?"

As he walked home, Mai and Pai, Esther, Miriam and Isaac all seemed to beckon from the other side of the Herengracht Canal. He could see them in lively detail. The jovial sadness of Pai, as if always concealing an injury. Only a year before his death, Pai had purchased, on credit, a fine wool coat, justifying the exorbitant cost by saying it would be used for decades. "My descendants," he joked, "will still be wearing it a century from now!" Baruch saw Mai's hands trembling. One sock was falling down. He heard Miriam's voice, as if she sat on the top of his ear. She said, "Our mother is only in your mind, Baruch. She no longer exerts a pressure on the earth. In fact, every person who lived in our time is gone, and you are one of the very few who lingers. It seems impossible but it's true. The socks are gone too, burned to dust, but father's coat survives, kept by a descendant of someone who used to be our neighbour but has now gone to the New World."

"The New World? Is that where you have gone?"

She looked at him with patient pity. "I only survive with you," she said. "Once you die, none of the millions on this earth will remember me. And soon none of those millions will be remembered."

The orange cat gazed into the night, mesmerized, but all Baruch could see were the usual things. Light and shadow, and the leaning, longing movement in the trees which was the embodiment of the wind. Could he love a chair or a bird as he loved another person? It must be, he thought, that the way we treat things, people, animals and even ourselves, is in accordance with our beliefs about them. What we do is a mirror of the ultimate unvarnished beliefs we hold. Was belief so fundamental, so powerful? If so, he mustn't let his thoughts rush by, automatic and unnoticed. He must attend to all that gives rise to belief.

Baruch loved the gloomy tenderness of the Third Man's bearing, and soon felt as comfortable in his presence as he did alone.

The Third Man had a commonplace book in which he copied passages from Descartes and others. To share these, discretion was necessary. He and Baruch took the precaution of meeting outside of the Jewish Quarter. For hours at a time, they paced the canals, past chestnut and acacia trees, beneath the ornamental facades, all the pilasters and caryatids, the stone Atlases carrying stone Earths, the great ships and flying dolphins, buildings soaked in moonlight. Amsterdam had already reached the future. Feathered hats and oily canals, street lamps and stuttering clocks! Restless Amsterdam, filled with drunks, world-weary women, gangs of roving youths, soaring beauty and rebellious and ugly paintings.

Tired yet still exhilarated, they eventually retired to the Third Man's room.

The Third Man liked to collect spiders. Now he moved two into a single jar. Constricted, they began to menace one another, and Baruch could hear the scrabble of their legs against the glass. It was a hobby of the Third, a remnant from boyhood.

The Third tapped the glass. "Remember those boys dropping their pants in the streets?" he said. "They just thumbed their noses as we went by. They pee in the canals and gamble in the open, yet I'm the one who feels that God will squash me with his shoe for daring to read Galileo."

We live in the freest city in the world, thought Baruch, yet here we are, whispering. He studied his friend's face, which seemed cloaked tonight. "Do you ever think of leaving our community?"

"Leaving!" The Third laughed and shook his head. "Where would we live? Whom would we marry?"

It was terrible to watch the spiders but also gripping. One seemed frightened and the other appeared to leer above it, pulsing as if out of breath, but it must have been a trick of the light and the round illuminations of the jar.

"We'd be outcasts in every quarter," the Third Man was saying. "The Dutch barely tolerate us as it is, so how could we live in safety among them?" He began listing the excommunicated of the last two years alone. "Those heretics might as well be dead, we can't even give them a crumb of mouldy food. And if you or I stood within a metre of these cursed souls, we'd face the same expulsion. The elders were merciful. Only one was whipped, remember?"

"But how is that right?" Baruch knew he should stop but still he persisted. "You said that you didn't want to follow another man's decrees, but to know, in the core of your being, what is good. What is true. The 'God' our community worships is pure superstition. Or maybe an utter fabrication."

A long pause. "Sometimes, Baruch, you go too far. Even for me."

He closed his eyes. He remembered watching Brother Orange, languorous, content to stretch out first one leg and then another, admiring his own bright ruffled body as if it were the most beautiful reality he had ever seen.

Wasn't it necessary for every creature to love itself, and to have faith in itself as the source of truth? Wasn't he, Baruch, also labouring under such an illusion? But how else could any living thing persist?

When he opened his eyes, the Third Man had turned back to the spiders who, locked together, had gone eerily still. He brushed his hand against the glass but nothing stirred.

In the night, Baruch heard the rattling of the wind. Stepping out of his room, he saw Pai wearing a woollen cap, surrounded by ledgers. Again and again, his father was writing out the same sums, seeking the miscalculation that would reveal the error of his thinking.

"Pai?"

His father continued to deduce and realize, before starting all over again from the beginning. "What did I miss, my child?"

"I don't understand."

"Just look!" Pai tapped the pages fearfully. "Time dissolves us, as if we're nothing more than sugar in water. Cells keep count of their replications. They have a memory, and with it they remember to die. It's all true, Baruch. But why? What's the meaning of it?"

"Don't upset yourself, Pai. You should rest."

"Upset?" His father pulled the heavy cap from his head. His hair was completely grey. "If my dearest boy chooses to go and stand in the rain, what is there to forgive? If my boy chooses to live in a world that turns its back on the redemption offered by God, how can I save him? You want to re-enter this life from another doorway. There is nothing to forgive, Baruch, but I mourn you. I mourn your soul."

He was awakened by the weeping of his own apologies. He drifted away again, thinking that the Third Man was at his bedside, trying desperately to rouse him. Baruch opened his eyes and saw the cupboards that still held his father's favourite cup and Esther's ornamental dancing swans. He remembered how, when he was eight, a man had been sanctioned by the community. The unbeliever, in his early forties, was tested in a long ceremony, and his groans had grown ever more agonized and terrible before dwindling to silence. The whip fell three, six, fifteen, twenty, twenty-five, thirty-nine times. In the end, the heretic was laid down at the entryway of the synagogue. One by one, the community walked over him. "Step on the lower half of his body," the elders had instructed. Baruch remembered the soiled floor and the way the man's legs had rolled, like logs in the canal. Baruch had stepped quickly over. The heretic was redeemed by this suffering and reconciled to the community. But a few days later the man hung himself. His name was said no more.

That night, the Third read, with increasing distress, the writings Baruch had begun accumulating. The Third put down the pages and picked them up again, like drink.

"Baruch, can't you hear yourself?"

"The teachings of our elders are a lie. God is not as we thought."

"Every word you've written is heresy."

"Heresy against our *teachers*, but not against God. We must stop confusing the two."

"If you publish this, you'll be saying that our elders, our greatest defenders, have led us to the devil." The Third Man laughed in astonishment. "Fine. If you really manage to strip them of their power, where will that leave us? We'll be at the mercy of the city. It would be the destruction of our community. The whole world we love, the families that nourished us."

"Yes."

"But you're still determined to publish it?"

"I am."

"Have you no pity on us, Baruch?"

Baruch knocked at the Third's door. There was no answer, just as there had been no answer for the past five days. He circled the neighbourhood and crossed the bridge, continuing to the bookstore, Under the Rose, but once there he only hovered, indecisive, at the window.

In the Papist, he drank a whole pitcher. His heart raced faster and faster, as if towards the sun. He considered his anxiety for a long while. He pictured it as a ball of yarn wrapped tightly around the spokes of his ribs. He imagined pulling the end of the yarn, carefully untangling it from one rib and then another. On and on he untangled and slowly he undid himself. At last the yarn came to an end and sat neatly in his hands. Relieved, he imagined setting it on the table. *Fear.* Was this what his doubt looked like, was this its size? *Look!* he wanted to shout. Madly, brazenly. *Look!* I am holding the disgusting wolf by the ears! It was growing inside me all this time!

He saw his reflection in the empty glass. The face of an unbeliever, a heretic? A son, he decided. The face of someone bereaved. Even so, what was right? What was good?

Tipsy, Baruch swayed home. There he found the note he had dreaded.

My cherished friend, we must talk. Come to my rooms tomorrow at dark.

The next night Baruch set out, moving comically slowly, hoping each step would lead him back to antiquity. The water chuckled against its banks, and the wind blew through him. Arriving at the door of the Third Man, he knocked so softly even his hand didn't hear the sound. Nevertheless it opened. The Third, smelling of tobacco and sugared bread—had he always been this sombre, this gentle?—embraced him.

Baruch was shivering and did not remove his coat.

Inside, two pillars of the community waited. They studied him in perplexed yet loving silence. Soon two more pillars arrived. All four were candles of varying shapes. Thin, tall, stout, thick.

The Third Man, retreating to a corner, merged into the shadows. On the table, beside the shallow Persian-Chinese dish, Baruch's pages lay in full view.

The oldest, who had once been the synagogue's cantor, made a declaration of forbearance and love, as if Baruch were suffering an illness for which, thankfully, there was a cure.

Despite himself, Baruch smiled. "So now you are doctors, too?"

Refusing to be insulted, the first pillar said, "My dear, dear Baruch, you've lost your father, mother, stepmother, brother and sister. In times of grief, good men feel surrounded by wilderness. As if their soul is being tested by God."

"And in this darkness," Baruch said, "they learn to strike a match and find light."

The pillar lifted Baruch's writings and, as if to summon some other Espinoza into the room, an ill version, he began to read.

How odd it was to hear one's private thoughts in another's voice, to be in one's own distorted presence. Yet I am standing right here, Baruch thought, diseased or not.

"What have you to say for yourself?" asked the second pillar.

"I believe there is no escape from thinking and from the repercussions of our own thoughts."

"Fine. Tell us what you think."

"I think that our sacred and revered texts were written by men not God. Our Holy Book is no more and no less than literature. It is a book of stories."

The pillars stared at him as if he had transformed into a chair or a bird before their eyes.

Baruch continued. "I think that you wise men, respected though you may be, are also only men. I think that each person must find the truth and therefore the beauty of this world for themselves. There is no such thing as an afterlife. This world is the only world."

"Tell us of your belief in God," the first pillar said gently.

"God does not exist as you have described him."

"Does he exist at all?"

"The world exists and is worthy of our attention."

"But God himself?"

"Himself? No."

The shouting began. Voices fell like hammers. Baruch felt oddly distant, detached, like a pipe lit and forgotten in a person's hand. The room, even in its dimness, hurt his eyes.

"Come back to us, my son," the first pillar said. "Do you not see that this hubris is an insult to all that is sacred?"

Baruch had the hallucinatory sensation that his family surrounded him, shouting and weeping. They were at his bedside, trying to wake him from a terrible fever and a fatal illness. It is you who are dead, he told them gently. Every human being is a piece of time. Your very cells have become part of the soil, other animals, the air. Your hours, minutes and seconds have long since dissolved. Ask Pai. He knows the truth.

The pillars burned the pages, which was a relief because frankly they were poorly written. He would do better on his next attempt.

They called him a radical, which was as good as declaring him dead. Before leaving, Baruch weakened. He whispered to the Third Man, "Don't turn away from something that is precious and necessary." Did he mean their conversations and ideas, their trust? He knew the answer only when he spoke the words. He meant their friendship, which he did not think he could live without.

The Third Man's face showed no expression, as if he had heard nothing, as if Baruch had already disappeared.

In readiness, he packed. Two sets of clothes, his books, a few cooking pots. Everything else, he discreetly gave away. His twenty-third birthday came and went without notice. He read Descartes, Maimonides and Averroes, and together he and these voices debated and joked as if the bunch of them were schoolchildren, lawless, with all their lives ahead of them.

"Movement and time are one and the same," Averroes insisted, pointing both index fingers at the sky. "Time is something the soul constructs in movement."

"Not a bit of it!" shouted Descartes. "Time is an obvious matter of circles, loops and straight lines. And you know it!"

Maimonides threw a dinner roll at him, which Descartes tried and failed to catch.

Averroes said, "One day Descartes stopped by the tavern. 'Want a drink?' the barman said. 'I think *not*,' Descartes answered, and *poof*, he disappeared!"

They hooted with laughter. "I think not, therefore I'm not— *whoops* . . . poof!"

The following evening, as Baruch paced the Herengracht, a shadow came towards him and spoke his name. The voice was a mere whisper, and for an instant he thought it could only be the Third Man. Then he saw the soft, almost liquid gleam, of a knife. Pivoting, his arms opened wide as if to embrace a friend, he did not comprehend the arc of the weapon. The knife cut through the darkness. He heard a rush of water, which was the long gasp of his coat ripping. A sound to wake the dead.

The shadow, insistent, drew his arm back and struck again.

But on the second attempt, the knife met no resistance, as if passing between the feathers of a bird, or an insubstantial being. Or the devil himself.

The assassin reared back in horror as if it were Baruch, not him, wielding the knife. The man cried out in terror and fled.

Baruch walked on, stunned, fingering the gash in his only coat.

At last, he was summoned. Before a row of community pillars, he was called, among other things, an animal. He knew he should have felt the sting. They compared him to a wolf that one takes into the home, nurturing, feeding and raising it, only to have it turn murderous. Baruch nearly smiled. They had found a long line of people ready to swear they knew his awful private thoughts. The Third Man's denunciations were the most detailed and intimate.

So this is betrayal, Baruch thought, feeling its hands for the first time.

This is the shape and weight of its fingers.

Everyone experiences betrayal, and perhaps everyone commits it.

But this is friendship, too.

His thoughts seemed to bend along a darkened track.

Betrayal is a risk of friendship.

Yes, but this risk is human and necessary.

Is it?

Isn't it?

The longer the Third testified, the more he seemed to grow in stature, as if from roots buried in the floor. "You must be saved from yourself, Baruch," the Third Man said, finally meeting his friend's eyes. He turned to the pillars. "You must do everything in your power to salvage what is good and beautiful in him. I beg you. I beg you to save him from damnation."

Will you apologize? the Third Man seemed to say. Have you no love, no pity? Apologize so that all will be forgiven.

But love and pity were not the same, thought Baruch, and should not be confused. That night, he went home and wrote out his apology. He presented it the following day. "The trouble," he told the community, "is not that I love God less, but that I love Him more than those who claim God's authority. I will gladly enter the path that is opened to me, knowing my excommunication is innocent."

The elders stared at him in horror.

Many other things happened after that. He went back and forth to the same warehouse-turned-meeting-room over the course of a few days, a week. "Your father was my friend," the cantor repeated, shattered. "Miguel d'Espinoza was a devout man who died too soon. He carried the light. Is it the hardship of grief and debt that has made you so blind, my son? We have raised you, Baruch, blessed one. We have poured all our learning into you."

"Yes," Baruch agreed. He was suddenly weary of the spectacle, and was surprised to discover a coldness or even a cruelty inside himself. "And in return," he said, "I am unexpectedly teaching you something. I am teaching you how to excommunicate someone like me, and how to remove all dissenters and freethinkers from your midst."

Overnight, the edict proliferated on notice boards and in the streets of the neighbourhood. Baruch read it six times before fully absorbing it. *He is cursed by day and cursed by night!* said the flowing script, borrowing liberally from Deuteronomy. *God will not spare him and therefore the community must liberate itself from his evil stain. The heretic was shown infinite patience and kindness, but from this day forward, we have no choice but to erase his name from the Book of Life. Be warned. Any person who communicates with him, reads his writings, sells him any item, or even comes within two metres of him will receive the same punishment.*

Baruch left quietly. He could at least attempt to spare Gabriel, whose business was thriving, and little Rifka, a new mother, further contagion. They refused to see him, in any case.

It was August. Carrying two small trunks into the street, he was immediately drenched in sweat.

He crossed the bridge over the Houtgracht and went directly to his acquaintance, Frans Affinius Van den Enden, a former Jesuit, who immediately gave him a room. Brother Orange followed them daintily up the stairs. To ensure that Baruch would not starve, Frans gave him a job tutoring Latin. The next morning, when Baruch woke in the narrow bed, he was unsure who or even what he was. In the mirror, he expected to behold a monstrous creature. Instead he recognized his father's long face and his mother's curious eyes. His curly hair stood on end, as if surprised.

A week passed. He was compelled by an ache, a longing, to see the Third Man, even just his shadow. On the tenth evening, Baruch, followed by the stray cat, returned to the outskirts of the old neighbourhood. They didn't cross the canal. Like ghosts they hovered at the foot of the bridge, gazing back to their former lives. He imagined that from one of those high windows, from a rooftop or a prayer room, the Third Man, too, searched for him. Baruch watched the sun set. The cat, emblazoned, seemed an apparition. Light filled the canals, an airy gold that arrived only in the seconds before twilight. If there was pain, and if at times the pain became unbearable, he vowed he would not speak of it.

ooooo

Around the table, we sat quietly, drifting in thought, the plates of food nearly empty, and all the bread gone.

The first to speak was Blucher. "Stubborn, isn't he?"

"Unlike us," said Jupiter.

The neighbours laughed and our table seemed to quiver in the moonlight.

"He's only stubborn about a few things," said Bento defensively, taking the last piece of steamed arrowroot.

"Which things?" I asked.

"Well, for example, Spinoza believes there are only a few things we can be certain about. But when something is True, it is always true—in all times and for all things. So a true thing must be surpassingly rare, maybe one of the rarest things we encounter. If a person is fortunate enough to intuit a truth, or deduce one, they shouldn't keep it to themselves. A true thing is a transcendent one in our mortal lives."

I yearned to understand. "You know when you feel happiness inside you," I said, "and you don't know why because there's no reason for it? It just lands in you, almost by accident, or because you happened to be standing in a particular place at some particular instant. Do you think *that's* a kind of knowledge? Is it a true thing, or is it totally separate from truth, just a part of living?"

"Mmmm," Blucher said. She drew a cigarette from her shirt pocket. "I think I see what you mean. It's as if there's no other place and no other moment. If unbidden happiness isn't a form of knowledge, what is knowledge?"

Jupiter lifted his cup, discovered it was empty and set it down again. "When I was happy, and also when I was grieving, I experienced a timeless time."

The room had blurred into darkness. Just a moment ago, hadn't bright sky and sun been everywhere? Tracing my finger back through the day, I couldn't recall the in-between before night fell. The teapots which had once been full were now empty. The neighbours had fallen silent, into their own thoughts, so I picked up the thermos and went to refill it. Before heading down to the boiler, I stopped at 12/C. Dad was awake and hungry, which was a good sign.

"We have food. I'll run and get it."

I brought him a tray and some tea, and pulled the curtains wide to welcome the starlight. Dad didn't like to be watched if he was the only one eating, so I continued down the stairs.

At the boiler, the line was long. A little boy ran up and down telling jokes. "Why should you never talk to π? Because π goes on forever!" He laughed so hard we had to hold him upright. His mother explained that these jokes were her son's belongings, like toys he carried from place to place.

"Why did the chicken get up and cross the Möbius strip?" someone asked him.

The boy leaped up and down, shouting. "To get to the same side!"

By the time I returned home, I had heard almost twenty jokes. Dad had finished eating, and the neighbours had gathered in our room to keep him company.

My three books sat on the table, looking battered and worn.

Jupiter still hadn't shaken his irritation over the volume on Du Fu. "This series can't have been very popular," he said. "It's all about failure."

My father examined number 3. "They were collectibles. All the kids read them."

I tried to change the subject by asking a question I'd overheard downstairs: "Is the moon older or younger than the earth?"

My father said the moon was at least four billion years old.

"How do you know?" asked Jupiter.

"Education," I said.

Dad cupped his mug of tea in his hands. Steam rose, fogging his glasses, and he pushed them up onto his forehead. His body was worn out but his eyes were almost too bright. My father explained that the moon was made of almost the same rock as the earth, so they could be sisters and near the same age. Or maybe our moon was one piece of a vanished meteor. Or maybe the moon, a solitary wanderer, had drifted near to earth and become caught in her orbit, their fates becoming one.

Moonlight rested on Jupiter's eye, cheek and part of his nose. "Three histories," he said, "but each one is a different reality. Is the moon at home or is it a foreigner? Are we watching its beginning or its ending?"

My father nodded. "I overheard you talking about happiness. When I was twenty-four, I met Lina's mother. Her name was Bee. I think happiness is an encounter. It's a kind of blessing."

Light slid across the table, as if searching for a spoon, or the finest rim of a glass. I felt a fracture inside me, not wanting to hear a word more about my mother and wanting to hear only about her.

The light touched Aunt Oh in our family photo. She was actually my great-aunt, the sister of my grandmother. We had taken this photo on Aunt Oh's sixtieth birthday. Leaning on her cane, holding my father's elbow, her smile seems to reach out and hold me. The ficus in Mom's arm, a fig tree, is the birthday gift Wei and I have chosen, a type of climbing fig whose name contains the character for devotion.

I said, "Do you think devotion is a kind of happiness?"

No one answered at first, and then Bento, following my gaze, leaned across and picked up the photo. He studied the faces of my family. "The ancients thought that we could confess our grief and pain to just about anyone," he said, "even to strangers, but we trust very few people with our happiness. The mark of a true friendship might be a complete readiness to share our happiness, and to receive theirs."

"I think friendship is time itself," said Blucher. "I think friendship is the homeland."

My father looked upset. "So when a man betrays his friends, is he destroying his home?"

Jupiter and Bento leaned forward, the sleeves of their house-coats rippling across the table. They began to argue amongst themselves.

My father's tea smelled of rose petals and sage. I stared at the photograph. *The notes disappear*, Aunt Oh once told me, but when and why? Was she teaching me to dance? I glimpsed us in the People's Park, sitting side by side, my small hand in hers. I remember the naps we took on the sofa, the eucalyptus scent of Aunt Oh's blouse with its pattern of joined and repeating circles. After she left with Mom and Wei, I hid in her closet among her clothes. The three of them had left in such a hurry, leaving behind so many precious things.

At the table, the neighbours bowed their heads and now my father's voice seemed to reach only me. Glancing at the photograph, he told me again the story of how, at the age of nine, he'd journeyed across the country by train, showing up unexpectedly in Foshan, at the door of Aunt Oh. His mother had died tragically and he had no one. He had been a shocked, grieving child. Aunt Oh had sacrificed everything to raise him. An expert seamstress, she worked endless hours, but still they barely had enough to keep afloat. Aunt Oh taught my father how to sew, embroider and repair. Detail, he realized, was structure itself. Detail, he said, prepared him for his future: the remaking of the materiality of cyberspace.

My father rambled and I struggled to follow what he was saying, and to fit all the contradictory pieces together. He had met my mother, Bee, when she was twenty-two. Inchoately, euphorically, he had pursued her the way a person pursues their destiny.

"When I was devoted to your mother," Dad said, "I was happy." Even as he spoke the words, I could feel his doubt.

Other things he had told me over the years: Your mother was exceptional from the very beginning. Your grandfather was an orchard worker. When Bee graduated from university, she accepted a job with the central government which involved going out to record, identify and classify every plant species in a given area. Your mother and I were the same, Dad said. We were children who grew up in the backwaters. Nobody had any expectations of us. We saw our loved ones discarded by this world. We knew we had to seize our destinies, no matter the cost.

Blucher said something that made everyone push their chairs back and go to the windows, and I was startled back into the room. The neighbours were talking, their voices running together like colours. The moon through the window seemed utterly still, yet I knew it was travelling faster than anything I could imagine.

"How much can a person learn with three books?" Blucher mused, picking up Volume 84.

"Each volume is a square of time," replied Bento. "Hundreds of mornings."

"And each morning is a universe," Jupiter said. "What's that saying again? 'Heavy is the root of light.'"

As if I were a pebble on the shore, I felt myself, bit by bit, dislodged by their words. Blucher picked up the story and continued.

7.

Hannah Arendt was in her good friend Lotte Sempell's Paris apartment, smoking in the bath. Exhaling, feeling blissful, she accidentally dropped her cigarette into the water. Hilarious! She splashed around trying to grab it. The typewritten pages of her manuscript were balanced on the rim of the tub. In one clumsy movement, she swept them into the water.

The water seemed to gulp three times—*plop! pllop! plllop!*—and swallow them.

Impressively, she had managed to grab the fallen cigarette. But when her right hand reached for the manuscript, it knocked over the glass of wine. Instinctively, she dropped the pages in order to catch the glass. Howling now, she climbed out of the tub, clutching both glass and cigarette, but no manuscript. The wine was turning the water a murderous red. She pulled the plug and salvaged what pages she could. *Ten years!* She had worked patiently, arduously on this biography of Rahel Varnhagen. Now here it was, her only copy. Bits of it were stuck to her legs.

She carried *Rahel* to Lotte's living room, knowing she could not be saved. Stunned, unable to fathom what had just occurred, Hannah dressed and fled the apartment.

At their meeting place, Walter Benjamin looked frantic yet still, like the horse of a carousel leaping in circles. "Late, late, very late," Benji said, pushing her through the tall doors. The auditorium was packed and they had to sit apart. Giants sat in front of her; all she could make out was the right arm of the speaker, Alexandre Kojève, which moved as if he were continuously tapping a child on the head. This awful day was the perfect time to hear a lecture about that goon, Hegel. She tried to relish it. Kojève was thrilling in an egomaniacal sort of way but other worries kept interfering, *Rahel, clumped on the floor of Lotte's apartment, moulding!* She had imagined an intimacy with Rahel Varnhagen, a kind of solidarity or even friendship that could exist despite the century that separated their births. She had dared to narrate Rahel's dreams. But even copying out a clean manuscript would be impossible. The pages would have to be trashed before they started to smell.

After four hours, everyone rose and walked stiffly out of the lecture hall. Benji, who couldn't wait to start insulting Hegel, was no longer upset by her lateness. Hannah was in the middle of re-enacting the bathtub farce when they ran into a friend of Benji's. The man, dressed in a suit, carried an umbrella even though it hadn't rained in weeks. He had a jaunty pipe. Terrifically handsome, terrifically cocky. Lovely eyes. A Berliner, it turned out. The pipe smoker curved towards her. He said to forgive his handsome appearance but he was in disguise.

"As what?"

"I'm a communist impersonating a monsieur."

"Well done. You're a natural."

He assessed her with interest. "And you?"

"I'm a loudmouth."

The great flock of friends—Benji, Lotte, Annie Mendelssohn, Erich Cohn-Bendit, Chanan Klenbort, and the faux Monsieur—went off to drink and yell at one another. She argued that Kojève was impressive even if one did not always agree. "He repels me," shouted Chanan. Benji declared Kojève's arms to be impressively long. Now everyone had something to proclaim. They moved on to Lotte's apartment where her friends exclaimed over the drenched *Rahel*, who had died a hundred years ago and now stood sopping. Hannah laughed and wept real tears. The friends argued even more. Finally, they lay on the floor like rolling eggs, singing in German, shushing themselves, bickering about whether it was clarity or passion that transfixed the world, thereby fixing it. They had a great many terrific thoughts, but no residency papers, passports or cash.

The faux Monsieur inserted himself like a comma at Hannah's elbow. His name was Heinrich Blücher, and he repeated Kojève's aside: "Frenchmen play chess whereas I, Kojève, play with people." She replied that, despite her antipathy to Hegel, it was refreshing to see Kojève study and actually seek to understand prior texts, rather than just utilize them, as intellectuals were wont to do these days, for their own nefarious purposes. This Monsieur, it turned out, was a sometime-journalist and also a former communist on the run. He fancied himself a string-puller. Not a Jew at all, although their friends teasingly called him The Rabbi. Like her, he'd fled Berlin and been living in Paris for three years. He had a wonderful voice, full, round yet anarchic, that sent chills down her spine.

It was passion between them from the outset. Heinrich said he would devour every bit of her, and Hannah replied, "Typical, between a German and a Jew."

Heinrich neither winced nor laughed.

"Love between us is completely out of the question," she said. Her husband had left for America in 1936 but had refused to divorce her, and she was still a married woman.

Heinrich loved to talk. Combat came naturally, but reaching across the distance for each other's thoughts felt natural, too. They attacked and defended each other's positions on the Jewish question, the Communist Party, Palestine, Berlin, fascism, the true meaning of education, the need to liberate liberty itself, and

Heinrich's insistence that one had to slam the books shut in order to live. Wrapping the world in language, he said, could make it vanish before our eyes.

"You need not always speak to me," he teased, "in such a doctoral tone."

She warned him, "In love, I treat you as I treat myself."

"In love with me," he said, "you'll come to treat yourself better."

Weeks later, he said, "I love you with all my soul, Hannah."

She shrugged. "The soul does not exist."

It was 1939. The news was grotesque. The International Brigade was done for. Every day, thousands of refugees fled from Spain over the Pyrenees, young and old freezing to death. Those lucky enough to cross the border into France were catalogued like specimens, and then shut inside barbed wire prisons. Women and babies had been interned in camps at Valence, and men were starving in Septfonds. Meanwhile, her friend Kurt Blumenfeld sent her a chilling letter. The Gestapo had forced three hundred Jews in Breslau, recently released from concentration camps, to charter a ship immediately and emigrate to Shanghai within the week.

"We must act," Heinrich said. "If we're too stunned to move, they'll round up every Jew and every communist in a single night."

But their friend Benji refused to consider leaving France. And Hannah did not want to talk about leaving him.

Time seemed to fall off a precipice. On September 1, Hitler invaded Poland. Two days later, France and England declared war on Germany.

On September 5, the notices came: all German males living in Paris must report to authorities at the Olympic Stadium. Benji, Erich and Heinrich obeyed and were immediately interned.

Hannah ran between lawyers and relief organizations, sometimes going back and forth a dozen times in a single day. Emergency visas were the best option but impossible to obtain. "The waitlist for an American visa is ten years long," she was told. "You should have applied years ago."

"What can we do?"

"Get to any country that will take you."

But for this they needed sums of money which they did not have.

Meanwhile, Heinrich wrote to her from the internment camp in Villemalard. His letter was formal, even cold, and was primarily a request for practical items: *Pants (Manchester velvet, beige or brown). My winter socks. A stainless steel kitchen knife (not a pointed one!).* Not a single loving word. Obviously whatever feelings he'd had for her were gone. It was her fault. She'd refused to admit that she loved him. Now, with the walls crumbling, how could he trust her? Then Heinrich, suddenly ill, was sent to the camp hospital. But instead of telling her, he wrote to Anne Mendelssohn! When Annie said, "Your Heinrich is very sick—" Hannah exploded. Exploded, via letter, at this hospitalized person whom, perhaps, she really did love. *You lie because you don't trust me to know.*

Silence.

Hating herself, she went to see his favourite paintings at the Louvre, as if she were visiting his circle of friends. But the buzzing crowds pained her. Giddy, empty talk, as if there were no invasion, no camps, no cruelty, no dead. Room after room of portraits staring over her head into a past moment that engrossed them. The war wasn't making her braver, only more broken. Courage and fear, jostling for space inside her, did not seem able to coexist.

At home, a letter was waiting: *My darling, I am still so happy. Especially when I think of the reservoir of love in our existence together. There's no reason for you to be upset. Of course there are many people here who think only of their own private fate—and in view of that I have fallen a little to the other extreme.*

In her next letter, Hannah apologized, which was dreadful for her, like opening her eyes underwater.

Three months later, Heinrich was given a release certificate from "voluntary work camp." It was the last week of 1939. He showed up at their door in Paris neglected, thin and stubbly. He took her in his arms. Over bread, soup, and a cake she made that suffered badly from the shortages and had the texture of ground beef, Heinrich described to her, in great detail, the conditions of the camp, the men, the situation. One day, a former officer of the Wehrmacht disdainfully lit his cigarette off the Sabbath menorah. The mix of German internees had made absurd, excruciating bedfellows.

As he spoke, the sun went down and the room darkened.

"Let us try to be together, Hannah," he said, "for our love's sake."

Suddenly the only official papers she had were divorce papers. Her husband, settled in New York, had finally signed the documents. The war had brought everything in France to a standstill yet somehow, Lotte, working her connections at the Paris civil court, performed a miracle: she obtained a marriage permit appointment for Hannah and Heinrich. On January 16, 1940, they wed. Their whole party was quickly drunk on the remains of a wine cave left behind by a fleeing Jewish merchant. These were friends, Hannah thought, with whom she could mourn and also rejoice, and wasn't the capacity to share joy, to entrust another with one's happiness, however fleeting, however complicated, an indescribably good thing?

They toasted the ridiculousness of their hearts. As the war readied its knives for them, she had hitched herself to an atheist German.

"I suppose reason cannot stand in the way of love," she said.

"Reason," Heinrich replied, "cannot stand in the way of very much."

Now if only the Paper God would float an emergency visa into their hands. First, one of them needed a job offer from a foreign country. This required affidavits, police reports, and all manner of replacement documents, without which an application could not even begin. London was their best hope, therefore she forced Heinrich and Benji into English lessons, proposing they read George Eliot together.

Benji was flabbergasted: "*Leave* France?" Paris was Benji's overcoat, hat and spectacles, his only pair of shoes.

Heinrich said, "Why on earth would I read a novel now?"

Still, they followed her to class, even though, each time, Benji made small dancing steps of protest. "I will learn exactly enough English to denounce the *ugliness* of this language!"

Air raid sirens sliced the night open. The shelter was a block away, deep inside the metro station. They crouched, surrounded by Parisians in gas masks, which of course they did not possess since they were not citizens. They could not even whisper to each other; their German words would open the gates of hell. She began to sleep through the alarms, and her dear Heinrich gave up trying to drag her from bed. They lay in each other's arms, waiting. The Greek philosophy she'd loved as a teenager came back to her, like rain into the groundswell of her thoughts: "For what purpose, then, do I make another my friend? In order to have someone for whom I may die, whom I may follow into exile. Ponder for a long time whether you shall admit a given person to your friendship, but when you have decided, welcome them with all your heart and soul. Speak as boldly to them as with yourself."

Money was what they desperately needed. What *did* they have in its absence? Walter Benjamin's library. Sundays, the group gathered at his home at 10 rue Dombasle, surprising Spinoza, Lazare, Heine and Kafka in their dainty quarters. Benji spoke in gusts. His boxes of scraps, bits, notebooks, photos, envelopes and general "stuff" were piled high. Incidental things, he earnestly believed, had the ability to unlock unnoticed doors. "In every disaster," he told them, almost happy, "a collector like myself is rewarded."

The spring of 1940 arrived, and with it a world descending to its knees. Now every foreigner, men and women, would get the opportunity to experience internment. What did it matter that Jewish and German *refugees* would be the last ones to welcome Hitler into France with confetti? Women were ordered to report to the indoor cycling track, the Vel d'Hiv, and men to the Olympic Stadium once more. Some were spared: Annie Mendelssohn, because she had children; Benji, too, thanks to a well-connected friend.

Still, Benji was a wreck. He was penniless! He would die without them! Oh, and excellent news, he had secured first editions of Kafka's early works! He would find the cash somewhere. But wasn't it suspicious that he was being spared internment? Was it a trap? Should he take his poison pills? Did Hannah need pills for herself and the Monsieur, too?

"Benji," she said with all the patience she could muster, which was limited. "They are interning men and women who are fit, whom they suspect of having fighting capabilities. Back in September, walking from Nevers to the Vernuche camp, you collapsed in a heap and had to be *carried* the whole way."

"But I *am* fit. I am totally fit for my purposes."

They smiled but neither felt better. Benji's excessive politeness managed to soften her bite. No one else had this effect on her.

They drank coffee as if they might never drink it again.

"In fact, I could have gone to England," he said, buzzed out of his mind. "But I told myself that no one could ever make me leave Paris."

"Well, what's done is done."

"I'm going to hide all my papers," he said. "Guess where!"

She rattled off a dozen places. He was mightily cheered by this game and finally told her, "In the Bibliothèque Nationale. Hidden in plain sight."

"Genius," she said, and congratulated him. She took one last look at his library, which was his most intimate circle of friends, for he had chosen from both the living and the dead, and bade him a hurried farewell.

Fear took everything, but there was no time even to be afraid.

Heinrich, a veteran of internment, gave useful advice. "In the camps, stay alert and bide your time. Choose your reading material carefully. Pack a book that can withstand a thousand readings."

He moved through their little room, touching the typewriter, the bed, the four walls which had given them shelter. He brought his heavy hands, warmed by the stove, to cover her shivering body. "I love you," he said, "with all my senses, with all my reason, and all my heart."

"And I, you."

They had long ago abandoned their souls. She breathed him in. They kissed and refused to say farewell.

At the Vel d'Hiv, the line was electric with rumours. When Hannah's turn came, she was questioned by a French commander who was so bored or drunk he passed out midway through. The assistant assigned Hannah a number and sent her off to find her "resting place."

The triangulated glass roof was coated in blue-black paint. The straw stunk of oil. The women had been advised to bring a fork and enough food for two days. Imagine, she thought, the velodrome empty of people, with two thousand forks glinting on its seats.

Horrible thirst. Horrible. It could not be helped. She busied herself by writing letters but words were flimsy, like hurling a carton of eggs at Hitler.

All around her, a sea of women. Mostly Germans, but also Austrians, Czechs and Poles. Communists next to Nazis, fascists beside pariahs, petty criminals, trade unionists and anarchists beside antichrists and politicos. Difficult to tell whose foot was whose. Hannah, for once, belonged to the majority—Jewish refugees whose German citizenships had been revoked, yet who remained German in the eyes of the French police. "Stateless no more," she joked to these acquaintances, but she was the only one who laughed. For the first three days, this was how she survived, drowning in ironies.

Air raid sirens, day and night.

The gorgeous roof, made of glass, was basically a grenade above their heads.

Dread was very draining. Therefore, practicality first! Sleeping configurations, food and water, care for the fragile and despairing, and please the gods, sanitation. Some women tidied obsessively as if maintaining their allotment turnips, others declared themselves magistrates and tried to boss the world. But what to do with all the young people? They, too, began to organize themselves by dominance, indifference, fear, submission and social status, like birds unable to resist formation.

Newspapers were forbidden. Rumours bombarded them: The Jews would be shipped to labour camps. They would be ladled into a bowl and offered to the Nazis. The waitlist for emergency visas to America was now 300,000. This last was no rumour, but miserably true. The relentless speculations were unbearable, as was the way gossip worsened terror. She spent the fourth day staring up at the dark painted glass and thinking of architecture, time, the Lecturer, trains, the world and everything in it. Her beloved Heinrich. My sweet numbskull, she thought. I feel you as close as if you were standing right behind me. *May the little world in which you and I make the rules live and prosper . . .*

On the fourth night, the dowdy woman sleeping adjacent rummaged in her suitcase and pulled out a chessboard.

"A chessboard?" Hannah said. "Shouldn't you have packed something edible?"

"Do you play?"

"Of course I do!"

The dowdy one was delighted. It turned out they were evenly matched, which was surprising because Gertrud was very nice and decent. Too fair-minded to be pushy on her own behalf. When elbows were handed out, she didn't get them.

As she considered her moves, Gertrud made a bizarre noise, a sigh crossed with a click, and this click-sigh was like a faulty clock. It irritated Hannah to death.

"How can you play at a time like this?"

She turned. The complainant was one of a group of Austrian communists, an icy girl with a blaze of golden hair.

"Boldness and strategy!" another woman huffed. "That's what our situation demands, not bourgeois games."

Gertrud blushed but was unbowed. "Boldness and strategy. Chess, in other words. Would you like a match?"

Five hundred women were plucked out and shuffled onto trucks. Off she and Gertrud went through the very centre of Paris, on transport slow as a hand-pulled cart.

How dark the Seine rippling against the morning.

Proper shops, mothers with provisions, boys on bicycles, apples apples apples.

Children staring up at them from beneath their handsome hats.

Nôtre-Dame reaching its tall ears to God.

What is this emotion, Hannah wondered, cutting into my chest. Panic? Self-loathing? The horror of fate?

At the station, their jailers had thoughtfully spread puffs of straw inside the freight cars. She and her fellow émigrés had considered themselves prospective citizens, so how nice it was to find they were, at least, good enough for straw. She wanted to shriek, curse and throw up on as many people as possible. Instead she bullied out a space for them, Gertie handing out apologies all the while. Somehow they landed on top of their suitcases. Thank God they were beside a door, where a tiny curl of wind touched her. The police bolted the doors.

For a long time nothing happened, except that someone actually did throw up. Some women cried, some rebuked the criers, some complained—"This car has thirty people but some of the others are nearly empty!" "They have seats, I saw them!"—some consoled, and some were silent. Finally the warning, a long whistle, and a hiss of steam, as if air were being let out of all the women. The wheels tightening, tightening into motion. They were off. A woman moaned, disbelieving. The waves of light began to change. Hannah closed her eyes. Gertie's click-sigh chafed against her panic. She would have throttled her companion but—how fortunate for Gertie!—she couldn't move her arms. They kept going and going and no one knew where.

When she finally opened her eyes, her eyelids were sticky. The ribbon of sky through the door whitened and abruptly vanished.

Better not to add or subtract time. The people in the freight car were very familiar to each other now, like a despised family. The transport halted in Tours. She discovered a new terror, the terror of leaving the train. Heinrich and I should never have registered ourselves, she thought. We should have left Paris immediately, we should have gone to London or Geneva with or without visas. If the law is lawless, a person can only become an outlaw . . . The train decided to keep going. She thought of her ex-husband, long settled in the United States, and the savage letter he'd sent: *It would be better if you do not make any use of the American visa and do not come. It would create an unbearable situation. You are right in your statement: I don't live alone. I have found a woman with whom I am together. I wouldn't want to give her up.* Hannah hadn't cared a dime about the visa. She had been exuberant because, after years of stubborn pettiness, he'd finally agreed to a divorce. Now her blouse was wet with sweat as if she'd been lying in the grass.

"We are in the south," someone said.

Conversations drifted and piled up.

Gertie clicked and sighed again, like some kind of fowl. "Eat this bread, Hannah," she whispered. "Don't be stubborn. You've had nothing all day and we have a duty to be strong."

A little woman, squashed into a ball, sang a German lieder. How rich her voice, how sublime the song. *A stranger I came*, she sang, *a stranger I depart*.

"Quiet, quiet, shut your mouth!" her neighbours said. "Singing in German! Have you lost your mind?"

But it was Schubert's *Winterreise* and they could all hear it even when the woman clamped a hand over her mouth as if the song had snuck out against her will.

The month of May blessed me
with many a bouquet of flowers

Gertie peered out at the slice of sky above the door. "Bordeaux," she announced as if performing a public service.

They waited on a side track for eternity. The train reeked of sickness.

After an interval, the journey continued.

Reprieve came in the form of music. What was it? So familiar, so near. A pattering, dripping, falling. It was rain. It was just the earth receiving the rain. Rain tapping insistently on their metal box. Through the crack in the door, she saw hills rolling past, puzzles of glistening fields, shining villages. Her body was cramped and in such great pain, she wanted to tear it away from her mind and fling it outside.

"Ponies!" a girl cried, as if she'd suddenly spotted her mother.

The child was half-heartedly teased.

The light, what was this tormenting light? Turning the air to liquid gold. The museums, remember them? Van Gogh wrote that *those who do not have faith in the light of the southern sea are the true blasphemers.* Heinrich said that Rembrandt's colours were tensions, contradictions visible in the chiaroscuro where synthesis is most alive. She had walked the Louvre's long galleries with him, arm in arm, the war sliding up to meet them like water rising over their hips.

At Pau, they were shunted into trucks. Her mind seemed to circle her body like a prayer. Villagers could be seen along the road and in the fields. Some were curious, some pitying, and others, convinced that the train held Nazi sympathizers, cursed them and hurled rocks. Could France fight a war if it couldn't even identify its opponents? Above and around was the blue sky, heavy with brightness. Sweet Gertie, kind Gertie, caressed her hand.

You do not suffer, Gertie seemed to say. You are biding your time. Life will save you.

No, a voice inside her warned. *Life saves no one.* Pull yourself together: only cunning and luck, not goodness and certainly not blind faith, can help any of you.

ooooo

On the twelfth floor, the moon had passed the frame of our windows. Everyone was facing a different direction, listening. I thought there was no more food to eat, but Jupiter got up and came back with a pineapple bun he'd been saving. We cut it into five pieces, and mine disappeared in a single bite.

"It's my favourite thing," my father said. "I loved pineapple buns when I was a kid."

"Is no one tired?" asked Blucher.

"Tomorrow we can sleep in."

"I feel like I dreamed about this night," my father said. "It reminds me of that book with Genghis Khan and Marco Polo. It was a story but also a poem. Our copy had a white cover . . ."

"It was Calvino," said Blucher.

"Right! The book was called *Invisible Cities*. We called the writer Ka'er Weinuo."

Jupiter touched his empty plate. The plume of his beard was so long it brushed his knees. "That's a nice name. It means 'the dimensions of a promise.' Or maybe, 'to safeguard a promise.'"

"Invisible cities," I said. "Was it a series?"

Dad shook his head. "Actually the father of Ka'er Weinuo was an agronomist like your mom. I remember exactly when she discovered this book. Your mom was doing fieldwork in Guangxi province, and she was out there for three or four months, sleeping in a tent. She read this book every night with a flashlight. Your mom told me the writer was describing China."

"Well," said Blucher, "wasn't he?"

"Could be. Lina's mom, Bee, also told me about this essay. It was called 'Ka'er Weinuo at the Chinese Station' and it was about the frame of things. The frame marks the boundary between the picture and what exists outside. The picture has a gleam that only separateness can give. But the source of that gleam is actually outside the picture because it's the light of the vast, endless continuum."

"I wish you'd packed *that* book," I said.

"You've got your imagination. That's a lot already."

"Some people have imaginations that have imaginations of their own," added Jupiter.

Bento wet the tip of his index finger and used it to lift tiny crumbs from his plate. He gazed at us like an owl peering through foliage. "Imagination without limits sounds like a nightmare."

"In that country," Dad said, "people would fight to the death over what's real."

"Great, that's *terribly* interesting," said Jupiter, "but what about Hannah, what about Gertie? What about people? I'm worried. Can't we go back to them?"

I, too, wanted to follow them.

"If I continue the story, don't forget what came before," Blucher said, looking straight at me. "Turning the page won't make it all dissolve."

The night slid past the window, and I felt a disturbing motion sickness. The water in my glass seemed to sway as if the floor were moving.

"What we call 'now' has no solidity," she continued. "We're always falling through it."

"It's not that a listener forgets, but that the one who survives to tell the story is always addressing a changed world. That's what this is all about, isn't it, Lina? Memory and its alterations. The storyteller shows herself through her errors and escapes. How much can a child learn from just three books? Maybe you and I should set our sights on the world that emerges between each and every person. Maybe imagination is a way to find that place."

In the room, I waited for someone to answer. But Dad had spoken so quietly, only I seemed to have heard his words.

8.

Now the trucks brought the women from the train into a town called Gurs. They rolled past double barbed wire fences, and into a military prison. The women were unloaded. Soldiers shouted at them, *Un-deux! Un-deux!*, and the women became a frightened herd, stumbling between rows of barracks. Gertrud, who had suffered polio as a child, could not run, so Hannah carried what little they had. They were ordered to push forward, past signs that read A, B, C . . . not knowing if they were running towards something or running away. At last, at the letter M, guards prodded them into an opening in the barbed wire. "Find a mattress, because if you don't," they laughed, "you'll have to sleep with us!"

She and Gertie entered the barracks in a daze. They sat across from one another on two pallet beds.

Gertie began to cry with a numb stillness. "It's nothing," she repeated. "Nothing. Just that my leg aches. It hasn't hurt this much since I was little."

The guards called this area, section M, an islet, an îlot. On the first afternoon, Hannah counted sixty pallets in each barrack. Twenty-five barracks in Îlot M. At least twenty îlots fenced off from one another by razor wire.

There were inmates here already. Hundreds of Spaniards had stood at the fences near B and C in silent greeting. A teenaged girl, malnourished, sent to assist the elderly arrivals, told Gertie that she and her mother did not expect to remain here much longer. "Last year," the girl said, "we were packed tight, like crickets in a jar. Everyone was here, Brigadists, communists, Basques . . . But anyone who could get out is gone. Mama and I have no money to buy our release, and nowhere to go." She had heard that they would be transferred to prisons in Spain.

The Pyrenees rose in the south, unreal, as if pinned magisterially to the sky. The barracks smelled of something rotting, but despite her earlier weeping, Gertie still clung to good cheer. "All will be well," she said to Hannah, meticulously braiding her hair for the night. Soon, rain hammered down on the wooden roof, which was covered by tarpaper.

All through the next day, people quarrelled. Some were determined to win what small comforts they could. Except Gertrud, of course. Gertie was as fierce as a puddle.

The wall near to Hannah was crowded with writing. In French, someone had written, *We were stupid. We trusted in international solidarity until it was too late.* In Spanish, another wrote: *What will happen to us?* Another answered: *Foolish question. Ask yourself instead what can we do.* Hannah's contribution was to write the date and mark the time, and thereby leave a clue to herself:

May 25, 1940, evening

She found herself longing to see Karl Jaspers, who ten years before had supervised her dissertation. His sunlit Heidelberg office appeared in her mind like a misplaced dream. She remembered the bizarre way Jaspers pretzelled his legs one about the other, entangling and disentangling as he considered problems without solutions and critiqued her writings on Saint Augustine. His wife, also named Gertrud, was Jewish, and the couple had fled to Zurich. Or at least this was the rumour, which she hoped was true. On their last visit, he'd told her, "The word 'German' is so much misused that one can hardly use it at all anymore." To which she had coldly answered, "The term is identical to misuse." He had neither argued nor agreed, but he had given up trying to persuade her that she, Hannah, was part of the German *essence*, a word that brought bile to her throat. Surely, she thought now, she would drink bitter coffee and argue with Herr Professor again. Her memory caught on the ink painting above his desk. A poignant Eastern painting, she recalled, where behind every mountain stood yet another mountain. He said it dated to the late Tang dynasty, eighth-century China. She had found the picture lovely but without heft. It was too delicate, too few brushstrokes to signify much of anything. Paintings shape the eyes. Give me Rembrandt any day! she thought. Rembrandt's subject is not beauty but transience.

She had not written to Jaspers in years. She had left a whole life behind. Frankly, she was done with universities, since the professoriate had turned towards Hitler as if to a new pillow in their beds and, as should be no surprise, they had done it collectively. But Jaspers was not like that.

More transports arrived from other parts of France. A guard complained there were six thousand of them, six thousand women! "Like a leper colony," he raged. Claudia in the next bed said that the camp commandant, on being told to expect fourteen thousand, had fainted dead away. The women in Îlot H, just across the muddy path, were agitating for a mass suicide in order to vex the French. They were almost persuasive until they weren't, only tragic.

Following Heinrich's advice, she had packed excellent books. But each time she opened one, the pages seemed blank, as if words had begun to erase themselves. She couldn't concentrate and was gutted by shame. She had been naive. She had convinced herself that the French would come to their senses: women would not be interned, certainly not children, and all would stand their ground against Hitler's cruelties.

Now, undone by her own errors, repentant, she listened carefully to each moment. Gertie talked about all things under the sun. Gertie made jokes when she shouldn't, and not even good ones. "Two men walk over a bridge," she said quite cheerfully, observing Hannah's futile attempts to escape checkmate. "One falls into the water, the other is called Helmut."

They bathed and washed their clothes under a thick pipe punched with holes which ran along the barbed wire fence. The water ran only two hours in the morning, and all fifteen hundred women in Îlot M had to push their way in. It took agility and fortune not to slip on the putrid ladder to the latrine. The guards stood like packs of wolves, enjoying the show. From morning to night, the women were ordered into the barracks and out again for no reason. What she needed to numb her panic—letters, newspapers, radios—was forbidden. Food was chickpeas in lukewarm water and one loaf of bread for every six women. Dividing the bread was the most volatile part of each morning, and fights regularly broke out.

The women went from fence to fence, making secretive visits to those in other îlots. "The name 'Gurs,'" Gertrud asked one day, "where does it come from?"

Minna in Îlot L said it was the name of a nearby town. "It's an old Arabic word, apparently, *gurtz*, and it means sinkhole. The Spanish girls say that, come summer, we'll see why. The whole place drowns in mud."

To sleep side by side with so many was otherworldly. It was terrible to wake in the night and hear women dreaming and crying out, trying to flee the terror they had swallowed.

There were other things, too. Humiliations and sudden brutalities that Hannah did not allow herself to put to words. Things she planned to expunge from her memory until one day, hopefully, the very worst was entirely forgotten.

Each twilight, she took refuge in an unnoticed spot where a breeze hurried between the buildings. Before the edges of all things turned dark, the mountains were outlined in gold. Momentarily, even the barbed wire dissolved. Noises from the road reached them. Bicycle bells, singing and fragments of conversation. Outside the camp, routines continued while inside time stretched until it broke.

She doggedly asked everyone who might know: "Where is the front?" "Is it really true the Belgians have surrendered?" "Any word from the other camps?" But there were no certainties, just speculation.

When Gertie shared the books she'd been carrying in her bags—seven volumes of Proust—Hannah laughed. Between the chess set, Proust, and a stack of writing notebooks, her friend was obviously no pragmatist. Also she was easily hurt, without inner defences, too honest and, despite all that, typically German. Gertie instigated idiotic fights over Hölderlin and Schiller, knowing that such fights could provoke Hannah and snap her out of her despair. She and Gertie had benefitted from the same excellent Weimar education, which gave them a sense of belonging. To what, after all? A set of books, a culture, to bits of philosophy, or a nation? To an inheritance that couldn't be withdrawn? The German poems they'd loved felt like lamps inside them, or maybe bitter pills, whose taste could not be dislodged. Damn this Goethe stuck in both their heads, which Gertie seemed to murmur without realizing: "But why confer on us, O fate, the feeling each can plumb the other's heart?" After a particularly hard-fought and humiliating chess match, Gertie soothed herself by reading aloud from her beloved Proust, that limitless passage about beholding the universe through the eyes of another, through a hundred others.

Hannah ignored her. She read instead from Heinrich's old letters. *I feel very close to you, and yet I miss you everywhere. I look for you every day and find you only in my heart, but at least that is completely certain. And that is why I hold on to the hope of finding you soon. I have patience, my love. Don't run away.*

—

Among the many impractical items Gertie had packed was a calendar, but eventually Hannah had to admit it was an inspired choice. Suddenly it was mid-June, and they knew it. Suddenly they overheard guards despairing over the news. The Germans were in France. They had bypassed the Maginot Line entirely and materialized at Sedan. Apparently the French had neglected to dynamite a bridge. In her fear, Hannah laughed out loud: Tant pis! Soon Hitler was on the road to Paris, trotting at incredible speed. Desperate families were caught in a traffic jam from Paris to Limoges. Really, the fighting was barely three weeks old, was this the end? France taking an axe to the knees. Every hour brought a more ridiculous and wretched story. Desperate civilians strafed by German planes, train stations bombed. Mussolini snickering as he declared war on France.

The hills turned green.

Panic. Except, of course, among the little clutch of Nazi internees, *actual* enemy aliens, shunned from the beginning, who now surveyed the camp with smug amusement. They spoke loudly to one another with aggravating cheerfulness. "Écoutes, have you heard?" they warbled. "Paris has fallen." An ironic smile. "Da kannst du Gift drauf nehmen." "The Nazi flag waves from the Eiffel Tower."

It was not even a month since the start of the real fighting. France had surrendered? Was it true?

The Gurs camp, still in the hands of the French, might be transferred to Hitler at any moment. Voices wailed around Hannah, but most persistently, she heard denial.

Gertie, with no identity papers and separated from her three sisters in Baden, was eerily calm. "Gurs is the safest place. Germany obviously doesn't want us back," she reasoned, "and the French would never deport us. Never. It is impossible."

"Impossible? Who interned us here?"

"To act precipitously is to err," the women of Îlot M insisted, foolishly, persuasively.

"Gertie, we must leave. Lisa Fittko and her group have gotten hold of release certificates. They'll forge documents for us."

"That's mad." Gertie sat on her mat and gazed at the chessboard. "What will happen to us if we leave?"

"An irrelevant question. We have to ask instead, *What can we do?*"

"Do?" Gertie's neck jolted. She looked at Hannah almost with spite. "Should I walk a hundred kilometres to heaven knows where, with no identity card, no money, nothing to protect myself, only to be left on the road—"

"Cowardice alone stops you."

"—nowhere to go except Paris, which Nazis now control? Or perhaps I should climb the Pyrenees into Franco's Spain?"

"You're no genius, Gertie. Your best hope is to trust me."

Silence. What Gertie had said was true: her bad leg meant that walking out of the camp, with no safe destination, was unwise. Was it also true that Hannah had no choice but to leave her behind?

"It does no good to express things so brutally." Gertie's voice was so gentle, it might mark Hannah forever. "It simply does no good."

They did not fight anymore.

There was no time, not even to try again or make amends. Gertie insisted on giving her a volume of Proust despite the added weight. "When we meet again, you can return it to me," she said.

But sentimentality was only a cover for the pain, the guilt and forgiveness, of saying farewell.

Safely tucked into Hannah's bag was *Time Regained*, which insisted that when *one has knocked at all the doors which lead nowhere, one stumbles without knowing it on the only door through which one can enter—which one might have sought in vain for a hundred years—and it opens.*

A commando of Austrian communists stormed the camp office, broke the file locks and grabbed the women's confiscated documents. Those women who had decided to depart, individually and in groups, walked straight through the gate and onto the road. The French guards, distracted by their own awful surrender, went on, dazed, with their tasks, except for one who chased after them, half-demented, crying, "Leave! Get out while you can!"

Yet nearly all the women, six thousand or more, elected to stay. Six thousand Gertruds whom the departing had failed to persuade. No more than sixty walked out.

Probably we're the fools, Hannah thought, but she kept going because the barbed wire terrified her more than the unknown.

Villagers in Gurs said the Nazis were advancing along the coast, and that the great encirclement was already complete. Villagers in Navarrenx reported that the socialist mayor of Montauban had promised shelter to political refugees.

"How far to Montauban?"

"Two hundred kilometres or so. Head northeast."

Some women got in a truck bound for Lourdes. Pulled in different directions, the group fragmented.

Nothing to do but walk. They crossed a stone bridge adorned with a heavy plaque, which proclaimed the village of Navarrenx a refuge, a sauveté, where man-made laws had no power and the unfortunate could not be pursued. Imagine if such a realm truly existed, Hannah thought. "Go to Montauban," said farmers on their way to Pau and Tardes, as they ferried the women to the next village in rattling vehicles like the skiffs of Charon. "You'll be welcomed there. The Resistance is organizing from Montauban."

The line of women—the Gursiennes, people called them, as if their ancestral homeland were an internment camp—was like a disjointed thought, stretching along the road, picked up and carried a small distance in farmer's carts, re-converging further along. It was June. In normal times they might have been ladies on a walking tour but today they were women who each carried a fork. They moved stubbornly, step after step, while the bloodshed, somewhere, around the next bend, leaped and curved instantaneously.

The land draped over itself, and behind one hill was always another one, achingly beautiful, a rebuke not to the gods but to the human world. Perhaps Hannah had been wrong about the ink painting in the study of Karl Jaspers, her lost professor. So few brushstrokes meant that the world wasn't covered over, and the page was inhabited by things that couldn't be seen, things that might be known but never would be.

Hannah trailed four Austrian communists whom she nicknamed Hertha the Good, Astrid the Virgin, Käthe the Wise, Rahel the Beauty. *Here is the pantheon of which I have dreamed.* She fell into step behind them. And you, who are you? *No one, only a loudmouth mortal. Hannah the Bellicose.*

Under the midday sun, it was folly to keep walking. This was the time for shade. She was desperately thirsty, but even that began to feel bearable.

Day after day, high thin clouds and no rain. Early mornings were a restoration. Endless sunflowers, valleys of quiet. She was startled by the yellows and greens, the hazy mountains. Brown ochre and cobalt blue, and between them nameless colours. The women followed streams and railway tracks, geometries of maize, vineyards, orchards, valleys. Hannah thought she smelled the sea, but it must have been the earth. How strange. The heat did not bother her as much as expected, but the light sometimes hurt her eyes. She wanted to bow down to the God of Shadows and sleep in his cold hands. The Gursiennes walked all evening. Farmers who met them on the roads sympathized, but stubbornly persisted in bringing unwelcome news.

"The surrender agreement," they said, "is harsh, very harsh. But we have no details yet. What disaster!"

The rooftops of Aquitaine had a foreign shape that appealed to her, upturned eaves made of thin bricks, which lent the little farmhouses an air of secretiveness. Food given or sometimes stolen—tomatoes, nectarines, a wheel of Tomme de Pyrenees—

tasted of a lost paradise. Things in the distance were fogged, gradations of blue confounded her eyes. Had the oceans finally swallowed the hills? It was hard to be courageous when all she could feel were the broken blisters on her feet, and the unrelenting sun. She thought of her friends, her cherished tribe, Annie, Chanan, Lotte, Benji, Heinrich, imagined them all walking towards one another on a crumpled map, and this gave her the will to keep going.

"The armistice agreement," the bad-news farmers said, "will return all German and Austrian refugees to Hitler."

"What?"

"It's in the armistice Pétain signed today. Article 19."

"But don't worry," another consoled. "It's not *you* they want. It's the Social Democrats and communists. About the German Jews, Hitler couldn't care less."

The women thanked the farmers for this information.

Hannah's throat was dry as straw and she felt an unearthly hunger. Some paths were pockets of emerald. Hertha the Good kept saying, "How beautiful, beautiful!" in stunned resignation.

Languedoc, or *langue d'oc*, the language of yes. Was that correct or had she misremembered the word, inventing a false meaning? But maybe the mistake was the key and held an answer. Yes to quenching her thirst, to life, to friends. Yes and yes again.

She was confronted by indescribable vistas. Famous paintings of this region—Cezanne's villages, Van Gogh's skies, all those fields of rapeseed and wheat—had furnished her mind with prior experience, so now she felt as if she were moving through her own memories and not an unknown place. She did not, to her surprise, feel alienated. Rahel the Beautiful taught them songs. They sang with gusto, as if their lives could be preserved by something as simple as joviality and good cheer.

The familiarity of the landscape, the old songs, made you believe that nothing ugly could happen to you, but of course hope was, as Baruch Spinoza had warned, an inconstant. Hope, he had written, arises from an image of something future or past, whose outcome to some extent we doubt. And was it Spinoza or another who spoke of despair receding, replaced by something which could only arise from a more shrouded realm: hopeless hope, nurtured in darkness, created by the freest part of each and every person?

Hertha, Astrid, Käthe and Rahel were certain, in touching ideological fashion, that Montauban could be reached as early as tomorrow. They had been walking for eleven days. Hannah hurried forward. Rain barrelled down. She glanced back to discover she had left the others far behind. Fine, the road was obvious and soon enough they'd reappear. It poured, it thundered. Gorgeous day, she thought, if you're a duck. She huddled in what seemed to be a provisions stall, except that it had toppled over. The cold menaced her. She fantasized she was playing chess with Immanuel Kant while a girl in a blue sweater brought them both figs and chocolate. They were on a train in the afterlife. Kant got bored. "Checkmate," he said. "Go away and return to your life." She wrote a long letter to Heinrich, ignoring the fact that she held neither paper nor pen and did not know where he was. She fantasized about the spongy almond cake she'd craved as a child. It had a German name which now felt painful on her tongue.

"Where are you running?" the trees asked.

"I left Gurs à la recherche de mon mari perdu," she replied and the trees tittered.

She breathed Heinrich into existence beside her. His warm heavy hands. His satisfying scent. They were lying in bed, memorizing a poem. Bertolt Brecht had sent it to Heinrich, tucked inside a long letter. In Brecht's poem, the Chinese scholar Lao Tzu chooses exile. He sets off for a solitary existence beyond the western pass. Brecht writes,

For in his country goodness had begun to fail
And evil once again was breaking through.
And he buckled on his shoe.

A child's rhyme in dreadful times. So Lao Tzu and his servant set out, carrying almost nothing. At the border, they're stopped by a guard:

"Precious items to declare?" "No, nothing."
And the boy who led the ox spoke: "Learning doesn't pay."
There wasn't any more to say.

As Hannah walked, a pinkish light radiated from the hills. She did not want words to come between herself and what she saw but still words proliferated in her mind and interfered.

In the poem, the guard asks Lao Tzu to write down what he's learned, because how else can an ordinary person find wisdom in these catastrophic times? The old man hesitates. "Do you really want to know?" The guard refuses to be offended. He says, "I may be just a poor tollkeeper, but I need to know about the mighty and the weak. If you know who'll win, then speak." Lao Tzu turns to the servant and gives him this lesson: "All those who put the question deserve an answer," and so, for the next seven days, the boy writes down what Lao Tzu tells him.

Whatever happened to that child, the servant who was also a student? But here was Brecht once more, insisting:

That gentle water, if in motion
In time can overcome unyielding stone.
So might, you see, is overthrown.

Now Brecht's poem was hidden in Heinrich's bag, endangering him. Her husband, a known socialist, a one-time communist, was exactly the kind of person French and German police wanted to annihilate. And she, a Jew? Well, there would be ample time to compare disasters, but not now.

The rain glistened and refracted in the sun. She felt as if she breathed inside a swirling glass. It was nonsensical to feel as she did at this moment—unbearably grateful, alive and at peace. Feelings that had no justification. It was strange, yet the fact of these feelings was real, a true thing in a world dense with untruths.

In the distance, she saw four heroic figures approaching. A dog barked in a rush of jubilation.

The Austrians approached. They pointed frantically down the road behind her and Hannah turned, expecting the worst. A rope, a giant knife, a three-headed dog. Instead, in the distance, shining with a silvery gleam, was a city from another time, heretofore disappeared by the rain. A long bridge and a series of towers, and through the heart, a river blue. The city, Montauban, miniature from this distance, glowed like a pink carnation between the folds of the hills.

9.

This morning, I woke early. Half in dreams, I heard the sound of the sea cascading along the shore, a pulse as steady as my own. There is no ocean here, though. I am fifty-seven years old, and I live in a crowded neighbourhood far from the past. My window looks out onto a burst of sky and a carpet of rooftops.

Outside, snow was falling but I distinctly heard my father's voice. "Even though I stand before the rivers and seas," he said, "my mind remains at the palace gate."

Why a palace gate?

My father had tried to explain by writing out the word mén 門. "The gate is the opening where everything touches. Inner and outer, yesterday and tomorrow, those with everything and those with nothing. The person I imagine I am and the person I turned out to be."

I got up and began my day. I spent the morning housekeeping and the afternoon running errands for the guests passing through this rooming house. For the last three years, I've worked as a caretaker here. It's an occupation in which I thrive: being able to procure things—objects and goods, medicines, as well as travel passes and documents—and solve problems. Sometimes the guests are journalists and I serve as their fixer and translator. Other times, I meet families trying to leave or return, people looking for work, importers and exporters, pilgrims and outlaws.

I still make paper from milkweed and other things, just as I used to do in the Sea. Life has given me an abundance of friendships and many makeshift homes.

This evening, a woman named Meryem hired me to repair the wheels of her suitcase. In return she gave me a pristine bolt of cotton; it was too extravagant a gift and I tried to refuse but she said she needed to lighten her suitcase. She was nearly ninety, and had come from the northwest. "And you, Lina," she said, "have you always lived here?" I said that I had left the city of Foshan when I was a child and that the outward journey, with many stops along the way, had lasted fifty years.

"An odyssey!" she exclaimed. "And where are your family, your children?"

"I was married for a time but it ended."

"A difficult subject, I can see . . . What about the place you came from? Foshan, I think you said." She was prying, but I liked her and tried to answer.

"Mostly I remember our apartment. The toys in my brother's room, for instance. He had a giraffe made of wood who sat on the edge of his desk. My mother was an agronomist and our balcony had pots of pink, blue and yellow flowers. Their scent was strongest at night. I smelled them even in my dreams."

"And your father?"

"He worked in cyberspace."

"Really? My wife worked there, too. Reyhan was a data scientist."

Meryem tested the suitcase. As she wheeled it around the room, she asked a favour of me. Would I mind keeping a letter she'd written, a letter for Reyhan, making a copy for anyone I met who came from the region of Khorgas?

I accepted the letter.

"Will you remember, Lina?"

"I remember everything."

"Great," she said, pleased. "Khorgas is the location of the Dzungarian Gate, so old even Herodotus wrote about it in the *Histories*. He called it the source of the North Wind. Do you know Khorgas?"

I shook my head. "I've never heard of it."

"That's okay." She thought for a moment, went to the wall, and began to draw a map with only her hands. "In my hometown, there's a mountain gate where the wind is constant, like a train that never stops running. The place we call the Dzungarian Gate is like a thin doorway in a huge mountain wall." She used both arms to express this mountain and it rose before my eyes. "This doorway sits between two countries which no longer have a name." She turned to me and her hand rounded into a cup. "I was born right here. My town sits on the oldest passageway between northeast and central Asia."

She stepped back from the wall and we both examined its emptiness for many moments. Then she moved her hand across the wall as if to wipe away the map.

"Before history," Meryem said, "a vast lake covered my hometown. It was called the Paratethys Sea, and it came into existence thirty-four million years ago. This sea stretched across Asia and Europe and overflowed into the Mediterranean. Over time, it began to dry up until its pieces became separated from one another into thousands of pools. The lake of my childhood, where I spent many happy years, was one repository of that sea. One rarely forgets beauty."

I could almost see this ancient water, a deep, shuddering blue.

In my pocket, I always kept small gifts. For Meryem, I chose an exceptionally beautiful constellation knot, tied from yellow silk. She studied it as if it were a code. When she looked up, she told me that she had not seen her family in more than fifty years.

"Reyhan and I were separated so long ago even our children would be old."

I nodded.

For decades, I had sought my mother, aunt and Wei in every passing face. I had kept going, convinced that life had promised to return them to me. How could I possibly grow old without seeing them again? Wei would be sixty now, perhaps with children and even grandchildren of his own. So I kept moving, certain that he longed for our father just as I longed for our mother. He was my double, my constant.

Not wanting Meryem to see my distress, which seemed such a minor thing in a world of endless flux, I busied myself with the white cloth, folding it carefully into my bag. She walked me to the hallway.

"Reyhan had grand, wonderful theories about everything. She believed the universe is an immensely complex thing born from a simple premise: it is the set of conditions for never-ending unrepeatability. She thought that, within the structure of the universe, nothing is forgotten. Nothing is wasted or without consequence. But . . . I'm not so sure. What do you think?"

I said I thought Reyhan was right, and that a hallway existed where all things cross over one another like an infinite string. That's what my father had taught me to believe.

"Is that a religious belief or more like a personal hope?"

I replied that I wasn't sure, but I suspected that we were surrounded by a room of forgetting.

"The room of forgetting," Meryem said wryly. "If only we could remember how to get there."

"It's at the palace gates," I said, "and no matter how far the body travels, the mind circles around it."

She laughed as if I had told her the most wonderful joke. She shook my hand heartily; she had a strong, almost ferocious, grip. But inside I was troubled. Even if Meryem's letter miraculously reached Reyhan, how could a reply be sent? Weren't some things too broken to be fixed, and didn't time become a mountain through which there was no path?

She reached out and held me for a moment as a mother might. "Goodbye, Lina. Take care. Remember, one rarely forgets beauty." I wished her luck and said goodbye.

In my own rooms, when the door clicked behind me, the twelfth floor materialized, just as shadows must when the lamps are lit.

I went up to the roof to wash clothes and hang laundry. It was hot and the ocean of my memory appeared like waves of silver bracelets dancing in the sun. I couldn't stop thinking about Meryem. As I pinned up shirts and trousers and sheets, the present and past encircled one another, like day enfolding night.

∞∞∞

Returning to the twelfth floor, I was glad to find Jupiter at his writing table. His scholar's cap was hastily tied, and the two loose ends dangled like ribbons off a kite.

"You've been out in the hot sun," he said, without looking up. "Keep me company. I made fennel tea."

I sat at his side and watched him work. Jupiter had tucked his long beard into his cloak, to keep it from disturbing the ink, and he looked like a tufted bird.

Here in the Sea, the written word was considered a kind of amulet, and travellers often hired calligraphers to copy poems, prayers, family genealogies, and sometimes the names of the dead in a book of records. The characters Jupiter wrote descended vertically in columns because, he said, words sink down through time. In the poem he was copying, the impoverished poet Du Fu undoes the strings of his coat to catch the night breeze. Describing a river of clouds, he says that the raft on which he floats could be a star in the night.

"Let us all go in song again," Du Fu says, calling forth his old life.

First, watching Jupiter, I'm standing on the edge of that piece of paper. Then Du Fu and I are side by side in his boat, which is a couplet floating on the page. His clothes are painstakingly mended, his face is haggard and sad, yet mischief lurks in his whole being. The wind makes a terrible mess of his thin grey hair. We are inside an old poem where no one can find us. I tell him that I am fourteen years old and that what I yearn for is something eternal, which I have named education, but what does education really mean? Du Fu says that education is a doorway that leads into things and through them, and through which others, too, will one day pass as if through a building of ten thousand rooms.

"Every time I leave this boat," Du Fu confides, "I'm afraid that when I return, the river itself will be gone. There will be nothing at all, not even land. The last words will have departed. And then what? Mortality seems an unbearable loneliness."

I say that his questions are my questions, too. I miss my brother who is my other half. My father is suffering, and I have no words to assuage my deepest fears.

Jupiter put down his brush. Around me, there was no river of clouds, no Du Fu balanced beside me on a boat. Just the usual things.

Jupiter got up and shouted at Blucher through Bento's doorway. "The banging of your typewriter is making me deaf! Please come and talk to me."

I could hear Bento complaining, "*Loud!* Everything is so loud."

Blucher kept typing.

"Listen!" Jupiter shouted. "That was a terrific story about Hannah Arendt, but I have news for you. This guy Lao Tzu is a total fiction. The story of his exile, the servant boy, the border guard? *Those who ask questions deserve answers*, yada yada? Nice touch, this Bertolt Brecht is an okay poet, but it's all made up! Everything the servant boy 'writes down' was actually composed by different people who lived in different centuries. That's how the text, the

Tao Te Ching, survived. It was all thanks to the work of various compiler-writers whose names are lost to history. Lao Tzu never existed! He's a figment of our imaginations to hide the fact that we don't know the source of the words we inherited."

In his room, Bento laughed.

Blucher's typewriter paused. "Are you trying to wake up Lina's father?" she thundered. "Don't you know he's not feeling well?"

Bento came and leaned over the doorway. He tried to play peacemaker by changing the subject. "Your Chinese poet, Du Fu, did he really . . . fail at life?"

"Life spat Du Fu out. But failure isn't the whole story," Jupiter said.

Bento shuffled in and flopped down on Jupiter's bed. The stray cat who loved Bento leaped up beside him, a puff of orange. "You know Du Fu's entire life story like the back of your hand."

"I read poetry. You should try it."

"You do know a lot about Du Fu," I said gently.

Jupiter looked mournfully at the poem he had just copied. "What am I," he said, "other than the things I know?"

I considered this as I began to sweep the floor around his desk. The sound of the tide was so near, it seemed only a matter of time before water soaked my feet. Outside the window, a cargo ship was visible on the horizon, and a line of people were carrying their children and belongings onto the sand. I peered out, searching for familiar faces, but none appeared.

Bento popped his slippers off and they bounced, one after another, on the floor. He was wearing the red socks I'd found for him. "A person is not what they know," he said. "A person is what they yearn for. Eternity has no longings. But for finite things, mortal creatures, longing is their very nature. Therefore desire is the inescapable essence of a human being."

Jupiter picked up Volume 3, which was leaning against the ink pot, and turned it upside down. "I am what I know," he repeated stubbornly. "What else do you and I possess?" He shook the book softly until its pages made a rushing sound. I was touched to see that despite his distaste for the book, he had glued it and repaired its spine. "Everything I know is aftermath."

10.

Du Fu was thirty-eight years old, ancient and without prospects. To pay for food, he'd had to rent out his beloved horse.

The neighbour girl set up his writing table. She unrolled paper, weighed down the corners with pebbles, mixed a dish of ink, and vanished outside.

Du Fu dipped his brush in luminous black:

Esteemed Shen,
Official Rectifier of Omissions!
Your goodness
is legendary. To a drowning man,
words are lost. I become
hope itself.

To compose an ode to a potential benefactor, an ode which was plainly an employment application, a resumé in couplet form, an exercise in self-promotion, and a letter crying out for spare change: could any use of poetry be more removed from art while also demanding the highest art? Distressingly, he was quite good at it, having practised this skill for several years.

He swished the brush in water, contemplating the curls of ink. Emptied of words, he squeaked his chair back and fled outside, to where the neighbour girl was meditatively sweeping.

"I live on the hundredth tier of a mountain," he complained, "on the edge of a precipice. I have no path to happiness. I am useless!" They stood facing the grey-blue world.

Then the girl gave him the broom and made him sweep. Soon, a dish of boiled turnips appeared. After he had eaten, she told him to keep trying. Back at the table, he wrote,

> *Shen of the Pure Reputation!*
> *Famous for rewarding*
> *merit. Yet even more heavenly*
> *is your*

"extravagant"? Or perhaps "enriching"? What about "kingly"?

> *limitless generosity,*
> *free of condescension.*
> *I presume to face*
> *your largesse the way*

a tattered pillow, a wingless bird, an old man with a runny nose?

> *an inconsequential*
> *shell*
> *faces the ocean.*

Working through the night, he managed to write a dozen such letters.

In the morning, Du Fu sealed the envelopes. He summoned the girl and told her to pick, at random, three volumes from the shelf. He couldn't bear to do it himself. By selling a few books, he'd have enough to pay the courier in the nearby town.

It was a long trek. The girl, running errands for her mother, accompanied him. On and on the road went, under the hot sun.

He was bemoaning his lot when, without warning, the ground began to shudder. They stared in astonishment as starlings exploded from the trees, driving upwards, shattering the sky. The girl yanked his arm and hurled him to the side of the road.

Horses. Hundreds of horses beneath yellow banners.

So brutally did the banners fly, slicing the air, they could decapitate a man.

Du Fu felt a sickening thrill. This was the imperial army bearing down on them. First he felt awe, then he felt ill. He pressed the sleeves of his gown over his mouth and nose. Dust, awful choking dust. A high-pitched howling turned out to be axles grinding against wheels, steel on stone. A demonic sound. Behind the cavalry came foot soldiers. But these conscripts were not soldiers at all. The arrows fastened to their hips bucked them sideways. Barely ten years old, he thought. Children whose faces wore a blood-curdling expression of terror and acceptance. On and on went this parade. The neighbour girl, horrified, had run further away from it, into a field. Now came real soldiers, hardened and poor. Tested young men who would have to carry the load. It was as if one man kept replicating and aging before his very eyes: the children turned into men, the men grew older, then older still until they were his father's age. Clothed in what? Nothing that could be called a uniform. Thin in every possible way, their chins, legs, arms, feet. Thin as slices of apple peel. They were farmers, hollowed out by hunger. Covered in mud, like open graves.

Conscripts enough for a war.

But there was no war.

Finally, at the tail end came the oldest men. Grandfathers. He began to run beside them, asking questions that came piecemeal: What? Where?

Passerby, they called him. Good passerby.

Impossible to see who was replying to him. It was like listening to birds trapped in a roof.

"No one to tend my field. My kids! When they conscripted me, I said I'd already served ten years. Laughed at me. *Pay some beggar kid to take your place. If you're too stupid to save yourself, whose fault is that?*"

"They herd us to a slaughter. There's a war going on that no one sees."

"First conscription, I was fifteen. Served twenty years before I got home. Now look at me."

"They've got fast horses and tax collectors, and we—"

"They want even more territory. Well! How else is a rich man to get richer?"

Du Fu scrambled behind. He heard the words *Why complain* like charging waves, angrier with every strike. *Don't waste your last breath complaining!*

"Ministers these days richer than kings. They have no limits, especially for killing."

"One egg is worth ten thousand of us."

"If it's not the army, it's public works. A son's birth makes you cry. You'll see how his life is wasted."

"Last year's bodies are still unburied. Their bones are bleached white."

The battalion kept going and going.

Du Fu's knees had buckled. He wanted to keep up with them, but couldn't. His face was caked with dust. The girl was beside him again. She offered him the flask of tea but the look on her face was damning: Is this the so-called perfect garden? Is this the centre you long to serve? Is this desire your very essence?

"Drink," he said, pushing the flask back into her hands. They stood still as the road settled and the horizon emptied once more.

He said, "For better or for worse, duty is my nature."

The girl examined her hands. They had turned grey with dust.

"If civil war comes," he said, "if the emperor falls, it will be the end of the world, and the hardships of today will seem a heaven compared to the horrors of tomorrow."

Her eyes rebuked these slogans. They told him that a dynasty is fated to fall when it loses the mandate of heaven. The collapse of the empire is the only justice available to the downtrodden and those with nothing.

"True, and then another dynasty will take its place. But if honest men don't serve, it will arrive at the same end. There's nothing new under the sun."

Her eyes turned away.

Du Fu thought but didn't say, A state without limits is a state ruled with indifference. Ruled with indifference, every crime becomes permissible. The abyss is approaching. And yet, he thought, my only calling is to serve. I have bent my whole life towards this redemption. All I have to offer is duty.

A month later, the Rectifier of Omissions replied, sending a letter, a poem, and three strings of copper coins.

Du Fu, Shen wrote, *I have a task for you. Do not embarrass me. Compose three essays, and I will deposit them in the Imperial Hope Chest. Keep it under your hat, but the Petition Box Commissioner is an old friend of mine! I advise you to confess all. Let the emperor know you're wrinkled now, nearly forty years old, but well-travelled despite all that, and you live humbly. Display your erudition! Dazzle us. I've placed the silk in your hands but it's up to you to cut the clothes.*

Hope and consternation crumbled Du Fu's heart. He asked the neighbour girl to find him some quality paper. When it arrived, he sent the girl away, unable once again to answer her questions.

Hours passed and Du Fu barely moved. He was listening to the fading sun.

As night fell, his shame and insecurity began to dissolve, revealing a clarity within himself. He lit a candle and began to write.

When, as a young man, he had sat the civil service examinations, he had been his own worst enemy. *I thought, of course,* he wrote now, *that I was extraordinary, and should immediately be elevated to a high position.* His failure had been spectacular. A few years later, he'd succeeded in failing again. Determined to diagnose his problems, he had wandered from river to river, becoming a thread in the ordinary life of the empire. *Twenty years have passed, and my sole desire remains to serve you and submit to your decree.*

All night and into the next day, he wrote.

Sometime in the early morning his father pulled out a chair and sat across from him. Somehow beloved Father, wearing the bright robes of the underworld, had entered from the door of the future not the windows of the past. He no longer seemed disappointed in his son.

"When you address the emperor," Father advised, "acuity is only half the challenge. You must let go of your fear. Our emperor is surrounded by flatterers, conspirators, opportunists. Intellectually brilliant men whose brilliance is in service only to their own advancement. For this world, they care nothing." Father rested both hands on his knees, suddenly ashen-faced, hopeless. "In the east, conscription has left thousands of villages empty. The fields are thick with weeds. This administration of lawlessness has collapsed the structure of things, destroying the pact between power and submission. This pact only exists by agreement, my son. When the reckoning comes, the price will be horror. There will be a rampage in which no life is spared. Pity your country, my son. Pity a people betrayed by its rulers."

The lines that slipped from his brush now surprised Du Fu. Love and dispassion, he believed, must exist together, like necessary beginnings of a single knot. Because of love, not in spite of it, he had an ethical duty to be dispassionate, to be objective. To the emperor, he acknowledged that his words could be judged treasonous. He hoped his sincere attempt to see the encroaching shape of things, and to raise a warning, would stand as proof of his loyalty to the realm.

Du Fu then offered the emperor a story, one through which to approach the possible. In this fable, the emperor meditates thoroughly and long, seeking to distinguish what is lasting from what is perishable. He sees that magnificent monuments in far-off colonies create an aura of power but are meaningless if the spine of the empire is broken. Impunity, permitted to fester, will outlast a leader's most glorious achievements. Even the greatest victories will become as dust. Time casts its judgments backwards. The emperor in the story understood this, perceiving how the ephemeral blinds us to that which is eternal. He chose to govern for the powerless and not the powerful, for the many and not the few, for the world that would arise from this one. The name of this emperor would echo in time, immortalised in the Mirror of History and the Book of Songs.

Forgive my indelicacy, Du Fu wrote. He had addressed himself to the ear of heaven and had taken liberties. *In all frankness, I'm terrified to think that I might die unknown and unrecognized.*

Two weeks later, a royal courier dismounted at his broken door, carrying a reply from the emperor's secretary. The scroll directed him to present himself immediately at the Academy of Talents. *The emperor has read your essays with keen interest.* Du Fu, his shoes open and broken, his long beard blowing ridiculously in the wind, read the scroll three times to be sure. If he allowed even one tear to fall, the ensuing tears might last for days.

After the messenger had departed, Du Fu embraced Big Red, his most faithful companion. The horse's eyes were universes in the twilight. They asked him: Will you believe in the things you've written after you have drunk the wine of the powerful?

"Don't worry," Du Fu whispered. "This time, my good fortune is real. I was patient, I was honest, and now I will seize my life."

Chang'an, the western capital, wrapped him in ten thousand colours. The city was a swirling cosmos of music and ceremony, order and whispers. At the Academy of Talents, Du Fu was ushered in to sign the register and a dozen ceremonial scrolls. The address he gave was the home of Secretary Du, his cousin twice-removed. "Temporary quarters," he assured the scribe, "until such time as I am settled in my new role."

He waited and a tea tray materialized at his elbow. The square of yellow cake tasted of heaven. At any moment, would he be shaken violently awake? Would he find himself shivering in his room where the window was made from the rim of a broken pot?

"The royal clerk arrives!"

A tall feather of a man appeared in a stunning robe. The silk was so splendid, he appeared to be floating in a liquid green.

Everything Du Fu had ever longed for muddled his vision. He stood dizzily, ready to receive his life. Would he enter imperial service at a novice's rank, or would he fly to an even higher stratosphere? Up to the twentieth rank, or even beyond! To take his place beside the great—

"An honour to meet you, Scholar."

Du Fu bowed, acutely conscious of his own thin white robe.

"The Academy of Talents requests that you sit a further examination. The exam, I understand, will be prepared by the prime minister and overseen by the minister of propriety. You will be made aware of the time and place."

"I see." His knees were wilting. "I wonder if—"

"Unfortunately, I have no further details. But allow me to say how honoured we are to receive one such as yourself, Scholar Du. I wish you . . . *luck*. I will see you out."

The smile flickered off. The royal clerk bowed, and Du Fu was ushered towards the door. A fan cracked open behind him, followed by the long sigh of a rustling gown.

How many futures, promising and horrible, now stood within reach?

He was led, one morning soon after, to his special examination.

A dozen Talents of the Academy surrounded him. The chair he was given did not permit him to sit comfortably. Tiny hands emerged from a long sleeve to add water to his ink dish.

He steadied his heart and lifted the brush.

The first question was read aloud.

Failure! his younger self hooted, half-crazed. *Chóngdǎo fùzhé! To follow in the tracks of an overturned cart, or bàngshā, using excessive criticisms to push someone to fail—*

"Stop it," he whispered.

The men around shifted, rearranging the daylight that had crept into the room. They read out one question after another, each almost comically simple. He began to understand it was a trap. Everyone knew that the double-dealings of the emperor's court could cost a man his neck. One day you were on the banquet list, the next the executioner's.

"Life," he murmured, wanting to weep.

Someone tittered, echoing a bird above the roof. He lifted his eyes and saw glances shoot across the room. Heartless. Duplicitous. *Focus, focus. Let go of your fear.* He described the state of affairs that confronted them. His brush curled and inked down the page.

When the sixteenth question was answered, he heard the time-keeper's steps in the outer corridor and the gentle swishing of the water clock. The hour was announced and repeated, repeated, repeated. The men of the Academy of Talents filed out without a backwards glance. The clerk in his bright green robe emerged as if through the wall.

"The special examination is concluded. We thank you for your presence. Good night."

Now he could only wait.

Cousin Du distracted him with board games, drinking games, poetry recitations, dice and riddles. One evening, at a neighbour's party, Cousin introduced him to the daughter of the former minister of agriculture. Miss Yang was a geometer and student of astral observation, skills inherited from her mother, author of a highly cited treatise that had been published under her husband's name.

"Both parents deceased," Cousin Du remarked the following day. "Yang Anyi is unmarried, for the obvious reasons."

Du Fu nodded, clueless.

"She's well into her twenties, just so you know."

He arranged to see the geometer's daughter again. He gave her some of his poems, described his circumstances, and said he hoped to soon receive an official post.

Throughout, Miss Yang was poised, even austere.

What kind of soul was she?

The following week, after visiting the Garden of Scholars together, they stopped for tea. Du Fu surprised himself. He asked if she might consider marriage and even—he continued recklessly, his chest infused by the morning light, delicate as pressed silver—love.

"The moon is round," she replied, "and so is the poem."

Du Fu gaped.

"I mean," she said, "we're alike. Our interests shade together—"

The wooden ruler in her book slid out and clattered to the floor. He bent to retrieve it but she was quicker. He was coughing, she was sipping tea. He was spluttering. Unable to speak, he reached out for the tea but she handed him the ruler. He blushed, lifted Miss Yang's cup and drained it. His coughing abated.

With a hint of a smile, she refilled the cups. "Yes," she said. "That's what I meant to say. Yes."

"Why would you marry me?"

He had confounded them both.

"I feel I know you," she said at last. "From your poems, that is.

The splendours of this world
All its beauty turns

Returns
To us
To earth as dust,
Mourn &
You go on mourning

Life bewilders

Death bewilders
An old Emperor lost his way

But beauty
One rarely forgets beauty

Being sentient
Not grass, nor wood
No
Not made of wood
Men love & regret the colours of
What passes.

She paused. "It's strange how, well, don't take this the wrong way, ordinary your poems feel, and yet how sustained, how daring, their meaning. I believe you are doing something new."

The old injury inside him quieted. As if, by simply turning around, he had discovered what he thought he might never find. "Miss Yang," he said, "do you also think about tradition and how it dies and yet survives in us? And how this loss or change can be felt between two lines of a poem or—"

An old man interrupted them, asking if they needed the extra chair at their table. The chair was lifted away.

"Won't you call me Anyi?" she asked, and added, "I have no dowry."

This must be the obvious reason Cousin Du had meant. Du Fu smiled. "Anyi."

She seemed touched, and gazed at him as if he were blooming flowers from the tips of his ears. "So we'll go forward together."

"Yes."

Not knowing what came next, he returned her teacup.

"Your nickname," she said. "*Jupiter*. Where did it come from?"

"My aunt, who raised me after my mother died and loved me like her own."

"It would have pleased my own mother," Anyi said. "She spent her life studying the movement of the planets."

The next morning, Du Fu was unexpectedly summoned to the court. Off he went, ecstatic. He remained waiting in an antechamber until evening when, at last, the clerk appeared. His face was glum and, once again, his fan cracked open, cracked closed.

"Scholar Du Fu, you have passed the special examination."

He held very still.

"But the pass was middling."

"Middling?"

"Mediocre," the clerk said helpfully. "Average. Ordinary. Nonetheless, you are requested to proceed to the Bureau of Appointments at your convenience."

"And then?" Du Fu said. He could barely hear his own voice.

Irritation spread from the clerk's eyes until it creased every feature. The man exhaled with his whole body. "A pity. Such opportunities are rare." Something else trembled behind his expression. A bitter smile, a flash of grief, but it was gone in an instant.

That evening, when he broke the news to Anyi, she took his hand in hers. How unlike himself Du Fu felt in her presence, like an egg lifted from a slippery surface and set into a cup.

"So we'll be patient, and wait to see what the Bureau holds. In the meantime," she said, "we have much to do."

—

After their wedding, they moved to an old tumbledown on the outskirts of Chang'an. It made a happy home.

Du Fu visited the Bureau of Appointments every day, and then every week. For months, he attended a great many functions where he was fêted, flattered and solicited for odes and rhapsodies. A permanent job, he told himself, was inevitable. Everyone knew that Emperor Xuanzong, the Illustrious One himself, had personally admired the sophistication of Du Fu's essays.

"Of course we know you!" Court officials twittered. "The scholar of the hour!"

At one evening's reception, gourmet dishes were paraded across the room, matched with rare wines. He watched winter plums, camel hoofs, and mashed kumquat circulate and finally exit, untouched and pristine on their gold serving trays. Beneath the trays, officials whispered vulgar stories about the prime minister, detailing sexual proclivities, scorned lovers, border failures, fabricated crimes, conspiracies, and uprisings ruthlessly put down. They spoke maliciously, as if testing Du Fu's loyalty with their theories. Perhaps, he thought, deep down they were disappointed by this world, or didn't believe in the reality of it. They entertained themselves by consuming it or defiling it, even tearing it to pieces.

He gave a half-hearted recitation of a poem. A purse with too few coins was dropped into his hands.

Outside, the wind was viciously cold. He worried the guards would smell the food in his cloak, which he had pilfered to bring home.

His horse was led out by the stable boy. "Your animal has the patient gaze of one who has walked the world."

Big Red stamped a hoof youthfully in the dirt.

"It's hard times." The boy rubbed his weary eyes. "But our good ministers must be doing what they can to bring relief."

Du Fu could only nod.

There were beggars everywhere. Homeless, they camped outside the city gates, cold as stones. He had a foreboding he couldn't shake, as if a tether were stretching to its limit. When it snapped, everyone's true face would appear and no one would be spared.

Hours later, he stepped through his own door. Anyi was at the astrolabe, studying the Dunhuang star map while a copy of *The Mathematical Classic* lay unrolled across the bed. They were expecting a baby and between these four walls their lives could only be described as blessed. It was stupefying, breathtaking, to think that in a few months he would be a father.

Undoing his cloak with frozen fingers, he felt buffeted by the greatest joy, itself perforated by the greatest fear.

"Here he is," Anyi smiled. "Laureate of the banquets."

"It is he. But I have made a new pledge. I will ask no more questions of heaven. I've irritated even the minor gods." He touched her hair, the softness of her arms. His wife's papers were alive with calculations relating to the current preoccupation of her field: a new symbol for nothingness, referred to as zero, an emptiness that had a value and from which meaning could, mathematicians hoped, be derived.

"How do you feel?" he asked.

"Perfect."

"I stole these dumplings for you."

He watched her eat, the moonlight bathing each item on her desk. Books appeared like fragile porcelain. The dumpling was held aloft, so perfectly folded, a white shell. With a dramatic flourish, he removed three oranges from his pockets.

She laughed. "Thieving the emperor's oranges! What kind of guest are you?"

"I am a husband. It is my true vocation."

Late into the night, as she wrote her miraculous, clear equations in a fine hand, he too added a poem to his papers:

I sing that which occurs, that which is neither
modern nor ancient, and my songs—rising

and breaking against the trees and shrubbery
of palaces that stand, in their lavish parade,
innumerable—accept their mortal heart.

∞∞∞

On the twelfth floor, Jupiter fell quiet. We listeners had voyaged
so far away that I began to understand there might be no way to
return. Bento went to the window and opened it.

I heard a very quiet sound. At first I thought it was Dad writing
in his notebook or tearing out the pages. Perhaps he had overheard
Jupiter's story, including the description of zero as *an emptiness
that had a value*, and, delighted, rocked by memory, reached for
his pencil.

In fact, it was the sound of the tide washing out.

From the window, I saw the shoreline and the bright clothes of
many foragers. The ocean delivered all kinds of driftwood, plants,
shellfish, plastics, metal and glass. Things cast overboard from
ships, or washing in from far-off places. Every day, we received
something unexpected. When I was younger, I thought that if I
threw something into the ocean, it would come back, transformed,
like something old surrounded by something new.

The neighbours were talking but my thoughts roamed. Other
centuries were falling down on us like rain through the trees. This
rain was everywhere, shading through the air.

Sometime later, after my errands, I returned to the twelfth floor
with a bag of shepherd's purse that I had foraged. They needed
meticulous washing, so I set myself up in the atrium where Dad
and I could chat through the open door. Lately, he had grown so
weak, he needed help to cross between the rooms.

"Last night, I dreamed of Beijing," he told me. "I said I would
tell you everything. Not now, but soon . . . but I dreamed of a person I used to know, Professor Tong."

I turned the jicai over, shaking the leaves free of sand.

Bento, carrying a wooden chair, came to join us in the atrium. He fished out a handful of greens, took a bite, grimaced at their bitterness, and immediately ate some more.

Dad continued, "I wish I had a second chance at life, a third, a fourth."

"Wishing the past away," Bento said, "won't give you any insight into your life."

Startled, I kicked Bento's chair. But Dad only laughed. "Nice way to talk to a dying man!"

The words disturbed me. On the windowsill, the blue covers of my books gleamed. I wanted to steer us to a different subject, so I said, "In *The Great Lives of Voyagers*, Baruch Spinoza encourages his friends to observe life with greater clarity, and in this way 'move towards freedom by degrees.'"

"How many times have you read those books?" asked Bento.

"A bazillion times."

"It's not good to be a three-book person."

I agreed. "But they're all I have."

We listened to the swishing of water as I continued to prepare the vegetables. I thought about the immensity of the ocean, how it might travel endlessly without ever understanding its shell.

"One day, Lina," my father said, "you'll have more books than you could read in a thousand lifetimes."

"I don't mind rereading. But . . . in Volume 70, a lot of things get skipped. There's almost ten years the book just ignores. On page 30, Spinoza is excommunicated and becomes homeless. But when you turn the page, he's a famous philosopher with a thousand enemies who want him dead." I splashed my hand in the water. "How did he adapt to losing his family and home, how did he survive loneliness? No one says."

"Lonely!" Bento laughed. "What makes you think he was lonely? Spinoza lived his whole life with big families. Children ate him up."

"I don't believe you."

"It's a fact. The sons of Herman Homan brag about playing mumblety-peg with him. That's a knife-throwing game where the loser has to pull a knife from the dirt with his teeth. With his teeth! They say Spinoza lost on purpose. That was later on, when he moved to Rijnsburg. Homan was his landlord there."

"Volume 70 doesn't mention that."

"Personally, I think a book that neglects its minor characters might not be trustworthy."

The doors on the twelfth floor seemed to slide open. I could see Blucher's shoes as she sat on her sofa, and Jupiter's hat as he leaned back in his chair. He had finished writing a tall banner which now hung against his door. *You and he are both dreaming. I who say you are a dream am also a dream. The question of who is the dreamer is as trivial as the passage from day to night.*

"Time never goes missing," Bento insisted. "I think the structure of reality can be no other way. Therefore to glimpse reality as best we can is the root of true happiness."

Dad adjusted his blankets. He said that forgetting was also a necessity. "What's the use of passing on a history like mine, for instance? It would only break my daughter's heart."

Bento considered this. His jacket, once black, had faded to a bluish-grey, and I saw that the elbows needed mending. "One way or another," Bento said to my father, "your child inherits your life, so let her inherit a true thing not a false thing. Isn't that the very least a father should do?"

Offended, my father turned his face towards the ocean and said no more. The colours of the sky moved across him, they tinted the blankets and wall a pale blue. Bento picked up Volume 70 and studied it for a moment. To my surprise, he slid it under one wobbling leg of his chair. He sat back, the chair perfectly balanced, and resumed the story.

11.

After the edict that erased him from the Book of Life, Baruch Spinoza left the neighbourhood that had raised him. He moved into a house on the Singel Canal that was never silent.

Why no silence? First, there was the family—Frans Van den Enden, Mrs. Van den Enden, whom everyone called Mother or Mem, six daughters, one son, three maids, one cook, one man-servant. Second, there were the boarders—Baruch Spinoza plus five more who slept in narrow rooms on the top floor. Third, eighty-two day students enrolled in the Latin school's multi-year curriculum. That made 102 people in the house. On Wednesday and Saturday afternoons, when no classes were held, the youngest, Baby Maria, cried bitterly. Too much quiet disturbed her.

The six boarders plus four of the Van den Enden daughters taught Latin. Baruch had charge of the littlest ones, who came on weekends to read Erasmus's *On Civility in Children*. Erasmus guided them to cultivate a calm face, not to stand around like storks, and to refrain from eating like wolves.

This morning, his room felt deathly cold, and for the thousandth time he imagined what it would be like to go home.

"Meneer Espinoza?"

The door stood ajar, revealing Sophy, the daughter of the washerwoman.

He stood, reached for his purse, and opened it despite knowing it was empty. "Forgive me, Sophy. Could you tell your mother that I'll pay my bill next week?"

The child, far more wretched than he, nodded. She vanished behind the door. From the third-floor classrooms, boys shouted in Latin, "I DO NOT FEAR the wheel of fortune!"

It was unconscionable. Baruch crossed the hall and knocked. Kerckring appeared, frighteningly tall, holding a clean scalpel. When not teaching Latin, he studied anatomy and took immense pleasure in dissecting organs.

"Kerckring, could I borrow three guilders? It shames me to ask but I—"

"Of course." His neighbour's neutral expression, betraying neither curiosity nor pity, touched Baruch. "Here. Take this . . ."

Outside it was pouring. At last, he caught up with Sophy. He must have looked a sight, sopping with rain, utterly bedraggled, but the girl's smile was like the sun.

Back inside, he squelched up the stairs. Clara Maria, tutoring Advanced Classics, turned as he went by. Seneca spoke to him through her clear alto.

"We are not given a short life but we make it short. You ask, *what is the proper limit to a man's wealth?* First, having what is essential and second, having what is enough."

But how? Baruch wondered. How to obtain what was enough?

That evening, Clara Maria, Margareta, and the twins, Adriana and Anna, gave their weekly household concert. At the height of Clara Maria's exquisite solo, the book on Baruch's knee tumbled to the floor, scattering its unbound pages.

Baby Maria wept as if she herself had fallen.

"Grant us thy peace," Clara Maria sang, "in this our generation." Her voice redrew the shape of the room. Imagine if music were the afterlife. If Isaac, Miriam, Esther, Mai, and Pai moved like notes on the air . . . To his great surprise, his eyes grew wet. The composer, Heinrich Schütz, had written sacred music addressed to man and God, mourning the five million dead of the Thirty Years' War and rebuking the silences that hid the toll.

On the carpet, Brother Orange rolled over on his back, lifting his upper third like a piece of dough. The cat proceeded with his evening toilette, occasionally lifting his head to yowl.

The performance ended. The four sisters held hands and were enthusiastically applauded. Baruch got down on his hands and knees to gather up his book, Cavalieri's *Geometry, Developed by a New Method through the Indivisibles of the Continua*.

Lysbeth, the housekeeper, built up the fire. Damius came around with brandy-wine. The fragrance of an orange, peeled somewhere behind him, sprang through the air.

"Did you enjoy the concert, Baruch?"

Clara Maria was gazing down at him on the floor. "But . . . you're weeping."

"Something got in my eye."

"Damius, get Spinoza some lemon cake!" shouted Mem. "He's homesick for his own kind, poor flower."

"No, his soul has been touched by Clara Maria's voice." Tall Kerckring reached down to tenderly squeeze Baruch's shoulder, but in doing so inadvertently tipped his brandy onto Baruch's head. Clara Maria, eyes widening, darted away and returned with a cloth.

Kerckring, oblivious, led Adriana in a jig.

Spinoza wiped brandy from his ears. He felt he might scream with irritation but how could he be angry at Kerckring, who had just lent him three guilders? Moreover his neighbour was always willing to share his beer and snacks, and was forever trying to interest Baruch in his anatomical studies. Kerckring's room was packed with horrors: the airways of a rabbit floating in a bell jar, an etching of an autopsy-in-progress, a bone saw.

Baruch, eating lemon cake, watched the gathering as if he were visiting from some distant star. The tenant in room three, a tapestry-maker, was playing chess with Frans, and another was hollering drunkenly out the window, "Good evening, ladies!" Meanwhile Kerckring was whispering in Clara Maria's ear. She looked up at Kerckring and smiled.

It was too much. He preferred his lonely room. Quietly, he slipped away.

Upstairs, Baruch opened his notebook and studied his drawings and diary. In Portuguese he wrote, *A morgen or morning of land is the amount of space that can be ploughed in the time of a morning. Can the time of a morning be measured by distance? Is time a kind of space?*

Somehow, I must direct my thoughts outwards, into the world. Otherwise my life will pass me by.

His bedroom was a bowl of ice. The previous tenant, a shipwright named Theodor, had died of illness. Was this Theodor's final view, this window smaller than a comb? Brother Orange leaped onto the bed. The cat circled, stretched, and finally settled his girth on Baruch's feet.

"I am a pelican of the wilderness. I am sad."

The cat yawned.

He fell into an unhappy sleep in which he ground his teeth. In his dream, he couldn't find his shoes. A girl picked him up as if he were a doll and said, "We'll drop this washing off and go have supper, Helga." Baruch opened his eyes, thinking he was a child again and his brothers and sisters were heaped around him. But all that was a past life and irretrievable; it was morning now, and students were thronging the house.

"The ancient gate is large," they recited, so loud it was as if they were kneeling on his pillow. "A lens is a series of prisms!"

A tall, tall man, Obissi the Venetian, appeared in his mind.

"Without a few friends," the students warned, "life is not strong."

Gasparo Obissi, a former butter-maker. He had set up a glass workshop in the Nieuwe Zijde, producing lenses for spectacles and telescopes. Years ago, Obissi had loved Baruch's father like a brother. What if the bond still held?

The harbour bell clanged, and the ships along the Damrak whipped and sawed, tilting like giant dancers. Baruch walked into the wind, crossing to the New Town, entering a street of rope-makers. The day was consumed by mist. Fog wiped out a street, and then revealed it, as if the street were rearranging itself behind thick curtains. He kept going, past a familiar thermostat shop. Now a bottle shop with its display of blue tumblers. Across the street, a sign read, *Clear spectacles help us see the common good.*

The wind knocked his hat off.

He chased it, the hat spinning like something possessed.

Pouncing, he snatched it up. Rooting it firmly on his head, he straightened and saw, through polished glass, a man in a leather apron, tall as an exclamation point, yellow wooden shoes anchoring him to the ground. Gasparo Obissi. Heart pounding, Baruch stepped through the door.

"Spectacles, microscopes, telescopes?"

"I—"

"From the Nightingale, aren't you? Tampion's got the bill of lading."

"My father—"

"Dropping off or picking up?"

"Apprenticeship," Baruch managed to say. "For a Jew who hopes to enter the business. Meneer Obissi, perhaps you re-member—"

The set of gauges in Obissi's hands froze in mid-air. He looked up and, for a long moment, contemplated him. "Why, Bento Espinoza," he said finally. "You're trembling like a newborn."

Baruch pressed on. "I came to seek your guidance. I've had some troubles lately."

"Yes, yes, I know. Miguel's debts were heavy even before Isaac passed." Obissi sighed and began flipping pages in his ledger, hiding his eyes. "You'll die of pneumonia in a coat as wretched as that . . . I heard you were chased out of the Vlooienburg. Is it true? All sorts of rumours have been flung about."

"Two months ago, yes."

"I heard you were expelled."

"Yes."

"Denounced as a heretic?"

"Yes."

"Oh. But . . ." Obissi glanced up, a little frightened. "Where do you live now?"

"In the Latin school of Frans Van den Enden. He's given me room and board in exchange for teaching the children."

They had a brief, awkward chat about Latin and Catullus. Behind Obissi, the workshop screeched. Lathes of all kinds, rows of glass rounds, a display of spectacles and spyglasses. A shiver ran down Baruch's spine. The workshop was exactly as he remembered; its unceasing labour catapulted him back to childhood.

"One moment," Obissi said, clomping off to answer a summons only he had heard. En route, he gave instructions to a boy and, moments later, the boy brought Baruch some breakfast ale and a hunk of bread.

It tasted of barley and sugar. He wanted to kiss the loaf.

The boy gaped.

Embarrassed, Baruch, mightily chewing, pretended to examine the goods around them.

The boy, following his gaze, moved with antelope steps towards a shelf. "This, sir, is our collection of laps." Proudly, he ran one hand over the brass discs, some small as silver coins, others wide as carriage wheels. "We use them for grinding lenses." The boy kicked at a sack, which sneezed up white cloud. "This isn't ordinary sand, but top-grade Vincentia. Over there, on the stove by Sonnius, that's Greek pitch. It's not for eating," he added helpfully.

Baruch managed to swallow the bread in his mouth. "I see. And what work do you do here?"

"I'm an everyman." The boy's whole frame seemed to shiver. He scratched miserably at his right hand, which Baruch now saw was tightly bandaged. "I'm in my second year with Master Obissi."

An apprentice. Ten years old, if that.

Baruch had been so small the first time he'd witnessed these machines and their inhuman racket. Labourers working treadles and pedals with their wooden shoes, polishing circles of glass with metal dishes. His Pai had come here to buy in bulk.

Obissi had once placed a peep-tube in Baruch's small hands. "If it were night, Young Master, you could bring the heavens near. You'd swear the moon was so close you could reach out and pet her nose!"

The tube had a velvet collar that tickled Baruch's eyebrow. He had looked down the telescope's hallway and seen, at first, only a whirl of colours.

"Focus, focus . . ." Obissi had said, showing him how to adjust its vision.

A thin man had appeared. He was putting on his overcoat. He was *right there*, close enough to sniff. As if Baruch had been whisked across distance without time. The man was cold. His shivering fingers fumbled with the buttons, straining to fasten even one.

"Some of these modern telescopes," Gasparo Obissi had said, "can leap your eyeballs twenty miles . . ."

The thin man was alone. Hands shaking, he tried to button his coat, and kept failing. Would no one come to his aid?

". . . anyone will be able to look into our spyglasses and leave this war-torn world behind."

"My boy will be your first customer. Look at him! He thinks he's on the moon."

Baruch blinked and looked up, expecting to meet his father. Instead he saw Gasparo Obissi, side by side with his apprentice. "Just yesterday, Fluweel here suffered a painful injury."

"I burned all my fingers and even the thumb. More bread, sir?"

"Thank you, no. I'm very sorry about your hand."

"Hurts like a big hammer."

Obissi gestured for Baruch to follow him. At a desk, he opened up a massive ledger.

"Miguel told me you studied Euclid, said you spoke the new calculus as if it were your mother tongue. He was proud of you."

Baruch quelled the emotion rising up. "I tried to improve myself."

"You hope to apprentice here, did I understand you right?"

"Yes, but I know—"

"Sonnius can do the honours. That's him—Sonnius, give a wave, will you?—best lens grinder in Amsterdam. I poached him from John Alt." Obissi gave a satisfied smile. "Now, as to wages, they are minimal. But enough, I hope, to get your coat mended and put a little fat on your bones. I can guarantee, at least, that the training will be first-rate."

"Thank you. Thank you for—"

"Thank me? No, I've looked high and low for someone with a gift for the new mathematics. Now . . . you've left the Vlooienburg and obviously they don't welcome you there . . . but to the guild it makes no difference. You're a Jew in their eyes and barred from permanent employment here. I can keep you for two months, no more. And we'll need a good story."

"Tell them my interest is the export trade. Brazil or Chile."

Obissi laughed. "Or both. When the guild hears the words 'New World,' they're pudding in your spoon."

He rummaged through a box, dragging out an apron. "In two months, if you're suited to the craft, we'll talk contracts and such.

Build you a lathe, get you set up. But let's not praise the day until it's evening, agreed?"

"Meneer Obissi—" Baruch's voice shook. "I'm in your debt."

"Hup hup, let's get to it. You've got oceans to cross in a very short time."

Each month, the workshop, with its eight craftsmen, two clerks, and one apprentice, produced 3,500 pairs of spectacles while, next door, a consortium built frames. "From here to Rome," Obissi said, "have you ever seen an engraver without eyeglasses?"

"No!" Fluweel cried joyfully. "All their eyeballs go mis-shaped."

"Prepare yourself, then. Everyone in our trade eventually becomes a customer."

Five of the lathes were as huge as donkeys, and two as small as cakes. The turners, moving with great delicacy, shaped one glass round after another. Glass dust coated their aprons in a winking, sparkling light.

First lesson: melting glass over the controlled flame of an oil lamp. Sonnius was a strict master. No new skills would be taught until Baruch could produce thirty single-bead lenses in under an hour.

By the tenth hour, he still could not do it.

Beside him, Fluweel drew an enormous eyeball and labelled it neatly. "Here's the *pupilla*, the hole in your eye," he said. "That's the baby door that lets light through."

Baruch mopped the sweat from his face. Around him, five craftsmen, their machines facing one another, seemed to dance in rows.

Fluweel picked up two convex lenses and held one in front of the other. "Look, Apprentice Baruch," he said, "this is how you get a telescope. Curved glass has heavenly qualities. It can make Saturn seem as close as your own nose. The hollow bends rays of light—*refracts* it, do you know that word?—and gathers them in a single point. *Focus*, that's Latin for hearth and home. A lens brings all the light home, as Master Sonnius says."

Baruch's head clanged with new learning. He had to learn how to make tools. How to mix pitch. Understand tempers of glass, know the many grit sizes of silicon carbide and emery, and the number of "wets" required for attaining exact curvatures. Simple eyeglass lenses could be made by machine, but a single telescope lens could go through twenty-four different changes of abrasives, with a painstaking wash between each. Machine work, followed by intensive hand polishing, could take weeks.

"Let us pray that you are a patient man," Sonnius said.

On his second week, he was allowed to touch the lathe.

The machine was an awkward, ugly thing. A spring pole, dangling above, that bobbed up and down. Its pulley rope was joined to a metal dish, and made it oscillate back and forth. A round of glass was affixed to a cylindrical handle and pressed against the oscillating dish. In this way, glass was gently hollowed to produce a lens.

"Off we go then," said Sonnius, his left foot caressing the pedal. "Turn, turn, look how we are turning!" Under his lead, the machine was swift and powerful. Meanwhile, Sonnius's right hand pressured the glass against the turning dish. His upper body, focused and quiet, appeared suspended in prayer. It was marvellous. Baruch half expected the machine to turn to him and speak. The lens was lifted up. A soft curve was already swelling through it.

"Give it a try," Sonnius said, pity in his eyes.

Baruch faced the beast. His foot made a jerking movement against the treadle and the spring pole lunged into motion. The dish spun, it made a terrible keening, a muscle popped in his back, and he was sure his left foot had somehow been lopped from his right arm. *Help me*, he struggled to cry, as dust garbled his vision. The machine was screaming murder, wanting to smack him to the ground.

"Wipe your sweat now," Sonnius said. "For you can hardly see."

Baruch froze, his foot in mid-air. The machine continued shouting, as if worked by demons. Finally it slowed, a rhinoceros out of breath. When Baruch lifted the lens, he saw a large crack.

For a moment, he and Sonnius stared at one another. The whole workshop seemed to pause. He heard the unfamiliar sound of Obissi giggling.

"It's simple, Brother Spinoza," Sonnius said kindly. "Just imagine that you're threading a needle while galloping upon a horse."

Sweat dripped down his back. "I see."

"I used to think it would swallow me whole," Fluweel confided. "Kick me down and make me lick its boots. But it doesn't hate us like that."

Sonnius said, "Here's a fresh piece of glass."

They carried on.

Each night, darkness fell instantly. At close of day, shopkeepers scrubbed down their patch of cobbles, leaving icy patches that took him by surprise. A dozen times he slipped, skidding on his bottom in ridiculous ways. But the worst was the wind. A new coat, some three hundred guilders, was beyond his means. Still, this winter, between teaching Latin on the weekends and apprenticing during the week, he would have enough to get his old one patched. Solitary lamps glowed like tiny suns at the foot of each street. He would endure the sleet and cold. Baruch stumbled to the Van den Enden house, frozen, hungry, exhilarated.

Four weeks passed. In the workshop, Baruch had a stack of orders assigned to him.

METIUS, GALILEAN TELESCOPE 20X−1

SANTINO, BICONVEX SPHERICAL +1.50 3 DPT QUARTZ

IPPOLITO, MICRO-BEADS−200

BROUWER, PIETER JAN, SPYGLASSES MILITARY GR.−16

"My opinion," Baruch mused, continuing his conversation with Fluweel, "is that each person's life has a form, and the form is created by what each person chooses to love."

"*Chooses* to love?" said the boy, incredulous. "But love chooses us!"

"Oh . . . do you think so?"

"Didn't you say," Fluweel persisted, "that sadness is just an emotion? And that happiness is *just* an emotion. But I think Sadness and Happiness exist for themselves, like water and sky. They alight in us, as if we were vessels for their travels. But hang on: why does Master Obissi call you Bento?"

"It was my father's name for me, my Portuguese name . . . well, hold on a moment. I need to concentrate . . ."

Bewildered, he studied the order for the tenth time. Metius, a professor of mathematics at Franeker, had ordered a replica of Galileo's 1610 telescope, a magnification twenty times the power of the human eye. A gift for his son, apparently. On Baruch's last attempt at the plano-convex lens, some leftover grit on his sleeve had gotten onto the lens and scratched it. After more than fifteen hours of work! He had crumpled over the little glass in despair.

"Boy, run these papers over to the Nightingale, pronto!" Tampion called.

Fluweel cantered off.

Baruch contemplated his work bench. Callipers, various dishes and basins, a pot of warm water, turpentine, Swedish pitch ready for heating, tins of silicon carbide powder in various grits, jeweller's rouge, brass templates, two glass rounds—one for the lens, and one to act as a tool. He talked himself through the steps: fix the glass blank (a) to a wooden disk, and the wood to a smaller piece of sheet iron, and attach the whole thing to the lathe to create a grinding tool; fix glass blank (b) to a cylindrical handle so that (b) can be ground into the plano-convex lens.

When he ground (a) against (b), it would result in a glorious parabolic curvature on a 38-mm-wide lens, which was the size of a rather small biscuit.

Adjustments, adjustments, a thousand adjustments!

Every detail foretells the future, as Sonnius never tired of reminding him.

His left foot set to work. The lathe woke and began its labour. The grinding tool swivelled, now clockwise, now counter-clockwise. Holding the cylinder in his right hand, he pressured the glass blank against its sibling. First, long movements as Sonnius had instilled in him, to rough out the curve. Followed by briefer elliptical movements. When the abrasive ceased to cut, he added another dusting of 80 carbo and a few drops of water.

Grounds of glass shimmered before him, all the world clarified into flecks, and he had an eerie sensation that dust was hardening on his skin. Soon he would be wearing a shining shell. Stay *focused*! The glass curved, and Baruch felt as if he, too, were taking on a crescent shape.

Carefully, he washed out the tool and the lens. He went out into the street, took off his shirt to the whistles of the frame-makers across the street, and shook it free of grit. Inside, he reattached tool and lens. He measured out a finer grade of abrasive. He pedalled the lathe into motion once more.

The glass was the softest vault.

Two hours passed in this way. When night darkened the windows, he removed the lens from the lathe, as tenderly as if it were a baby kinglet. Everyone had gone home except Obissi, who was sorting tomorrow's orders. Baruch washed his equipment, set a paper cover over his work-in-progress, and walked home. The hours of his life felt compressed, like the sky's horizon reflected in a cup of water. Clara Maria's voice was stuck in his head, her voice serenity itself: "How can you wonder that your travels do you no good, when you carry yourself around with you? You are saddled with everything that drove you away."

The next morning, he resumed.

Intermittently, Sonnius came to inspect his work. "Every day you grow a little more patient. That's nice to see."

Baruch began to polish the lens by hand, wearing it away, turn by turn, with an abrasive of washed emery. When the morning sun speared through the window and landed on his chest, he knew he could rise to a finer grade.

Sonnius circled around again. "The mirror is all," he said approvingly. "No matter how fine all the other telescope bits, if the mirror is poor, the thing is helpless. No action, however small, is minor."

At midday, Fluweel brought him a plate filled with cheese, figs, roasted parsnips and bread, and also a pot of kandeel. After lunch, Baruch had a small nap under Tampion's sorting table. He woke refreshed, in the gentlest of spirits.

Hours curled around him, as if surrounding him in a parabolic form. What were minutes to him now, but the slow curvature of this circle of glass, the working out of a question of form, which must be a kind of essence, so that the final curve would contain, inside itself, the whole history of its polishing. *Every detail foretells the future.* So the afternoon vanished.

Finally he prepared a cloth, more like a pillow, filled with tripoli. He continued to polish. His body was so tired, but his mind felt focused—at hearth and at home—and free.

There came a moment when he could almost hear the perfection of the lens.

Heart in his throat, he brought it to the testing room. He lit the lamp and closed the door. Distances, used to gauge the point at which the lens focused, were marked on the table. He set the lens on a stand and peered through. He studied the items on the far end of the table. First, the landscape painting. Second, the map of Amsterdam. Third, the page of Biblical text.

His heart beat wildly as the lens, and his own eyes, filled with clean, sharp images.

Baruch put out the lamp and exited the small room. He carried the lens to the window. Fluweel hurried to join him. Baruch lifted a strand of horse hair and cast its shadow against the upraised lens. He examined the shadow for interruptions, breaks, nicks, ruptures. He shifted the horse hair and looked again. He searched for the most minute imperfections, certain they existed.

Sonnius was here now. Baruch handed the lens to him, and he, too, examined it.

At last, Sonnius said, "The arc is true, the lens is perfect."

Fluweel let out a whoop of joy. All the craftsmen turned like figurines rotating on a dish. His friends stomped their feet and hollered, inaugurating his glorious lens. Paired with a convex partner, it would be able to see not just the planet Jupiter but its many moons, and wasn't that a wondrous, almost unbelievable, thing?

Afterwards, in the soft spring air, he hardly knew who he might be.

Before he realized it, his feet had carried him to the Rieuwertsz bookshop. In the display window, Tables of Contents beckoned him inside and through the entry. He skirted the shop's reading room, where men sat at long tables flipping the tall pages of the latest bulletins. Baruch was gripped by a loneliness so ferocious he had to lay his hand on the table, ever so gently, as if it were the table that needed comforting.

He scoured the offerings. A title caught his eye, jolted him, made him turn. *Don Quixote*. When Baruch's family was still one, Cervantes' hundreds upon hundreds of characters—the Knight of the Mirrors, Dapple the donkey, sweet Rocinante—had crashed through their rooms and into their dreams.

Jan Rieuwertsz bounded towards him. "Speak of the devil. If it isn't Spinoza himself!" He clapped a hand on Baruch's back. "We wondered if you'd gone into hiding. Jellesz, Simon de Vries, Pierke Balling"—he ticked them off on his fingers—"not a single person has seen you all winter! All we've got are crazy rumours. Come to study circle next Saturday, alright? We're holding it right here. Ibn Khaldun's *Book of Lessons, Record of Beginnings* is our book of the month."

"Thank you, Jan. I'll be there."

"Your hair is glittering, did you know?"

"It must be glass dust from my workplace."

A customer called the bookseller's name. Rieuwertsz brushed particles from Baruch's hair, concerned. "That can't be good for you. See you Saturday!"

Don Quixote, unbound, cost half a florin. Giddy, almost disbelieving, he received his copy. Isn't it true, he wanted to ask, that words can never be as precise as rays of light? That words can never be as prismatic, as close to truth, and therefore, as close to God? And yet, for reasons that seemed to have no words, the novel comforted him. He protected it in his arms and hurried home through the darkness.

Two months passed quickly, and in the blink of an eye, summer would return. His little room in the Van den Enden house now held a lathe, glass blanks, bags of sand of varying textural classes, and eight brass laps, all delivered last week. Baruch missed the turners, especially Fluweel, who had a mind like a butterfly net. But Obissi assigned him a steady stream of orders, and Baruch was grateful. All day, he laboured. In the evening, when Kerckring returned from dissecting corpses, Baruch repaid him the three guilders long owed.

With this debt erased, he felt at home in himself again.

He was almost asleep when he heard the clavichord.

The notes were richly patterned, and yet so precise, so purely moving. Awash in tears, he pulled on his coat and stumbled out to find out what it was.

Clara Maria gave him the name of the composer but no matter how many times she repeated it, he couldn't make sense of the name.

"Don't struggle," she said kindly. "The music is foretold but the composer is not yet born. He will arrive with the future."

Baruch sat somewhere above her, in a hollow of the wall. The music rejoiced through him, unspooling feelings for which he had no name; how revelatory this sound was, and yet how perplexing.

My thinking is haunted by my actions, he thought, and my dreams are haunted by my life. What if happiness never graces my future? *Futurus*, about to be, on the cusp of existing. Clara Maria, if offered all the paths of this world, which would she choose? And for myself, isn't it inevitable that I will one day go back to the elders, to Talmud Torah, that I will go back to my only home on hands and knees, begging forgiveness? Might they accept me and love me again? Wouldn't it be better, in this short life, to accept the joy that only belonging can provide? Why did I run away, tail between my legs, to loneliness and ridicule? Isn't it far easier to lose oneself than to remake oneself, and isn't the remaking of a new self as difficult as the creation of a new world?

Mai, Isaac, Miriam, Esther and Pai had died more than three years ago, but it felt like three seconds and three centuries. Baruch was stuck in mourning. He no longer existed for Gabriel and Rifka.

"But what is mourning?" he asked the music.

"Mourning is the painful letting go of a certain and once credible future." Clara Maria had lifted her hands and the clavichord was playing itself.

All the intelligence in her eyes leaped out to touch him. "Baruch, the lenses you make, aren't they a kind of machine, a machine for seeing?"

"Yes, perhaps that is so."

"The human eye that looks through a lens, is it also a machine?"

"In a manner of speaking, yes."

"And the mind that interprets what the eyes perceive, wouldn't this also be a machine?"

He shook his head. "I don't know."

"The quality of a given life depends on what a person chooses to love, isn't that so?"

But what did such words actually mean?

Clara Maria did not belong here either, he thought. He, Baruch Spinoza, could cease to live the outward life of a Jew; he could survive when expelled from his community. Perhaps. But Clara Maria, despite so radiant a mind, could not flee and find employment in a Latin school, apprentice in a workshop, or recklessly borrow money from the anatomist next door. Such things were forbidden to her. But why? Didn't widows live that way? Were some people condemned to be secondary in this world?

Clara Maria quieted the clavichord. She said, "There is never a moment, never a time or space, in which something is not acting on another. Even the mere act of perception changes us. It changes both the perceiver and the perceived."

After that, she continued playing, but how unreal the music was. He could not hear. He could not see. Terrified, he waited, expecting at any moment to be reduced to nothing. Without any memory of the sequence of events that took him there, he was back in bed, his nightcap soft against the side of his face, and then it was morning.

ooooo

The neighbour's daughter was washing the windows. Bento hadn't heard the door; he must have fallen asleep in his chair. Something felt out of order, as if days and months had been removed from his memory. He looked down at his table and saw notebooks, tools, and a glass blank still attached to its cylindrical handle. Orders, many orders, thanks to Gasparo Obissi. But he was confused. His chest had a pain as sharp as little knives.

He tried to pick up where he'd left off. He ground the lens a hundredth of a millimetre more.

"Are you okay, Bento?" the girl was saying. She had turned away from the shining window and was assessing him critically. "Your cold was getting worse so Dad sent me to get these mulberry leaves—"

"I'm nearly finished."

She drew near, until she was peering over his shoulder. "What are you writing? What's a 'scholia'?"

"Writing? I'm not writing, I'm polishing a lens for . . ." But when he looked down he was indeed holding a pen.

"There's soup and bread here. You haven't eaten since Wednesday afternoon. That's two days ago . . ."

He stared down at the pages in his hand, on which someone had scribbled the words, *Caution! Beware of malice in the guise of zeal.*

He was aware of the tide, the creaking building, the smell of a burning cigarette. Music was pressing against the walls. The girl had stepped into the next room, and he could hear her conversation with her father.

"Is what you remember always behind you?" the girl's voice asked. "Because I also get confused by—"

"Don't think about past and future, think about frame and picture. Something is inside the frame but only a part. The frame itself is made of the present day and the picture appears unchanging but in fact . . ."

The voices drifted off.

Blucher came in. A string of pearls had crept out over her black brocade coat. Her grey hair was carefully brushed, curling back on one side and sweeping out on the other. Like a handkerchief in the wind, Bento thought, waving farewell.

Perhaps she intuited his pensive thoughts. She tapped fingertips, irritated, on his rounds of glass, leaving smudges. When she pulled a chair towards her, dust particles rose from the cushion and shivered in the light. The music from the next room felt as if it were coming out of his own ear. She picked up a brass template and said, "This is Beethoven's last piano sonata. Number 32. Do you know it?"

"Beethoven . . . someone I know was just mentioning him."

To his bewilderment, she slipped the brass piece into the pocket of her black coat. When he protested, she said, "People thought Beethoven was refusing to hand over the real ending, that he'd sent an unfinished sonata to his publisher. But that wasn't true. He was deaf by then, did you know? The second movement, which is the final movement, is monumental and simple. It has an inner inevitability that frees you as you listen." She paused. "Whenever I hear this sonata, I know who I am."

Bento felt himself in the grip of someone else's memory, a memory that was at the root of this building and which seemed, relentlessly, to surround him. "I feel very odd. I wonder if my old malaria is coming back."

Blucher touched a cold hand to his forehead. "Could be. That's definitely a fever. I suppose . . . none of us is getting younger. Should I close your door and let you sleep?"

"Where's Lina? I'm afraid to close my eyes."

She was startled. "I am, too. Let's talk. Maybe it will take your mind off things."

"Yes. We're voyagers, after all."

They laughed. Beethoven's distant music was like the sun setting on the moon. The girl returned with a basket of laundry and began to fold it. Jupiter came in and lay down on Bento's bed. Soon the stray cat arrived to take his usual place. When Blucher spoke, they fell quiet while the world, streaming through clouds, refracting off the waves, never stilled.

12.

In the summer of 1940, people kept arriving in Montauban. Hungry, frantic, they held on to rumours—that Russia had declared war on Germany, that Mussolini had been felled in a coup—that fed unreasoned hope. The facts were cruel: France had been severed into occupied and free zones. Yet even here in the free zone, refugees could be rounded up and deported to Nazi Germany.

The mayor's office kept a list of empty rooms, and Hannah Arendt was given a place on the rue de la Comédie, above a photography studio. The ration system kept her fed and clothed. She was grateful, despairing, and sometimes indifferent. The latter frightened her. Indifference would numb her fear and make her incautious. In a moment of carelessness, what might happen? Endings she dared not imagine.

In *L'Humanité* and *Le Populaire*, thousands of personal ads crammed the pages. People searched for mothers, children, friends, pets, all lost in the chaotic flight from Hitler's invading armies. Overnight, two million French soldiers had become prisoners of war.

The sun crept over the hills, whose shadows lengthened like things recalled. Hannah wrote letter after letter. Beforehand, the group of friends had all agreed to use Lotte Sempell's Paris address as their routing station for messages, but so far Lotte had received nothing from Heinrich. No one in the group knew where he was.

Well, there were so many camps to choose from! Life would be acceptable were it not for world history.

But Hannah could take no comfort from her own jokes.

How to joke when, on the radio, collaborators gave righteous speeches, blaming the weakness of France on sex, foreigners, pastries, Jews, degenerates, and a hidden enemy within. Marshal Pétain, glassy-eyed, shook hands with Hitler. "I dedicate all of myself to France to appease its agony," he proclaimed, declaring collaboration the high road to honour. A fool, but it was unwise to underestimate even the biggest buffoons.

She longed for Gertie. Only Gertie could distract her with truly bad jokes. "All the children are playing with a knife, except Hannah. She has it in her head."

July, a sky of searing gold.

Lonely, she haunted the long rows of a nearby bookstore, The Rose, which was nestled into the arcades of Montauban's central square. The spectacled bookseller, wearing a shop coat of pure Prussian blue, dusted the shelves with an enormous ostrich feather. Drifts of music washed in from an unseen record player: Handel, Tallis, Monteverdi, otherworldly and impossible. Qualities which struck her as achingly real.

One day, the bookseller appeared under a sign marked *Romans*.

"Forgive this interruption, mademoiselle, but are you an admirer of Georges Simenon? No? You have never even heard of Inspector Maigret!" Delighted, he dropped a stack of paperbacks in her hands. "Please, I insist. It is overstock. Maigret is a strategist. Read and you'll see what I mean."

Within three days, she had devoured them all.

The French police system was now alive to her, Simenon having shone a torch over the whole order. "Every race has its own smell," Maigret thinks, "and other races hate it." A line that made her recoil in disgust, which gave way to horror, and then fear, and bit by bit, a painful clarity. French police were ordering all stateless foreigners to register at the gendarmerie. She *would not* register. Once the lists were compiled, they would be trapped. Survival required disobedience, and each of them must become an outlaw. So be it.

Beloved Gertie managed to send a letter, forwarded by Lotte. A fire, Gertrud reported, had befallen the Gurs administrative office and consumed many files. *A German commission came to review the camp and left us as we were. The Reich authorities are not interested in us since Jews are not considered to be Germans. Their focus is on politicians, communists and the International Brigade. We are told that Jews must wait for emigration visas. I, of course, miss you. Every day I looked forward to trouncing you at chess.*

Hannah laughed so that she would not weep. She could feel the censor's greedy presence devouring the lines. How could Gertie not see the danger? But there was no way to rebuke her, to protect her. The ground had turned to mud. She did not write back, hoping silence would grant her friend protection.

From Heinrich, not a whisper.

She took to playing chess with the photographer's assistant downstairs, a handsome man named Remi. They discussed ad nauseam the affidavits, certificates, promises of employment, bank statements and more that every Jew needed before they could even begin the applications for exit permits and visas.

"We are forbidden," Remi joked, "from entering the next circle of hell without the proper forms, stamped and signed by our own enemies."

He suggested they play Marseille chess, which he had learned in prison. In this variation, a player made two moves per turn instead of one.

"One more rule," he added. "Checkmate cannot be declared with the first of the two moves. Shall we try?"

Two sequential choices instead of one turned chess into an entirely different proposition, a derangement. Squaring off against

Remi, she was disoriented and even repulsed, as if the board had grown a terrifying third head.

"That's a normal reaction," said Remi. "This simple mutation generates a different universe. With two moves, the player is faced with more freedom. Greater freedom equals greater incoherence. When the dimensions of the world are transformed, our trusted strategies are revealed for what they are: ridiculous."

"Nothing is recognizable."

"The player, too, by necessity, becomes unrecognizable to herself."

They played until Hannah could stand it no more and, in a fit of rage, flipped the board, shocking them both. But a scorched earth policy changed nothing. After the massive destruction, the board was simply reset, according to the very same rules.

August was stiflingly hot. On Saturdays, she roamed the market even though the stalls were distressingly bare. Now and again a table was graced by blushing tomatoes or a creamy wedge of cheese, packs of cigarettes, and sunshine persistently cascading over the National Square.

Pick a cheese, she told herself, any cheese. But whatever you do, don't pick the wrong cheese. What was happening? What would happen? She was sweating and full of grief and walking in circles. At last, coins departed her right hand and a reblochon landed in her left. Its softness gave way against her fingers, as if she squeezed the waist of a goldfish.

"J'ai le Rouge parfait pour ça." Spoken in a haughty bourgeois tone, with a cave-dark German accent. *I have just the Red for that.*

Needles. She had never before realized that tears were needles. Not for all the world would she turn around. If necessary, she would stand in place for eternity, squishing this lump of cheese. Anything to avoid the abyss of disappointment.

Two heavy hands on her shoulders. Gently they warmed her until her feet unglued, gently they turned her around.

Heinrich stood there, except it was as if he had been forced through increasingly narrower doors. Depleted. Sickly. Where had he gone? He was holding the same battered pipe. The delicate cheese seemed to collapse in her hands.

"Careful, careful," he whispered, extracting it from her grasp. "Soft cheeses are very vulnerable."

"Where on earth have you been?" she asked, as if she were angry.

"On a glorious walk through the countryside."

She hardly dared to ask. "But how have you been?"

Smiling, he thumbed the sweat from her brow. "Never better."

He had nothing but what he wore, and went with her at once to rue de la Comédie.

Inside, he lay his face against her neck, breathing her in. For a long time they said nothing. From bed, they watched the curtains chased by the breeze. They ate the cheese with their fingers and held one another.

She learned that Heinrich's camp had been evacuated when the Germans reached Paris. At first, French guards had herded the inmates south at a quick march, but on the second day German planes strafed the road. In the mayhem, the prisoners fled.

By then, villages in every direction were occupied, and France was not only surrounded but perforated. Heinrich could be caught out in an instant.

"First we escaped as a single group and then we separated," he told her. "At the time, I was wearing my best clothes, Manchester velvet pants and a white shirt because, in the camp, I'd put off doing the wash. So as I ran I stole clothes off a laundry line and left my own as payment." Hiding among the displaced French was impossible; he could see over the heads of everyone and everyone could see him. He asked himself: In paintings, what do our eyes pass over? How can I hide in plain sight? He experimented with walking alongside a car which had a table and three mattresses strapped to its roof, but the human flood was so great the car made no progress. He chanced on a cow that got separated from its group. Thinking its bulk would camouflage him, he tried to lead it but the cow refused to move in straight or purposeful lines.

"I persevered," Heinrich said, as if survival were nothing more than a puzzle to be solved. Everywhere, he saw parents desperately trying to keep hold of their children while balancing whatever food and precious items they could carry. At last he saw an old woman walking ahead of a donkey. She'd been beside him the whole time but he had failed to notice her before.

Immediately he approached and offered assistance: she could sit atop the animal and he would lead it.

The old woman laughed. "Dressed like a farmer except for your Sunday shoes. The Germans aren't idiots, you know." She shouted to a passing man, who immediately traded his disintegrating sandals for Heinrich's loafers.

"Now," she said, "help me up, Sancho," and climbed onto the donkey.

For the next nine hours, they walked together.

Matter-of-factly she told him, "This isn't my first war." She taught him how to wear the face of a paysan, how to change his walk, where to find stores of food, which locations to avoid even if you were at death's door. Knowing when and how to bluff, she said, will save your life a thousand times. A refugee must learn to be a master of disguises. He who is being pursued must camouflage himself inside other people's worlds. But be warned. It takes only a moment to don a series of costumes but a lifetime to take them off. Grief comes later, she said, when you finally pull down all the masks and discover how little survives at the core.

Heinrich paused to boil coffee and bring it to bed. Morning had come, softening the air. One last story, he said. I met a boy on the road. A year ago, the child had been a refugee from the war in Spain. Both parents murdered. He'd escaped alone over the Pyrenees without even a sweater to warm him. It had been winter. One freezing night, he collapsed on a mound of paper. When dawn came, he saw he'd been sleeping on a huge bed of money. Banknotes of the Spanish Republic. The currency was so devalued it could only weigh people down, and they'd thrown it all away. "I filled my pockets," the boy said. "I stuffed it into my clothes until I was round as a balloon."

"But why?"

"I refused to leave my country empty-handed."

"What happened to the money?"

"I took it to a bank in Perpignan. Everyone came to stare at me. The manager gave me a hamper of food." The boy laughed. "I gave them millions. Millions. It was the most expensive food I ever ate."

At last letters began to reach Hannah and Heinrich in Montauban. One came from Walter Benjamin, who had fled south to Lourdes. He said that he was busy with a long rumination, which he called "my Baudelaire," a term he was applying to everything he wrote because all the fragmented pieces belonged to one another. He confided, "I am studying to be a Jew because I've finally come to the realization that I am one." This letter was followed by a postcard mailed earlier, but which had lagged behind,

I found the aphorism that is most splendidly appropriate to my current state: *His laziness supported him in glory for many years in the obscurity of an errant and hidden life.* I cite this in the unspoken hope of causing Monsieur sadness.

Your old Benji

Soon Lotte Sempell, Chanan Klenbort and their newborn arrived in Montauban. They were followed by Annie Mendelssohn, Fritz Fränkel, and Gabriel, the son of Erich Cohn-Bendit. In cramped rooms, they shared meals and built a routine of sorts. What did they have? Almost nothing. Friendships that would outlive the times.

"Let's play chess with our backs to the board," Heinrich suggested one night. "We'll announce our moves like bulletins from the war office."

In this way, blind chess was born. The room exploded with guffaws and stomping feet. Laughing never hurt so much. The chess board they couldn't see grew more and more hideous until it dissolved into farce, re-emerged as comedy, and twisted back into life.

"So this is how the French command is run!" cried Chanan.

Fritz waved a fallen horse. "It's the backwards road to escape!"

"It's the German essence," said Hannah.

Heinrich tried to sound clever. "The board is only a distraction. It's in the soul of your opponent where the game is played."

"Let them have my soul," countered Fritz. "It's a petty thing anyway. Just let me keep my life."

Nothing could have been more hilarious.

An ancient mail carrier could be seen passing by the house each day, an aged Pegasus who had the wings to deliver letters from loved ones as well as identity documents, police certificates, financial affidavits, statements from guarantors, encomiums from people of influence—chapters in the files the group of them were forced to compile on themselves. Without such a dossier attesting to their usefulness, no future would be granted them. They had no rights, not even the right to have rights.

Two paths lay open: the camps or flight. Along both paths, life could disappear.

At the Saturday market, Annie traded a pen given to her by her father for an Artur Schnabel recording of Beethoven's last piano sonata. Number 32. She and Hannah lay together on the floor, eyes closed, listening. It was this music, not a pen, Annie said, tears wetting her cheeks, that made her father live again. Critics had insisted this sonata was missing its third movement, its finale.

How very wrong they were, said Annie. It was a lesson for the ages, that the sublime could meet you on the road and you might look away.

Hannah held her hand. Tell me the lesson.

There is necessity and there is beauty, Annie told her. There is survival and there is life, and I will hold them both.

The spectacled bookseller, he of the Prussian blue coat, gave Heinrich a copy of Kant's *Critique of Pure Reason*.

Now Heinrich was reading each and every one of Kant's prefaces and introductions, interrupting the silence to muse on the gulf between the act of thinking and the fact of knowing, and to provide comical stories of men who thought things far beyond the scope of reason.

But Hannah was distracted. She said, "Is the sun arriving or departing?"

"I heard that in the beginning, gases and minerals spun together, forming the planet. Today the earth keeps spinning for the simple reason that there are no forces to stop it."

So the most ancient attribute of earth was its turning. What to make of that?

Only that occasionally Heinrich's arm around her shoulders made her so unhappy because love held one fast to a world that sometimes had very little to recommend it. Even her own breathing, her own pulse, often felt like a cage. Life, with its brevity, its limited visibility, its depths and its cruelties, saddened her.

"The abyss," she said. "How near has it come?"

"Let us hope we're not already encircled."

"Should we dare to hope?"

"Only if it moves us to act."

All night, as Heinrich slept, Hannah continued to think. Alone with herself, she argued with the future as if trying to examine the contours of a blindfold she could not, no matter how she struggled, undo. A blindfold that claimed to be life itself.

In the fall of 1940, an American emergency visa was issued to Hannah Arendt.

Chanan toasted her with a baguette. "Spare a thought for the Romanians," he said. "I heard the visa waitlist for them is forty-three years long. Your visa is a miracle."

Heinrich, usually allergic to religious sentiment, agreed. "A miracle." He had been included in her visa. But, Hannah thought, what if things had turned out otherwise? Only Lotte Sempell's interventions at city hall had made it possible for her and Heinrich to obtain French marriage papers. Without that official certificate, Heinrich's visa application would have disappeared down the well, like more than 300,000 others. A former communist like him was despised by Vichy France, the Nazis, and the Americans. *What if?* The words rattled around in Hannah's nightmares.

To receive the visa, they had to immediately go to Marseille, five hundred kilometres southeast. The journey would require a safe conduct pass they did not have, so taking the train was out of the question. Remi, the photographer's assistant, managed to procure two bicycles.

They set off for Marseille with a basket of provisions, water flasks, and Proust and Simenon side by side in a little suitcase. Heinrich had also packed a bottle of wine and a little elbow of cheese, as if the two were travelling sweethearts out for a pedal on the Canal du Midi. They rested at noon, stretched out like two cats with a view of the universe, or maybe just Toulouse. Hannah's body ached and they'd covered barely a twentieth of the distance, yet she felt alive for the first time in months. Finally, they could do more than fret. At last they could take action.

Along the road, nobody harassed them. Instead, French farmers offered truck rides and bread. A kindly chaperone pointed out a slender river. "We call this the Seuil de Naurouze, the Threshold of Naurouze. Some rains flow west and stream into the Atlantic. Some flow east and empty into the Mediterranean. Quite a different outcome, no? Deposited in the sea or pushed away to the limitless ocean."

"But who decides?" asked Heinrich.

"The bureaucrats, who else!"

"*Naurouze,*" Hannah said. "What does it mean?"

"A beautiful word. In Arabic it means a narrow passageway."

The five-day trip, begun on Sunday morning, ended sooner than anticipated on Tuesday night. *Marseille.* They collapsed in a windowless room three blocks from the office of the Emergency Rescue Committee. As usual, Heinrich fell asleep instantly. Hannah listened for the sound of the port, for the sound of childhood, the Königsberg shoreline, endless circling trains, the Lecturer, youth, her ex-husband, departures, singing, a page turning. Who dreams the dreamer? she wondered.

What we know with certainty is exceedingly rare, came Benji's voice, mumbling in her ear. It comes in such brief flashes. By certainty, did Benji mean truth? Did it come from within or without, from ourselves or the world?

Heinrich turned over in his sleep, kicking a leg free from the blankets. "When the time comes," he murmured, "*jump.*"

On boulevard Garibaldi, in a windowless office, the American visa sat in Hannah's hands.

A man by the name of Gemähling, who looked as if he had

not slept in centuries, gave her a sweaty handshake and a stern warning about the fickleness of exit permits and transit visas. He was blond, soft-spoken, had a runny nose, and spoke without stopping for breath: "Timing is everything. Therefore, let us proceed with caution. I will be blunt: we've processed twenty-one thousand applications in the last three months, and how many has the American government approved? Not even two hundred. And of those two hundred people, I'm sorry to say that some were arrested and interned before we could get them out. Therefore we must wait for the right moment before assisting you across the Spanish border to Portbou and onwards by train to Portugal. For now, the borders are closed. We must wait."

Back at their small hotel, they celebrated the visa by drinking a gallon of coffee. For an hour or more, they did not see the message that had been pushed under their door: Monsieur was to report to the front desk at once, and should please bring his documents.

It was the *please* that chilled Hannah.

"So that is how it is," Heinrich said. Colour flushed his face and then subsided.

They understood everything. The hotel register was being checked for enemy aliens and Jews. Heinrich had escaped the internment camp at Nevers but his file must still be in circulation. The Gestapo, then, under the guise of Marshal Pétain's newly created Armistice Army, was casting its net. With the hotel's collaboration, of course.

They formulated a plan instantaneously, having silently anticipated this moment all along. Heinrich tried to make her smile. "I don't know why, but the Resistance casts me in the same role every time, that of a charming, *incredibly handsome*, but rather dull flâneur. "

Dry-eyed and smiling, she held him. I am determined to be spared the unanswerable question, she thought. There will be no *what if.* I will not lose.

Heinrich put on his hat and coat. Pipe in hand, he went magisterially to the front desk as if he had not seen the message, deposited his room key with the on-duty clerk, and strode out. A Monsieur par excellence. She kept the door to their room ajar, listening. Her heart was breaking and pounding in the same instant. The creak of the stairs, an unfamiliar voice, a tinkle of bells, heavy steps. The noises subsided. In her head, she pictured Heinrich vanishing into the sidewalk crowds. She imagined it so fiercely she could feel the sun touching his heavy hands. He was unlocking his bicycle with panache. No one accosted him. Picturing him was her way of praying: he was pedalling away like a gentleman of leisure off to buy a copy of Le Temps. A perfect performance.

Complete stillness. She gazed into the hallway until her hands ceased their shaking.

Hannah packed their small suitcase. She picked it up, went downstairs and checked out. The quavering of her voice made it difficult for the concierge to understand her. She entered the hotel restaurant, requested a table for one, and picked at the omelette that arrived.

The hotelier came to her table, radiating smiles. "Enjoying your meal, Madame?"

She touched the napkin to her lips.

"And how is your husband today? Will he be joining you?"

Hannah set down her fork. "Why do you ask?"

"I personally sent a message to your room. If he could spare a moment to identify himself to the front desk, we have a message which can only be delivered in person—"

"What message?"

"A formality, I'm afraid. Just a simple document check."

"A simple document check," she said. Her voice found its strength. She was strangely, quietly, shouting. "In these times, does such a thing exist?"

"I beg your pardon?"

How the hotelier smiled at her, how he seemed to swell in his duplicity.

"My husband," she said, "is already at the prefecture. Was it you who reported him?"

He lifted both hands in negation, as if he did not want ice cream with his cake. "Reported him?" A look of pity crossed his face, or perhaps a look of scorn.

The other patrons were staring now.

Her voice sounded pristine in the newly quiet room. "You are a true French patriot, indeed."

"I assure you—"

"Do you always share your guest list with the Army of the Armistice, which, as we all know, is under the direction of the Nazi command? Do you share even the names of the courageous sons who chose to lay down their arms rather than serve the Nazis they were bravely fighting just a few months ago?"

"Don't be absurd. I would never . . ." But he looked behind him, as if fearing his shadow would overhear.

A murmur of distaste swept the room.

"If anything happens to my husband," she said, "*you are responsible.*" She had not intended to weep or cause a scene, but here she was. The tears streamed down her face as she gathered her things. Her hands were shaking as she counted out money for the bill. "Is this how you serve your homeland?"

She was near the exit now. Her tears fell freely, and she could not have stopped them even if she wished. She, who never cried, now sobbed as if the floodgates had opened. All her friends, her whole life, she thought, thrown away like so much garbage. And so many others just going along. Who would answer for it in the end? Nobody at all? The other diners were watching rapt, horrified. A young woman at the window began to weep, too, and a man leaped up, incensed, and began to approach the hotelier.

"If anything happens to my husband or to any of your guests," Hannah said, "if any harm befalls them, *you will bear the guilt*." Shaking, she turned and fled.

At the café they had agreed upon, she found Heinrich with his hat on his knee and his pipe balletically raised. He was reading not Kant but, to better complete the picture, Proust. A copy of *Le Temps* was folded crisply beside his noisette.

"C'est réglé?" he asked in his comical French.

"C'est réglé."

"Have you been crying, my darling?"

"Yes."

They retrieved their bicycles, secured their belongings, kissed, and embarked on the smoothest path out of melancholy Marseille and back to Montauban. The midday sun seemed to burn straight to the centre of her. "Away, away," Heinrich sang, his voice enveloping her. She pedalled and pedalled. She had the strange sensation that the wind dried her tears before she even wept them. But of course, against her will, they still fell.

She was thirty-five and too old for sentimentality. Enough, she told herself. *Enough.*

13.

The word *enough*, lingering on the twelfth floor, drifting through the rooms, reaches me now in the present. It is midwinter, the eve of the solstice, and I am travelling, having boarded a train that will carry me to the coast. It struck me suddenly—this need to see the ocean again. I'm fortunate to have a little savings, friends by the shoreline, and a welcoming place to stay. The entire journey, lasting through the night and into the morning, will span almost twenty-four hours.

This train carriage is divided into compartments, and for the moment mine is empty. Small outposts, glimmering between fields of snow, occasionally appear.

The door opens and a boy in a red uniform steps in. He tells me that around midnight, when the train reaches the city, it will fill to capacity. "Until then," he smiles, "stretch out! You'll have the whole palace to yourself." He stamps my ticket, makes sure I know where the carriage's hot water boiler is, and wishes me a good journey.

Soon the world outside darkens and the window becomes a mirror. A series of infinitely smaller compartments shimmers inside the glass.

Beside me, or somewhere along the corridor, familiar voices approach.

I confess, Jupiter says. I don't fully believe in the reality of the future.

The past, present and future walk into a bar, Blucher begins.

Bento, seated across from me, covers his ears. Please, don't say it—

It was tense . . .

Laughter rolls along the windows.

Does anyone know, my father says innocently, why Beethoven got rid of his chickens?

Then, after a pause: They wouldn't stop saying Bach, Bach, Bach!

Jupiter slaps his knee, laughing. Enough, please!

I can hear someone dipping their hand into a bag of sunflower seeds. The crunching begins.

My father says, "It's my turn now to continue the story, isn't it?"

The train carries me ever forward alongside a bright moon above the shadows of trees.

Up on the rooftops of the Sea, my father once taught me history, mathematics and the laws of physics. He told me about the Dunhuang star map, the oldest surviving atlas of the stars, drawn on a scroll that, when unrolled, was twice as tall as me. A millennia ago, it charted thirteen hundred stars visible to the naked eye; it showed, through various calculations, how to translate the near and the far onto a flat sheet of paper. My father taught me these determinants when I was a child, demonstrating how Von Neumann algebras are built from the simplest of structures.

On the last night we went up to the roof together, he didn't return to his usual subjects. He said, "Tell me something you learned today."

I told him that I had met two sisters who spoke Hakka, his own mother tongue. They were nurses from the Malay Seas and were headed west. They hadn't wanted to talk about the past but had been overjoyed when I spoke to them in the old language.

I told him, too, about the journalist Khun and his wife, Srey, who were travelling with their seven children, two uncles, five aunts and two great-aunts, none of whom was a blood relation. They were a created family, having adopted one another along the way. A half dozen times, the family had tried to set up a permanent business, but drought, hunger or people had chased them out. "I worry we'll never stop moving," Srey had told me. "My dream is to have a garden. My father had a flower farm in Preah Vihear that supplied the local temple. This was our family's work for generations."

"Your mother grew up in the orchard where her father worked."

"Did she?" I felt my mother's hand on my wrist. Even on the roof, the sound of the tide felt very near. In a moment, I feared, it would sweep over my knees and wash me away from here.

"I promised I would tell you everything," my father said.

"It can wait. I know you're tired now."

He shook his head. "Some things you might only understand later. Maybe you will write it down. Not all of it. And not now, but afterwards, when you're older. When you have a whole life behind you."

"I could."

"But you'll write it differently?"

"I'll write it word for word, I'll remember it exactly the way you tell me."

"No," my father said. "You won't. The only way to remember is to forget, to let time fill the story up, and create it all over again. But if, one day, you leave the Sea and you have to let it go, don't grieve. Life is fated to be left behind."

I wanted to lift his spirits. I reminded him of what he had taught me: that Spinoza said that time never goes missing, that the universe keeps track of the sequence of things, and the sequence of things is the material of reality.

"Your mother loved you," my father said then. "No matter what happens, don't confuse the facts. Another fact. It was because of me that she had to go."

part two

ooooo

THE
ETHICS

In Foshan, the rain was torrential. Bee, drenched, pulled Wui Shin under a shop awning. Her presence filled him with euphoria, and he wanted to stand between Bee and the world, to be with her and be needed by her. From across the street, the grocer, Ma Deng, came running for cover. She knocked Bee sideways and into his arms.

"Flooded again," the grocer cried. "When did our home become hell on earth?"

"Ma Deng, squeeze in closer or you'll be soaked."

"These bastards are drowning the city again."

Across the street, two figures lounged in the doorway of the Pearl Tower Hotel, smoking in the careless way of all public security men. Years ago, when Wui Shin first came to know them, he'd thought them witless and nicknamed them Big Fish and Big Meat. Now Big Meat tossed his glowing cigarette into the gutter, caught Wui Shin's eye, and waggled his fingers in an ironic wave. Big Fish called out a greeting but his words were swallowed by the rain.

Fortunately, Bee was distracted. She was wiping the rain from her eyes with a pale blue handkerchief. She said they might as well make a dash for the subway because this deluge would last hours. Then she pushed the sodden handkerchief under her sleeve until it disappeared completely. This was an old-fashioned habit he had noticed the very first time they met; months later, it still touched him.

Ma Deng was staring at him, alert and wary. Wui Shin did not falter. He radiated calm and moved to shelter Bee from the rain.

A month later, on Bee's twenty-third birthday, Wui Shin gave her a set of eight linen handkerchiefs which he had sewn and detailed by hand. "Stitching," he explained, "is the first skill I learned when I was a child. Sewing and embroidery prepared me for my studies, for engineering, and the detail work that creates the materiality of cyberspace."

He felt he had surprised her with this gift, and that she was reappraising him.

They were on the boardwalk beside the Fen River, and he was holding a paper bag of roasted gingko nuts. He had talked a great deal that day, he had talked like a fool. Now he told her that a building is engineered so that it *knows* how to stand. "To me, engineering is the structuring of knowledge. It reveals the function, and therefore utility, of both object and user."

Bee studied the eight ornate handkerchiefs he had given her. "Is utility our essence?" she asked with a wry smile.

Wui Shin felt as if he had walked clumsily into a door and, to avoid answering, popped a gingko nut into his mouth. She laughed.

Bee was only a year younger than him. Valedictorian of her graduating class. The recipient of a dozen job offers including a coveted position at the Ministry of Agriculture. The work, she told him now, would send her out to record, identify and classify species richness in ecologically sensitive areas. An accident in childhood had injured her right hip, but she was determined to make fieldwork her life. She smiled, "It's my function, I suppose."

On her tenth birthday, she told him, a car had run a red light and struck her. She'd been on her bicycle. When she'd looked into the driver's eyes and seen only a blank stare, time had stopped.

She knew that this might be her last image, her last breath. A child's voice, completely unfamiliar, sounded in her ears: *Go up*. The car filled her vision and she jumped. She had lifted her whole being, even her thoughts, skywards, and somehow rolled overtop the hood of the car and onto the pavement. The car kept going, crumpling her bicycle beneath it. She remembered lying on the ground, unable to move, seeing the tire of an oncoming truck stopping inches away. It was so close she could see matted grass and specks of plastic on its front wheel.

"I still think about that voice," she said. "Is it what people mean by a soul? Was it a past self, or even a future one, coming to warn me?" Bee met Wui Shin's eyes. She looked at him with complete trust.

Above them, the flying dome of the People's Hall of the Greater Bay Area curved like a shell. Bee tucked a blue handkerchief into her sleeve. The gesture was achingly familiar. Why did it awaken all his tenderness, as if he had been seeking it all his life?

Wui Shin did not tell Bee everything. He did not, for instance, detail his life in Beijing, where he had lived between the ages of seventeen and twenty-four. He didn't mention the kinship he had found there, and still nurtured, in a circle of researchers who called themselves the Floating World.

Like him, they were fascinated by open and closed systems, and therefore the covert architectures of Beijing and the country. And fascinated by the relentless flow of information within data pathways which, like rivers, could breach every entity, minuscule or vast. Debates with these friends—Bing, Feng Mei, Locksmith, Chen and others—had energized and infuriated him.

"The older generation controls the structures of this country," Bing said at one of their weekly gatherings, which took place in his cramped apartment, where papers, journals and books were piled everywhere, even on top of the fridge. "But the younger generation controls its culture. The structure and the culture exist in disequilibrium, and this imbalance is the engine of political change."

Feng Mei would have none of it. "Sure," she said scornfully. "Little crumbs like us drive the politics of the most powerful nation on earth."

But Bing nodded, as if she had agreed with him. "Exactly. Our generation has a deep-seated belief in perforation. The fabric is what it is, but the pressure of new culture stretches the system. That's the beauty: new culture stretches the fabric according to the logic of the fabric's own structure." After expounding at length, he raised his beer, grinned, and waited for praise. But everyone rose up as one to demolish his argument. Locksmith and Chen kept adding greens and meat to the steamboat, all the while shouting, and no one ever went home hungry or upset. On the contrary, these gatherings were their true education.

Conversation, *ha la*, was like steam, Wui Shin thought. New worlds made from air, transformative, dangerous and impossible to pin down.

Each member had grand ambitions. They belonged to applied and pure sciences, research, development, technology. It was Bing who had named their group the Floating World and declared themselves its engineers. Wui Shin would trust these friends with his life.

After the November riots outside the Ministry of Education, Wui had posted geolocation images to his message board with detailed analyses of crowd formation, clustering and fragmentation. He was nineteen years old at the time. His post caught the attention of a distinguished professor, who messaged Wui Shin to express his admiration.

"I would like very much to meet you."

Flattered, Wui agreed.

In person, the Professor was a surprise. Stooped and grizzled, quick to smile, with rheumy eyes that seemed half-closed to the world. It was a peculiar, almost spiritual, encounter—and Wui felt as if he had known Professor Tong all his life but was failing to place him.

Long into the night, the two of them argued about crowd systems, mechanisms of movement and flight, and whether the intra-architecture of physical- and cyber- spaces could create a field of predictable actions. "You see your work as a branch of philosophy," the Professor said, a little tipsy towards the morning.

Wui had the hubris to think so, and the wisdom to keep such thoughts to himself. He didn't answer and the Professor murmured, "You want to know how we outwit the world's constructions, how we appear and disappear, because there are always alternate possibilities, escape routes, that even the most cunning programmer will not anticipate. Your mother, of course—"

And here the Professor stopped. Embarrassed, he looked down. He had made a grave error.

Wui almost let it pass. The silence lengthened and grew awkward. Then: "My mother?" he said.

The Professor's voice was gentle. "Your mother died in that catastrophe, but you walked away."

"I wasn't there. Hundreds died that night."

The Professor waited.

"What happened that night was an accident," Wui said.

The Professor looked at him with great compassion. "It was a systems failure by our government. One of many. I am not afraid to say so. Are you?"

Such things could never be said aloud—yet here was this distinguished man offering him a true phrase, a clear-eyed understanding, without a trace of fear. Wui could not answer, either to agree or to disagree.

"The deeper you travel into the architecture of a system," Professor Tong said, "the closer you come to reality. This is true not only of finite field algebra, but also of society and governance."

"I don't understand."

"We need a pure genius like yours. For the good of the country, but most of all, in service to the future. Moral failure has been built into our system for too long and it has become inhumane. We need someone who will never forget that every grain of rice and every millimetre of hardware is the result of labour by ordinary men and women."

As if removing a mask he had been wearing all along, Professor Tong no longer seemed tipsy or even elderly. "Child," he said, "I have been looking for a survivor like you for a long time."

At first, Wui Shin did not submit written reports, and nor was he paid. He simply met Professor Tong on the first Sunday of every month. The Professor brought him many gifts and rare books. Occasionally they discussed ongoing events, like the protests in the outer regions and in Beijing itself, or Wei's classes and professors, or his circle of friends, but mostly they talked about interfaces and control systems. This was exhilarating. The Professor seemed moved by his ideas and their potential to reinvigorate a dying world.

Wui Shin told no one but Aunt Oh about this new figure in his life.

"Your mother is watching over you," she said. "I miss her every day."

The first report Wui wrote down for the Professor was brief. In content, it was no different than other things he posted on his message board: an analysis of structure and permutation in a specific locus of affairs. Professor Tong found holes in the analysis but also conceded that Wui's insights could reshape decades of

THE BOOK OF RECORDS   193

cynical thinking in the fields of public safety and surveillance. He said he now wished to initiate a small salary for Wui, a form of respectful compensation. Wui refused, but later relented on the condition that the money go directly to Aunt Oh in Foshan, who still worked long hours and had no savings. The very next day, a generous payment appeared in her account.

Aunt Oh sent Professor Tong an exquisitely tailored shirt, but he would not accept the gift.

"As a public official, it's impossible." The Professor insisted on purchasing it instead, because the shirt was fitted for him and no other. To Aunt Oh's horror, he paid an exorbitant sum. The Professor politely disagreed. "I would have paid far more in any Xidan boutique." It was all handled so elegantly, with such respect for Aunt Oh's expertise, that Wui felt everything to be in balance.

Month after month, Wui wrote his reports, and Professor Tong began to suggest problems to which Wui might, as the Professor put it, apply his philosophy. "There are several matters at the conjunction of information security, privacy, education and governance where your analysis is striking. You are considering reality from an entirely different vantage point. Your work is superior to that of all the well-paid minds in my department."

"When I complete my dissertation, I would be honoured to work beside you in the Ministry of Information," Wui once ventured.

"Oh no," the Professor said. "Oh no, no, no, no. The ceiling there is too low for you, Wui Shin. You'll rise much higher." The Professor's pride was that of a father. Wui felt all the doors of his future slide open.

At the age of twenty-four, despite his attachment to Beijing, Wui Shin decided to uproot himself.

By this time, the weekly reports had begun to feel onerous. And recently, Professor Tong's colleagues had developed an unhealthy interest in Bing, Feng Mei, and a few others in the Floating World. Meanwhile Professor Tong was ailing, and rarely left his apartment, and the notes he sent Wei were increasingly incoherent. Going home to the south, Wui thought, would send a clear message. There was nothing of concern for the Information Office—and certainly not when it came to the researchers of the Floating World.

A few weeks before his departure, the Professor and Wui walked together through the crowds in Tiananmen Square.

Aunt Oh had turned sixty, Wui explained, and he wanted to be at her side. "Family is calling me home."

"Of course, this is a great loss to me, but I cannot quarrel with your instincts. The south has always been where, in my opinion, you might undertake your greatest work."

In the Square, they paused to gaze at the towering obelisk, the Monument to the People's Heroes. Visitors flocked up and down its shining stairs.

"I happen to know of an enterprise in Foshan that would suit you perfectly," Professor Tong said. He hoped Wui Shin would give it serious consideration. "The firm has a whimsical name, Days and Months Technology Corp Ltd. Its engineers are frontier scientists in every sense of the word. The company is interested in questions of governance: What will happen when the territorial space alters its dimensions in ways we currently find unimaginable? Territorial space is limited but the mind is adaptive and potentially free. Computational territory must also be defended."

Wui was only half listening. In recent months, Professor Tong's illness had made him more loquacious, yet confused. He once told Wui he was trapped between the world he had helped design and this current world, which was an iteration of that design.

Tenderly, Wui touched the Professor's elbow. "What kind of employment is this really?"

Professor Tong blinked and brushed one hand across his cheek, as if waking from a stupor. He named the salary and benefits.

"Additionally, if you serve as a bridge between the firm and the Information Office, we can provide you with the deed to a modest apartment in the centre of Foshan, in gratitude for your patriotic efforts."

Wui looked down, shocked. "Forgive me, professor. That is not for me."

"One way or another," Professor Tong said, as if Wui had not spoken, "the fate of the many and the few are one: urban and rural, sea and land, computational and terrestrial. Such relationships build pathways and therefore prosperity, it's all a closed system, you see? Therefore the deeper the system knowledge, the less danger of human error. Knowledge is our only guardrail, and surveillance is the father holding the hand of the child. Look around you." He gestured at a family coming towards them. "Remember when we were small? Remember the dimensions of the world? I'm an old man, Wui, but even I still hunger for that sense of faith. For the child, the father is a giant. That is where we stand in this universe. We are insignificant and under threat. For our own survival, we must gather knowledge."

They sat on a bench to rest, and Professor Tong rested his hand on Wui's knee, a display of tenderness that elicited a wave of feeling in Wui, an onrush of memories.

"With every technological leap," the Professor continued, "blind spots accumulate. Blindness is an inescapable aspect of perspective. But what we fail to foresee can be catastrophic. People like us, Wui, are menders. We sew the safety net, repair it, we do the detail work that no one notices unless . . . unless . . ." Professor Tong shook his head. "Your mother was in that crowd in Wenzhou. They were surrounded, and their gathering was illegal, criminal, but still the crowd grew. There were far too many to be manoeuvred into that space. What happened wasn't malicious but it also wasn't an accident. Hundreds died, and even the survivors were not saved. The system decided, and mistakes were buried. I saw this open grave with my own eyes. But when people like you and me have the training, expertise, and *most of all the memory*, should we leave governance to unprincipled fate? It's the survivors, the children of the mistakes, who understand. And because we know better, we bear responsibility for the future world. The technocrats of the last century were almost right. The most ethical way to predict the future is to invent it."

The Professor had misleadingly described Wui's apartment in Foshan as "modest."

A glass elevator brought him up to the tenth and highest floor of a turn-of-the-century building. Light cascaded off the surrounding skyscrapers. At night, advertisements burst off the facades, packet after packet of wild colour. A dreamworld. But inside the apartment, it was like stepping back into the past. Smooth surfaces and stainless steel appliances. Biometric locks, white walls, plank floors. Windows that could be opened wide like swinging doors, curtain panels that slid soundlessly across the room.

The first time she entered, Aunt Oh had been astonished. "But . . . this is a replica of the furnished apartment of my childhood. Our parents slept here . . . and your mother and I and two cousins shared this room, and we had a dog, Pele, and three cats . . . actually, Little Wui, isn't this the *very same building*? . . . Gosh, that's bonkers. For sure that building was demolished decades ago. I guess they're all made from the same plan. But it makes my hair stand on end . . ."

She touched the couch with a bewildered look, pleasure and suspicion mixing together.

Professor Tong had been right about the work at Days and Months: it was irresistible. The deeper you travel into the architecture of a system, Wui thought, the closer you came to reality.

He couldn't help but write to Bing and Feng Mei, describing how "perforation"—Bing's keyword—had become a method of both security and disruption. Cyberspace was tightly woven, yet plasticity was its nature. It had star patterns, galaxies and places of "nothingness." It had highways and urban clusters, but also tunnels, unpaved roads and remote wilderness. How did a designer or programmer prevent, or perhaps create, catastrophic change? Change could be a slow encirclement: a pattern that did not register as a pattern until its damage was irreversible.

Bing, intrigued, came for a visit. Looking every part the gentleman scholar, he arrived at Foshan station with a box of jujube flower shortbread, a satchel stuffed with papers, and gifts from their Beijing friends.

For hours the two of them walked along the Fen River. You were right, Wui told him. The culture of the younger generation is writing a new set of codes for existing structures. These "codes," like paths trodden by many people, perforate the fabric in unanticipated ways. Wui suspected that the root system of the Chinese Internet was under threat. If so, society was on the brink of radical transformation, even peaceful revolution, without anyone, even its makers, realizing it.

After listening to Wui's excited monologue, Bing's reply was brief. "You're naive. I said the forces were in disequilibrium and always have been. The watchers are always being watched. The structure has safeguards." Bing looked at him with a knowing sadness. "You of all people should know this."

A chill along the back of his neck. "I don't follow."

"Picture the Canal du Midi of the twentieth century," Bing said, "or the Grand Canal of the eighth century. Picture a system of 'locks.' There are ways to manage the force of the water, to divert, fragment and break its energy. The locks harness the power of gravity: verticality controls the flow and energy of the water. Strategic containment is the key to power."

"And I of all people," Wui said hesitantly, "should know this because logarithmic worlds are a system of locks and containment."

"Precisely. Someone has to watch the guardians, isn't that so? All the way up the ladder. Anyone who thinks he functions outside of this observatory is deluding himself."

"So who, or what," Wui said, "is at the top?"

"It's a closed system. A loop. No one goes unwatched. It cycles through and around again."

Wui was stunned. Of course it was a loop, and yet . . .

Bing lifted his hands, as if holding a giant melon. "Yes, this is what I've been interested in. How does anyone find their way out? It's not a question of cutting a hole in a fence. The only way to outsmart a closed system is to surround the whole loop, and to do it imperceptibly, strategically, piece by piece. All the outliers must appear to be random until, in a single move, they close the circle. Chokehold—not just here or there, but everywhere. The more the target resists, the tighter the knot becomes."

When Wui returned home, he wrote all this down. To the best of his ability, he transcribed the conversation as he remembered it. He wrote for over six hours, reliving his walk with Bing along the Fen River, and at last slid thirty-six pages into a hidden compartment of his desk. The following day, Wui saw his friend off at the train station and promised to visit him in Beijing soon.

Days and Months Tech Corp Ltd. was a small outfit: eight researchers and two administrators. The company was interested, at least on paper, in defence strategies in the aftermath of a catastrophic Internet root system failure. Also: information warfare. His co-workers were innocents, child-like, Wui thought. They preferred to address each other by handles. There was KingTut, LiBai57, Wingnut, WhiteRabbit, JerkCat, Byteooven, and Tonsil.

To understand how an entity could perforate or surround a system, they experimented with living, working, dreaming, dressing, and socializing as black ops. One of their missions was to infiltrate the anti-hacker patriot community, the red ops, distract them with fake ops, and send them on wasteful scavenger hunts. This was the expertise of Wingnut and Tonsil. But LiBai57, JerkCat and Wui Shin—who went by Taikonaut—had a more theoretical problem: the infinite, and infinitely subtle, steps by which one surrounds a computational territory. How to create endless halls of mirrors, with authorizations within authorizations, until the territory itself was perforated and destabilized.

Taikonaut's idea was to use their most powerful weapons to split the root, a knife to the brain of the whole system, and let nature do its work, *but only as a distraction*. This kind of catastrophic system failure was something the government had surely foreseen; they would possess counter-weapons for precisely this scenario. Wui agreed with Bing's observation that someone always guards the guardians. Thus splitting the root was only a decoy. The real warfare required scrambling the information, security clearances, identities, blueprints, hierarchies, the whole logic of the system. Then, when the system came back up, the library would be empty of meaning. All the books would still be there, but the referents would be new, wrong, absurd. This was the "surrounding" move—not to break the system but to enclose it, occupy it, make it unusable for the governing authority, turn its logic to madness.

LiBai57 argued that this was a fantasist's illusion. An interesting idea, but unworkable in practice.

JerkCat, on the other hand, felt it was holistic and therefore supremely destructive. "It's a form of system dementia," he said. "If the system were a person, it wouldn't recognize its memories as its own, be able to form new memories, arrange them in time, or connect them to a stable centre. It's an attack on syntax and language models."

The idea had become so alive to them as researchers, they already felt it to be real. Once an idea is in the air, as JerkCat said, it's only a matter of time before someone puts it into practice. As soon as you pinpoint the kill point of a structure, the structure will change, one way or another.

"Ludicrous," scoffed LiBai57, always the doubter among them. "We can *imagine* the end of the world but so far as I know, the idea hasn't set the ending in motion. The opposite, in fact."

But how to test their ideas? The obstacle to continuing the research, even theoretically, was that they worked within a closed system. They would have to step outside it in order to test it fully, and they would never be granted this permission.

In the meantime, Wui continued writing his reports and serving as a go-between with the Information Office. He was nothing, he thought, a single synapse, a redundant thread between lived reality and systemic reality. The reports were almost a kind of philosophical practice, he joked to himself, like those famous words found in the Tao Te Ching,

For the vastest of all structures is formed
by the great cutting and carving
that severs nothing.

His submissions to the Information Office were less field notes than meditations. They were essays on ring theory and topologies, and the purity of the mathematics therein. It was true that sometimes he did not attribute Taikonaut's thoughts to himself. It didn't matter, he reasoned, who said what. All of it was just cloud, just words.

Upon his move to Foshan, the Information Office had assigned him two handlers: tall, rifle-thin, ever-smoking men. They were stupid items, Wui thought, dàyú-dàròu, big fish-big meat. Typical public security hacks. His monthly meetings with them gave him no difficulty—unlike his interactions with the Professor, who seemed able to read his deepest thoughts and pilot him effortlessly in any direction. How freeing it was to be two thousand kilometres away from the Professor's grasp; he'd managed to escape a confinement he'd mistaken for home.

Wui Shin had been back in Foshan three months when he met Bee. She was the daughter of Aunt Oh's childhood friend, a man known as Old Flower. She'd grown up in her father's orchards, applied his learning to her education, and devoted herself to agricultural studies. She had a photographic memory and heartbreaking eyes. When they met, she was still in mourning clothes, grieving Old Flower's passing from an aggressive cancer.

Through Bee, Wui realized that he had been blessed. Life was a creature that could show kindness. Happiness felt overwhelming when the world around him was crumbling.

The Professor had just retired, but not before Bing was detained, disappeared and, after several months when his friends could get no word of his fate, charged with subversion of state power. Bing's study group, it was reported in the papers, had a project of disruption whose aim was to bring chaos; this group called their method "perforation"—pulling apart the seams of society and governance. Wui dropped everything and travelled to Beijing to find out more about the case, but at the High Court he was denied entry. He wandered, stunned, along Jianguomen Road, and was surprised to look up and see Big Fish and Big Meat across the intersection. They did not pretend to be tourists or otherwise feign their own surprise. They simply observed him, bored expressions on their faces. Wui pivoted and kept walking, down one alleyway and then another, always ending up in a wide commercial street that mutated into iterations of the same squares and pavilions. He had lived in Beijing for eight years but still couldn't find his way around a corner. Yet Big Fish and Big Meat, from the south, shadowed him through the capital unruffled, like boys tormenting an injured dog. He couldn't risk visiting Feng Mei or any of his old friends; for this, he felt relief coupled with shame.

What choice did he have but to seek out Professor Tong?

They met in the bar of the Great World Hotel. A shining bullet of an elevator propelled Wui Shin forty-seven floors up to what felt like the doorstep of heaven. The Professor was already there. He shuffled forward with his cane, clasped Wui's hand, congratulated him. A table at the cliff's edge waited for them. Wui tried to find a break in the Professor's facade—that brief instant when a human being, in all his complexity and malleability, accidentally slips out from behind the mask.

But the Professor's wizened face was completely free of guile.

When Wui pressed him, he shook his head, almost lovingly. "We have all the evidence we need. Too much, in fact. Your detailed notes, for instance."

Wui felt as if he were toppling. Behind the Professor's back was an impossible view of Beijing.

"The Floating World," Professor Tong mused. The afternoon light had turned him into a portrait, an unreal presence. "A beautiful name, rich with literary history."

He seemed to be moving, imperceptibly but instant by instant, away from Wui, vanishing even as he was draped in light. "Ah, I see why you're anxious. You're worried that *your* identity will be revealed. Not to worry, my child. From the beginning, I went to great lengths to protect you. We've sowed enough doubt that each suspects the other and no one can untangle the truth. Randomness, noise, false fronts, spectacle—as I've told you, these weapons never get old. In fact," he continued gently, "you could petition to be a witness at his trial and defend Bing Lihai, as you see fit. I'm sure this performance might be arranged. The verdict is a foregone conclusion."

"This case is fabricated. You know as well as I do that nothing criminal occurred."

"Nothing criminal?" Professor Tong looked confused. "Don't you remember your own reports? *Strategic containment is the key to power.* Or this: *A closed loop where even the guardians are guarded.*" He shook his head sadly. "Poor man. Such delusions make a person a danger to themselves. We had no choice but to take measures for his own safety. Your friend Bing Lihai is one of the most gifted minds of his generation. And you . . . Taikonaut," that smile again, without guile, shining with compassion, "how can I convey our gratitude?"

Everywhere Wui went in Beijing, Big Fish and Big Meat followed. On the third day, new funds appeared in his accounts. The Information Office had doubled his salary. Again he demanded a meeting with Professor Tong, and they met in yet another bar at the top of the world. The old man said, "I know nothing about administrative matters. You'll have to speak to the financial managers."

"Who are they?"

"I've no idea."

"Then how do I reach them?" Wui persisted.

"Perhaps you can ask at the Public Security Office in Dongcheng District."

The Professor stepped out of the light. There was something so clean, so refined about him, like a new sheet of paper.

Who was this person Wui had known for more than a decade? To whom was Wui truly speaking? Could a human being be fabricated in a shop, in a neighbourhood, in a time?

That night, in his hotel, he dreamed, for the first time in two decades, of the crowds in Wenzhou. It was the city of mathematicians, the eastern capital of chess, the city of canals and seawalls, the place of his lost childhood. He saw his mother with her pamphlets and her smile, the tissue she slid out from the sleeve of her blouse to wipe the sweat or tears from his face, the way her hair curled and shone, liquid black, in the summer sun. But then he was sitting with Professor Tong in a room made of paper. In his dream, the Professor said, "A country cannot develop and transform this fast unless it leaves the souls of its people behind. Your mother, of course—"

"My mother?"

"She died in error, but Wui Shin . . . you walked away."

"Hundreds died in that catastrophe."

The Professor looked at him with great tenderness. He withdrew a tissue from his sleeve, held it between his fingers, and folded it into tiny squares.

But Wui hadn't been there, at the scene of the tragedy. He had been nine years old. He and his mother had lived in an apartment beside the sea, and he'd stayed up until morning waiting for her to collect him from the neighbours. She had been part of a crowd that had been forced into a smaller and smaller alley. People tried to get out, eventually crushing down a stone staircase, the only exit they could find. Panicked, they trampled one another to death. The bodies were collected, confiscated and, afterwards, Wui Shin was visited by security agents even though he was only a child. Was it possible his mother had been sent to prison and was still alive? Why had no record, no burial register, no list of the dead, ever emerged? How had hundreds of people been scrubbed from memory without disrupting the whole fabric of society? No name, no memory, no existence. His mother had vanished forever. Had he been with her? Wui Shin could not recall. His one clear memory was sitting in the apartment, watching the sea, and waiting.

Mistakes were made, people had whispered, mistakes that had resulted in a sequence of calamities. No one could have foreseen this tragedy. The crowd had lost control of itself. An accident, just a terrible accident. But this wasn't the first such episode and it wouldn't be the last. Had bodies fallen on top of him? Had he been there and found an opening through which to crawl away? Was he the only survivor?

"The deeper you fall into the architecture of a system," Professor Tong was saying in his dream, "the closer you come to reality. This is true not only of information, but also of politics, love and existence. These are haunted spaces where hidden codes guide our thinking. Child, I have been looking for a survivor like you for a long time. Open your eyes. Wake up. See the world for what it is. Only then can you begin to change it."

Wui Shin panicked. Then he was suddenly, violently, awake, and the radio blared. His hands swept the blankets, desperate to mute the sound, but he could not find a switch anywhere. The noise seemed to pour down the walls. The news reader was detailing a story Wui already knew by heart. Bing Lihai, a professor of physics at Tsinghua University, and leader of the Floating World anti-government group, had been found guilty of subversion of state power and sentenced to fifteen years in prison. At his sentencing the man had declared, "Imprisonment is not my shame. It is my honour." The rise of such high-level destabilizing efforts, the news reader continued, posed a grave threat to the economy and the nation. Government sources said these cells were directed and funded by foreign actors. A heroic years-long effort by the Ministry of Information had led to the infiltration and encirclement of the Floating World group. Bing Lihai and his collaborators had never suspected they were compromised until it was too late. Further criminal charges were pending.

The news carried on. Daylight swept up along the walls. Wui couldn't move. He eventually slept again, dreamless.

—

He opened his eyes to silence. Somehow he had slept through the entire day and into the next night. The other half of the bed had been meticulously made. A glass of water with a crenellated paper lid gleamed on the nightstand beside a room service menu.

He got up and washed his face. A thump against the door. He expected police, but instead it was a girl in a burgundy apron hanging newspapers in cloth bags from the handle of each door.

Wui brought the paper inside, unrolled it to find what he expected, a front-page story, a police image of Bing, and images of his own unsigned witness statement. It was impossible that Feng Mei, Chen and Locksmith wouldn't know that it was him.

He opened the curtains.

For a long time he sat on the bed unmoving. It was easy to make even innocent acts appear criminal. To demonstrate that violence is the monopoly of the rulers, that justice is a possibility not a right, that the creation of reality is child's play.

What could he do but make a ledger of the sequence of events that had destroyed Bing's life? Wui's deceits, which had seemed so minuscule, almost comical, took on a new appearance. It is alarming, he thought, to step into this vantage point, the point of view of the ledger. Information analysis reveals data errors which are mistakes of truth. The ledger, drawn from facts available not just to himself but to others, was a mirror, and the mirror was ruthless. If one examined it dispassionately, many things became clear.

All his life he had withheld information from his closest friends, and held a life-and-death power over them. Yet he had never noticed.

The ledger demanded a kind of emotional reckoning. He saw the devastated boy who had come to live with Aunt Oh; the teenager who did piecework and embroidery at night, and studied for his classes by telling Aunt Oh stories of history, philosophy and science to keep them both awake while they cleaned offices and shopping malls; the seventeen-year-old who excelled in the national examinations despite having no money or tutors—who was admitted to the top-ranked science and technology university in the nation, perhaps the world, and who devoted himself to numbers and codes the way others explored ice, stars and oceans. He had mistaken Aunt Oh's goodness for his own, and the tragedy of his mother's death as his right to a pain-free existence, a world shaped towards his own redemption. Ambition had been his right. He'd had no moral centre because he'd taken it as a matter of fact that he could not be corrupted.

What should he do now? He could recant and face the consequences.

Or he could go on. He was imperfect. In an unjust world, he was only a person like all the rest.

He logged in to his computer, told LiBai57 and JerkCat that his cardiomyopathy had worsened, he couldn't travel, and he sent a variation of this message to Bee and Aunt Oh. At first light, he took the subway to the Tsinghua campus and wandered aimlessly, arriving hours later at Beijing South train station. He watched the ceaseless waves of students and tourists, families and workers, in a space designed to direct their movements. He imagined a life in which Professor Tong had never called him, imagined not feeling enlivened by this flattery. Imagined that, a year later, he had rebuffed the Professor's suggestion to listen and surveil, to report on his friends. Imagined that he had emigrated, like so many of his peers, left the country for good. Imagined that his mother, instead of joining the demonstrators on that day long ago, had instead entered Wenzhou South station as she had intended to do that weekend, travelling three hours to Fuzhou to visit her only sister, Little Oh, and had emerged into the wet heat of the south. That this life in which he now stood, bewildered, in the melee of the train station, was a mistaken iteration, and all he had to do was hit undo. Undo, undo, undo, undo, until he arrived at the proper crossroads and turned in the proper direction.

Then he told himself that, from this day on, he had no choice. The most ethical way to predict the future is to invent it. He went to see the Professor. The old man put his hand on Wui's shoulder and called him son, and promised him that only absolute security would create a lasting peace. "What the government is after, and what we loyal souls must achieve," Professor Tong said, "is the happiness of the many. It is inevitable, a fact of society, that some people fall to the wayside."

Ten years later, Bee was at the top of her field, their two children, Wei and Lina, were thriving, cared for by Aunt Oh, and Wui was happy.

Bing Lihai had been released on parole and had chosen, foolishly, to remain in Beijing, causing trouble, agitating for the release of the still-incarcerated Feng Mei. It was only a matter of time before Bing landed back in jail. Locksmith had resurfaced in Australia. Wui Shin, now the general manager of Days and Months Tech Corp Ltd., had survived the arrest of JerkCat for matters unrelated to the firm. LiBai57 had left without notice, never voicing his suspicions, and cut off all contact. The company now employed thirty researchers, though of the original group only Wui remained.

There were government moles everywhere, Wui learned, but most only burrowed into the superficial exterior. Inside, like the rings of a tree, were encircled worlds. Triple agents and spies with no loyalties. Consultants who sided with the angels, the devils, or the highest bidders. Disrupters driven by revenge or just boredom. In this hall of mirrors, one encountered adventurers and career diplomats, missionaries and do-gooders. It wasn't the digital realm that was perforated, he thought. Rather the vastness of any space worked its way, day by day, month by month, into every individual until each person was stretched thin, pulled as far as they could bear. Until they became only surfaces and finally were no more.

Depths that were surfaces, wasn't that the driving paradox of life? LiBai57 used to say that cyberspace was the physics
of thought, not the physics of things, but Wui now considered
such poetry fatuous. Things ruled the world, not thoughts.
Information was not an empty space, it was made up of *things*.
Only a fool would deny it.

One day, he was informed that Professor Tong was dying. Wui
travelled to Beijing, where he found that the Professor did not recognize him. He could have walked away. Yet even custodians, Wui
thought, need care. Wui couldn't help it: he loved this man like a
father. For three months, he stayed in Beijing with the Professor,
shaving his whiskers, adjusting his blankets, helping him drink
through a straw, managing the caregivers who came and went,
paid by some unknown entity, an endless passageway of faces the
Professor could not recall even if they left the room for only an
instant. More astonishingly, Professor Tong spoke as if he'd lived
his life in some other country, a wilderness where he'd survived by
his wits, learning to read the soil and the stars. The emaciated man
described marvels too fantastical, Wui thought, to be real. Peacock
spiders, five-foot-tall storks, creatures that were a cross between
piglets and rabbits, deer with human faces, antelopes that walked
on two legs.

There were some moments when the fog in the Professor's eyes
lifted. "I don't expect you to forgive me," he said once, before sliding back into dementia. And another time, "Once you become a
revolutionary, there is no retreat. Wui Shin, you and I had only
two paths, escalation or betrayal. But both are ultimately useless.
Neither can change the nature of the game."

And once, "Thank you for accompanying me in my dreams."

The apartment was filled with photographs of a family that
Wui never saw; in the last three months of the Professor's life,
not one relative came to visit. The photographs stood on book-
lined shelves. Endless works of history, philosophy and religion,

hundreds of novels, and even more poetry. But Wui found nothing on mathematics, and not a single scientific journal. This couldn't possibly be Professor Tong's home, he thought—and yet somehow the rooms embodied the man he knew. The books were not separated by truth or fiction or any particular category; they were like a single creature, a world of infinite divisibilities made manageable by their unity. Almost against his will he pulled a volume from the shelf and opened it. *In the long run,* he read, *every lie that survives into the future becomes a truth.*

He felt his stomach turn.

Still, Wui Shin fulfilled the duties of a son. Caring, weeping, and finally burying. Only eleven people attended the funeral, all colleagues from the university, and there was no discernible government presence. Professor Tong, who had always presented himself to Wui as a data scientist, turned out to be a professor of literature. Before his death, three plainclothes officers cleared away his files, including identity documents and family photos. They left the books and furniture untouched.

Wui, present at the time, had watched as the caregivers continued their work, tending to the Professor as if the noisy, disrespectful commotion of the officers was not occurring at all.

Back home in Foshan, the Information Office assigned Wui Shin a new custodian, a woman named Royal Shen, who was younger than him, disconcertingly pleasant, and took a hands-off approach. He submitted his reports as before, on the official letterhead she gave him, and received his payment. Big Fish and Big Meat still trailed him, often on Saturdays.

"Be honest with me," he teased them. "You *like* me. That's the only reason you keep coming to see me."

"Actually," Big Fish said, "it's your wife we're trailing."

Laughter all around.

Wui Shin, it turned out, had grown into his own complicated skin.

Power, he thought, doesn't rest in the information itself, but in the way it is arranged, filtered, labelled, and utilized. This power was as true for nations as it was for individuals. The value of his own existence, his own livelihood and self-determination, rested on the management of power: the arrangement of information.

This fact he knew: his heart was Bee, his happiness was their home, the children. Wei with his nose in a book, Lina napping on the sofa with Aunt Oh. This part of his life would be protected at any cost.

At work, he enjoyed pretending to be a simple node, directing and redirecting data, seeking optimal conditions for parcelled information, mapping the fluctuating dynamics of computational territory.

But within the privacy of his mind, he worked incessantly on a single theoretical problem, the problem of perforation.

Power demanded absolute control of the root of cyber-systems: a tiny, almost invisible, surface like the head of a pin. The minuteness of that root gave it its strength.

One morning, Wui Shin was smoking on the balcony. Bee was helping Wei with a school project, and the two were turning pages on the dining table. Wui knew that his son didn't need any help. At ten years old, the boy was an ingenious yet sorrowful prodigy. Wei was terrified of being alone. He relied on Lina's presence, on his younger sister's adulation, and seemed to shrivel when she went away. Now Wei and Bee were discussing set theory as a means to analyze topology. In the living room, Aunt Oh played a game of Go with Lina. When they dipped their fingers, now and again, into the bowls of stones, a soft clattering filled the room.

A scientific household, Wui thought, intricate, loving, rational. He, alone, was unfit. A deviant within his own life.

Outside, traffic fumed and radios seemed to sing the same worried song.

It had been raining for months. There had been insufferable heat domes. The atmosphere was wet, chilled, steaming, like a kitchen with all its windows sealed. The water coming out of the taps was a frighteningly beautiful bluish-gold. Bee was being sent further and further afield by the Office of Agricultural Diversity, sometimes for weeks at a time. When she came home, she laboured over data and charts with descriptions that seemed pulled from the *Classic of Mountains and Seas*—a catalogue of bizarre findings and new wild-ings. Bee said that what was happening was catastrophic, accelerated evolutionary change. Many of the interior regions were slipping into the unfamiliar, the unknown new. Sudden change was now the only norm. In the space of days, entire valleys had sunk into the sea.

"And you," she said to Wui Shin one morning, her eyes full of that familiar gentleness and gravity. "You hardly talk about the firm anymore. Whenever I come home, you're reading history."

These days, cyberspace, which had once seemed so rapid and unpredictable, was stable. In any place, at any moment, the author-ities could shut off the flow of data, as simple as turning off a tap. This was Professor Tong's legacy, Wui thought. He had always been convinced that cyber-territory could be secured, made sta-ble and intelligent, no more complicated than a ball moving along a groove. The task for authorities was merely how to make the groove invisible.

"Cyberspace has become dull," he said.

"You used to say that engineering was a structure of knowl-edge. A cup is designed for the hand that lifts it, the eye that is drawn to it, the mouth that receives it."

He shrugged. "I was romantic about things."

"But now?"

"Only pragmatic, like everyone in our generation."

"Your systems," Bee said, "forget that every human being is, by nature, a predatory animal. Foolishly or wisely, our instinct is to dominate."

The two of them often spoke like this, taking an aerial view of their divergent fields. Even after all these years, his need to dazzle her had never gone away. He said, "Our instinct is to secure territory. To be predatory is only one of humanity's many strategies."

"But in every group," Bee replied, "you'll find at least one member in whom the predatory response dominates. Every group, in every branch of learning, action or governance, is infiltrated by individuals who act purely in this way: self-preservation as a cover for predation. Malice in the guise of zeal."

"I suppose," he said.

Bee looked at him with such love that his heart felt wounded. He knew she was under tremendous pressure, that her reports were meeting with stunned resistance. He wanted to tell her that he would make any sacrifice necessary for the family and for her. *This* was—they were—his floating world, an exception from all the rest. Hadn't he done everything for love? She stood up abruptly, as if remembering something on the stove, and left him.

At work the next morning, Wui was struck by a severe headache. Returning home, he was surprised to find Bee in his office. Papers glowed on his desk. He saw the ornate letterhead given to him by Royal Shen. He would never have left this particular file—a morbid collection of all the reports he had ever submitted over the last fifteen years—on his desk. How long had she known of its existence? An hour? Days? Far longer? The papers sat in rows, absurdly neat.

She turned at his footsteps but was not startled.

He felt his soul fly out of his chest even as his body moved with utmost calm towards her.

His wife was habituated, he thought, to operating in the dark and green of remote geographies. Her body never betrayed its fear.

"Hello, my darling," he said.

She gazed at him. She did not apologize for prying. And she did not seem alarmed.

He took off his jacket, folded it over a chair. He could hear Aunt Oh calling the children to lunch.

"What horrifies me," she said quietly, "is that I have been living on the profits of your betrayals. Not just me, but the children and Aunt Oh."

"What nonsense are you saying?" He could not find the words that would save him. He was a fool.

He walked over to the desk. Smiled at that ridiculous baroque letterhead. Should he pretend to be angry, or clueless, or rational? "What possessed you to look at this pile of junk?" he said with a laugh. "This is . . ." A diary? A novel? A meditation on the nature of research? "These are personal notes."

"All these arrests over the years. I wondered how we would escape them . . . I never guessed that you had nothing to fear."

"Don't be ridiculous. All this is nothing, just a game."

Bee touched her sleeve, the only sign of her distress. Stared at her arm, relaxed her hands, looked towards him again. Examined Wui as if he were new to her, a recalculation that changed the features of her face and the very light of her eyes.

"Your son is convinced he doesn't have a future here. That a systems failure is happening before our eyes, and we must change the form of our governance. Will you put that in a memorandum? Your own son harbours these thoughts."

"Yes, it would be my duty to report them. Do you harbour these thoughts as well?"

Silence. Finally he had succeeded in surprising her. This person whom he knew and loved far more than the world itself. "If I'm really the disgusting traitor you're imagining," he said, "I would do my duty."

"How do you know, Wui," she said after a moment, "that you're not the person who was always the target? That it's not *you* who is surrounded and caught in the trap?" Her voice was so familiar, as if it came from outside of them both. That unflustered, unerring inner voice.

"I've protected us. If only you knew."

"Mistaken beliefs are powerful," she said. "Sometimes, in the end, they're more powerful than love."

He could not understand what this meant. And did not understand what it meant when she said, "I will never forgive you." When she gathered up the papers, put them carefully back in the file, and walked out of the room with it.

He was, Wui understood, too frightened to react. His soul, after all, had flown out of his body minutes earlier, and now it was only his shell responding. Had it been like that for Bing Lihai when officers broke down his door and cornered his family in a single room? Or for Feng Mei, Locksmith and LiBai57, and the others, when the police smashed through their homes? You watched the world for signs, Wui thought, numbly. You saw concrete skyscrapers beginning to crack, repeated flooding that destabilized a city, how the salt got in everywhere and undermined the stability of a world. You saw the first leaves falling, and that's when you knew you had to act.

A person's life took decades to realize itself, and to be revealed to the person.

Days and Months Tech Corp Ltd. was not really an entrepreneurial entity. Although it had been set in motion decades ago by Taikonaut, LiBai57 and JerkCat, under Wui's stewardship it was an illness, an invasive life form spreading through the Chinese Internet. There is nothing so dangerous, Wui thought, as that which is camouflaged as a joke. Almost his entire life, from the moment he was nine years old and saw the distraught crowds and the vans full of bodies in a video that went viral for a few hours before it was wiped from the Internet forever—the very cellular structure of the images crumpled and dissolved—he had never stopped working on the only problem that mattered to him: how to pull down, imperceptibly, quietly, achingly, the entire structure. If those in power had given him a grave to mourn his mother, that might have been enough. But they had vanished even her lifeless body. Bee's misunderstanding, even the loss of her love, could not change the trajectory he had chosen. His life stemmed from that tiny, invisible root and was his very identity.

The rain continued, and wouldn't stop. Wui wrote up his monthly memorandum for Royal Shen and left it, in plain view, on his desk. In the memorandum, he described his argument with Bee exactly as it had unfolded, including the criminal thoughts harboured by Bee and his son. He had imbued it with what he felt to be literary flair, a terse dramatic quality. Such stylistic choices were nothing more than theatre, a complicated trick to make Bee understand that *everything* was theatre. He could not risk telling her about the nature of his work at Days and Months, and the recent stunning advances he had made. Soon, when the program culminated, its consequences would be visible for all the world to see.

But what had Bee meant, he wondered, when she asked if *he* had always been the target? Why had she been so calm, so unsurprised?

In the morning, the memorandum had vanished from his desk. He wrote it again from memory, and once more left it in the open. Again, it disappeared.

He was now in a strange game of cat and mouse, in which the woman he loved seemed a figment of his mind. Professor Tong, too, kept appearing in his hallucinations.

"You've confused the dead for the living," the Professor explained; he looked rested and jubilant, younger than Wui Shin had ever seen him. "Didn't it ever strike you how simple Bee's career path has been? All the doors opened for her immediately!

Just as they did for you. And the two of you, from know-nothing
backwaters." The Professor laughed. "Don't you remember her
father, Old Flower? How did this speck of life, this impoverished
apple picker, manage to raise a child prodigy?"

"We rose high in this world through hard work and genius,"
Wui said. He wanted to say, *It was our destiny.* He said, "The system
is structured so that talent has a pathway to fulfillment."

The Professor looked at him with tenderness. "Is it?"

"I know you," Wui Shin said. "You're my guilt, my paranoia, my
self-loathing. Nothing more than a false mirror. Leave me."

Royal Shen called him, requesting a meeting. He said there was
nothing of note to report. She asked many questions about Bee.
She asked about his son. He ended the call.

Soon after, it was announced by the government that Foshan
would be included in the five-year plan, known as the New Era
of the Imperishable, or Daybreak, headed by the Infrastructure
Office and the Ministry of Security, supported by the Ministry of
Industry and Information Technology. The five-year plan would
secure the Pearl River Delta for generations to come, while redraw-
ing land and sea borders to create a stable perimeter, the Blue
Thread. Existing coastal and river defences had proven inadequate
against storm surges and major flooding, and a third of the region
was now below sea level. A geographical area that totalled more
than 100,000 square kilometres, and included eighteen major cities, had been left outside the Security Perimeter. These regions
would instead be refuelled by nature, while oceanic military
zones would be maintained for mineral recuperation and military
training. The national data centre, as well as the data centres of
Huawei, Tencent, ZTE, BaShi and others, would all be relocated.
Speed and efficiency were crucial.

The day after the announcement, Wui came home from work
to find Lina sitting at the kitchen table with a glass of orange
juice. It was a few days after her seventh birthday, and balloons

still drifted through the rooms. He opened every single closet in the apartment like a man who is certain that what has been misplaced can only be here. It must be here. Within these four walls, his family was safe; this place was the exception to the rule. But even though the closets were still full of their clothes, Bee, Wei, and Aunt Oh were gone.

Bee had left him a note, folded inside a beige envelope beside his rewritten memorandum, the one he had insisted on redoing each night. Her goodbye, unsigned, was brief. *The family is now in two parts and the root is broken. Tell Lina I love her and always will.*

Aunt Oh had left nothing for him, only a sealed letter for Lina. He didn't open it but some shame inside him, the terror that Lina would learn everything, made him destroy it. And so, unread, it was gone forever.

"There was no part of you," Professor Tong said in his dream that night, "that was hidden from any of us. There was never a private world that was invisible. You are nothing but a programmed entity, a piece of code, like everything in this universe."

The only constant is change. That old truism of calculus, thought Wui, now frightens me. For days, he wandered the apartment, and one night found himself staring at Bee's bookshelf. It was overflowing not just with oversized volumes on botany and agronomy, but with Bee's elementary and high school textbooks. One was upside down. On a bookmarked page, he recognized her handwriting in the margins: *Software is engineered so that a user knows how to function. A building knows how to stand.* Even if she had loved him when she wrote those words, now they could only serve as a rebuke. The very page seemed to mock him.

Thirty spokes share a single hub—
the function of the cart happens where the absence is.

Doors and windows are chiselled out to make a room—
the function of the room happens where the absence is.
So profit lies in the having of something,
in properties possessed,
but function lies in the having of nothing—
in possession of no properties at all.

Meanwhile, the rains never stopped. As summer dissolved into fall, all manner of ailments spread. Even Big Fish and Big Meat had wheezing coughs. No one was evicted, no buildings were declared uninhabitable, nothing was demolished. And also: no one was ordered to pack up their belongings, cross the Security Perimeter, and take up residence in what was now being called the Central Land. No one was forced to receive their compensation package, or to rebuild their lives elsewhere. Force was completely unnecessary. Instead, each week another school closed, another wing of a hospital, another government office. Devise strategies to your heart's content, thought Wui, make your moves, resist, weep, deviate, refuse, but the chessboard remains set. Foshan and half the region now lay outside the land border.

Every day, the authorities filled the airwaves. "We cannot transform a vast urban area, an urban geography—designed to be rooted in the ground—into a floating city." The host, laughing, said, "Naturally. You cannot change a dog into a fish." "Moreover," said another, "to do so would be to ignore the new wildings, the miraculous permutations and adaptations already under way that are ushering us into a prosperous future."

The radios all repeated the same story: a century ago, when the Three Gorges Dam was built, three cities, 114 towns and 1,680 villages, some of which had thousands of years of history, surrounded by 1,283 archaeological sites, were deliberately flooded. More than four million people were relocated in a program of national solidarity. But as the years passed, the dam didn't protect the higher ground as hoped. The Yangtze basin continued to flood, and over fifty million people were moved again. The Three Gorges Dam, one of the most ambitious engineering projects ever undertaken by mankind, had turned out to be a teacup against the floods. Engineers and scientists had learned from past errors. The land was an entity, an organism, whose permanence required cycles of reconfiguration. In the New Era of the Imperishable, citizens must learn to live on the back of a dragon. Flourishing demanded agility and sacrifice. The history of this country, commentators said, *was* the history of managing its waterways: understanding their nature, navigating their byways, harnessing their power. The history of water was embedded in ancient mythologies, in the Tang poems, in the character of the people. The day was always breaking.

"Ten thousand years ago," said a gentle voice, "England, Germany and the Netherlands were not separated by a sea. That whole area was dry land."

The voice belonged to Bee, Wui thought for an instant, but of course this was impossible. Yet how familiar it seemed, this voice sliding from the speakers. All the voices had become hers.

"The North Sea," she reminded listeners, "covers an area that was once inhabited landscape. Twelve thousand years ago, this was fertile land. A person could go from what is now England to what is now the Netherlands by foot and cart. This land had countless towns and villages, it had dunes, lakes, rivers. What is now the Seine, the Rhine, and the Thames were all one. They flowed into the English Channel and out into the ocean. Myriad species thrived, deer, boar and so on, and all manner of plant life. *This was reality for five thousand years.* It was the richest environment in continental Europe. In the seventh century BCE, floods became more frequent. The sea permeated this area. What was once irregular flooding became predictable, regular, but inescapable. Rising water turned the land to islands. Eventually the islands themselves disappeared. People relocated along a changing shoreline. Within a century, what was once land became ocean, and all those prosperous towns lay tens of metres below the water.

"The rise and fall of oceans is the breathing in, breathing out of the planet. It is not government cruelty that drives us to redraw the map of the Pearl River Delta. This is simply the shape of the earth in our time. We must live and flourish in our own age, not in the map of the past."

Later, Wui lay in bed, confused and believing he was in a hotel room in Beijing, trying to track down his lost friends. During Bing Lihai's trial, he had told himself to emigrate as others had. To begin again. Now he blinked and saw rain sleeting down the windows. He was in Foshan and the ground itself was retreating. "The ground is emigrating!" he shouted, laughing. He heard his daughter moving through the apartment, picking up books she could barely read and putting them down. The voices of Big Fish and Big Meat echoed through the apartment. They had brought groceries.

"Don't upset yourself," Big Fish was saying to the child.

"Your mother, brother and aunt will come home," said Big Meat, "and Father will be himself again."

Wasn't it ludicrous that Big Fish and Big Meat should now become parental figures to his daughter? But why was it ludicrous? They had stood outside the hospital at her birth, walked behind her to school, they had carried Wei home in their arms when he crashed his bicycle. They had appeared to be everyday men of the neighbourhood, appearing and disappearing at will. *Uncle Fish and Uncle Meat*, he thought, laughing again.

Wui Shin closed his eyes.

He reminded himself that he had power. He could demand that Royal Shen locate his wife, son and aunt. He could find them on his own, explain himself to Bee, explain everything.

But there was something else on the horizon, something that paralyzed him. Days and Months had grown, in its patient, lethal way. The towers, nodes and junctures, and most of all the root system, appeared healthy, but the information and procedures of cyberspace had become tangled up within themselves. Days and Months, it turned out, was a kind of system dementia that had been permeating for decades. And in a matter of months now, it would entirely perforate the Chinese Internet. There are thresholds that must be respected. Once crossed, a cascade of rapid and unpredictable effects cannot be reversed. System collapse would be as continuous, as implacable, as the setting sun. When Days and Months connected its last few moves, an inevitable outcome, it would envelop the Internet, atomizing its pieces. Was Days and Months a poison, a virus, a disease? They were all effectively the same thing. The structure had lost the capacity to adhere to a sequence, in the same way that a person could lose the capacity to remember, swallow and breathe.

An all-too-natural death, Wui thought.

How poetic that external and internal structures were being attacked at the same moment. Soon the cables, transmitters and data centres of the Pearl River Delta would lie outside the Blue Thread. But they were not going to perish alone. Bing Lihai, Feng Mei, Locksmith and JerkCat had been visible dissidents, but he had been clothed in the night itself.

"My principles," he reiterated to himself, "were always pure."

Bing Lihai seemed to uncurl, phantom-like, from a nearby chair. This vision was so tall and wide it barely fit inside the room. That great mane of hair, those falling spectacles. "Come on, Wui Shin! Stop deluding yourself. When you started work at Days and Months, system perforation was already in motion. Frankly, you didn't understand it. You're not the genius you think you are."

Wui swatted him away. "Bing Lihai, you've got a warehouse full of stories."

"Don't be ashamed to admit your limitations. Whoever pro-grammed it must have been a friend of yours. He knew you inside out."

In all honesty, Wui Shin could not remember which pieces he had understood, or at which point in time. Yes, it was not impossible that Professor Tong or Bing Lihai or any number of programmers had hacked into Days and Months. Or even someone unknown to him, an enemy operative from outside the territory. But he had a strange and certain feeling that both he and Bing Lihai were right. That it was Wui Shin himself who had set the pieces in motion, but without comprehending their repercussions. That it was almost an accident, or human error.

His thoughts were confused.

"Your own network virus has infected you," Bing Lihai joked.

They laughed and laughed. The whole situation was a riot! Function lay in the having of nothing! Which one of them was actually in prison? Wui couldn't stop giggling, impressed by the appalling absurdity of it all, only laughing harder when Lina appeared in the doorway. Even when she ran to get Big Fish and Big Meat, who hulked into the room and spoke in soothing tones, the scene struck him as surpassingly stupid.

"The days and months are on their way out the door!" Wui Shin proclaimed. "Who needs one billion useless devices and all these wasteful base stations? Now we can stop gobbling up all the yttrium, gallium, arsenic and antimony to feed this chip or that component. Time and space, life and land, are not perpet-ual. All the old problems have ceased to be problems, don't you see? The digital realm is dead, and we can close every factory and mine that fed its bloated carcass. Sorry Big Meat and Big Fish, even you'll be out of a job soon."

Big Fish knelt at his bedside.

"The phone, the phone, Uncle Fish! Hurry and answer it!" Wui pleaded.

"There's no phone ringing," Lina said.

"It's that criminal Bing Lihai, he never stops calling. He wants me to join his 'movement' but I told him he's a stupid sponge. By the time he manages to convince one paltry court to uphold even one word of the Constitution, Days and Months will have done all the dirty work for him!"

He ordered Big Fish and Big Meat to help him dress, and somehow persuaded them to go on an excursion. The three of them, plus Lina, set out into the downpour, the packed streets and honking melee, the smear of lights across raincoats and sopping awnings, into a Foshan that was drowning before their eyes.

"Dacheng Peak!" Wui shouted from the front passenger seat of their car. Traffic was at a crawl, and everyone seemed to be out visiting friends, or taking advantage of the sales, stocking up and saying goodbye. They inched across the interchange and at last left the gridlock behind. The car swam across highways oozing with mud, soared over the Shunde Waterway, swirled ever higher into the clouds. Dacheng was the highest of the seventy-two peaks of the ancient Xiqiao Mountain. Big Meat complained it was useless to visit a historic site when the world had turned to fog.

"We won't even be able to get out of the car," Big Fish whined. "The rain is torrential."

"You should be thanking me!" Wui joked. "Even if I didn't invite you, you're still obliged to follow me through this bad weather."

"What's there to see on Dacheng anyway?"

"Don't listen to them," Wui said, turning to Lina. "These mountains were once revered as deities. Xiqiao Mountain is fifty million years old, an extinct volcano. Its history is its structure."

How clueless everyone was, Wui thought. Deep in this mountain range, in what had once been a missile silo, was the motherlode of servers and system mirrors, a data centre wrapped inside rings of bomb shelters. Tens of thousands of units installed in a modular platform, secured by robots, drones and AI. But all that was surface modernity. He wanted to stand on the peak of a mountain and look at the wavering moon as it slid across a lake of ink. He wanted to look far into the distance, towards the karst mountains of Guizhou, where the Chinese Academy of Sciences had buried its data centre, uprooting eight thousand people from their homes and villages in the process. Buried underground was data collected from their astrophysics telescope, which reached half a kilometre into the sky. A giant finger pointing at the heavens, Wui thought. An arrow extending from the earth's core. But what was it, in the end? A mere whisker on the face of the earth.

"I'm doing you a favour," he said. "We're going to see the old world one last time before it dies."

"Grumble grumble squirt squirt," said Big Fish. A local expression that meant *stop your muttering*. Everyone laughed.

"Listen," Wui said. "We're the last generation who will know, that is, touch, the reality of this world before it disappears into dysfunction. This is the world in which we came of age, and the only world where we'll ever feel at home. As with any death, one should say farewell properly, with all of one's heart and mind."

He felt warmth on his shoulder and had the wild sensation that it was tears. Tears falling from the roof of the car onto his shoulder. But it was his daughter's hand reaching over the seat.

"Your mother was my heart. My happiness," Wui told her. "She was the one I neither understood nor deserved."

Lina gazed at him. She didn't move at all.

"My mother, your grandmother, survived a massacre," Wui Shin said. The desperation in his own voice stunned him. "She's still alive somewhere."

Was it true? He didn't know. No one could be certain. That was the crime of it all.

Big Meat asked, with a sideways glance at Lina, "Who reported your wife and son? Wasn't it you?"

"I was trying to save them."

"Just like you saved the others?"

Trees twisted in the fog, leaves seemed to reconfigure themselves like flocks of birds. Lina had started to cry, and wouldn't stop.

"The higher you go," Big Fish said softly, "the more time slows. That's what we learned in school when I was a kid. All the memories of the world are high above us. Far above the atmosphere, all is preserved and nothing is forgotten."

When they reached Dacheng Peak, only Wui Shin left the car and braved the rain. In the seconds it took to pop open his umbrella, he was instantly drenched. He walked across the parking lot, past a placard, around a cordon of yellow tape, up two flights of wooden steps, and onto an immense viewing platform. Perhaps, he thought, the others assumed he was planning to disappear forever and they were letting him go.

Good night. He listened as his words were swallowed by the rain.

Wui Shin felt everything flickering into a new pattern, and then the pattern bit by bit broke down. So few people witnessed the end of a world and survived. Was it happening to him one last time?

He waited for something to change. The rain fell.

The target of Days and Months was not the physical network, but coherence at the most basic level. How long before anyone noticed that the network of roots in a vast forest was diseased? Or that an ice sheet, larger than a country, weighing a trillion tonnes, existing for tens of thousands of years, was on the verge of irreversible collapse? Patience was the engine of revolution. By hiding knowledge from everyone, Wui told himself, he had been closest to reality, which existed in pure form at the root, which was life and death itself.

Or perhaps he had only ever been a stranger to himself, just one more piece willingly put to use and discarded. Was that the final truth? Around him, the sky was fog. His life's work was complete and yet his life kept going. He couldn't think how to survive this fact. Was he—and everything he had ever loved— nothing more than water thundering into the valleys below? Were they anything less?

part three

ooooo

1.

I have been on this train for perhaps six hours. It carries me ever forward alongside a bright moon above the shadows of trees.

My brother appears at the edges of my thoughts. Wei was ten years old when I last saw him; in my memory, he is showing me how to paint with ink and water. I hold the brush and Wei rests his hand lightly over mine, guiding me, and we dip the brush into darkest black. Soon a mountain emerges as if dissolving from the world onto the sheet of paper. If other moments arrived after this one—if I saw him leaving with my mother and aunt, if we were permitted to say goodbye—those images have disappeared.

Now, another train draws up beside us, travelling in the same direction. Full carriages and empty ones appear like windows along a building; wagon after wagon drums by. The tracks curve, and the other train slows. For a moment it seems as if neither of us is moving. I see a man wearing a pale yellow sweater. The man's glasses rest on his forehead, and he is leaning towards something, or someone, I can't see. The light of the moon floods our two compartments, sharp as a silver blade. He turns and meets my gaze. His eyes are so curious, so near. He looks healthy, joyful and at peace. *If I could reach through the frame, would I touch my father's sleeve? Have I returned at last?*

I touch the glass.

As soon as I feel its solidity, the man is gone. The other train keeps going, pulling further and further ahead. The night explodes back into view.

The compartment door bursts open and two passengers, a man and a girl, freeze in the entryway; they apologize for startling me.

"Not at all," I say, embarrassed. My hands are trembling. "Come in."

The man and the girl settle into two seats facing one another. I sink into my own thoughts, and when I finally emerge, I'm surprised to see a sheet of paper unfolded on the table. A grid, hand-drawn in blue ink, covers its surface.

They are playing Go, or wéiqí, the game of surrounding. The grid on which they play is so familiar, as if it came from my own belongings.

"Does the light bother you?" the man asks, noticing my surprise.

"No, but . . . long ago, I used to play this game with my father. I had forgotten."

The girl says, with all the confidence of youth, "I never lose. I'm the best."

She tells me they are headed home but the journey has been hard. Still, the man adds, there is reason for hope: their village is recovering, and things are starting to grow again.

I hear the faintest *clack* of a piece set down.

It's your turn, I hear my father say.

The game of Go, I remember, happens stone by stone. The aim is not to defeat one's opponent but to hold territory securely. Groups of stones form shapes—my father used to call them stars, eyes, rooms—which will survive or die together. A player seeks to encircle her opponent while not being encircled herself. The game of Go is full of suppositions about the strengths and weaknesses of ourselves and others. The board can only contain suppositions because time never ceases to alter the way the stones stand in relation to one another. If a player attempts to make their suppositions certain by increasing their hold on territory they occupy, the value of their territory will decrease. This need for certainty, which reveals a weakness, will be tallied in the final scoring of the game. Go is full of such switchbacks.

As I watch the girl considering the board, the train lulls me with its rhythm, connecting innumerable points of space.

The game can end if both players, knowing there is nothing more to be gained, give up a turn; or if one player resigns. The resigning player, according to tradition, takes one of their own pieces and entrusts it to their opponent's hand.

"Tell me something," the girl says.

"What do you want to know?"

"Everything."

"Always the impossible with you."

"I want to know everything that wasn't meant for me."

It must be a shared, beloved joke. When they laugh, tears pool in my eyes.

"When two people meet in conversation," the man says, "each surrenders their weapons to the other." He lifts a single white stone. As the light in the compartment wavers, he places it in her hand.

It is late and, in these hours, the Book of Records always takes on a new form. The train continues, a sound that blurs into the tide of water against the shore.

ooooo

In the Sea, the board on which we played was drawn in blue ink on a sheet of notebook paper, and the stones were buttons my father and I had gathered.

In his pyjamas and slippers, Jupiter paused to study the game Dad and I had left unfinished. Soon, Bento joined him, followed by the stray cat; he curled up on Bento's foot as if it were his throne. For long moments, as they contemplated their moves, nothing stirred. I poured tea and watched the steam folding up.

A weight pressed against my chest. Alone, I went up the stairs and climbed onto the rooftop. A storm was coming and the wind immediately agitated my clothes as if I were flying. The moon was immense. I knew it was held in place by its own motion and by the force of the earth, as if the earth were a parent spinning its child. The ocean seemed to beckon me forward, a tidal urge, a mother's touch. On the roof's edge, I felt as if I were made of air. This loyalty to my father, a loyalty I could neither carry nor refuse, filled my vision. When I looked down, when I searched for my own hands, they blurred into the night.

"Lina?"

Softly, Blucher asked me what I was doing and why I was crying.

Without turning, I heard her footsteps—and heard them pause when I said that I missed my mother. That I was certain she was gone from this world and that my brother survived alone. "I don't know how, but . . . I can feel his loneliness. I know it's real."

For a long time, nothing moved except the sea. I heard Blucher's footsteps again, and felt her hand take mine and slowly draw me backwards. My knees were unsteady. A cold sweat rushed over me.

Blucher gazed at me for a long moment. She told me that if I couldn't bear to imagine their suffering, I must learn to imagine my mother and brother another way. *What other way?* Feel their presence elsewhere, in another "I" and another "thou." *Would that change anything?* Every movement within our minds, she said, changes us into something we can't yet see. She said that every person is housed in the word "I" and in the word "you." Every single person no matter where they lived or when or how. If you forget everything else, Lina, remember what these words hold.

In the morning, returning from my errands, I found Bento reading to my father. I made a porridge from dried amaranth seeds and topped it with wild mulberries. They were so ripe that a gentle shaking of the branches the previous day had yielded a whole bag. Soon Jupiter and Blucher joined us. My father raised himself to sitting and reached for his glasses. Jupiter tried to persuade the stray cat to vacate the softest chair; but even when Jupiter addressed him, with great solemnity, as Brother Orange, the cat refused. On the windowsill, my three books sat atop each other like a staircase.

The day grew hot. Blucher and Jupiter argued over whose turn it was to continue the story, and while they were bickering Bento stepped in. "Through the windows," he announced, "snow fell in thick bundles."

I saw my father turn towards the window. I saw snow gathering on the waves.

ooooo

In the Van den Enden house, Baruch Spinoza hid in a corner of the salon, trying to remain unseen. Damius was serving slices of cake while Adriana and little Jacob thundered overtop each other, "Who's got it! Confess, who's got the bean?"

With an arm that seemed to extend forever, Damius gave Baruch a piece of cake.

Baruch couldn't resist. He took a huge bite. Oh, it was wonderful! A cloud of egg, milk and vanilla. But then his tooth hit something hard, jolting his whole face. He cried out in pain and Damius gave him a pitying look.

"Ha ha ha!" Jacob shouted. "Baruch got the bean!"

The Van den Endens charged towards him. Adriana snatched the hat off his head and fixed a white paper crown there instead, crackling it over his ears.

"Hail, hail!" the children howled. "We Three Kings are here with our huge star! Through sand and dunes, we've travelled far . . ."

Mem, waving a paper star hitched to a pinwheel, joked, "The Almighty never fails to shower our Baruch with blessings!"

Baruch had already downed two tankards of ale. Twelfth Night, this Christian feast, was a perplexing event. Apparently, he had won the beancake lottery to be King. Now lots were being drawn from a bag, and other roles were being handed out: Cook, Messenger, Doctor, Singer, Servant, Carver, Pastor, Nun and on and on.

"But what is it for?" he asked. The paper crown, on which someone had scribbled *Epiphany!*, fell from his head and had to be refastened.

Kerckring laughed. "Roles for the table play, of course."

"The what?"

Shouting erupted from the street. Adriana, *Servant* card on her hat, galloped outside to meet the noise. The door hung open like a mouth. Damius glided forth, holding aloft a second beancake. Outside, a crowd was heartily singing. Baruch was half dragged, half thrown across the room, into the arms of a tall chair. The household circled him with offerings: a bunch of grapes, a mug of ale, one pork chop.

Baruch wished to be lighthearted. He tried to dance with the children but baby Maria bit him and Jacob kicked over a table. The King would be mortally wounded soon, but maybe that was the point? Here was Margareta now, whirling Maria up into the air. The baby, held aloft, dribbled down on them. Everybody careened drunkenly sideways, a joyful capsizing ship. He could not *possibly* be as drunk as they were. Kerckring, *Pastor*, cleaned Baruch's face with a handkerchief and presented him with a fresh goblet of wine.

"Everyone yell together!" Frans was yelling. "I, the Fool, am here to take a swipe at anyone who refuses to cry out, 'The King drinks!'"

"The King drinks!!"

Who was petting his ear now? And who was putting coins into his hand and telling him to enrich the poor? "Baruch, it's time to pancake now," whispered Clara Maria soothingly.

"Hail the Fool who dances round the King!" Frans pirouetted. Little Jacob, *Carver*, dangled a slice of beef above his mouth.

"Can't I stay here?" Baruch asked the noise. "Can't a person be merry forever?"

"King's candle," the girls cried, "lick my boot!"

He wandered out of the front room and found himself in a passageway that led nowhere. Clara Maria, cross-legged on the floor, beckoned him to sit. In the candlelight, her skirt was an emerald river. "Come and rest quietly," she said, "and maybe you'll feel a little better."

He obeyed, a wilting flower. The room spun clockwise and slowly slowed.

"Baruch, have you really *never* celebrated Twelfth Night?"

"Who am I again?"

She laughed. "On this night, children command the house-hold." Her voice was summer rain. "Everyone in Amsterdam loves the Thirteenth Day. I'm amazed you managed to avoid it."

"It wasn't celebrated in our community. We were a family of five children," he said from between his knees. "Isaac, Miriam, Rifka, Gabe . . . Miriam would have loved these paper crowns."

"Your Rifka and your Miriam, won't they come and visit you? Though I suppose they must be quite different from you . . ."

He found he could no longer explain a thing in words. Now she put her hand upon his heart. She deftly straightened him. It appeared he had fallen to the floor.

The Fool sprinted past, wearing a necklace of sausages.

"I think . . . I think I can understand something of that, Baruch. It must be difficult to live so near to one's family and yet be cast out, as if an ocean separated these streets and the Vlooienburg."

Portuguese, which he had not spoken in a long time, accidentally escaped his lips. He had fallen between languages and into a sky, and he was Bento again, hiding in his father's study. Clara Maria's hand upon his chest was a sphere resting for a moment, hindered, like his memories, from moving on.

The carousing braided into choral singing, and its coloured threads wove him back together. Something was sliding down his face. It was his crown, crumpling to his chin.

"I sometimes wonder if I'll ever leave this house," Clara Maria said.

"But one day you'll marry, won't you?"

"Oh, Baruch." The flurry of her fingers against his knee. "It's as if you never noticed my difficulties. My illness. I do not know if marriage should be my future."

She smiled when he protested, but he had no idea what she meant.

"An unbeliever is supposed to be worse than a murderer," she said. "And here I am sitting beside a cold-blooded excommunicated heretic."

"There are many things I believe in."

"I want to believe in something more than words. I can recite Seneca today, Epictetus tomorrow, countless plays and poems, ancient and new. I used to imagine a whole life, many existences, but none of them will ever fall to my share."

He asked, "What kind of life do you imagine?"

"Such as . . . reinventing myself in New Amsterdam, or mastering a new craft, like you. Learning a new skill. Having a second and even a third life. I would like that."

The word *Messenger* fell into her lap. He helped to re-pin it. Was she playing her role, or had they fallen through a mirror that was in fact a window?

He closed his eyes. Thoughts waiting in the wings of his mind came loose. "Descartes," he said, "tells us that there's the world we can touch and the world we can think. He says they go along like two marbles—the marble we can touch and the marble we can think—rolling side by side. He says they meet one another only faintly, as if through a magical veil. Descartes calls them physical substance and thinking substance. Matter and thought . . ." Clara Maria holds my hand, he thought, and I am seized with feeling. She *touches* me and my heart *aches*. A sequence in one dimension gives rise to a sequence in the other.

"Father knew him well," she said. "Monsieur René was kind whenever I met him."

"It's snowing!" Anna announced from some distant star.

"But in either dimension," Baruch said, "who or what moves the two marbles?"

"Who moves the marbles?" Clara Maria smiled. "Who keeps the Book of Records? I suppose people wish it to be the hand of God, or maybe God's mind. But what if it's just the slope of the incline, or the gravity and physics of our world? What if such visible rules can give rise to the kaleidoscope of our thoughts? Maybe they all belong to the same order of things, even God."

"What if thought, or the thinking substance, is deeper than even the ocean, and I am just a droplet inside it?"

She laughed drowsily. "A droplet who believes that the way it exists now, in this moment, should last forever."

The party moved to a new key. From the sitting room, the feathering lute and Adriana's voice made him shiver: a song of unrequited love from the mouth of a child. Who are you, the song asked, slumped against the wall like that? What in God's name is the point of you? The tempo changed, smuggling him into a new world. Adriana sang a dancing tune, now giddy, now light. Was beauty a truth or a faith? And wasn't all of this, all of these festivities, this shimmering family, almost too much happiness to bear?

Baruch needed to crawl out from the ocean before he vanished inside it. An atom of water escaping the water! Was there no one who could save him from being consumed? He should live alone. He must . . .

Adriana came and begged Clara Maria for a duet.

Now, as he floated sideways to the floor, her voice cascaded towards him and swallowed him whole.

In the morning he was so dehydrated and feeble he wanted to die, but sat down to work nevertheless. Gasparo Obissi was providing him regular commissions. The appetite for specialty lenses appeared limitless.

By early afternoon, six objective and ocular lenses, as well as lenses for a high-grade microscope, shone on his table, and he sat beside them like a boy among brothers.

A knock and the door inched open. Clara Maria in a dress the colour of marigolds.

"May I come in, Baruch?"

"Of course."

Brother Orange took the opportunity to squeeze discreetly through the open door.

Her eyes fell immediately on the lenses.

Unable to contain his pride, he said, "A morning's work."

The room felt very small. From lens to lens she proceeded, as if enacting a ceremony from childhood. He noticed her limp and the concentration in her eyes, as if she held at bay a continuous pain. It seemed impossible, yet he had never, not even for a moment, registered these most basic facts of her life. Was it possible that the ones we love are the ones we most powerfully imagine, the ones we create, continuously, inside our minds?

He lifted two lenses and held them up.

"Rays of light," he said, "don't intersect at a single focal point. So we must combine multiple lenses for use in a high-grade telescope."

"So that they remedy one another."

"Yes. Together, they compensate for certain aberrations. Not entirely but significantly."

Clara Maria's interest was unwavering. From what materials are the grinding moulds made, she asked, and how does one go about checking the spherical figure? Like him, she was drawn to an algebra at the heart of things.

After a time she grew quiet, even though she had not run out of questions.

"What are you thinking, Clara Maria?"

She moved cautiously to the other side of the table. "I was thinking that when a man lifts a telescope to the sky, what he sees will trouble him. He will know that our senses perceive only mere slivers of things. He will be forced to reconsider truths that have shaped his existence . . . but which are demonstrably *untrue*. Galileo wrote that Saturn has ears, or that Saturn has swallowed its children somehow. I was thinking, What kind of universe is this really?"

Long ago, in the Vlooienburg, the rooms had overflowed with noise as Mai chased down Isaac and Miriam, and Baruch had fled into his father's room. "Love reveals our death," Frans had said to him this morning, in a kind of warning. Or had he misunderstood? "Death reveals our love." What propelled one's actions finally—was it past or future time, was it eternity or mortality?

Clara Maria was at his desk now, before the microscope he had built himself.

"May I?"

"Of course."

She seated herself, smoothed a strand of hair from her face, and bent towards it. On the glass plate was a dead spider he had found on the windowsill three days ago. If only he had something more to offer her: a blade of grass, a butterfly's wing, a grain of sand.

Watching her, he imagined the edge of the microscope's eyepiece against his own forehead. He pictured the bulbous nodes of the spider's joints, horrifying yet utterly familiar, reminiscent of the joints of a human hand. When one slipped into the microscope's hallways, ordinary vision dropped away like a false world.

"And this must be . . ." Clara Maria said, "its insides?"

"The viscera. It's almost as if the creature has been turning inside out since it died."

"It is even more unspeakable than I imagined."

He recognized his own emotions in her voice, a kind of hair-raising, horrified fascination. A kind of satisfaction.

Noises crashed around them, pots banging, students practising or singing. Clara Maria sat in wonder. A feeling he loved. That feeling which arises in us when something singular detains the mind.

After a moment, she stood. Her hand on the back of the chair steadied her.

"Baruch, when I'm in your presence, I feel happiness. I ask questions you seem to understand, and I hope that your questions, too, might find some answer in me." She flushed, her hand released the chair and she took a step forward, unsteadily. The pleasure that washed through him had a growing shadow, as if joy and sorrow were joined at some inescapable root.

"When I think about next month or next year," she said, "I feel that my future was already set in motion by things long ago."

"I know this feeling," he answered. "I have this foreboding now."

"That I've stood in your room before, like this?"

"Yes."

"That I've taken your hand, like this."

In a single glance, he took in the room, the bags of silica, the single bed with the tiny window, the decaying spider in the dish, the table with his endless writings, his weathered hat, his book of Hebrew grammar, all of which stood in austere contrast to the softness of Clara Maria's dress. Some truths were inescapable. Why had he accepted his excommunication? What was driving him on, really? Was he a marble, rolling along a groove? The groove itself foreclosed his every escape.

He thought, I could never allow her to join her life to mine.

She told him that Kerckring had proposed to her a month ago. She had delayed and delayed, imagining a different kind of future for herself. A future she did not know how to describe. This morning, her parents had given their blessing if Kerckring converted to Catholicism, and he had accepted. Marriage, motherhood, family would be her vocation. She understood that now.

Somehow, Baruch thought, all paths led to the same necessity: his life and Clara Maria's life must separate.

"I am happy for you both."

Her eyes moved across his face. If you study all the cells of a person, he wondered, every single fibre of their physical being, what falls outside your knowing? Almost everything.

"Forgive me, Clara Maria. I must return to work."

"Are you unhappy, Baruch?"

"No, I am never unhappy."

"Never?"

"I'm blessed." Reveal nothing, feel nothing. He wanted to hurry her from the room so that he could be in solitude. "Ever since my father died, I have given up a great deal so that I might be free."

"Freedom," she said. A small lamp of a smile. "That's what I would wish for you."

Baruch began housing the lenses back into their fitted boxes.

She was at the door. "What I want to say is . . . how beloved you are to us, Baruch. Sometimes I worry you'll slip away from us, into shadows. When a person is completely free, others might cease to understand what drives them, their motives and feelings. When the world that once raised you, that educated you, makes you an outcast, the refuge of introspection can seem to fill a life. Don't confuse that loneliness with freedom."

Clara Maria looked at him, at the spider, as if all three had made a pact. And then she was gone.

Baruch was at the mercy of emotion. He closed his eyes, but it only made the world within him more vivid, so he tried to picture himself between the stars, unburdened of all sensory feeling. Still his thoughts cascaded as if driven by a force, a torrent, all their own. Time was a whirlwind. It was grinding him down to dust. The world intervenes in everything we do, he thought, and we turn and stumble in its innumerable fragments.

In the evening, Baruch could hear the happy couple conversing through the walls. He heard a new firmness in Clara Maria's footsteps down the hallway, the pious ardour of her music rising from the piano. *Before the day breaks and the shadows flee, I will make my way to the mountain of myrrh and to the hill of frankincense. Come with me from Lebanon, my beloved. Rise up and come away.* The words, from the Song of Solomon, transported him.

His room was a perfect square. The window, the size of a holy book, let in only a blade of light.

"Exquisite!" Kerckring shouted. He thumped the adjoining wall so hard that Brother Orange, startled, fell off the bookshelf. He pounced at the wall, hissing.

"Eh, Spinoza, what's that you say?" Kerckring yelled.

—*in the open pathways, I will seek him whom my soul loves.*

Kerckring again: "Your new lenses are first-rate! This microscope is the birth of a new age. Clara Maria, come and look at these exquisite lymphatic vascular bundles. Marvellous, marvellous!"

ooooo

The following morning, when I returned from my errands, I found Blucher in the atrium between our rooms, packing a suitcase. Among her clothes and precious objects were my father's notebooks, decorated with the purple logo of Tsinghua University. A round piece of metal rested on top like a crown.

Blucher picked it up, annoyed.

"It's a brass template," I said, crouching down beside her. "A lap for grinding lenses."

"I know, but how did it end up here?"

"It must be Jupiter. Yesterday, he said he didn't have enough room for his plants. He moved a lot of things around." I reached into my bag. "Look, I found this coat near West Gate. Isn't it nice? Last night, you said your room was getting cold . . ."

Delighted, Blucher held it up. We searched its pockets and found two paperclips, a pen, and half a lottery ticket.

Birds raced past the open window, the patterns of their flight entangling like dozens of invisible wheels. Unable to quell my anxiety, I touched the suitcase and asked Blucher if she was preparing to leave.

"The world is only worldwide. Who can leave when everywhere is the Sea?"

I nodded. "Is that a riddle?"

"No," she sighed. "I haven't even had breakfast yet."

I went to get the leftover porridge, and when I returned, we sat on the floor and ate together. After we had finished, she asked me if it was true that time was both a dimension and a line.

"Yes, but I don't really understand what that means."

She agreed. "Maybe a line is a sea sailing on a ship of dimensions. Or have I got it upside down?"

I thought of my father. I knew that he still dreamed of my aunt, my mother and Wei, and that he grieved not knowing what had

become of them. Would I, too, pass away with my deepest questions unanswered? I said I wasn't sure I could bear this outcome,
and the heartache of an infinite uncertainty.

Blucher picked up the coat again. She ran her thumb over its
gleaming silver buttons, and in her eyes I saw both wonder and
longing. "I feel the same," she said, after a moment. "I know I'll
leave this place with as many unanswered questions as stars in the
night. Still, I think it isn't true to say the earth was silent. Or that
the world offered no reply."

Sunlight warmed the top of my head, and I had the strangest sensation that Blucher's suitcase was the size of the room.
Impulsively, I took the coat, opened it and wrapped it around
her shoulders. The touch of her hand on my wrist felt as real and
weightless as the hours themselves.

∞∞∞

Here was the situation for Hannah Arendt: the only plausible way
out of occupied France was to cross the border into Franco's Spain,
pass through Spain to Portugal, and onwards to America by ship.
French exit permits, necessary to exit the country, were not being
issued. Meanwhile her and Heinrich's Spanish exit visas, acquired
with such difficulty by Jean Gemähling and the Emergency Rescue
Committee, would expire in one week, on January 10, 1941.

But this morning, the French government had unexpectedly
announced that the requirement for exit permits had been waived.
How long would this grace period last? No one knew. Their friends
in Montauban had fled in every direction, truth and lies were
impossible to separate, and disastrous news kept arriving.

Two days later, Gemähling showed up at her and Heinrich's
door above the photographer's studio. A forger working for the
Americans in Marseille had been arrested and the whole operation

could be exposed at any moment. It might already be too late.

She turned on the radio, the music creating a curtain of sound. *Before the day breaks and the shadows flee, come with me, my beloved. Rise up and come away.*

"You have three options," Gemähling began. "One: trust the French police. They say exit permits are no longer required. Therefore you can attempt to cross the French border under your real names and hope that you'll be allowed out. Others have done so. It has been successful."

Hannah fumbled for a cigarette. "What else?"

"The Gestapo has a list of names. So, option two: carry a different passport and present yourselves to French border guards under false names. They might let you pass. Or not."

"And option three?"

"Avoid the French checkpoint entirely and go over the Pyrenees. This is risky. French patrols are shooting trespassers on sight. But we have an experienced smuggler who can accompany you to the Spanish checkpoint. The smuggler risks execution so only consider this option if you are physically and mentally capable of making the crossing. You'll go under false names. Once you enter Spain, you'll have to get across by train, all the way to the Portuguese border. In Lisbon, we'll get you on a transatlantic ship. If all goes well, you'll be in New York two months from today."

Gemähling stood and turned the volume on the radio higher. Sat down again and looked at them with stern eyes. "All these methods have succeeded. All these methods have also failed."

Hannah was certain of one thing: she did not trust the French authorities. They could not risk travelling under their real names. If Heinrich were to be arrested? If he, a former communist and organizer, were to be sent back to Germany? And she herself? She exhaled and watched the smoke returning.

"We choose the third option."

Heinrich nodded. "If anything goes wrong, it gives us the most room to improvise."

"Good," said Gemähling. "We have no time to waste."

In the town of Banyuls-sur-Mer, ten kilometres from the Spanish border, the smuggler met them in the empty Grand Hotel. *Ein Spargeltarzan*, Hannah immediately thought. A pale Tarzan, slender as a stalk of asparagus.

Through the windows, the Mediterranean wavered.

The Spargeltarzan was someone they knew indirectly. Hans Fittko, the husband of Lisa Fittko, who had helped to steal release certificates for the women interned in Gurs. Lisa was ill, Hans told them, but did not elaborate. There was no time to say everything they wished to say to one another. Business first. "At 5 a.m. tomorrow morning, walk to the corner of avenue Puig del Mas. You will see me up ahead. Follow at a distance. No speaking. *Not even a whisper.* I will join the vineyard workers on their way into the hills, and you will fall in behind. We call the wind in this season the transmontane, and it is the devil's wind. You have good sweaters, I hope? Do not wear overcoats, you will appear incongruous and Spanish agents will be obliged to stop you. I will have your belongings retrieved from your rooms. They will be sent separately and you will retrieve them at the Portbou train station on the Spanish side. No more than two bags total, please. Be cautious. The Armistice Commission sends collaborators to make trouble here. If we run into problems, you must bluff your way out."

Heinrich pressed his hands together, priestlike. A sure sign of excitement. The months of waiting, unable to move or act, had been excruciating.

Their passport, made by an Austrian cartoonist, gave them new names: Margarethe and Otto Ebermann. They were Czech shopkeepers, leaving to join their children in Panama, and who could blame them? The Ebermanns had lost their livelihood and been forbidden from withdrawing their savings. Thinking of them, Hannah found sleep impossible. Terror mixed with the hope of change kept her eyes open, alert to every sound. At last, thoroughly exhausted, she rose and dressed.

Escape is possible, for us if not for everyone. That she and Heinrich should be exceptions to the rule, that they could be saved while others were not, was an immoral thought. It shamed her, but she also could not bear to think otherwise.

On Puig del Mas, they glimpsed a villager in a Basque cap carrying a spade over his shoulder, from which hung woven baskets. Hans Fittko, the Spargeltarzan.

They trailed him into the hills. Above, on a jutting ridge, vineyard workers turned, registered their presence for a moment, and dissolved.

The wind was cruel.

This world, she thought, tangles you up. What could they do but slip lower, always lower, beneath the net, to get away?

There was no moon and the sun would not rise for several hours yet, but little by little her eyes adjusted and she found that she could distinguish solid from less solid things. How right the poets are, she thought. *The day is beautiful but the night is sublime.* The blackest night contained within itself limitless gradations, and these expanding registers of darkness touched emotions she had long buried.

They ascended. Breathing became hard, so hard.

She glimpsed precipices and endless space. One misstep and they would plunge to their deaths as if off a balcony. Each time Hans disappeared behind an outcrop or ledge, she panicked. Without him, they were lost. She couldn't help but love his form—it seemed as if the very dark created him and needed him. Hans was not following any visible path, only perfect memory. The wind tore at his hair and clothes, giving him a poignant air, and each exhalation released a faint white cloud.

There was no path, only dense scrub, frozen earth, and sheer rock. Uphill ice.

Slipping, she seized at branches which, naturally, were covered in thorns. Her hands were cut, yet what could she do but grab hold again and again? Fog rolled in, a new misery.

If they did not rest, she would not be able to go on. She tripped, slammed to her knees, and felt an explosion of shame. "Careful," Heinrich murmured, his hand alighting momentarily on her back. "You wouldn't want to lose a shoe." She had to gulp down her laugh. His heavy hand almost kneading her up the mountain, as if she were a stubborn loaf.

After months of playing chess in Montauban, what a shock to find she was out of shape. But Gemähling's words hit her like a slap: *the smuggler risks execution in order to help you. Consider this option only if you are capable of making the crossing.* Three months ago, Benji had crossed these same mountains. She'd heard everything from Dora, his sister, who remained trapped in Lourdes. Even though it was late September when they made the journey, Benji's group had faced a brutal summer heat. It had taken hours of climbing, with Benji needing to rest every few minutes. He'd never been a sturdy walker, let alone a mountaineer. At the apex, strangers, appalled at his condition, rushed to find him water. He had been entirely exhausted, and his companions feared a heart attack. On that day, the Spanish border guards refused entry to all who arrived, without exception. Despite their pleas, the group was sent to a hotel in Portbou, the Fonda de Francia, rumoured to be crawling with Gestapo. The following morning, they were to be returned, under guard, to France to be imprisoned. In the night he swallowed his poison pills. A doctor came. Benji was apparently bled. By mid-morning, he had ceased to breathe. Dora's letter had reached her in Montauban four weeks later. In all the time Benji was dead, he had been entirely alive to her. She had imagined he was already in Lisbon, and even pictured him pale and miserable on a New York-bound ship. How easily she had envisioned it! Benji on a shining deck, glum because he could not read without seasickness. When he was downcast he became secretive and paranoid. Before the letter arrived, they had heard rumours of a suicide but she had insisted to Heinrich it was gossip. Despair fuelled outlandish, desperate stories. But the facts were true and must be faced. She could no longer speak in euphemisms. Jews were dying in Europe and being buried like dogs. This was how things stood. Benji had not made it.

For heaven's sake, she reprimanded herself, watch your feet. Look straight, why don't you!

She picked her way over the rocks.

At the very instant she decided to give up, the wind turned yet more vicious, spitting in her face. Snow reached her knees. Intolerable. Fuelled by rage, she went on.

Up ahead, Hans was almost jaunty. He did this three or four times a week, he'd said. The refugees were sometimes called *parcels*. The word now struck her forcefully.

Benji's ghost was chattering in her ear, saying something she had difficulty understanding since he spoke intensely yet at a whisper. He had dreamed of the letter *d*. "I could only see the arm," he said. "Its elongation revealed an extreme aspiration to achieve spirituality. Appended to it was a small sail with a blue border, and the sail was billowing as if filled by the wind."

"Of all the nice things one might fantasize, you dream of the letter *d* and this is what gives you pleasure?"

He said, "A German stands before two doors. The first door reads: *Entrance to the Kingdom of God*. The second door reads: *Lectures on the Kingdom of God*. Which door does he choose?"

She laughed and Benji, overcome by his own joke, let loose the most inept chortle, bending over double, shouting, "Open up and receive me, door two!"

His grey hair, bouffant in the wind, was completely ridiculous. Benji showed her his Spanish entry permit and shrugged with ironic formality. A self-conscious smile, an awkward motion of his foot to kick a stone into the abyss, and he was gone.

A manuscript Benji had given her in July was wrapped in her bag, to be gathered in Portbou with the other luggage. She was duty-bound to retrieve it. Therefore she had no choice but to continue walking over this ungodly mountain.

They could enter Spain legally but only if they exited France illegally. They could arrive but not depart, as if the two were not the same motion, the arm of the letter *d* uncurling from its small sail. I have a joke for you, she wanted to tell Benji, of a folded-up world, a Möbius strip of tomorrow and yesterday. She wanted to laugh and laugh, which of course was weeping. Turn everything inside out to find its secret, the paradox it tries to swallow. I have never felt so happy to be alive. Or so she told herself, forcing her body on.

Night began to withdraw, giving way to a fine pale morning. The steepness of the climb increased but Hannah felt somehow renewed. Assisting refugees of military age across the border was punishable by death, yet Hans seemed cheerful. In normal times, she wondered, what kind of man was he? Perhaps someone for whom charity was no empty word. *Thus shall no fellow being remain alien to me.* Yesterday, before departing, he'd spoken of a grotto nearby which had hidden people on and off for some twenty thousand years. "People here," he said, "observe without looking, know without knowing. This is, by nature, a secretive place."

She had begun to understand Banyuls-sur-Mer differently then: the vineyard workers who appeared indifferent; the wrinkled old men playing boules beside the sea, tipping their hats on the street, pretending she and Heinrich were locals; the stern woman providing twice the cream their ration tickets allowed. But not a smile from anyone. Incuriosity as the perfect camouflage for the duty of protection.

Light ebbed towards them, as if the horizon, like a sheet of paper, was beginning to tear. It was intoxicating, it was beautiful. No, beauty was unfailingly an inadequate word. She could see distances now. They were nearing the summit, endless ranges at their feet, the colour starting to awaken. Her eyelids were packed with snow but her memories seemed like water released from melting ice. Remember the yellow mittens her grandmother made. Remember her father bedridden, unable to recognize his only child. Father and daughter in the morning light. His name, Paul. His delirious eyes. The blue eiderdown. The pendulum that Mother took from his room. The white basin and pitcher for washing. No longer, not yet or not at all. Paul, a beautiful name. Falling wind. A death so near.

And still they kept climbing this endless ladder.

"I am not at all frightened," she whispered hoarsely.

Behind her, Heinrich laughed. A soft laugh, a sweet lament.

Cicero says that the man or woman who is pained by another's misfortune is also pained by their happiness. A true yet awful thought. Was anyone pained or disappointed that Hannah Arendt stood here now, Portbou in sight? Did any human being begrudge her the chance of survival?

The transmontane, Jean Gemähling had told them, was not just the icy wind but all that comes over the mountain, a foreigner or a barbarian. Someone, perhaps, like Heinrich, clothed in snow, look-ing abominable. Meanwhile Hans was pointing to the future. They had avoided the French checkpoint and arrived near a sentry post. Now they stood on Spanish ice. Hans was nodding at them. He did not speak but heartily shook their hands, as if saying farewell out-side a café. Yesterday's parting words at the Grand Hotel unfurled in her mind: "Be alert," Hans had warned them. "Even with all your papers in order, the Spaniards can refuse entry. They can send you back for no reason, into the arms of the French police. Give the sentry these Camel cigarettes. Remember: *Descend. Customs post. Entrada stamp. Train to Portugal.* The overnight to Barcelona leaves at 3:15 a.m. Here are ration coupons, pesetas and escudos to get you through. Our friends from the American office will find you once you arrive in Lisbon. Use your common sense and be determined. Good luck."

Away Hans went now, almost skipping. There were exceptional people, Hannah thought, and there were exceptional minds. It was the former who created and carried out escape lines, and the latter who were fooled, time and again, by events.

Her hands had been badly cut by brambles. Heinrich washed them tenderly with snow. The two of them shook off the cold, waited for a moment, as if resting between planets, and continued on. Her thoughts were fragments. *My soul often flies back and forth between the seas that, to the right and left, cool the feet of glowing moun-tains.* Strange how memories arrived and departed like vessels.

The Spanish sentry post was no more than a shepherd's hut. It sat on a sheer white rock whose colour echoed the moon, still visible in the new sky.

She was nauseous with dread. The torment of hope was the fear that salvation would not come. It was Spanish policy, she knew, for suspected communists to be sent immediately to the Miranda de Ebro concentration camp. She and Heinrich should bypass this outpost, pretending they hadn't seen it. "Wait," she breathed. "Don't knock on the door. Don't—"

But her husband, her terrible husband, knocked. Heinrich was the kind to sprint towards battle. Difficulty came if he had to seek safety.

Out stepped a boy in a plum beret and severely belted uniform. Wool blanket draped over his shoulders, face like a small apple, black boots with a wet sheen. A volley of Spanish. He was only asking for their papers, but it was as if he were squeezing her heart between his hands.

They gave him the Czechoslovakian document. Orange-red cover, a coat of arms featuring a lion. All in order, perfectly replicated, down to the stamps, including one for a trip to China in 1936. The work was stunning. Inside, Otto and Margarethe Ebermann wore the faces of Heinrich Blücher and Hannah Arendt. One could not forge more perfect papers, radiating dull respectability.

The border guard examined the passport very slowly, particularly enjoying the Chinese stamp, which took up a full page and seemed to float like a blue footprint. But he was not satisfied. He wanted something they did not have and began pointing uphill. Go back to the French border post, he seemed to be saying. Look, do you see? They forgot to stamp your exit visa. It is important to follow the steps. First you exit and then you enter. That's how it's done.

She pointed at the words *Bon pour se rendre à Portugal* upon which sat the round seal of the Portuguese Consulate in Marseille. She unfolded the ship tickets to Panama, also forgeries.

The young border guard had been writing documents of some kind and, behind him, in the tiny shepherd's hut, the papers shivered like feathers. How did one write with frozen hands? He had a small fire fed by pine cones, and its fragrant heat wafted over them.

Lightheaded, she stumbled backwards. The border guard's hand, small as a child, darted out to catch her.

He began to speak again, but in Catalan. Maybe he said: What a storm last night. This is not the season to cross unless you have claws and wings. Or maybe your back is to the wall?

He stepped back into his sentry box, half closing the door. The sun grew rounder, its edges more distinct. She could not bear the cold. Every border post was furnished with the Gestapo's wanted lists, those names were everywhere. The boy emerged. Still holding their documents, he banged the frail door three times until it finally closed. He locked it with a key attached to his wrist by a white string. "We go," he said first in French and then in Catalan. He descended along a path that only now became visible, a furrow trod by goats, the faintest indentation. The guard's blanket, wrapped over his shoulders, swayed before them.

She was afraid and wanted to turn and run. They were on the list, they were inescapably on a list. Trembling overcame her. The border guard was leading them where?

Downhill. She followed the crumbling sound of mismatched steps.

He was leading them downhill.

It was a difficult trail, a steep slide into the wind, clinging to boulders and branches.

They arrived together in Portbou.

At the customs house, the boy handed their passport to a man with an artillery belt and a hat that looked as if it had been run over by a truck. Desks, carts, the smell of wet papers. The tinge of something burning. The man said two words, the boy said three. The boy helped himself to coffee. Before he left, he looked fleetingly in her eyes. In a flash, he was gone forever.

There were others in this room, waiting. Two old women, their stockings in shreds. They were so disastrous in appearance, Hannah's heart swelled, but they stared back at her with even more pity. A voice blustered through a swinging door, *Shall we breakfast at the hotel and not disturb him?* It took her a moment to realize she understood the words. Everyday German words, sharp as tacks in the mouths of Nazi officials. *The wife is with him after all.*

Her heart died in her chest.

The man with the artillery belt waved them forward. It turned out that the boy, the border guard, had stamped and validated their entrance visas. He must have done it in his sentry hut. How was it that something so simple, a boy choosing to stamp a piece of paper, could cut a hole in this net and possibly save their lives? The passport was handed back to them.

The man held Heinrich's gaze for an instant.

"Go," he said, and turned away.

In the train station, where they picked up their single suitcase, an old porter hovered. Darting here and there like a bumblebee, he tried to assist them. They had nothing, so a porter was unnecessary. Still, he followed them out of the train station and let loose a plaintive cry in French: "See these streets, bombed by Hitler's planes! What did England and France do but spit at the ceiling while we suffered? Now the fascists are everywhere and refugees who fled one way are coming back the other."

They could say nothing, not even to agree.

"Be cautious. Good people do despicable things. Morality is secondary when people are starving and nothing is certain. Here in Portbou, the devil's spies are everywhere."

The old porter pivoted and returned to the station, upset by his own words.

They had departed France. Hannah realized it only now, feeling an incongruous, bittersweet longing for Paris wash over her.

There were many hours to wait in this town filled with German officers, double dealers, and a billowing sun. *Use your common sense and be determined.*

—

Up in the town cemetery, it was ever so cold and she was exhausted.

She told her husband, "I feel like something that has been slimed along the ground."

"You look it, too."

The tide below seemed to laugh and laugh.

In her head, a voice reminded her, I am Margarethe Ebermann née Lendl. My husband is Otto Ebermann, a shopkeeper. We are from Brno, where once upon a time we met as students and fell in love beside the Svratka River. My favourite book is *The Good Soldier Švejk*. I have lost myself in its thousand pages many times.

They tried to find Benji's grave but they could not, and at last she and Heinrich stood still, side by side in the open-air mausoleum, facing the sea. "Under circumstances such as these," Benji had told them, "happiness equals hope for me."

To be stripped of hope yet retain happiness.

To be in despair yet know joy.

These contradictions were possible, she felt them even now, and this, too, caused its own particular pain.

"One day soon," Heinrich said, "we'll stop fretting our lives away. We won't run anymore."

The cemetery was a series of terraces carved into a cliff against the waters. It was one of the most fantastical and beautiful places she had ever seen in her life.

Benji had eaten all the chocolate he had been carrying, and which she, too, had been instructed to carry. Intended for bribes or currency, in order to make one's way to Lisbon. Eating all the bribery chocolate had been his last act before dying. Damn him, she thought, and refused to cry.

In her memory, she was sitting beside him in Paris, the city he had not been able to abandon. Such choices only reveal their shape after the fact. There they were, Heinrich, Lotte, Annie, Chanan, Erich, Fritz, and Gershom visiting from Jerusalem. They had all come of age during the earlier war and felt deserving of cheap, plentiful wine. Fritz gave a memorable treatise on happiness, which he warned they should not confuse with either bliss or melancholy joy. Benji and Gershom wanted to dance with Spinoza, Buber and the Chinese, but they kept getting tangled up in the present, and levitating towards mysticism to transcend the hard fact of the now. Benji's neck always seemed to bend like that of a goose. He and Hannah were sharing his last cigarette before sending her Monsieur to buy more. Heinrich said their problem was not that they over-valued books but that they valued almost nothing else as highly.

In any case, she and Benji would not speak again.

Memory's habit is to dissolve what it can't contain. She feared that something within her was already dissolving before she'd had a chance to feel it and thereby know it. In his suicide note, Benji had written, *There is not enough time to write all the letters I had wanted to write.* It was to be expected they could not find his grave. He must have been buried discreetly or not at all. *No one knew anything of the dead man, only that he came from the frontier.* Was that Heine, or Brecht, or someone else whose words had floated free from their name?

I have reached the summit, Benji, arriving to see the panorama when the light is best. I wish that you would, too.

She and Heinrich tried not to attract attention, sitting near the station, moving with the shade. But after a time, the porter reap-peared and convinced them to follow him.

The man brought them to his home, and suddenly there were grandchildren who, holding hands, seemed glued together. But, then, *pop!*, they unclasped and went about their play. A grand-mother entered with a basin of water. Bananas and grapes appeared, and soup, and this seemed the most incredible food she had ever beheld. The children stared, especially at her—she must look awful—but the old porter clucked, clucked, clucked, until the little ones waddled out. To the very end, the children smiled at her, as if to comfort the stranger eating all their food. There was no bread, and certainly no meat, but here was wine. How to thank them? The porter vehemently refused money but finally they managed to saddle him with French chocolate.

After they ate, mats appeared and Hannah instantly fell asleep. She was pursued by the black-winged coats of Vichy police who, when they caught her, asked mockingly, *Who believes in their own death?*

I believe, she dreamed.

When she opened her eyes, it was evening. Heinrich was sitting with the grandmother, a pot of coffee between them. The woman addressed Heinrich as *tu*. He had been given a blade and was newly shaved.

"The best disguise," the grandmother said in flowing French, "is to be smooth, tidy and bourgeois."

This family, she understood, welcomed her and Heinrich as comrades because they belonged to the same side: those who face defeat. It's true, then, that to survive our own particular situation, we should direct our attention to the universal. Otherwise, the alternative was to give up hope. Could such an ethics take root in her? Could she learn to exist in this way?

It was time to leave, and the porter insisted they take a thermos of coffee and a bag of dried figs. Hannah disliked figs but did not say so. Heinrich was pleased by her good manners.

Holding hands, they walked downhill to the station. The lamps were all blown out. The cavernous station stood in shocking disrepair, though Franco's portrait gleamed unblemished. Chunks of roof hung like drapery. On the walls, initials of the revolutionary parties, though scrubbed out, remained visible. The round clock face was blasted out.

At last, a train pulled in. The Civil Guard began to ransack it, car by car, top to bottom. They did not seem to be searching for anything in particular; their aim was to intimidate. Catalonia had been the last region to fall to Franco and must now suffer for it. The manhandling of the train took three hours. The railway workers, in shabby uniforms, watched placidly until they were ordered to reload the cargo and to be quick about it.

It was so cold Hannah couldn't feel her feet.

"Shall we board, Otto, my darling?"

"Yes, my only Margarethe."

Names are eternal, she thought. They persist across centuries and millennia. Mortal things are but namesakes.

She and Heinrich lined up at the document check. The officer barely looked at them. Just as he was hurrying them along, there was shouting everywhere, and the crash and thump of suitcases. Behind them, at the next wagon, a family of six had been yanked from the line. A guardsman was waving papers in the father's wretched face. They were German Jews—Hannah would know her own anywhere.

"Go with God," the officer said.

She turned towards him in confusion. He was offering his hand to help her up the steps.

She entered the carriage, hearing the voices of the agonized parents and their four small children.

Inside, there was no glass in the windows, giving the wind free play. Only half the wooden seats were occupied. Nobody spoke. The family on the platform was taken away. She had to shut her mind to them. The wagon doors were sealed. Heinrich folded his hand around hers. The train shook into life and she was still breathing, overcome by relief, sick with shame. They were moving.

Eventually, jolting side to side, she fell asleep. She dreamed they descended below ground, into frigid waters. Now they were swimming without moving their arms, they were breathing without lungs.

∞∞∞

In the Sea, the neighbours brought pots of flowering plants into my father's room, hung scrolls that could act as amulets, and set up the record player. He grew energetic and talked like a man pulling books down from the shelves, wanting to hold everything at once. "Your brother was born early," he told me one night. "In the beginning, he cried non-stop, it was terrible. I had never held a baby before. He looked at me, panicked, as if I were the newborn not him. When he grew older, speaking to him gave me such happiness. He had your mother's eyes."

At one point, my father looked through me and said my brother's train had arrived. I turned, spine tingling, feeling that in some distant place my brother was dreaming of us. When Wei and I were very young, Aunt Oh had given us a book with a hundred myths. We'd devoured every page: a boy who swims in a sea of milk, a girl on a raft in the River Styx. Children born from a giant egg; crack it once, twice, three times, and out comes chaos. Heaven sliced from Earth with a silver knife. An ancient river named Okeanos orbiting the world, marking the very limits of existence. I read that when a person dies, their limbs untie so that they might rise to Hades. I read about a woman with a mind made of clay.

One day, surely, I would meet the stranger who was my brother. *It is granted him to see the ones he loves beneath his own high roof in his own country.* I would ask him for the title of our book, and when he answered, "The Record of Beginnings," perhaps my questions could finally be answered. *Did our mother say my name? Did she think of me until the end? Tell me everything.*

Around me, conversation rippled. Blucher went to the window, leaned out and said, "What's that rumbling?"

"My stomach," Jupiter said.

"The glass workshop," said Bento.

"The train coming in," my father replied.

I stood at the far window, listening.

ooooo

On the train, light seeped through Hannah's eyelids. She forced her eyes open, unsure where she was.

Through the windows she saw blue hills behind towns of scorched earth. Rubble. Never-ending destruction. Heinrich was staring out, eyes red. Police could be heard in the next carriage, demanding documents. She braced herself, but only the ticket collector came through the rattling door, followed by an aproned woman, selling crackers for almost nothing. They tasted of air, which calmed Hannah, as if ghostly Margarethe Ebermann could only eat ghostly food. At a local station, the train doors stayed locked while people on the platforms cried out for bread. Houses had no roofs or even walls. The looming shell of a church was shocking.

In the next car, the police were searching every person, shouting questions. These questions were all superfluous since the Civil Guard could arrest anyone they wished, without needing the excuse of a reason.

When the train reached Barcelona, she stepped down onto the platform, expecting at every moment to feel a hand dragging her backwards. Her legs tottered as if she wanted to dance but had forgotten how. Turning, she saw no police, only endless ramps and concrete barriers.

On the next platform, she and Heinrich were searched again. This guard had a thin head on a frying-pan body. He threw their papers back at them. Heinrich knelt to pick them up.

As he came to standing, his eyes met hers, and she felt her husband's tenderness washing over her.

The train for Madrid was just as broken-down as the previous one, but it had, thank heavens, unbroken glass in the windows. They were eight squeezed into a compartment, unnaturally quiet. Heinrich opened a book on his knee, the same dog-eared copy of Kant. Close your eyes, she told herself, let Margarethe keep the night watch. Let Hannah daydream something else—Baruch Spinoza, maybe, in a black coat, grinding lenses, glass particles glittering in the air. *If space is taken to be a thing in itself then Spinozism is irrefutable.* This was Kant's warning, and Hannah largely agreed. Time and space, Kant argued, are how the human mind experiences existence. Otherwise, if space-time were an essential part of God as opposed to mere aspects of human perception, then Spinoza's beliefs—that we are bound by necessity and our idea of free will is an illusion—would be unarguable. A shame, she thought, that Kant and Spinoza had not lived in the same age, on the same street. Separated by a century, they seemed to see each other in their imaginations. They would have enjoyed a long walk together, or at least pretended to.

The train began to move. Outside, the world softened as it fled past.

Spinoza's family had gone in this direction, fleeing Spain for Portugal. But safety was short-lived. They were Marranos, Jews who had converted, or been forced to convert, to Christianity, and the Spanish had labelled them swine. Soon the family was forced to run again; in the Netherlands, at last, they could practise their faith. Spinoza's stepmother had arrived there from Lisbon at the age of forty. Esther, her name was, but she had not lived long. Solitary Baruch Spinoza, an outlaw in his little room. This pariah with his love of fate, or at least his faith in its necessity, and his acquiescence to *that which is.*

Here now was the city of Lleida. Vanquished, as if the gods had stamped it out, the new gods being German and Italian bombs. Was this the future for all the cities that she loved? Had past and future, as Spinoza suggested, long been determined, as if everything, in the mind of the universe, was just a single moment? Her whole being reviled the thought.

After Lleida, the landscape grew calm. Hilltop fortresses and stubble fields, churned-up mud, and a sky so colourless it seemed a page of eternity. It hurt her heart.

Now it was Heinrich who slept, his bulky weight against her. The others in the carriage began to drift off, too. It was comic how regularly someone was awakened by another's snores but not their own. Night fell abruptly.

In Madrid, they found a small room in which to wait for the Lisbon train, two days hence. In the morning, Margarethe Ebermann woke smelling horses, putrid water, and the sweet perfume of an unknown flower. Outside, buildings had been stripped of their doors and shutters, burned, it seemed, for fuel. A line of women and children extended far down the road, waiting for rations. An argument erupted but ended almost as quickly. The combatants, two mothers, turned away, shoulders slumped in mutual defeat.

Every hour she and Heinrich stayed in Madrid felt reckless. It was shocking, escaping war via a war-shattered country.

Their acquaintance Arthur Koestler used to say, "It is necessary to shrink down to what one can carry." Hannah hated to agree with him but now felt it to be true—not only about belongings but about beliefs. For weren't beliefs possessions? One had to stop giving transport to one's own lies. *Discredit thyself first.* In 1933, fleeing Berlin, she'd carried a suitcase of books, poems, a bundle of letters from the Lecturer, the draft of *Rahel*, and the firm belief that the imminent political disasters would be overcome, for how could it be otherwise? This unwarranted, unscrutinized certainty had come so naturally when she was twenty-seven. Death, at least her own death, had been inconceivable back then.

Heinrich, rolled up like a cigar in the blankets, mistook her silence for fear. "Tomorrow is another life," he said. "Every day is a new life. So why not be happy today?"

"Yes, why not?"

She pulled her husband to her. All of this—visas, escape, flight— was necessity and not misfortune. In order to focus on survival, she must, at least for now, see it as such. She had never been so tired and yet, and yet. *I am for you, I am with you.* The green curtain and the blue light, the almost suffocating weight of her husband, pleasure heightened by fear, quieting her voice, making words meaningless, and the exhausted aftermath, the breaking of her heart, footsteps barging up the stairs, running past, men shouting and then finally quiet. A thread of ecstasy fighting through. She loved Heinrich, who must do for life itself.

Finally the hour approached for their onward journey to Portugal.

Madrid was rumoured to be the nerve centre of the German spy network, and filled with roving mercenaries. She and Heinrich had to don their disguises once more. They gave their clothes a neat brush, and Heinrich shaved and sponged his head. The street to the train station was plastered with headlines. British forces advancing on Italian-held Ethiopia. Vichy France victorious in Thailand. Plymouth bombed overnight by the Luftwaffe.

Here was the station. Once more, Otto and Margarethe Ebermann waited placidly as their papers were examined. They were waved briskly through. She could almost hear the plash of water as they crossed another circle of eternity.

They paused to put their documents safely away.

An altercation erupted on platform six. A group of exiles were encircled by shouting guardsmen. Overhead, pigeons gathered, knowing crumbs would fall as bags were pulled from hands and families torn apart.

"Look away, Margarethe. You can do nothing."

They walked on, eyes averted.

The train to Lisbon was delayed and the platform unbelievable. Waves of voices in Spanish, French and German. "Luis, Rosa! Stop kicking each other!" "Darling, my umbrella please." An unreal world, in which every person adhered to class conventions, or appeared to do so, and thus hid themselves in plain sight.

Waiting had never felt so busy. Finally, there was a change in the air and the train arrived, a grimy thing. People seemed to tumble out of it headfirst, in a mad rush, embattled, and then in slow motion. Suitcases bumped down, porters bent double under the weight of giant trunks. A dog gazed out from a crate, floating above it all as if he rode in a sedan chair. This train had largely retained its windows, though some were broken.

They plodded in a line. She had the sense of people softly shouting.

Their compartment had two wooden benches. Three passengers— a middle-aged man, a boy, and a foreigner, Japanese, maybe—were already there, facing the direction of travel. She and Heinrich took the opposite seats. She bustled and rearranged herself, all the while stealing glances at the strangers.

The man was perhaps thirty-five or forty, wearing a faded black suit. Portuguese, she thought. His dark and curling hair was like a sunburst around his head. His travelling companion was a boy, no more than twelve years old. Not his son but perhaps an apprentice or an orphaned charge.

The third passenger wore a blue cloak. He was old, almost gaunt, with a very long, very slender grey beard, and a jaunty expression in his eyes. On second thought, he might be Chinese not Japanese. There had been a handful of Chinese in Paris to whom she had grown not acquainted but accustomed. The man's cap was unusual: a piece of fabric tied ingeniously with the ends extending like two fluttering legs.

She tried to stare without staring. The boy held a small box in his hand, its lid painted with a picture of olive trees, rolling hills, and blue light tinged with gold.

Outside, that magisterial dog barked from his sedan chair.

A woman shouted, "Clever, Clever, where are you?"

Now the boy took out a book and began to read. Archimedes, *On the Equilibrium of Planes*, of all things. She doubted he understood a thing.

Heinrich, exhausted, drew his hat over his eyes. Who on earth could nap in these conditions? Herr Ebermann, that's who. Immediately, he began to snore.

The Chinese man opened a little pouch and withdrew a handful of sunflower seeds. When he extended the pouch to Hannah, she surprised herself by accepting. She had not eaten sunflower seeds since the age of five. Each tiny snap brought her a wallop of pleasure. As the man ate, he dropped the empty shells on the ground and, with a shameless nod of his foot, swept them under his seat.

Hannah gave him a disapproving stare, but he continued, oblivious. He kicked more shells away.

"I've been travelling forever," he confided to her and to the carriage. "The strange thing is, even the longest journeys seem to evaporate from my memory. This trip, for example, will last eleven hours through the night. But when I try to recall it afterwards, I know the pictures in my mind will barely fill an instant."

Unsurprisingly, no one answered him. "I suppose," Hannah said, not wanting to be rude, "recollections take up space in our minds but they have no duration."

"Here's the whistle," the Portuguese said, stating the obvious. The train began to move.

The boy, immersed in Archimedes, murmured, "'The centre of gravity of a parallelogram is the point of intersection of its diagonals.'"

Everyone gazed at the boy, who ran his finger across the page and sighed.

Hannah felt a cold chill go down her spine. The Chinese gentleman could only be a diplomat or an emissary. But the Portuguese must be a spy. Therefore the boy must be his cover. But a spy for whom? Sweat gathered at her hairline and she swiped an index finger up to catch it.

The Portuguese man was fixated on the Chinese emissary. "Tell us, sir, where you've come from? That blue cloak of yours is marvellous. It looks like it's seen the world."

"I'm afraid so. I'm headed to the western port but it's been one calamity after another. I just hope my vessel will sail." He made another quick motion of the foot, brazenly sweeping more sunflower shells under the bench.

"Did you enjoy Madrid?" Hannah asked.

"I stayed mostly in my room. Every time I went out, the rubble saddened me. After war comes famine. I know it all too well."

Through the windows, a rocky canyon rose up and subsided, replaced by a white thread, which was a road.

The Chinese emissary continued: "I've heard that the Spanish have no word for evening because, in this land, darkness falls the moment the sun goes behind the mountains."

"There's *la tarde, el anochecer, la noche*," said the boy, surprising them all. "I guess that's afternoon, darkening, night . . . maybe there really is no word for it."

"If the word for evening vanished," said the emissary, "I think people would invent it again and again."

"But words go missing all the time," Hannah ventured. "Names, for instance. People no longer introduce themselves. Evening has been disappeared, along with our names."

"We know your names," the Portuguese spy said. "It's written right there on your suitcase."

The emissary nervously gathered his cloak around himself.

"Just now," the spy continued, "we said that a train journey of eleven hours is reduced to a few discrete moments in the mind, until even those dissolve. We retain images of experience but not the experience itself."

Hannah despised pomposity. This spy, with his faux-serene look, was surely a failed priest. She could just see it, his brethren evicting him from the monastery, hurling his books after him, waving their relics and shouting, Good riddance! May your tiny little mouse squeak along!

"My memories," he burbled on, "do not pass smoothly before my eyes like these Spanish towns filing past our windows. Nor do my memories sit beside one another like parcels on a shelf. They must come to us in flashes. The past is relived, and maybe even disorganized, in the act of remembering it."

The word *parcel* pricked her, a trap door to the heart.

"Memories don't sit on a shelf like jars of pickles," she snapped. "I come towards them with my consciousness, which is a kind of torch. This light catches on images in my mind—"

"Like the focusing of a glass—"

"—and I create a new sequence, and a new order and disorder, each time I do so."

The Chinese nodded politely. "It seems you both agree on . . . something."

"Hardly," said Hannah. Then, out of nervousness, she laughed.

The boy turned the page of his book. "I'm counting the hours until we get to the ocean. My mother and aunt sent me ahead but I wish I could turn around and go back. There's something important I forgot to tell them."

Quiet gazes among the adults.

Outside, night had fallen suddenly. Hannah had the feeling of rushing forward, though in the darkness a direction could not be verified.

—

The Spanish police locked the train doors, and chains rattled against the metal. Hannah was scared and could not sleep. Meanwhile, Heinrich continued to snore. He could not resist sleep when he was sad.

The carriage lamps were extinguished. The boy made a noise of irritation and shut his book.

The dead of night—what an unhappy phrase. It was as if a blindfold had been pressed against Hannah's eyes. To anchor herself, she put one hand on Heinrich's knee, and the other on the grey buttons of her own coat.

"I wonder how people commit crimes in the dark," mused the spy.

The boy laughed. "What?"

"I mean, in a total blackout. Isn't it strange how often this happens? The criminal cuts the lights and eliminates vision, yet still manages to locate his victim."

"Don't expect us to solve this riddle," said Hannah. "We're all the custodians of this boy." She wasn't sure where she got this idea but it was obviously correct.

"Once, not long ago, I was unlucky and had to escape in the dark," said the emissary peaceably. "In the forest, like a deer, I listened. The parts of my mind used for language grew quiet, or maybe they were put to use by other senses. For example, every vibration in the air was monitored by my skin—as if it were thinking. What I mean is, thinking is not just words. Your senses adapt to the world hidden from sight. In these moments, language doesn't come naturally; it's too simple, just an approximation."

"I can't feel the train moving right now," the boy said. "Can you? I read that time is movement."

"That's Averroes," said the Portuguese approvingly. "When the windows are dark, the surrounding world vanishes and we can't be certain that we're in motion." The more animated he got, the quieter his voice became, as if he were whispering state secrets.

"Descartes says, 'I think, therefore I am.' But I would rather say, 'There is something outside of me. The existence of another is what calls me into being.'"

"Well," said Hannah, also whispering, "that explains . . . not very much."

The emissary agreed. "Not catchy."

They laughed, and even their laughter whispered.

"Fine, tell me this," said the Portuguese. "If the outside world is erased from all five senses, what is time?"

The world before I existed, Hannah thought. Space before time.

"Your heartbeat."

Hannah, startled by the boy's words, put her hand to her chest. She felt the buttons of her coat. She had a vivid memory of pain, of heart failure so terrible it could only be a death. Hadn't she experienced that once, the realization of her own ending? The thought frightened her. She pressed her hand more firmly against her chest, but all she could feel was the vibration of the train car.

The train lurched, pitching them left then right.

"Sorry, sorry," everyone murmured.

Through the walls of the compartment, other voices rose and floated past.

"Do you have children?" Hannah asked the emissary. "A family?"

"Four children. We were separated by the war. It was impossible to cross the different fronts. To travel east, I had to become like a tangled thread, going west and south at the same time."

Hannah nodded. "Actually I feel like I've been here before but not exactly. Can you return to a moment you haven't lived yet?"

"After this place, time comes apart. That's what my mother told me when I was young."

The emissary began a story, and the spy told another, full of exaggerations, encounters and exotic details that made her laugh, and now and then, in the privacy of the darkness, weep. The company of these others was a comfort. They took turns recounting impossibly real things, and in this way the night passed through them.

Trees, silvery in the dawn, squat and dignified, dotted the landscape. Olive trees, Hannah realized, centuries old.

The darkness of the carriage softened. Now she could see her companions again. The Chinese man was lost in thought. The Portuguese man looked as refreshed as ever, which annoyed her.

The boy was turning the Archimedes book over and over in his hands. It had a blue cover and had been read so many times, the pages were sliding loose.

Archimedes of Syracuse, Hannah wanted to tell him, was the first to measure the circumference of the earth. Two thousand years ago, before his life was taken by invading Roman soldiers, he had been writing his spectacular equations in the sand, at the mercy of the encroaching sea. In the stories that outlived him, the geometer turned towards his executioners. Instead of pleading for his life, Archimedes tried to protect these writings. "Pray," he said, "do not disturb my circles."

She couldn't stop looking at the boy. His hair, unkempt, needed to be combed.

"After we cross the border," Hannah asked him, "where will you go?"

"I heard a rumour that my sister passed through this area and went out to sea." The boy turned the book in his hands. "You're trying to reach a ship, too, aren't you?"

"Tickets are impossible to buy," said the Portuguese. "But others will help. In times like these, friendship is one of the only certainties people can give each other. People are obliged to rescue one another."

Was that a belief, Hannah wondered, a belonging? *Thus shall no fellow being remain alien to me.* She remembered the figs she had been given in Portbou, pulled them from her pocket, and offered them around.

"I can't bear dried figs," said the Portuguese, yet immediately he took three. "My father imported them from Damascus. When he died, we had to eat up the stock."

"So you're a merchant, then?"

"Not me. But my younger brother exports dried fruit from Brazil."

"I wish I could prepare a meal for us," the boy said. "I'm a good cook."

"I have chocolate." Hannah knew it was meant for emergencies, but still she withdrew the precious bar from her coat.

For a few minutes, all that could be heard was the excitement of the wrapper and the emissary noisily eating all the figs.

When the food was gone, the boy turned to the emissary. He said, "When we were telling stories last night, you said that you write poems. Can we hear something?"

As Hannah listened, she felt another plane of existence arriving, and with it her own buried memories. Heinrich woke. Drowsily, he reached out to hold her hand.

Where would one go?
The world is only worldwide.

The train rolled her this way and that. Sleep was coming, like rain on slippered feet.

One petal in the wind diminishes spring.
Tens of thousands cast adrift,
A sad sight;
Doesn't alleviate
The pain.

Marvel at each
As it goes

—It goes
That drop of wine you are about to drink,
Is never too much.

Why tie
The body by a name tag
To this floating world?

When the poetry was done, the emissary gave a gift to the boy. Mesmerized, the boy held it in his hands. Pale yellow with dots of blue, it gleamed like porcelain.

"Keep it," the emissary said. "I no longer need it. It's a cowrie shell."

"But what was this night?" Hannah murmured.

The emissary touched a rip in his cloak. "Have you heard the story of the painter who disappeared into his painting? I think this journey has already happened, and we disembarked long ago."

"But even if that's true," said the Portuguese, "for us it's the first and only time. Within this carriage, then, we're free."

"Even if the train long ago arrived at its destination?"

"Even so."

The train ascended through Extremadura, high cliffs, ruined castles, the wide curve of the Tagus River, all bathed in morning light. Hannah saw bulbous rocks gathered together like slumbering creatures.

The others had drifted off, but Heinrich was alert and cheerful.

The world outside the train bewildered Hannah. Dry mountains and rippling hills of hidden passageways, as if a voyage here could never be completed.

Soon they arrived at a border. Abruptly, border agents burst onto the stopped train, waving rifles. "Passports, passports!" An awful cold slid through her. Could they have made it this far only to meet disaster? It had happened to others. It would happen again.

Once more, the passports of Margarethe and Otto Ebermann were offered up, this time to a man in a dark uniform and a cape. He rubbed his thumb over the doctored stamps, determined to find fault, and perhaps he would have if the emissary had not alerted him to his own crime: littering. He adjusted his feet imperiously, and the discarded sunflower seeds crunched like twigs.

The officer was horrified.

The emissary managed to appear ashamed yet indifferent.

Furious, the officer threw their passports on the bench.

The Portuguese intervened with just the right note of decorum and complaint. "How awful, but I'll see to it that this compartment is set right, and the train can get on as it must, and be kept in good order, et cetera."

Now the officer was staring at the emissary's passport but could make no sense of it. He was apoplectic, insulting the incomprehensible marks, the pea-brained stupidity of foreigners, and the barbarity of the world as a whole. "This disgusting troublemaker will be fined, make no mistake, such behaviour is depraved!" and so on. The officer stormed out. Shouting resumed in the next compartment, where a family had hidden chickens under the seat.

The boy got up to help clean. But the Portuguese told him to rest. Soon the mess was gone.

The border police exited, and the train groaned into motion again.

"Are we in Portugal?" It was the first thing Heinrich had said in ten hours.

"The line is beside that olive tree," said the boy. "We're not far from the sea now."

A few minutes later, at Vilar Formoso, the Chinese man, the Portuguese, and the boy wished Hannah and Heinrich well and disembarked. Through the train window, Hannah saw the boy help the emissary down from the steps. No one was there to meet the child. He turned once or twice to get his bearings before merging into the crowd.

A conductor appeared and asked if they were headed to Lisbon.

"We're replacing this carriage," he explained. "Head over to that customs booth over there. When you're done you can wait under that tent. It's raining and what's the point in getting drenched?"

The papers of Margarethe and Otto Ebermann produced a warm welcome from a belted, buttoned Portuguese customs agent who seemed to enjoy meeting new people. The Ebermanns were on no one's list, being wholly imaginary, and he duly stamped their passports. Hannah did not know where they stood, or what they were. It was as if, from place to place, she became someone else's dream.

A woman and her little girl brought them coffee, waved away their money, and smiled when Heinrich marvelled that it was real coffee and not the stand-ins they had grown used to.

"It's only coffee," the woman laughed, while her little girl chirped, "Cream?"

At midday they were told to board the Lisbon train. There was nowhere to store baggage except on one's knees. The wagon was packed with travellers who greeted one another with kisses and gossip, who shared food and wine and recommended places to sleep and promenade, as if she and Heinrich were arriving at a party that never ended.

Each door they passed through dissolved the room behind.

"A stone is thrown into the air," she remembered her father saying. This was long ago, when Paul was ill, when he was dying, and seemed to exist, painfully, unwillingly, between worlds. Hannah had stood at his bedside, teetering between love and fright and incomprehensible sorrow. "A stone hurled into the air suddenly wakes into consciousness. It has no memory of what set it in motion. All it knows is what it senses: the wind, stars, birds, trees, and other stones. Every second is unanticipated. The trajectory of the stone was determined, long before it woke, by the force and angle of the throw. Yet it experiences each day as if nothing could have been foreseen. Is the stone free?"

Three long months later, in April 1941, letters began to reach Hannah Arendt and Heinrich Blücher in Lisbon. Via the Central Post Office, they received updates on their friends. Very few had gotten out, some were in detention camps, or prisons, or were mentioned, in heavily censored letters, as "gone."

They were staying in an unheated room, a sort of maison de rendezvous, on the Rua da Sociedade Farmacêutica. The concierge, Matilde, was a cheerful presence. She was aided by a housekeeper who, three times a day, used the outdoor water pump to fill a huge plastic drum, which needed at least three tenants to haul inside. The rooms were painted mint green. Six of the boarders were Jewish refugees, their rent covered by the aid group HICEM. En route to the icy toilet, they all murmured the usual exchange— "Any luck with the American line?" "Nothing at all, hoping for the Greek ship"—plus lewd witticisms about the freezing of delicate parts. Such sacred routines made life almost enjoyable. All were trying to obtain places on any departing ship but the berths had sold out months ago. Gloominess was not irrational. In a lending library run by Quakers, Hannah nabbed Kafka's *The Castle*, which no refugee in their right mind wanted.

The words of the Portuguese stranger on the train continued to trouble her. Human beings, he had said, are obliged to rescue one another. Was this fear camouflaged as hope, or did it truly touch the root of things?

She joked to the clouds and the birds that Hitler would take Spain in a day. And Portugal? He would occupy it by telephone. The birds had no sense of humour, and shouted denunciations at her. They were know-it-alls who woke everyone at 5 a.m. with their demented singing. They did not understand why only laughter seemed to touch the deepest source of her pain.

"It's just a joke," she shrugged. "I heard it at the post office, where hard truths are delivered. By the way, have you figured out if Hitler is substance or accident?"

The birds seemed even more appalled, but inside she could hear Heinrich giggle, spill his coffee and curse.

Shortly after that, it was mercifully done: another two-week extension of their Portuguese permits. They celebrated by sitting on a bench on the wide avenue that led to a proud statue of the Marquis de Pombal. Bare branches tangled the sky, like arms thrown up in the middle of a laugh. Matilde had promised that, come June, these trees, jacarandas, would bloom glorious purple flowers.

"I may not last until June," said Heinrich.

On Avenida da Liberdade, a stout man with a leather purse strutted past. He had a tremendous moustache, and looked around him in a contemptuous yet beseeching way, as if he had no clue who he was and yet also couldn't understand why no one knew him. But I, Hannah thought, will always recognize my own. This stranger is like me, a German Jew and a refugee, forced by circumstances to become illegal and thus an outlaw. Would stating this help him live? You must defend the space of yourself, she wanted to tell him, the German as much as the Jewish. *I am exactly what you say I am.* You must defend your identity, you must not mistake it for a humiliation to be used against you. Shame will make you disown yourself and see this as your fate.

The man passed on, walking quickly to nowhere.

Because she was bad company, Heinrich proposed that they go down to the water, and gaze upon the ships that steadfastly declined to take them.

Through Rossio Square, noisy with all the displaced languages of Europe, she and Heinrich walked arm in arm. Further south, the streets grew narrow. They saw grocers arranging marvellous fruits, they saw grandmothers with overflowing shopping bags, they saw mischief-makers and all the honking, laughing and easy swagger of everyday Lisbon life.

The Praça do Comércio, the final square before the western edge of the European continent, was also, conveniently, the location of the Central Post Office. The Square was a giant antechamber, filled with anguished chatter.

"—since the boy died he refuses to leave his room. Says it's all his fault because he blasphemed God."

"—he finally gets the job he wants and *bam!*, the whole world collapses . . ."

There were others, too. Refugees so wretched even the poorest avoided them, unable to risk the contagion of further bad luck.

Friends you'd thought lost forever could magically appear. Last month, they'd met Fritz Fränkel, whom they'd feared dead or worse. Such shouts of joy! "When did you arrive?" "How?" Even passing strangers, an elderly Portuguese couple in matching green, cried a few relieved tears. "They got me in Valencia," said Fritz. "Stuck me in prison in Madrid. Lotte intervened, I got out, no idea how, three weeks of absolute hell, a crazy scramble, awful beyond words, impossible to transit unless you have papers for your final port . . ." Heinrich was overcome. Hannah couldn't bear to look at her husband's naked grief mixed with his naked joy. Fritz had secured passage for Cuba and would leave two days hence. It was drizzling on the morning she and Heinrich waved goodbye to his ship. On the faces of those leaving, people who had gone to super-human lengths to escape, she saw disbelief or, sometimes, only fear.

Departure hurts, even if one has long desired the leaving. People sobbed when they turned their backs on Europe, where everything they had ever experienced had occurred.

"After this place," Fritz had said, "everything breaks apart."

Today, the post office line circled the building. One after another, people faced the clerk, hoping for a letter. She and Heinrich inched forward. At last, they reached the front. Nothing, no letters, no news. Saddened, they slunk away.

England would be the next to fall—everyone said so, as if it were already fact. And in the end what hope was there for Portugal when every safe harbour in Europe and Asia had given way?

Beyond the square was the Tagus, whose steel-blue waters flowed blithely into the Atlantic. At the cusp of the shore was an enormous monument of a king on a horse. He was racing towards the ocean, victorious, snakes underfoot, as if believing that having crushed the snakes he could gallop on water. That was the state of affairs.

Another week passed. The family across the hall was next in line for Matilde's typewriter and then, at last, it would be Hannah's turn. Only when she was good and done would she share it with Heinrich and the other neighbours.

She *needed* that typewriter.

"Stop pacing," Heinrich said. "Go outside if you want to stomp around."

Down she went. The sole of one shoe flapped like an innocent she was constantly crushing. Their street ended abruptly at the back entrance of Santa Marta Hospital, which might prove convenient.

Above: pink and yellow buildings, gossiping birds. Then, seemingly out of nowhere, an orange tree beside a lemon tree. This pair, so verdantly alive, upset her. She felt a wrenching desire to stop running, to hold her ground and spit in the face of the enemy. Everyone knew this chasing after visas was meant to stop the flood of migrants to third countries. They expected Jewish refugees to act *normally* and be interned and die politely as if their lives had come due. Last night, when Heinrich said he was ashamed to be German, she had snapped, I am not ashamed to be German, I'm ashamed to be human. She remembered the train from Madrid, the freezing wind of the Pyrenees. A life that led back to Gertie, to Paris, to that house sitting on the border between Germany and Czechoslovakia, to Heidegger, to childhood, to the Baltic Sea.

I want to love the world the way a person loves their home, she thought. This world is not alien to me. I will not renounce this love, even at my very last breath.

"Senhora!"

She turned. The housekeeper, holding the typewriter in her hands as if it were a roast chicken, was gazing down at Hannah's feet.

"Senhora, we must find new shoes for you."

Grateful, Hannah cradled the typewriter in her arms.

Upstairs, popping off the case, she found that the neighbour across the hall had left a page in the roller. She pulled it out, read glancingly, *I imagine old age nurtured in a thousand-year shade*, and flipped it over to use the clean side.

Typing was freedom. Her fingers leaped between German and French on the Portuguese keyboard. The noise was such that Heinrich, feeling attacked, went out to smoke.

Kafka, she wrote, *an employee of a workman's insurance company and loyal friend to many Eastern European Jews (he helped obtain permits for many to stay in the country), had a very intimate knowledge of the political conditions of his country. He knew that a person caught in the bureaucratic machinery is already condemned; and that no person can expect justice from judicial procedures where interpretation of the law is coupled with . . . the control? . . . the administering . . . of lawlessness.*

She paused to warm her fingers, looked up through the wedge of window. She kept going, besieged suddenly by the feeling of the Baltic Sea washing over her feet.

Where was she?

She was a child in Königsberg, so small as to be made of paper. In this way she could slip herself through some window in her mind, extend out onto the roof, and observe the seven hills of Lisbon, and surrounding them, the crumpled hills of the ocean. *All of Kafka's employees*, she furiously typed, *all his officials and functionaries, are very far from being perfect, but they act on an identical assumption of* . . . authority? Right? No . . . *omni-competence*. Omni-competence is the motor of the machine in which . . . in which we now live. *It is senseless and destructive but nevertheless functions without friction*; its very functionality is the object of its worship. The conditions people made were perhaps the things people least understood.

It had been so long since she'd attempted to compose herself in this way. Too long since she'd written any words that were not spoon-fed to a form. Kafka, in friendship, helped her face her fears. As she typed, she experienced the freedom that only structure could create, as if she were the very tip of a bird's wing.

People were more terrified by the horror and terror expressed in The Trial *than by the real thing. Kafka depicted a society which had established itself as a substitute for God, and he described people who looked upon the laws of society as though they were divine laws—unchangeable through the human will.*

The sheet of paper was now bludgeoned. She removed it, heart racing, and tucked it in her notebook.

Now her correspondence. She absolutely must respond to all the letters.

Notes, postcards. To Annie in Switzerland, to Salomon Adler-Rudel in London, to others with whereabouts unknown.

Date, addressee. Her heart shivering.

She wrote the first letter with good cheer, dismissing all her personal worries. *We've hardly been bothered at all. I was in Gurs less than four weeks.*

In the second, she joked: It's like that board game we always played, Mensch ärgere Dich nicht, remember? Each roll of the dice moves you forward or back, or hurls your silly peg back to square one. *The American committee paid for our tickets, and HICEM, the Jewish organization here, is supposed to obtain them. We have faint hope. But enough of the personal, no?*

When so much was at stake, individual problems must not become the whole matter. Was this possible? To look away from her personal fate and try to see the entirety? Or else how could she live without shame, that humiliation in which a person cannot face themselves? And what of vanity, that thread of vanity upon which shame feeds? No, she could not think straight. But she must think. First, rid yourself of shame, and afterwards see what comes. *We are hearing reports that Hitler aims for a complete evacuation of Jews from the whole of Europe, and their resettlement to closed territories overseas. Are you able to obtain a photostat or clipping? Rumours here are of ten thousand dead and hundreds of thousands expelled, but we are without information.*

The last card began, *Your letter of 6 March arrived with me a few days ago and I was very happy to have direct news from you. And since I was able to find a typewriter again today, I want to write a little more in detail.*

A month passed and there was still no space on any ship.

In the late afternoon, falling light slid Lisbon into a new dimension. Hannah walked with Heinrich beneath spring trees, between shadows sharp as geometric forms. Light stood on the cornices of facades, as if on the tip of a nose. Even the eternal café-goers, the pensive men and women with their crumbling cigarettes, seemed like liquid silver, emptied of all durability.

The shadows faded and the glow of the lamps deepened.

It was May 1941. Three days earlier, Hitler's army had reached Athens and on the southern shore, seven thousand Allied soldiers had been taken prisoner. Letters from friends reported resettlement in the east, roundups, forced labour and death. Letters returned unopened. This afternoon, Matilde's typewriter had come back to her again. When Hannah opened the case, she saw that the neighbour had again left a sheet in the rollers. The neighbours were a destitute family with four small children. She removed the page, unable to stop herself from reading:

The cotton quilt is cold as an iron sheet, and wrecked because our kids have torn it open. They sleep restlessly and kick their feet. In our last room, the roof leaked onto the bed. I haven't slept well in years.

What would make it bearable?

I imagine a huge house with many millions of rooms open to anyone who is cold. Even in a hurricane, this building would be as reliable as a mountain.

Make it appear, let me see it for a brief instant and I'll be content with my life. Maybe I'll even stop complaining.

Hannah stole the sheet and hid it in her notebook.

After she had finished writing her letters, Heinrich made her put on her shoes. In downcast silence, they walked to Rossio Square and then, like pendulums, turned around and retraced their steps.

Along the way they passed a couple reading from one book. "The term *sacred*," the girl was saying, "in its old Roman meaning, in archaic law, means something destined to pass away. All things consecrated and offered to the gods share a trait the gods themselves do not possess: mortality and the capacity to die."

"Eureka," she said to Heinrich. "I never approved of offerings."

But he didn't smile as she'd hoped. He was grieving. So many of their friends had disappeared. The sickening news from home tortured him.

Back in their room, she saw him try to shed his sadness. He picked up Kant's *Critique*, which he had started back in Montauban, and which he attended to as if it were current employment.

"You carried that curmudgeon on your back over the Pyrenees," she teased.

"Kant led an extremely dull life. I did him a favour taking him with us. And who are you to criticize? You carried Proust in your pocket."

Gertrud's battered copy of Proust, with her handwriting in the margins. Gertie, who had faced her across the chessboard, fingertips alighting on the crown of a castle. Hannah fled the memory. "We were fools."

"We were fooled. It isn't the same."

Hannah remembered how, in Paris, among their friends, they had been raucous, as if argument could exalt them. Now she and Heinrich had become like two chairs whose existence made a room possible. He had shown her that four walls, a home in other words, was not anchored to a building or a place. It could be made of time. It could be made of something as intangible as a promise.

He took her in his arms and asked, "Are you fooled now?" He kissed her deeply and asked, "And now?" The back of her head tingled, desire rushed over these strange days and nights which had changed what she suspected of love. Love could be fierce but also solemn, it could come so near to freedom, become a part of experience known only by faith, forever inexpressible, impermanent yet, somehow, as known and reliable as anything in this world.

"And now?" He undid her blouse and pulled it free.

—

Still they waited.

They had been in Lisbon nearly four months, ships were full and nothing could be done. Today, outside the soup kitchen on Travessa do Noronha, Hannah felt faint. They hadn't had a proper meal in days. "Our room is winter," she said to Heinrich. "Life is trying to evict us."

The shaking of the leaves of so many high trees made a great racket, as if Lisbon, wanting to dissociate from history, was preparing to levitate from earth.

Hannah and Heinrich, in their Portuguese guise, Ana and Henrique, walked holding hands. *Namesake*, she thought, an old word. For the sake of a name.

They went to Chiado, with its impossibly lovely streets. The bell on a shop door tinkled and the bookstore's narrow facade opened into passageways of ever larger rooms. She stood at a shelf reading Pessoa . . . *the philosophy spreads and the religion propagates, and those who believe in the philosophy begin to wear it as a suit they don't see, and those who believe in the religion put it on as a mask they soon forget* . . . She looked up from the book. The world slid across her vision, as if reality were ultimately smooth and empty. Only what is actively remembered survives, she thought, but even these bits of memory are changeable. What am I holding on to, then? Perhaps all the lives clinging to my memory.

Back home, she and Heinrich climbed the dark stairwell.

Matilde, hearing the thump of their footsteps, burst out of her room. "Ana, Ana! Henrique!" Her brown dress crumpling and flying as she ran up the steps behind them. She thrust a note into Hannah's hand. A note from HICEM. Berths had been secured on the SS *Guiné*, which would sail to New York on May 10. Three days from now. They should pick up their tickets in the morning.

Hannah glanced up and saw the family in the next room, the four children and their parents, congratulating Heinrich. They were still waiting for vouchers, for a passage to anywhere. Their faces were joyful even as their eyes gleamed with tears.

Inside their room, Heinrich gathered her in. He smelled of coffee and pie, of sweetness and bitterness. His hands, his heart, his head, his breathing. These were the four walls that sheltered her. And hadn't she, too, become a home for him and thereby been transformed? They undressed and lay in bed. Sleep came. In the middle of the night, she woke to the sound of the neighbour drunkenly singing to himself,

I ask, What's philosophy to us now
when the old philosophers are dust?
Let's not sadden ourselves with this kind of talk!
So long as we're alive
let us drink this cup

She fell asleep again. Early the next morning, when she asked the housekeeper what song it was that she'd heard in the night, the housekeeper shook her head.

"It was dead quiet last night. Actually, I was out here all alone, sitting on the roof, looking at the stars."

2.

I descend from the train into rolling hills suspended in blue light. Standing in this familiar station, to which I have returned many times over the years, a dizzying hope lifts me: everything moves, the white plastic chairs, waiters in long aprons, colourful shade umbrellas, quarrelling pigeons, countless bristling leaves. The air smells of the ocean and tastes of salt.

A waitress sets a cup of coffee down in front of me, pulls a silver spoon from her pocket, and turns to greet a customer. The spoon turns out to be a marvellous pen. The pattern on the woman's apron is unusual and it takes me back some fifty years to the Sea, where all cloth was precious. Circles of the same size meet and overlap at precise intervals, repeating up and down, left and right, in an orderly yet affecting geometry.

Sunlight touches the tables and happiness alights in me.

This afternoon, a local bus will bring me to the coast where I will be reunited with my friend Marie. I met her and her sister, Yilan, on the voyage out. The two sisters and I cared for one another and lived as family for almost a decade. Eventually they settled in this region; but I kept going, searching for my mother and Wei. The sisters and I never lost touch, and whenever I could, I returned to see them; over decades, and despite distance, we remained as one. When Yilan passed away, Marie raised her sister's two sons. They are grown now, with families of their own.

Now another cup of coffee arrives, pitch black, so strong it gives me new senses.

The waitress brings me a plate of sponge cake. Each bite is heavenly. As the sun warms my shoulders, I watch the waitress pause, as if listening. Something in her expression summons the past. I have a sudden, vivid memory of the young girl who wore the necklace with a wooden rose and of the boy Reza who once played the santur, and who fell to his knees weeping, refusing to relinquish this last piece.

Before my bus departs, I visit the old temple that sits across the street. Above its entryway, a wooden plaque reads 爾來了 ěr lái le, which can be translated many ways. I've come. Or, You're here. Or: You've come at last.

When I was fourteen, I stood in this entryway mourning my father. Beside me, others bowed their heads and offered up their private prayers. I thought: maybe I can't forgive him. I thought: I love him like life itself. High in the rafters, a tall abacus, carved from dark wood, swayed beneath a warning: *The calculation of right and wrong is difficult to bear.* My father sought to educate me with three books he had plucked from the shelf in a moment of chaos and derangement. "I chose the names I recognized," he told me, "and the books that looked unread. I wanted to teach you what I could. I wanted to lose my life. I thought that all I could give you was a new beginning."

I had promised myself then that if I never found any trace of my family, I would return here one day and leave my own Book of Records, something of my own making. I would wrap it in a blue cover and give it the number 91. It would wait for them, a true story hidden inside an imagined one, an unbroken love hidden inside a world of betrayals, so that they would know I had never stopped looking.

Decades have come between then and now. There are birds in the eaves now, and the paint is fresh and bright. I imagine my mother, brother and Aunt Oh stepping inside and meeting those words. *You've come at last.*

oooo

In the Sea, it was morning. As Wui Shin drifted in and out of consciousness, the three neighbours took turns telling stories, embroidering them together. All the episodes were disjointed yet somehow this felt freeing. Each time Wui Shin opened his eyes, the story had jumped forward or stepped sideways, leaping across centuries.

The neighbours kept interrupting one another. When Wui heard their voices, he knew he hadn't died yet, and this fact made him laugh.

Insulted, Blucher said, "Am I boring you?"

Keep going. Stay with Lina.

Jupiter sighed. "After creating the world, do you think the gods fell fast asleep?"

"Sometimes they jolt awake," Bento said with great confidence. "They peek through a window into our world and glimpse fragments."

"That's why they get everything wrong," said Blucher. "They see slices of time and leap to conclusions."

"Are you talking about the gods or us?" Jupiter's words were mumbled, as if he were eating something and trying to pretend he wasn't.

"We are to God as waves on the ocean."

"You're reading it the wrong way round. God exists to us as waves on the ocean."

The stray cat had settled on Wui Shin's feet, an earthly warmth. I am a pelican of the wilderness, he heard Bento say. Wui Shin recalled that his son had begged for a cat, and he could no longer remember why he had refused. What had happened to his son, his family? To leave this life without knowing was unbearable. He lingered, hoping still to turn and find Bee.

What remains surprising, Bee had told him, and he had tried to tell his daughter, is that we come into this world at all. We inherit stories never intended for us, sometimes to the surprise of those who left them behind. No matter. Let things fall to the one in need, who takes it upon herself to care for them.

I'll tell you about the SS *Guiné*.

"Lina?" my father asked.

"I'm here."

He opened his eyes and gazed at me.

A steamship carried them across the ocean.

My father closed his eyes. Tell me everything.

∞∞∞

This steamship carrying them across the Atlantic was three thousand tonnes of steel, but it might as well have been dinnerware against the ocean. This salvation, Heinrich said to Hannah, is a real wobble-pot.

There were 408 passengers and only a hundred cabins. Cots filled the decks below, where passengers had one minuscule towel each and one muslin sheet. Two days out of Cadiz, they'd hit a storm. Now, on the sixth day, which felt to Hannah like the six thousandth, they were still riding out rough waves. The Atlantic Ocean was a thick thing, the heavy back of a universe.

Heinrich looked terrible. "Is this a ship or a shoe?"

Clementine, also of Berlin, said, "This tub is meant for 196 passengers at most. But we've got twice that, and you can smell every one."

Clem was an unnerving girl, newly fourteen, constantly polishing her glasses with a frightful shirt that needed mending. Surprisingly, she had grown attached to Hannah. The girl bounced from incandescent anger to stupefied sadness and back to good cheer. She was travelling with her mother, Frau Kotzin, who tripped over cots or nothing at all, and was forever being caught—"Ouf, Mama!"—by her daughter's quick reflexes. The father, named Wolfgang, had left for America two years earlier. He was present through his wife, though, who liked to end arguments by saying, "Well, as Wolfie says, you'll think that over, Hannah, won't you?"

"Our ship's regular port," said Clem, "is Bolama, Guinea-Bissau. Now instead of cereals and peanuts, she's got us. That's what Officer Barbosa told me, so it must be true."

The hold was chaotic with rumours of U-boats, typhoid and German planes, and its passengers seemed to anticipate ever more calamitous news. This was not irrational, since calamity had touched every part of their lives. In six days, Hannah had managed to meet and dislike a whole shipload of refugees: the opera director, butcher, plenty of professors, a linen man, and a Freudian. But interesting conversation could be had with the cattle dealer, Hirsch, and the Polish priest, Wolkowski. Together, they played cards or chess in a shaded area at the stern.

Heinrich was trying to put on a brave face by persisting with Kant, but it was only making him feel more nauseous. Tricky Kant, creasing one leg over the other, reaching his hands out to maul the objects in your suitcase, insisting that a "sense of space" and a "feeling of time" are structures of the human mind.

Fine, whatever.

Pitch and roll, roll, roll. As if some toddler god had reached through the sky's curtain and was shaking the ship. She and Heinrich lay still, sweat dripping from all parts of them.

"Where in hell are we now?" asked Heinrich.

"You both look awful," said Clem brightly. "Are you going to throw up? Maybe . . . definitely!" Clem had a pack of children with her, wards of the children's relief agency. The group examined Heinrich as if inspecting a house pet.

"When travelling on moving things, a person should also be moving." This was Jentje, twelve years old.

The rest of the children, Raisa, Johanna and Bert, didn't even crack a smile.

What was Hannah seeing? Orphans in dark clothes. Between their shoulders and over their heads, a dizzying rumple of movement. The ship spun, taking Frau Kotzin with it.

Now Raisa was stroking her hair. She began to pet Hannah's nose, running her finger along the bridge. Raisa's tag, clipped to her shirt, read *US Committee for the Care of European Children*.

After all this time, Hannah thought, I can't help but mistrust hope.

Raisa held her gaze, unshaken.

The waves began to subside, and the passage, for the first time in days, calmed. Beside her, Heinrich looked monstrous but was otherwise alive. Hannah found the smell of her own skin revolting. The two of them got up and attempted the ladder-way, pushing through stacks of heavy doors, emerging up a slimy staircase.

Outside, at last, a cool wind embraced them. They stood on deck, awestruck: more stars than she had ever imagined possible within an ink-black sky, so dark it seemed the source of light. Beside them, a man and his dog contemplated the world. "Now, Bruno," the man said. "Isn't this fine?" With a shock, she recognized him. He was the very same refugee she had seen on Avenida da Liberdade, clutching a purse, looking humiliated. Bruno the boxer gazed at the vanishing smoke from his owner's cigarette.

"I'll never go back," Heinrich said. Words that had been bottled up. "It's impossible now."

Where was the place in the future where all the past could meet? Hannah had left behind, she suddenly remembered, those two heavy copies of *The Good Soldier Švejk* given to her as gifts. *To Hannah, we hope to meet again in better days.* "When the war's over," Švejk and Vodiçka repeat. We'll clink our glasses and pick up our lives again. We'll carry on.

No land in sight, no war, no peace, except what they carried with them, or what they were. I would go back tomorrow, she realized. I would go home forever.

∞∞∞

From the Sea, I saw a line of boats approaching. It started to rain and the boats were blown in, tipped side to side until, mercifully, they reached the shallows and the shore. All the while Bento and my father spoke, sometimes finishing each other's sentences and sometimes falling still. I watched a mother and child disembark, make their way across the sand, enter the Sea, and begin again.

∞∞∞

Only the reckless were travelling to Amsterdam. It was October 1664. It was a plague year. It was, Baruch knew without thinking, Tishrei 5425. When the barge docked, he stepped down and felt an unexpected, almost incomprehensible, happiness. The chestnut and acacia trees, the pilasters and caryatids, the noise of this city that had once been his whole world, surrounded him with aching familiarity.

Three years ago, he had left the Van den Enden home for a rented room outside the city, in the village of Ouderkerk aan de Amstel.

Baruch was barred from entering the Jewish Quarter but could not be prevented from settling beside Beth Haim cemetery. All winter, he had remained in this room, sheltered by his papers and books, by his lathe and glass blanks and the fine white dust of silica sand. Beyond his door, processions appeared: a barge pulled along the river by a white horse, sometimes two; a family of mourners accompanied by pallbearers and by the men of the Chevra Kadisha, the sun sliding across their wide-brimmed hats. Sometimes he felt moved by the funerals, and sometimes he felt bitter, but most often prayers came unbidden to his lips. When spring arrived, he once again prepared his father's trunk, the same one Baruch had carried to the Van den Enden house when he was twenty-three years old. After leaving Ouderkerk, he had kept relocating, each time further away from Amsterdam. Now, at the age of thirty-one, he lived on the outskirts of Den Haag.

Hat pulled low, Baruch walked rapidly away from the Amsterdam port. Merchant ships flung tall shadows across the walkway, and up against the stone facades. Despite everything, the city still clanked and heaved, a ceaseless machine, as if every canal house had been transformed into a shipyard or a warehouse.

Jos Bouwmeester was waiting for him on a stone bench in the courtyard of the Old Church. After his illness, almost unrecognizable. The slightest gust could punch him down.

Seeing him, Jos shouted in joy. They embraced and interrupted each other in their longing to say everything at once. "You're so thin, so thin!" "I'm twice the size of you!" "Braggart!"

Jos pressed a pouch of medicines into his hands. "For your malaria. But listen to that cough! You haven't rested at all and wasn't that the whole point of leaving city life?"

Baruch could not deny it. Wearily, he sat down, Jos gently assisting him.

The bells rang, ten knocks that clattered the sky and left behind a hollow of silence.

"How was the journey?"

"There's not much to tell," said Baruch. "I left Voorburg yesterday and stayed overnight in Leiden. The barge was jammed with goods but empty of people. Even the crew was hiding."

"Anyone with the means has fled Amsterdam and taken refuge in the country. But now we hear of plague even in remote villages and doctors unable to reach them."

Only last year, Baruch remembered, Jos had been so plump that the buttons of his coat would spring open. Now he had to hold the loose fabric closed. Jos caught him up on old friends, one after another. All this news hurt the heart. Jos said, "Rieuwertsz tells me he's planning to publish your *Ethics*, despite the threats. Says he's only waiting on Pierke Balling's Dutch translation. Is it finished then?"

"I'm not sure . . . I'm worried about Pierke. He doesn't answer my letters."

Jos paused for a long moment. "I have to warn you: he won't open his door no matter how long you stand there. Did you know that, a decade ago, Pierke's wife died of the very same illness? It shattered him. And now his son, too. He loved that boy beyond reason. His only child."

From a nearby tree, birds emerged, swirled up into the sky as one, extending like a necklace. They vanished upwards.

"None of us have seen him since March," Jos continued. "You know our study group has reached part three of your *Ethics*?"

"Dare I ask how it goes?"

Jos laughed. "You won't be surprised to hear that every meeting ends in a shouting match. In the spring, a few insisted on going back to the very beginning. To the preface. We went over it so many times I know it better than my own children . . . *Nothing which happens in nature can be attributed to any defect in it, for the laws and rules of nature—according to which all things happen, and change from one form into another—are always and everywhere the same.*

In response, Thyssen flung his chair across the room. He kept shouting, 'So there's no such thing as evil, eh? That's the "ethics" I'm supposed to learn? No such thing as good or bad, moral or immoral? No point to suffering and cruelty except the trustworthy "laws" of nature?' When he threw that chair, it crashed into the dining table. Thyssen is strong but has no aim. I thought someone was about to get flattened but it was just the bread!"

Their laughter startled a grey cat who skittered from the grass and fled through the open door of the church.

"Be careful," Baruch warned. "Thyssen used to be a fighter. A wrestler, if I recall."

"Well, soon he'll be a carpenter! I told him he can't step foot into my house until he brings me a new table."

They talked until the bells sounded a new hour, until Jos's words became nervous and roundabout, like a man searching every pocket for an object that was already in his hand. Around them, linden trees stretched their shadows upon the ground.

Finally, Jos said, "I know that your *Ethics* is not just a text, it is a practice book of sorts. Pierke told us that, proposition by proposition, we must work at it, the same as we work at any craft. In this way, by heart and hand, your geometries help us recognize errors. Our understanding of the world, and of goodness itself, will be transformed. He said we have to labour over it . . . But even after years of study, I still find myself in the dark."

A wind came, and Baruch coughed for a long time. Jos rested a hand on his back, soothing him.

"I shouldn't upset you . . ."

"No, Jos. Whatever you wish to tell me, I won't take offence. Speak freely."

Jos's voice fell to almost a whisper, fearing to be overheard. "In the *Ethics* . . . I know your aim is to study that which is eternal. Through a geometrical approach, you prove that we are mortal creatures. It can be no other way. No part of us, and no soul, will outlast death. You say that we do not possess free will. Our lives are brief. They pass. All this is certain.

"You say, also, there is no God as we imagined him. That we are part of a chain of events, consequences of an infinity of consequences. Everything that will be is determined by everything that was. Yet you insist that freedom and blessedness are within our reach. I've repeated your words a thousand times, trying to know their meaning. You write, *But all things excellent are as difficult as they are rare.*

"Baruch, you know I would defend you against every slander. But I fear for your life. The situation has become dangerous. They say your book denies the Almighty and is the devil's work. Vicious rumours fly everywhere . . . And there is yet another thing, more personal, that troubles me. I am afraid for Pierke. I think his present suffering would be bearable *if only he had not lost faith in God* . . . A God who redeems, who says, 'In my father's rooms are many mansions' and promises us that not a single bird will pass from the earth without His knowing. There. I have said it. If only Pierke had faith in God, he might survive his pain."

Jos pulled his coat more tightly around himself. His neck was emaciated, a softened stem. "I'm not as gifted as Pierke or Lodewijk or any of your other students," he said, flushing with embarrassment. "I'm an ordinary person with no special insights."

"No, Jos. I depend on you so that I might understand."

From a window came the sound of children fighting. A woman shouted and then a girl echoed the woman's words.

In Amsterdam alone, Jos said, the plague had taken twenty-four thousand in a single year. Entire households dead, no one left to bury them, not even a servant.

"When we were small," Jos said, "the war was murderous. Ten million dead and thirty years of killing! After the Peace of Westphalia, our parents had to get on with life. Who had time to grieve? War ended, but then came the plague, wave after wave, it never stops. How can this be the result of the unerring laws of nature? It seems a curse or, at the very least, a warning. Prophecies are everywhere. 1666 will bring the apocalypse, they say. Last year's comet was a sign. Everyone shouts for their own true religion. People on every side seem to yearn for destruction, they call the collapse of this world 'freedom' and destruction of this world 'good.' Money keeps rolling off the ships, yet somehow our losses deepen. In Amsterdam now, a man without a religion, without some shelter of beliefs, is a person entirely alone. Pierke is alone. He has no God, and now he has no son, and no way to explain these losses to himself. He doesn't know how to live, or what living is for. Pierke is dying even as his body goes on. Baruch, what if there are things that only faith in God can remedy?"

Spinoza watched the grey cat re-emerge from the church and the tall trees bending as if towards a beloved sound. This world, he thought, was made of every instant which had ever occurred. This place, this nature to which all living things belonged, remembered. Its existence was its structure. "To have any hope of truth," he said, "we must put aside our fear. Perhaps our deepest fear is that there is no one and nothing to remember us but God."

Out at sea, in the middle of the Atlantic, the SS *Guiné* pushed on.

Each morning, Hannah and the cattle dealer, Hirsch, and the Polish priest, Wolkowski, distracted themselves with card games. The game Schwimmen, for instance, which made them laugh hysterically as they won extra lives or 'went under' and drowned.

Today Hirsch was indisposed, having eaten bad potatoes. Hannah and Wolkowski were playing chess. The priest owned a superb set with nice big pieces and was not, as Benji would say, "a mere wood-pusher." A good twenty minutes would elapse before his fingers emerged from his soutane to pinch the head of a horse or the tip of a pawn.

She and Wolkowski were evenly matched. Trouncing him would provide exactly the lift she needed.

Serious Raisa, who seemed eighty not eight, came to observe. The girl, too, had been interned in Gurs. When it rained, she had told Hannah, the mud was so thick it would pull you down to your knees. "We were in Îlot K," she said. Gurs was now under Gestapo control, and Raisa's mother had not been allowed to leave with her daughter. Hannah, unable to think of Gurs without feeling everything give way, had listened but said little.

Now, Raisa leaned against her arm.

Wolkowski gazed at the board as if all else—ship, passengers, Atlantic and war—was mere distraction. Intermittently, the ship jolted, but Hannah's knights, which she had developed into lovely, strong squares, stood firm.

"Nothing is more persuasive than the beliefs of others," Wolkowski was saying. "And that is a great misfortune for society as a whole. Groups are the creators and arbiters of beliefs, and a person standing alone is a fragile creature, barely credible."

"I wonder how much longer you'll be a priest." No matter how cleverly Wolkowski tried to distract her, Hannah thought, no matter how he searched his strategic imagination, her victory was drawing near.

He had her checkmated in three moves.

Heinrich happened to come by just then. He studied the board and laughed, "You fell for that old trick, did you?"

Hannah was devastated.

Wolkowski beamed. "God is with me. You were expecting Nimzovich but I have my own theory on bishop endings."

Raisa giggled.

"Let me tell you," Wolkowski said kindly to the child. "Chess is time's greatest voyager. It originates from India, where the queen was formerly councillor, and the bishop the elephant. The game travelled from India to China, thanks to Buddhist travellers, and from the Arab world to Spain, where the Moors passed it on to the Christians. Now, no part of the world is unfamiliar with this first line of defence, the sacrificial pawns."

"You should not be allowed to speak to children," said Heinrich.

It began to rain even though there was not a single cloud in the sky, and this struck Hannah as the most incomprehensible of all the inexplicable things around her.

Raisa lifted a fallen horse. She said, "The greatest voyager is the cowrie shell. It was used to buy and sell everything, and for protection and memory. My mother told me. These shells come from the Pacific and Indian Oceans, and were used in Africa, India, Oceania and China. I used to have six of them, but I had to leave them all behind."

ooooo

In the Sea, my father was cold and the neighbours brought their blankets. The fabric of Jupiter's quilt, with its blue circles, seemed to meet and overlap as we breathed. "Circles in the sand," Blucher said, as the sun slid down and met the rising moon.

"In all directions," Jupiter said, adjusting the quilt. "*Shipo*, I think it was a Japanese word. That was the name of the pattern."

ooooo

Chang'an, in the distance, was barely a smudge on the horizon. Under a shelter beside his home, surrounded by a drenched field, Du Fu watched the rain.

A wheel shaft lay in sixteen pieces at his feet. His neighbour's son, a stringy boy wearing pants but no shirt, had taken it apart in order to repair it. Now the boy crouched on the ground smoking while his father began the reassembly.

Du Fu's expertise did no good here, so his only contribution was to regale them with stories.

"Last night, I got caught in the storm," he said. "For the hundredth time, I was leaving the Academy of Talents empty-handed. There I was on my faithful horse, totally drenched. And then, my belt snapped! These old hands were so frozen I couldn't knot the thing back up. Picture it! My glorious self parading down the grandest avenue of the grandest city: my clothes flying open, rain slapping my bare chest, hat ripped from my balding head. But I had a function! The road was a swamp and my horse was making a usable track, for which other creatures gave thanks. Behind me came a regal procession: one camel, five donkeys, and a family of ferret-badgers."

The father, Zhou, did not laugh. "When your last shirt has blown away and even a donkey knows better than to follow you, the emperor in his wisdom will say, 'Remember that old geezer, Du Fu? What did we do with him?'"

"The fate of some people," said the boy, cigarette pinched between his lips, "is to be ill-fated."

"Don't listen to this know-nothing," Zhou laughed. "Mark my words, Du Fu. You hoped to be an eagle but you'll turn out to be a whale."

All three of them drank to that, lifting high their cups of wine.

For three years, Du Fu had been haunting the Bureau of Appointments. But after all this time, he had received neither job nor salary. Meanwhile, the world was unpredictable. Drought had been followed by torrential rains which drowned the meagre harvest. Every week, he stood in line at the imperial granary, but even paying welfare rates he couldn't get by.

Du Fu hoisted the wine jar and topped everyone up.

No one I care for
is about

I lift my gaze
& my goblet
To the moon.
My shadow & I with nobody
That makes three.
The moon will drink to nobody
A shadow was sent me
In apology.

Zhou nodded approval, "Pretty good!"

"It's Li Bai's poem."

"I heard the emperor served him a bowl of soup with his own hands," said the son. "What a crock of shit."

"It's true." Du Fu set the jug down and rubbed his shoulder. "I used to know Li Bai."

Father and son exchanged glances.

Sadness rocked Du Fu. In fact, despite many letters, he'd had no answer from Li Bai in years. Li Bai was as free as the night wind. It was the nature of a great poet to be free.

We who got together sober
No longer drunk,
Shall part company
Having been merry;
A pact like
None other
Forged under the Moon
Men are put through.

& if booted out of the earth
To the stars above?

Traffic of the spheres, permit
Celestial clouds & river of mercury

Li Bai shall not go entirely friendless,
— See you.

Drawn by the singing, Du Fu's son wobbled out the door towards them. He burped, tripped, fell flat on his face, laughed mightily, and pretended to be a pony. The cassia and pines Du Fu had planted, bowed by the wind, seemed to rest in one another's arms. A gust blew the boy back inside as if he were made of petals.

Little by little, the wheel shaft was repaired and fitted into place. Father and son stood on either side of Du Fu, propping him up. It was funny how he kept swaying.

"My wise friend," Zhou was saying, "I must tell you some hard facts. There's no harvest, the cold took everything. Rations might feed your household for a month, but then what?"

The boy said, "Two small kids and another on the way. Let's put our heads together and think things through."

"This next famine will be worse than the last two years combined."

Du Fu nodded, glad that he had fallen to sitting. "But isn't the rain everywhere?"

"The world and nature are lawless right now," agreed the boy.

They talked about granaries, irrigation, lost friends, and a candy made of figs. The wet field swayed, as if mistaking itself for a river.

"My kids are happy here," Du Fu said.

"Kids can be happy anywhere," replied the son.

Zhou cackled. "Listen to you. Sixteen and still not married. What do you know about anything?"

"How can a man get married in times like these?"

That night, the wind ripped a hole in Du Fu's roof. It was unbelievable. Were the gods shouting and weeping upstairs, were they stomping and dancing? Shouldn't they be ashamed and speechless? Du Fu tried to comprehend his world. His little boy startled awake at each thunderclap, while his girl slept calmly on, smacking her lips as she dreamed. Li Hui's commentary on the *Nine Chapters of the Mathematical Art* lay unrolled at his wife's side, but she wasn't reading. In another two months, a new baby would be born. Du Fu and Anyi talked softly, listening with one ear to the children's rumpled snoring.

She told him about her mother's arithmetic, and the treatises her mother had laboured over while the four sisters sat unmoving, afraid to disturb the rocking of her brush. Her mother had discovered things about constellations that were difficult for her to communicate. Knowledge, Anyi had realized, could make a person lonely, bereft of landmarks. Her mother taught the girls to tie complicated knots, each in a different coloured silk. The knots, black, white, qing, white and yellow, symbolized time without beginning or end. The procedure had so many steps it was like finding one's way through a building of ten dimensions.

On the table, two red flowers sat in a cup of water, glowing in the moonlight.

"Zhou says we should leave here and go to my father's village. Fengxian is on higher ground so maybe the harvest was spared. It could be famine again this year." The words left a bitter taste on Du Fu's tongue. "I'm sorry."

"Are the heavens sorry?" Anyi asked. "The skies? The men in the capital?"

He touched her cheek. "No, but Du Fu is sorry."

Like an egg in a cup, he remembered. That's how he had felt when he first rested his life against hers. But how could she not be disappointed in him?

"Zhou can read the weather," she said. "If he believes we should go, we must listen."

He nodded. In the night he woke up sweating and panicked, and she reached over, touched his chest, held on.

The family squeezed into a covered cart while Du Fu and the hired boy, Aduan, sat up front with Big Red. The whole operation was a cosmic joke. They were blinded by rain. The cart got stuck. He and Aduan dug out the wheels, fell into the mud, pulled each other free. He could hear the children reciting poetry, continuing their lessons.

The cart pushed on.

Du Fu searched his soul for an answer. His last three essays, deposited in the Imperial Hope Chest, had been met with cold silence. He had no choice but to compose something exceptional and timeless, yet it seemed the hearts of influential men could only be softened by flattery.

"How about this one," he said to Aduan. "'Respectfully presented to Honourable Minister Liu . . .'"

Rain cascaded off Aduan's hat as if over a waterfall.

"'Kind sir, bend your ear to this penniless man. For thirteen years, I've eked out a living. Four years ago, summoned by the emperor, I hoped to . . .'"

"Unfurl my wings!"

They laughed. "'*Unfurl my wings.* But, flightless, I plummeted to the ground. I am reduced to begging meals in the homes of the rich. A literary man such as yourself can surely put an honest scholar to use . . .'"

Six days passed like this, unbearable, crossing abandoned villages and destroyed fields. They saw geese, wings heavy with water, sinking through the sky. When they reached Fengxian, Du Fu's heart froze. This once prosperous village had not been spared. But his childhood friend, Sonny, ran out to welcome them, not even stopping to pull on his cloak.

The only shelter available was an unused room in the mausoleum. The mausoleum! Du Fu wanted to laugh maniacally. The children were so cold they were like baskets of snow. Aduan could barely move. Sonny and his children brought quilts, clothes, food, and a green-onion wine they had warmed on the fire.

At last Du Fu and Anyi lay down. She took his hand and rested it against her belly and they felt their child kicking. "This one fights and fights," she said. Her exhausted voice was barely an exhalation. "He's ready to touch this world."

"A little longer," he consoled his unborn child. "Your house isn't ready just yet. Wait just a little longer."

"Don't be afraid," said Anyi. "Dad and I are here, waiting at the door of beginnings."

Their son was born early but he hung on, tiny and embattled.

Perhaps the child brought good luck from the netherworld because, at last, Du Fu was summoned to the Bureau of Appointments. Immediately he and Big Red departed, picking their way through the mud. Two weeks later, they arrived in the capital.

The royal clerk did not seem to notice his desperate appearance. "Esteemed scholar," he beamed, ushering Du Fu into the reception room. "Please honour us by signing this register."

A family of ten walked past, so extravagantly clothed even the toddler was wrapped in sable.

Papers were unrolled. At last he was being offered a job and salvation. He could not believe his eyes when he read the words *Commissioner of Police in Husi District.*

"We wish a man of your talents to set a firm example. Collect what is owing from tax evaders and ensure that every man fulfills his military service and corvée labour. As you know, the punishment for draft dodgers is death."

Du Fu's heart sank to his knees. When he thought it could drop no further, it fell right through the floor. Stunned, he nodded politely and thanked the clerk. Out he went again. He and Big Red slogged through cramped roads, back to the distressing room far beyond the city gates which he could not afford.

I am forty-three. Is this the moment when I must seize my life?

In the morning he returned to the Bureau. He waited until nightfall for the royal clerk to see him again.

"I beg forgiveness. The position of Commissioner of Police in Husi District is unsuitable for me. I am unable to accept it."

"Unable to accept it?"

"The emperor and his council elevated me into service on the basis of my written and verbal examinations. In those essays, I analyzed the ongoing uprisings in the border regions, and detailed the ways in which agriculture is once again being used as a weapon of war. I said we must remember what time has taught us, that every grain of millet and every inch of silk are the result of labour by men and women, on whom all hope of stability rests. I laid out designs for reform and future growth. I'm ashamed to say that my physical condition makes me ill-suited for the position I have been offered. Moreover, the lauded skills I possess will go unused. My sole desire is to serve the Son of Heaven and the realm to the best of my ability."

"Fine."

"Fine?"

"The position is rescinded."

"May I ask . . . what I might hope for?"

"You can ask, but what is there to say?"

Nervous shame washed over him but Du Fu held his ground.

The clerk laughed, startling them both. "You're a learned man, Du Fu. Can you really not see the state of things?"

Du Fu went out. To save money, he paid his bills and left immediately. This done, he and Big Red turned away from the imperial
city. The sky was one long cloud, impossible to tell something
from nothing. A day's journey north, he stopped at one roadside
stall after another, attempting to buy rice or cereals of any kind,
but the stalls were empty. "Nothing here, nothing anywhere," a
woman said. Her cotton head wrap had worn so thin it barely held.
"What little we had was requisitioned."

"Requisitioned by whom?"

"The prime minister, of course."

"What can I do?" He was soaked through and could barely see.

"Pray to the gods for sun." She turned her face away.

Had he lost his mind? Was he feverish again? Swirling com-
ets of heaven, he had just refused a job in the emperor's service!
A disreputable job fit only for a violent, merciless brute, but a job
nonetheless. "I have a newborn child," he said.

The woman looked back. She was younger than he first thought,
only a girl.

After a long moment of listening to his weeping mixed with
rain, she said, "You could trade your horse for rice."

Aghast, he said, "Impossible."

She stared into space. "What's in that big bundle saddled to
him?"

"Bedding." It was the bedding he used when he boarded in
the capital.

"Let me see it."

In a dream he did as he was asked.

As the girl opened the bundle, he noticed a small room behind
her where a man lay on a low bed. The girl's father, perhaps. The man
reached up now and then to prod the air above him. Was he reaching out for something? Was he writing on the heavens? The man
was talking or dreaming, saying, "There are thresholds that must
be respected. Once crossed, a cascade of rapid and unpredictable

effects cannot be reversed." Hearing a faint thud on the table, Du Fu turned unsteadily back. A small bag of rice had materialized.

"Give me the bedding and you can have this." There was no apology in the girl's voice, only resignation. "Money doesn't help us these days. The medicines we need can't be found."

He reached out, lifted the sack. Barely a day's worth. Anguished, he shook his head. The bedding was worn but it was made of good silk, with a pattern of perfect circles, impossible to buy again.

She began folding the sheets, fitting them back into their cover.

"This measure of rice will only feed my family for a day," he said. "But I'll give you the bedding for three days' worth."

"We can't spare that much."

Under a dripping shelter, Big Red turned and water sloughed off him. He loosened one hoof and then another from the soggy ground, shaking the mud free.

"Two days," the girl said. "Two days' worth of rice and it's settled."

Du Fu agreed. The rice was his, so light in his hands.

"When you're ready to trade the horse," she said, "come back."

The baby boy would not receive his name until he grew a little stronger. He was tiny, the smallest ripple on the ocean. His brother and sister took up positions around him. When Anyi turned her back, they liked to sniff his little body.

"Of course you couldn't accept that position," she said when he told her everything.

"What will we do?"

But neither of them knew.

The baby kicked a little leg, cried out as if someone had pulled it, kicked the other leg and stared up at them in amazement.

Anyi laughed. "So many legs. Where did they all come from?" She held their boy's tiny hand. He looked at them with a wisdom that was confounding.

At the end of the thirty days, they named him. A name whispered from father to mother, from mother to father, to keep it private and safe.

Sonny's youngest brother had left for the frontier, and the now vacant room was offered to Du Fu. He and Sonny moved the family's belongings across the village. He felt embarrassed by the largest chest, containing nearly six hundred poems, and tried to make light of it: "I've only kept my best ones."

Sonny paused. "You should have kept them all."

This was something only a friend could say, and it touched him.

Sonny shifted a table towards the light. "The news out of Chang'an is terrible. Do you know much about it? There's some kind of exodus from the capital."

"I only know the rumours."

"My brother went to school with Adjutant Zhang. He says the court is out of control. Every week someone else is brought up on fabricated charges. Anyone remotely capable has left to serve at the frontier. Even worse, Zhang says there's upheaval in the northeast, not from invaders, but within the army itself. Treasonous talk." The room seemed to glow with cold. Self-conscious, they both fell quiet, but there were no spies to overhear them, just rain dripping from the eaves. "My brother says the outposts need reliable men. Administrators who may have been overlooked by the court. Du Fu, this could be your opportunity."

"I'd have to leave my family here," he said.

"What's ours is yours."

It was November. Once more, he prepared to leave with Big Red for the capital. On the day of departure, the sky cleared. This aquatic light seemed like something foreign to his nature and yet he felt bound to it. What was unfamiliar was his. What was unfamiliar belonged to them all. He saw his son hold the hand of his little sister. The baby, too tired to open his eyes, was the lightest bundle in his mother's arms.

—

He took a room at his regular inn, trusting they wouldn't turn him away. The innkeeper, Homan, drooped and pale, needed a deposit. "The times, you know," he said, apologizing.

"Of course." Du Fu handed over a small leaf of jade inherited from his mother. He should have sold it long ago. Inside his room, he couldn't avoid his reflection in the glass. His clothes were threadbare, his shoes were mulch. What remained of his grey hair was falling out, as if he were his own ancestor. "Truly distinguished, with hair as fine as silk!"

The reflection smiled back, eyes wide in wonder.

Without formal attire, he could not present himself and must therefore rely on letters. They were written in strict formal verse, employing a patterning so elaborate, Du Fu felt both dazzled and embarrassed by his gifts. All three were odes: one to a duke's horse, another to a sheriff's painted silk screen, a third to a magistrate's toddlers. Finally he wrote a long poem to General Geshu, commander of the northwestern armies, begging for a military post.

Three agonizing weeks passed with no reply. He decided to submit a poem-essay to the Imperial Hope Chest, and thereby alert the Rectifier of Omissions to his continued existence.

For many days he perfected his submission. Big Red had a runny nose and a cough, and seemed exhausted still from the long journey, so Du Fu decided to go by foot. But when he arrived at the palace to submit his poems, a pair of guards refused to let him cross the road. The older of the two looked embarrassed when Du Fu said he had business at the court.

The other laughed outright. "Of course you do, and I'm the emperor's mom."

Du Fu smiled. "Do you know how many phrases we have for humiliation? I do. For instance: to allow the spit on one's face to dry in the breeze. Also, to drain the cup of humiliation. Also, to be dishonoured, mortified, shamed, sullied, or to be forced to crawl, as the celebrated General Han Xin is said to have done, between another man's legs."

"Move along," the elder said, bored.

Du Fu had a disquieting image of himself standing in the road, waving his hands like a chicken.

The world is ungenerous. Luckily, the wealthy kept multiplying. There were still some to whom he had not yet appealed. Thus sunlight slid through the rain.

"Who can compete with your eminence?" he sang, as he turned away. "You, you and you! Under your banners, let all talents unite. Your legacy reaches the dark heavens! One word of praise from you rewrites destinies!"

Shuffling home, he passed a bookstall with a sign that read *The Rose of Time*. The longing in him could not be repressed. In he went. Three shelves of books encircled him, like friends he no longer saw. Du Fu's eye fell on a critical poetry anthology: twelve poets, the finest of the age, selected by a revered literary scholar. He knew better than to pick it up. He backed out of the stall, turned left, and walked at speed for ten minutes before spinning around and rushing, hat flying, back to the very spot. He could hardly breathe. Sweating, he lifted the anthology from the shelf. The wrinkled bookseller, smoking his foot-long pipe, exhaled. Smoke curled between Du Fu's hands. He combed through the book, as if leafing through his very soul. At last he returned to the beginning and concentrated, slowly, painfully, on the table of contents. He recognized every name. Seven he considered close friends, including Li Bai, Gao Shi and Meng Haoran, and the rest he knew in passing. A critical introduction preceded each poet. His eyes welled up. Some poems were lustrous, some were masterpieces, but some were empty. He wished he could afford to buy it but was also relieved that he could not.

The bookseller said, "That's Volume One. Are you looking for Volumes Two and Three?"

His heart leaped. He must have been included in another volume. He was certain of it.

Slowly, impossibly slowly, the old bookseller stood. He reached up towards an ornate box. Down came the two heavenly collections.

Du Fu picked up Volume Two and opened it to the table of contents. He closed the book and picked up Volume Three. His eyes moved quickly through the names, before returning again to the beginning. He kept studying the lines, full of hope. Was he there? Years ago, he had been celebrated and admired by these poets, his friends, his peers. Was he truly not there? Truly?

He felt his heart collapse to something weightless, a small blossom. "Thank you," he said to the bookseller, returning both volumes.

"This anthology will serve us for the next century," the bookseller said brightly. "Our thirty-six finest poets, masters of every form."

Du Fu retreated back onto the street. "We are very lucky."

"Walk carefully, Grandfather!" the bookseller said.

"Thank you."

Out he went into the sunshine. He chided himself for his self-pity. All existences in this universe, he told himself, whether rich or poor, fulfilled or unfulfilled, must be lived. What could he hope for? No, that was a foolish question. What was his due? Even worse! Still a question remained: What could he understand?

The following day, Du Fu was summoned to the Bureau of Appointments and offered the post of Registrar in the Right Commandant's Office in the Palace of the Crown Prince. It was a long title for a low position—administrator in one of the imperial guard units—but dignified.

The clerk wore the shadow of a grin. "Would such a posting be acceptable?"

His knees trembled. "I am grateful."

He signed all the papers, approved the meagre salary and benefits, received various instructions and went out, once more. He found Big Red and whispered, "We are saved."

His faithful horse bowed his head.

Back at the inn, an attendant to the duke was waiting for him with a gift of money in return for the ode to the duke's new horse. Soon after, the sheriff's servant came to invite him to a banquet that very night. The sheriff had sent along a gift, a simple yet elegant scholar's robe. There was money in both pockets, more than enough to pay his bill at the inn, and see his family through another month. Giddy, setting out with the sheriff's servant, wearing new clothes, Du Fu almost felt like a person again. The old bookseller, packing up The Rose of Time, didn't recognize him. Nor did the two guards, shivering in the cold, or the homeless families, street vendors, petitioners, or the ill and unfortunate who called out blessings and begged coins. The sheriff's banquet was opulent. Starving, he ate too quickly and felt queasy. *My stomach can no longer tolerate expensive wine but that's a blessing, isn't it?* His new robes smelled of sage. His host called on him by name and entreated him to recite the praise song he'd written.

"Of course, Excellency."

"Quiet, everyone, quiet!"

He cleared his throat. "Song in Honour of the Painted Landscape Screen of Sheriff Liu."

His eyes felt itchy, and someone handed him another cup of wine so that, oddly, he held two. Were they laughing? No, it was only so many eyes shining joyfully towards him, officials and great men who had his best interests at heart. The hall, bedecked with endless ornaments, twinkled in glee. He saw a great platter of oranges which must have ripened in the frost.

"Painters are legion yet Sheriff Liu's artistry is rare," he began. "His brushwork transcends ancients and moderns—"

"Louder, louder!" Cups were raised towards him like temple bells.

Du Fu swallowed. "This . . . humble viewer finds himself ferried to another world: the vigorous cold of the summits, the cries of gibbons, the paint still wet with the mist of the original fog . . ." The poem seemed to go on forever. At last, the wine ran out. His words, too.

He was escorted back to his lodgings where the innkeeper's son helped him to his room.

"Are you ill, Honourable Registrar?" the boy asked, invoking Du Fu's new title. "Won't you take a cup of this? It's nettle tea and very soothing."

"Thank you, child."

The son lingered, unsure what to do as his guest cried.

"Not to fear, not to fear," Du Fu said. "There's a night flower that makes me sneeze. All is well. We're saved."

In the morning, he paid his bill and Homan returned the leaf of jade. The boy saddled Big Red, and they saw Du Fu off, calling after him, "A good road, Honourable Registrar! May a strong wind carry you home!"

Everything appeared to be breaking. It was the ninth month and the air, white-blue, blurred like submerged glass. Big Red exhaled, then struggled onwards, tired, a stove losing heat.

"The hundred grasses in tatters," Du Fu sang, "wind-shaped ridges and knife-edged stars. It's year-end on the imperial highway, this cold road too many armies have polished smooth . . ."

They passed the summer palace, closed for the season. They passed luxurious spas, six courtesans descending from sedan chairs, and in the distance, bolts of new silk, dyed and drying in the sun, ready to be cut by seamstresses whose husbands and children darted like herons through the wet fields. The rains began again. A man was being whipped by imperial guards. A line of draftees stood shackled and defiant together. He saw empty stores, a load of lumber, a luxurious cart as high as a six-floor pavilion. The journey pulled his mind to pieces. Big Red must have taken shelter, they must have rested together somewhere. When they reached the Jing River crossing, the ferry landing had vanished. There had been a flood, and nothing was left but a few floating planks. Big Red detoured east, searching for a safe route, and at last they came to a trestle bridge. A line of terrified people was crawling across its planks. Du Fu didn't understand what he was seeing. He dismounted. Villagers waited to cross this bridge, afraid to overload it. The wind was howling now, buckling the trees, and the very spit of land on which they stood was drowning. They had to cross, there was no choice, the bridge was as thin as a child's wrist, and at any moment the river would swallow everything.

Big Red was the subject of great concern and even anger among the villagers. It was decided that all of them should cross, but that the horse must stay behind. Leave Big Red on the other side? But what else could Du Fu do? "Wait," he whispered to his horse, before he turned to go. "Wait and follow." His old companion looked at him with trusting eyes.

Du Fu went on foot with the last group. The village men tried to shelter their wives and mothers, who carried shocked children in their arms. An old man had to stop every two steps to cough his life away. Du Fu wanted to shout at the river, "Don't you know who I am? I am the newly appointed Registrar in the Right Commandant's Office in the Palace of the Crown Prince!" He could hear the river laughing, unhinged, crashing its banks. The trestle bridge swayed, tossing them maniacally from right to left.

Yet they made it to the other side.

Big Red approached the bridge. How small he seemed. The bridge creaked as Big Red set his weight on it, and howled as he began to move. Du Fu could barely watch as his old horse moved steadily, bravely, over the water that terrified him. His horse walked towards him, never unfixing his gaze. Bit by bit, he drew near, growing slowly larger. With a last wail, the bridge seemed to rise and unclasp. Big Red hesitated for a moment, and abruptly extended in a desperate leap. He was falling through the air. He was landing. He was touching solid ground. For a moment, they all watched the bridge swing wildly, like a broken toy. The bridge fell away. The horse remained.

When Du Fu touched Big Red, the horse was vibrating, overcome like a clanging bell.

The villagers continued on, moving in drenched slowness. Some of them shouted angrily at the horse, as if the bridge would still be standing if not for him. A few gently caressed Big Red for luck. Du Fu climbed up and he and the horse continued on.

The road passed under them. Soon a graceful, familiar willow came into sight. Fengxian's name had a gorgeous meaning, the ground of first devotion, a place of spiritual beginnings. His family had lived in this county for many generations and his grandfather had been a celebrated literary man. Du Fu thought about these things in order to repel a chilling sound that was growing ever louder. "Wind in the fields," he said to Big Red. "It's nothing. Only rain collapsing the trees."

Big Red seemed uncertain—rushing towards home yet also, in fear, slowing down.

He could hear voices in the distance, Du Fu realized. There was a strange hollowness on the village path. The rain turned to silver, and finally slowed, stopped. Sonny's house came into view. They saw Sonny's children, ragged and shivering, Sonny's mother and sisters crying openly in the road. Big Red slowed even more. Du Fu's children were shadows in a doorway. The sound of the weeping did not retreat but grew louder and louder. Big Red stilled. In a daze, Du Fu heard his son saying, "Our brother died, our baby brother died." How had he died? Of course, what could anyone say? They all stood there, starving and bedraggled. Barely enough food to keep them alive, let alone a tiny baby who had struggled from the first morning. Sonny sat on a stone, weeping. Du Fu rushed into the little room and at first could see nothing, only a fierce white light pouring through the doorway. On the mat, Anyi lay pale and shivering. She held her arms out to him when he spoke her name.

After leaving Jos in the church courtyard, Baruch continued through an unnervingly quiet Amsterdam. In the ports, the hustling never stopped, but further north along the Singel, where the Van den Endens had once made their home, all was silent. Quarantine markers, made of straw and tied with three bands, were stuck to doors. House after house looked abandoned though sometimes a maid could be seen, ghostly, in the window. He knew that Frans Van den Enden had been chasing dreams. The last time they'd met, more than a year ago, Frans had talked wildly of crossing the Atlantic and building a utopia in New Amsterdam, but whether he had really departed, Baruch didn't know. Frans had been grieving. His youngest ones, Jacob and Maria, had been lost to the plague. Clara Maria, Kerckring and their children had moved to the countryside, but Baruch had not heard from them in months.

He followed the path of the Damrak, the bells of the Old Church tolling in his wake. He kept walking almost against his will. Over the little bridges and sluice gates, past the massive warehouses of the Dutch West India Company, the cloth-makers and the drapers, between the ramparts and over the last bridge until he came, finally, to the Vlooienburg and the Jewish quarter.

Could it really be so painful to walk away, but so effortless to come back? He felt he had changed so greatly in appearance that no one would bother with him. But what was he doing? Nothing he could easily explain.

The faces of children appeared before him. They were fence-riding on the balustrade where he and Isaac had once also played. In fact, now Baruch longed for someone to recognize him, and even curse him or denounce him, but nobody did. He saw the same shops, synagogues, rabbis, students, servants—all of whom of course were not the same. He walked ever more slowly. He glimpsed, through a door swinging closed, a group of men reading in murmured prayer. Had he really forgotten what it was like to hear Portuguese spoken with Pai and Mai's rhythms? He saw Brazilian shipbuilders, servants, adventurers. He heard Hebrew, Spanish, Dutch, German, Javanese. Now he stood at the door of the Third Man, lost in time. There was a quarantine sign on it, tattered and sun-weathered. The straw had wasted away. Who lived here now? The rooms had been very small, very cold. He remembered two spiders in a jar, and one victor. He thought it need not have ended in the way it did. He thought the Third Man had truly understood and loved him.

He kept walking, waiting to be perceived. But life had moved on. "Avôzinho," he heard someone say. "Baruch." He turned, prepared to face his beginning. But there was no one. Perhaps it was he himself who had said it, out of desperation. Out of all the possibilities for his existence, this was his. The consequence of innumerable consequences, and yet, astonishingly, inescapably, his alone. For each and every face he saw, no one would walk their particular path again, no matter how long the universe existed. That path was their true possession, which no man or god could take away.

3.

Finally, I am at the coast. It is a wild place, a realm of tides and change. Yilan's little grandchildren surround me.

"Lina, Lina, here's more coffee!"

"Eat peanuts!"

"Lina, let's play mumblety-peg!"

I have hardly put down my bag when these small bodies are draped across me, clinging to my shoulder and hanging off my hip, and I feel wide and gargantuan like a tree. Marie plucks them off, one at a time, telling them to get water and fruit, and *go and get that gift you made for Lina*, and so on.

Immediately I am swallowed into family life and the metronome of the tides. The days pass as one.

Each morning here, when it is still dark, I open the old notebooks, their covers emblazoned with the purple logo of Tsinghua University. I touch my father's drawings and notes, and lose myself in the words I and you, *I* and *thou*. At some point, Marie brings in coffee and sugar and bread, but I am so submerged I barely rise to the surface, coming awake to find a cup in my hand.

This afternoon, as I sit thinking, Yilan's granddaughter, who is my namesake, sidles up to me. "Lina," says this smaller Lina, "what's that you're reading?"

I look down at the forgotten book in my lap. "Archimedes."

"Why?"

I smile. "He's an old friend of mine."

The child doesn't question this. She goes on with her playing, in which nothing in the world is alien to her. Shells, stones and plastic pots have been made into a tower. She takes the book to use in her game.

"Is that a door?" I ask.

She laughs and says no, shaking the book. "That's a long name. Arch of . . . How did you meet?"

"The same way I met your grandmother. We met on the journey out. That was ages ago."

"What happened to him?"

"Life, I suppose."

She nods and offers me her last candy. "Did he have a good life?"

The candy, perfectly round, sits in my hand like a shell, as real and weightless as the night. "Yes," I tell her. "I think it was. But what's a good life?"

Without any hesitation, the girl says, "Flying like a bird and sleeping in a nest. Dad said you're coming to live with us."

"Maybe."

She moves the book into another position. "Now it's a window," she informs me. "How come Teng didn't come with you this time?"

"Well, we went our separate ways," I said. "We don't live together anymore."

"Do you miss Teng?"

"Not so much."

"Me neither!" This makes me laugh despite myself. The girl keeps adjusting her tower. It looks like a boot. She asks, "Did you find your brother?"

"Not yet."

"What was his name again?"

She steps into my arms and her dark hair smells of rosemary. I have an enduring memory of three doors standing ajar and a cross-current ruffling the papers in my hand. I stood there for centuries watching the light touch the objects in each beloved room. "His name is Wei."

"Oh yeah," she says. "I knew that. He was a voyager."

When she uses the past tense something stings behind my eyes, but I don't correct her. In the last few years, I have had an abiding, inescapable feeling that my brother and I have become untethered. That Wei is gone. "That's right. He was lost at sea but after many adventures he came home. He was saved many times and when he could, he saved others."

"Was he an orphan?"

"No, he had a family that loved him."

"Nice," she says. "What are you writing?"

"I don't know yet. Something for Wei. What do you think I should call it?"

"Ummm . . . call it *Lina and the Sea*. That's nice, isn't it?"

"I like it."

"If you come live with us, we can play Go and mumblety-peg all day long."

"I'm the best at mumblety-peg. I never lose."

The girl laughs and laughs, waving her arms. All the laughing makes her tower fall down, and to my surprise she bursts into tears. Her siblings come running out of the water, as if they've just been born, and off they go again, chasing something or fleeing something. The tide crashes over jagged rocks, bringing shells and particles of life and carrying them away. As I prepare to leave pages for Wei, I try to listen for his questions. I suspect that our lives have run in parallel, that the two halves of our story can never end without the other. At last, I think I hear him but he bears no questions and no answers. Instead, he tells me that because it is forever unfinished, we have sought each other in the faces of strangers, among the living and the dead, among the mothers and the fathers, and he tells me that his journey appears everywhere I look. Love, he tells me, like devotion, leaves everything unfinished.

ooooo

On the night when news of the rebellion reached Du Fu, there was no moon, only a low fog that had frozen and crystallized in the cold.

He wanted to curse and weep but instead he laughed. Du Fu laughed so hard it was like a river rushing over a wall. He was nothing, a scholar's robe drying in the wind, a touch of colour in a falling world. Power was a farce. Two hundred thousand men, under the banner of their rebel leader, had caused the collapse of nearly every major city east of Luoyang. This rebel leader was none other than An Lushan, the adopted son of the emperor. Instead of readying a defence, the prime minister had overseen the execution of An Lushan's eldest son. Now, in retaliation, ten thousand surrendered imperial officers in Chenliu had been executed by the rebels.

And I, Du Fu, must immediately report for work in Chang'an because I am fortunate enough to have a job. He laughed.

Nonetheless, he had to go, riding away from his family who were still in mourning for the baby, and who still had so little to shelter them from cold and hunger. It took nine horrible days to reach the capital, and for what? He made the rounds of banquets which, poisonous and frenzied, had descended into mayhem. Two celebrated generals, brought up on fabricated charges, were arrested and brutally executed. Pernicious gossip ricocheted through the court. Every minister was an opportunist. Du Fu asked for and received permission to return home. The war raged on, and the rebel army advanced inexorably towards the capital. Then, once more, he was summoned back to Chang'an. He saw rivers breached, roads closed, bridges destroyed.

Spring came, a renewal and a wilting. Formerly occupied cities were suddenly resurrected as imperial strongholds. An Lushan, rumours said, had retreated. An Lushan was surrounded. An Lushan had been murdered in a coup. Yet somehow the rebellion only grew.

Du Fu had enough money to buy necessities for his family, he was fortunate. He was given permission to go home again.

It was summer now. Everything seemed precious and fleeting. Around the table, his wife and his son read. The boy's finger trailed down the handwritten page. Unsteadily he identified the characters—"We look up at the sky to find the images of heaven. We look around us to find the . . ."

"Patterns."

". . . patterns of the earth."

Anyi continued, "We look at the markings on the birds and the beasts. We look within ourselves. The book says nothing that is not already . . ."

The boy's eyes were so close to the page he looked as if he might fall in. ". . . from the start in the mind of the diviner."

When Du Fu was a child, he had dreamed of voyaging down endless pages until they carried him into the heart of knowledge. Instead, such knowledge had moulded him into a man who pledged his life to the palace gates, as if such edifices stood forever.

My idea of life got in the way of living. *Turn your life around,* he thought. *Unfold it now and find its worth.*

In the evening came the news they feared.

Ten days prior, fighting had reached the Tongguan Pass, one hundred miles out from the capital. The pass was a chokehold, deemed impossible to breach. But in a single day the emperor's army had lost 170,000 soldiers. Fewer than ten thousand had managed to escape and sound the warning. The road to the capital lay open and undefended. In a headlong rush, the emperor and the entire court had fled Chang'an. On the road, the emperor had abdicated. The crown prince had ascended the throne and was attempting to regroup north of the Yellow River.

The rebel army, seizing the imperial palace, had murdered the families of those who had fled. One week. That was how long it had taken the rebels to march in and subdue the centre.

Along the Wei and Yellow Rivers, all the counties were now in rebel hands. By morning, their own village would be surrounded. They had to run—out into the night, with almost no provisions. Only those who were too old, too sick, or who, like Sonny and his family, refused to part with their homes remained.

Soon the fleeing families were a scattered line, vanishing in the dark. No choice but to swing west, bypassing rebel outposts, and try to cross the marshlands. On and on Du Fu and his family walked, Big Red carrying all they had. On the fifth day, his daughter bit him, and then bit her mother, the hunger was too great. It thundered and poured, as if stores of rain were being forever emptied. Without Aduan, their hired boy, they would have died of shock and cold. They walked over ten hours each day, carrying the children.

They reached Lu-Tzu Pass but the uphill climb to safety proved impossible. Du Fu had no idea whether to turn back or move forward. Every choice was perilous. As night was beginning to fall, a boy in a mud-drenched tunic reached them. He said he was a servant of Sun Tsai, whose household had received word that their great friend, Du Fu, the Honourable Registrar in the Right Commandant's Office in the Palace of the Crown Prince, was sleeping in the open.

"In friendship, Sun Tsai begs you to shelter with him."

It was the dead of night when Du Fu and his family reached the compound. Moment by moment, the lamps flickered into life. Bolted doors swung open. But Du Fu's family was so broken, they entered in mute stupor, as if into the afterlife. Sun Tsai himself wrote words for them on paper banners to call their souls, their crumbling minds, back into their bodies. Servants, pulled from sleep, carried buckets of heated water and warmed the children, and then the adults, back to life. Du Fu finally fell asleep at dawn, holding Anyi who held the children, and in his dreams he returned to the company of his elder brother.

"I tried to tell you," the ghost brother said, "but does any living person believe in the future?" This boy had died too young, he seemed to have never aged. "The era into which you were born is ending. The ground has turned to water. From the highest to the lowest, all things must change their places. No life will be left undisturbed."

ooooo

In the night I woke with a start. I couldn't hear the ocean, or the tide coming in, or the waves cascading against land. I could only sense the presence of our two windows, the curtains open, the windows waiting like two frames. I went to my father.

The neighbours were already beside his bed, speaking quietly.

"Have you seen Lina?"

"She's here."

My father was talking, trying even now to tell me what he had seen, what he had hoped. Bring the little horse in from the rain. Take these notebooks and maps. They'll help you wherever you go. I promised I would take them with me, and he reached out and held my hand.

ooooo

Baruch climbed the narrow staircase. His friend, Pierke Balling, opened the door. They passed through the sitting room and entered the study. Baruch could smell oranges. He had brought gifts for Pierke: dried figs, candied ginger, and a bag of double-salted licorice, which had always been his friend's favourite.

"It was selfish of me to want your company," Pierke said. "It's too dangerous to travel now."

"You didn't ask," Baruch said gently, "but I came."

Jos, he thought, had been a vision of health compared with Pierke, who was thin as a line and aged beyond recognition.

They talked, at first, about outlying things: Casearius, the student who seemed to be stealing Baruch's papers. Baruch's upcoming move to Schiedam, to shelter for a time with friends. The Rieuwertsz bookshop. The seizing of Dutch merchant ships and the growing agitation for war with England.

But Pierke's rooms seemed cut loose from all that, drifting in some other world.

"I've missed you, Baruch," he said. His voice was groggy. "Your friends, you know, continue to study your work. Every time you send us new pages, we're keen to discuss them. We try to do as you taught us, to be thorough and patient, to understand each Proposition and Demonstration before moving on to the next." He got up and went to the desk, on which sat the Dutch translations he'd made of the *Ethics*. Almost all of parts one and two. He had even, somehow, begun part three. Baruch touched the first page of the Latin original.

Definition One: By that which is self-caused (*causa sui*), I understand that whose essence involves existence, or that whose nature cannot be conceived *except as existing*.

"We argued endlessly over this definition," Pierke said. "Do you remember? My son was just a baby back then, no bigger than my forearm. And later, after Saskia died, I kept returning to this first line."

Baruch, finding no words, said nothing.

"This definition is a seed," his friend continued, as if talking to the page itself. "Essence, existence. Everything that follows in the *Ethics* grows from this seed, as if all the other Propositions are a vine already curled within the first word. That's what you tried to explain to me: this book will unfold this vine, which is connected to the eternal, and the eternal contains what we are, by necessity, in our mortality."

"Tell me how you are, Pierke."

But his friend only shook his head. "This vine, Baruch. It twines round and round me. The *Ethics* demonstrates that free will, as men have grown accustomed to defining it, is an illusion. That all things are determined. You say there is no afterlife, and that God is not as we imagined Him. It is difficult to conceive . . . You are my best friend, Baruch, and my wisest teacher, and now here you are, in my hour of need. I would like my son to be in a better place than here. The plague is an evil illness. My child does not exist anymore."

Baruch put his hand over the pages, as if to cover them. He guided Pierke to a chair, sat him down. Sat beside him. "Your boy," he said, "was loved and he felt that love all his life. Such a thing matters."

"Do you know, Baruch, my child asked me to intervene on his behalf. That was his word, *intervene*. Intervene with whom? With what? I know for a fact that I could have saved him, but I erred and offended God."

"How, Pierke?"

"One night, when I was sleeping, God sent me an omen. This was many weeks before my child fell ill. He couldn't breathe. *I heard it so distinctly*. Chasing his breath, desperate for air. I woke up instantly. The whole house was quiet but I ran to his room and was relieved to find it was only a dream: my boy was calm and breathed easily. But, Baruch, this was the very same sound he made in the last hour of his life. God himself warned me to save him! But I did nothing because I didn't understand the prophecy. I failed my child and because of me he suffered a cruel death."

Quiet lay between them.

"You know what I must tell you," Baruch said at last.

Pierke looked at him with such hope, such despair.

"You see it as a prophecy," Baruch said, "because you are searching backwards for a cause, and you are trying to understand what cannot be accepted. But the reason for his death is clear. There is a plague. He became ill. He died. You could neither stop it nor prevent it."

"You don't want me to blame myself."

"No, Pierke. I am telling you the truth."

"Others have lost more," he said. "Entire families buried. But in my small world, it was just us. I should be gone, and he should know a full life."

Baruch had a terrible foreboding that he could love Pierke but not save him.

"I want my child to be with God," Pierke said. "To be held with kindness and benevolence in a better world."

"It is our bodies alone that suffer."

"And the soul?" Pierke asked.

Baruch said nothing.

"There is no soul, that's what you believe. My child has no soul. We're superfluous in this universe."

"The world doesn't belong to us," Baruch said, "but we belong to it. I am certain of this."

He heard voices on the street outside. He poured his friend a glass of brandy, and some for himself.

Pierke drank. But it was clear he did not taste it, or even perceive his own hand. "A free man," he said, "does not dwell on death, and his wisdom is a meditation on life, not on death. That's what you've been saying to me all these years. But I am not free and I am not wise."

"You think you can't go on."

"I can't, Baruch."

"Believe me when I tell you we are all a piece of that lasting thing, existence. Me, you, and your dear, beautiful son. Even though we are mortal. Because we are mortal. I believe, and I hope you too will come to believe, that we hold within us the remedy to sorrow."

Later, on the barge leaving Amsterdam, Spinoza saw almost no passengers. A Jewish couple spoke softly in German. There was a family with four children sitting all in a line. At the back, a father and daughter faced the shore. The father, very frail, was tying a complicated knot. Untying it and tying it again while the girl watched intently. The world slipped by along the banks. Windmills burst out of the fog, first just a wing, and then the whole machine with its circling blades.

One of the children was reading and her mother was correcting her when she couldn't recognize a word. Baruch closed his eyes. He was tired of books, tired of trying and failing to see.

"Good," the girl read, "is the reckoning that uses no tallies and does no counting. Not one thing is found worthless, not one is . . ."

Her mother gave her the word.

". . . abandoned. Failure either to value the teacher or to cherish the material is the vast confusion found even in wisdom."

He knew this text but no matter how he searched his memory, its name escaped him. In his travelling bag were the first hundred pages of Pierke's translation of the *Ethics* from Latin into Dutch. My words didn't reach him, Baruch thought. I failed my friend. Why didn't I help him to study the stars, trees, machines, optics, light? Or to understand that through them we can begin to know the turbulence within us. What is sorrow? What is hope, greed, love? Everything within us follows the same necessity and force of nature as all that exists. Nothing in this world is too small, nothing is immaterial. Nothing human is alien to us.

All of the world seemed to be passing by on the opposite shore. But in his mind he was still talking to Pierke, still trying to hold his friend close. *The striving by which each thing strives to persevere in its being is nothing but the actual essence of the thing.* Desire is our essence, but what is desire? To exist, to continue, to actively persevere. *Joy is that passion by which the mind passes to a greater perfection.* And sorrow, and melancholia, and pain? And one who imagines that what he loves and what he needs is forever destroyed?

The barge went on, pulling him further south. The other travellers gazed at him with curiosity and pity. He was crying, it seemed. Pierke was his dearest friend, and he was leaving that friend behind. But the wind was taking his tears away even before he felt them. He glimpsed a funeral procession moving across a village road, a child in a feathered hat leading the way. Just a few months ago, sick with malaria, Baruch had thought his own life was coming to an end, yet somehow time was growing wide again. The book he had thought complete was incomplete, had only reached the halfway point. He must go back to its beginnings. What was the meaning of a philosophy like his, an ethics, if it could not walk beside a good man in his time of need? The plash of water against the barge filled him with memory, like a future unfolding within him from a seed that had no beginning.

On the SS *Guiné*, 408 destinies moved ever forward.

"When we dock at Bermuda," said Clem, "Captain will bring fifteen thousand oranges aboard. That will cheer you up and also save us all from scurvy."

These wards followed Hannah like goslings.

"Did you know there are seven sailors from Java and twenty from China in the crew quarters? They were on a Dutch ship that got exploded by three torpedoes. They floated in lifeboats for twenty-eight hours." The boy, Jentje, appeared very proud to report this.

The man she'd recognized in Lisbon went by with his boxer. The dog had a bright, intelligent look, and the children heaped praise upon him.

"This is Bruno," the man said. "The two of us are joining Albert Einstein's group in Princeton. I work in the field of nuclear physics, specifically cosmic rays."

Hannah snorted. He'd lost all his marbles.

"What is physics?" Raisa asked.

The man had been waiting so long to be asked, on hearing her question, he appeared to soar like a paper plane flung into the sky. "Children, this evening, after dinner, I invite you to join me here at the stern. I will tell you what I know."

"And what is that exactly?" said Hannah rudely.

Beside her, Heinrich murmured, "Darling."

The man's face shone so brightly it almost hurt her eyes. "I will explain something very common to all. I will explain the night."

Darkness arrived and many stars became visible. The children, longing to be told something true, gathered.

"The world," Père Bruno began, "is not always as it appears to our senses. For instance, we commonly say that things are either in motion or at rest. But friends, the truth is: there is no such thing as 'at rest.' Even stones, even handkerchiefs, even a book on a shelf, are all in motion. So let us begin. Would you please puff out your cheeks with air . . ."

Obediently the children puffed.

"Everything is made of molecules. When you puff air into your cheeks, you are crowding the molecules into a confined space and this crowding, children, is air pressure—let your breaths out, that's fine, breathe all together, *I said breathe!*, excellent . . .

"I entrust this theory to you," he whispered, as if sharing a secret. "The theory of the Law of Mechanics of Moving Bodies. But where can we, fleeing through the night, having lost all our possessions, observe the physics of moving bodies? The answer is *always with us*. The sky is a time machine of the universe. Tonight, my aim is to describe the world to you in new and more accurate ways. Chance itself is subject to law. There is no doubt, no doubt whatsoever, of this truth. That is because all laws of nature are laws of chance in disguise."

"What a muddle," said Heinrich. "We are subject to a strict nature subject to strict chance."

The children shushed him.

As Père Bruno spoke, Hannah felt as if she were walking across the painted ceiling of the Vel d'Hiv into a dark sky which turned out to be the most reliable witness to one's life. In her suitcase was Gertrud's copy of Proust and a manuscript from Benji, things given to her for safekeeping. Benji's manuscript was only a few pages, written on various cut-open envelopes and other scraps, paper being so precious to him. This courteous man with his odd staccato laugh, she thought. These true and faithful friends without whom she herself might have lost hope. The dark sky seemed to give her memories back to her, as if entrusting her with her own self. She saw the forest behind the Lecturer's office. She saw the yellow-brown paintings of plants and telescopes on the walls of a Berlin train station. All the little Paris rooms over eight years. Her father's paranoia before he died, when he had begged her to climb up on a chair and take away the clock. Disjointed memories which hardly seemed to exist in the same earth or the same century, let alone the same life. Yet there they were, filling her thoughts as if they were a single image.

The ship was insignificant, and its passengers even more so, but hadn't they moved heaven and earth to reach this moment? Hadn't they, by chance or fortune or advantage, taken the places of others? Where in this world could memory or sorrow persist, except in their heads and hearts? Things pass away but the fact that we live, she told herself, that any of us appear at all, is also a truth of our world.

"Tomorrow evening," Père Bruno was saying, "we shall discuss the sea. The laws of physics are vividly apparent as we look upon the ocean. Children, let me leave you with one last instruction. Tomorrow when the sun rises, I encourage you to look up at the sky and take note that, the higher one looks, the darker the blue you perceive. This is because, if we travelled higher and higher, less and less air would exist around us. If we were to rise so high we escaped the earth's atmosphere, what colour would the sky be? Even drenched in the full power of the sun, in its full luminosity, the sky around you would be dark. Richly, brilliantly dark. The sun-swept atmosphere would be the colour of that which we call the night."

ooooo

My father said that I could go ahead and untie the string that ran from these rooms to the Sea. Isn't it true, he added, that only those alive in the present can undo the knot?

Crying, I said I didn't know.

Bee was my heart. She was the gift I neither understood nor deserved.

I could hear the tide against the rocks. He was delirious and soon he would leave me.

One more story, Lina. The last one.

I searched the breadth of my memory. It was the eighth morning, I said, when she awoke.

My father smiled. *Of all the parts, this one is my favourite.*

∞∞∞∞

On the eighth morning, Hannah woke early. Morning seemed to travel in from the edges of the world. Bermuda was expected that afternoon, and Staten Island within three days. New York, hardly imagined, was approaching.

She had a letter in her hands. The last time she'd seen him, Walter Benjamin had given her these papers. "It's not meant to be published," he had said. "It will be misunderstood."

The essay was divided into twenty sections, each no more than a paragraph or two. It was a series of moves and countermoves, the slow turning of a misshapen key, whose hopeless hope, she now believed, was to pause, however briefly, the game of life which was no game.

There is a story told, Benji begins, of a chess-playing puppet, an automaton whose actions determine the outcome of a game it always wins. The automaton, controlled by strings, is in the service of a man curled beneath a table which itself is falsely transparent. This automaton, he writes, might be thought of as the forces of capital and labour which drive human affairs, and the string-puller under the table, shrivelled and concealed, is theology. Benji has chosen to face the automaton and play a game he cannot win. As in all games of strategy, the field of play is the opponent's mind.

"I don't want these pages to be misunderstood."

But, Hannah argued to herself, what if everything we leave behind can only be misunderstood? Isn't that the nature of anything that outlives its maker? And even Benji, who wished language to do what the human mind could not, and transcend itself, could not escape this outcome.

When she was joined by Wolkowski and Hirsch, and later by Frau Kotzin and Père Bruno, Hannah asked these questions of them. They decided they would read the pages aloud together.

Raisa, Clem, Jentje and the other children joined, filling in the spaces between them. The ocean was everywhere nearby.

The essay was not only Benji's last surviving work, but the testament of a friend who described hope where he experienced none. Hannah could no longer foresee who would be the one to comprehend, and no longer trusted that it would be her.

The expressions on her companions' faces lay in shadow. Heinrich read aloud the second section. *There is a secret agreement between past generations and the present one. Our coming was expected on earth.*

Had Benji himself wandered into their gathering by chance, as if the SS *Guiné* were a ship for which he held the winning voucher?

Hannah leaned towards him, his voice:

Benji takes the empty chair. His pinkish shirt, a favourite, is rumpled and stained with chocolate. He is not seasick but is deeply concerned that soon he will be. Hannah suspects he is hiding something, smuggling a bird under his sleeve to ensure that the irrational will have the last laugh.

We have a raft of ideas about the future, Benji is saying to Frau Kotzin, but rarely do we envy those born after us. The only thing we know with certainty about the future is that it contains our death. Thus our image of possible happiness is inseparable from the lives we see around us, and the present in which we live. I submit that our image of happiness is in fact the hope of redemption, therefore redemption can only come in our own time. Redemption is an act of necessity for every living generation.

The gathered listeners ponder this.

"But what does the fellow mean by 'redemption'?" asks Wolkowski.

Benji, having realized that his true opponent is the theologian hidden under the chess table, and thus himself, is looking at everyone sideways. He offers a fragment of one of Gershom Scholem's poems. *My wing is ready for flight. I would like to turn back. If I stayed timeless time I would have little luck* . . . His glasses are sprayed by the ocean. Shaking out a handkerchief, he tries to force the chair to grant him comfort, which is impossible.

Père Bruno asks for paragraph six to be read again. Heinrich obliges. Benji's words, clear on the surface, dart away, suddenly reappearing like a breeze behind Hannah.

Benji asks her to find out how to prevent nausea, of which he is morbidly afraid.

It is Hirsch who answers. "Turn your chairs a little," he says, "and face the direction of motion." That Hirsch, the landlocked cattle dealer, should have this wisdom is comical to all the others. "Just focus on the horizon," he insists, "and you won't get sick."

Benji tests his forehead for fever and stares fixedly at some distant point. He says, I know what you feel at this moment because I feel it, too. But in all times, and not just ours, catastrophe is the rule, not the exception. This state of emergency is one we hoped would bypass us, and so we failed to react. Don't lose sight of this as we turn history over and over in our hands. Or, rather, as you do, since I am dead and thus indisposed.

"Isn't it just as the poor man writes?" sighs Frau Kotzin. "In our country, even the dead aren't safe."

Hirsch says, "Not safe from that clown we've all had to flee."

"I can't really follow these words," says Clem. "I mean, it goes in circles, doesn't it? I'm fourteen already, and even I can't understand."

Hannah smiles, and Frau Kotzin sighs, "Heavens."

Nobody remarks on the fact that Benji has wandered away from their gathering, drawn to higher reaches of the ship in order to attain a different view. His shoes are ill-suited for such attempts, Hannah thinks, and if he falls he cannot swim.

Père Bruno muses, "It is true that if Bruno were placed inside a sealed room and dropped through the cosmos, he would not know if he were falling or rising. The reason is simple. There is no gravitational field in his immediate vicinity, and the same would be true for the chew toy he happens to be chasing. Bruno and his toy would be in uniform motion and therefore appear to be 'at rest.'"

Precisely, Benji says. A fragment torn from its context is free-floating in space . . . But his words drift. He is too far away now for Hannah to hear him.

"The past is the shape of the world into which I was born," says Heinrich. "Benji is saying that our lives become the shape of the past's fulfillment." And here her fine husband makes a big circle with his two lovely hands. "Our lives are the redemption of the past, in other words. And future generations will come of age in the shape we have left behind." He relights his pipe with one hand while the other keeps circling. "Each redemption is short-lived and weak, but this weakness turns out to be its power. Each generation must enact a new redemption. This is the only basis for hope. Benji was in love with contradictions. How does he put it? Weakness is redemption's divinity."

"Weakness as the form of divinity," repeats Wolkowski, doubtful. "I cannot agree. When I was a child, I visited the Orient with my father. On the walls of a thousand-year-old palace in Kampuchea, I saw paintings depicting an ancient Sanskrit epic. This mural enclosed the viewer within four walls. The painting or the epic was always happening, happening again, and the viewer, no matter who or in what century, remained surrounded."

It's like this, Benji says, having returned to their circle. It's taken me forty-something years to see the things most decisive to me, and now when at last I perceive them, well, bad luck. I stretched my hand out to write the answers, but as soon as the words began to appear, my eyes opened, and I awoke. The attempt to breathe something into life again is the root cause of our sadness.

Hannah found she could not catch every word of the group's recitation. A wave would crash and blot out half a sentence, or ringing voices would erupt around them and drown them out. Meanwhile, Benji could not help but pace. He would pivot and come back with his peculiar gait, seeming to walk without advancing.

Before the group dispersed, he offered his light and lovely smile. He said, What is paradoxical about everything that is justly called beautiful is that it appears.

It turned out that it was not the season for oranges in Bermuda. Instead, crates of watermelons were brought aboard, shocking as bright green meadows. The shipwrecked Chinese and Javanese came on deck to help cleave the watermelons into wedges. As they worked, seagulls materialized out of the sky, squawking and shouting.

Someone, Hannah thought, will slip and break their neck. A tragicomic end to their heroic escape.

Whole faces disappeared into melons. Shells were flung overboard. For the last ten days, passengers had eaten mostly bread and potatoes, and drunk only stale water. Who knew that plenitude could unite them? Men and women huddled over their wedges to fend off seagulls. Children took voracious bites, as if plunging headfirst into bowls, then tossed each wedge aside to get their next piece. The seagulls dived to catch the discarded pieces in mid-air.

She and Heinrich ate so much Hannah knew there would be intestinal consequences. Meanwhile, the shipwrecked Javanese and Chinese seemed to be making a world of their own. One was juggling watermelons, which seemed to pause in the blue sky before being caught as softly as infants and flung up once more. The passengers laughed at these impossible sights. A few wept, unable to make sense of a joyful act in the middle of the ocean, in the midst of an ugly, unspeakable war.

Jentje remained subdued, staying near the Javanese sailors with whom he could speak Dutch. "On this steep shore," someone sang, "cliffs rise a thousand miles. The river drinks from ten thousand streams. Dark waves contest and surge. Here on earth, all living things contend . . ."

Jentje's father had been born in the Dutch East Indies. As a young man, the father had left Jakarta and settled in the Netherlands, in a village a stone's throw from the North Sea. Now, it was as if Jentje found himself on the original shore, returned to a place that did not know of his father's death.

Finally the deck was clean, and the crew, one by one, disappeared down the stairs. Heinrich, Wolkowski and Frau Kotzin gathered again to continue interpreting Benji's essay, eventually joined by Clem and Père Bruno.

"The brief flare of illumination," Wolkowski was explaining, "arises when images of one's own time are struck like a match against the time of an earlier era. We are the match and they are the ground. One day we will be the ground, and the future will strike its match against us. Sequences of events do not succeed each other like the beads of a rosary, history is not empty time waiting to be filled. History is the time of the now, perforated with fragments of redemption. Isn't that what your friend here, your old Benji, is trying to tell us?" he said to Heinrich.

In the corner, Jentje sat so deep in shadow that no one except Hannah noticed him, as if he had become part of the metal plating of the ship.

The seagulls had risen en masse and now appeared like storm clouds.

"I forgot to answer yesterday's question," Père Bruno said, as if continuing his lessons for the children. "What if Bruno were to chase light while running at the speed of light? The answer is this: light waves would appear frozen in space and time. Perfectly still. Bruno, as a result, could not know if he were moving."

"I knew it!" said Clem. "That's what I thought because, if two trains were running at exactly the same speed, and the windows were facing each other, how would you know that you were moving at all? You're in suspension."

Hannah sensed Benji walking away from her.

You could say farewell to someone in this way, you could let them leave, and so return to the necessity of day-to-day living. There were debts of love, she thought, that became memory, never to be repaid.

"I promised myself that no one would make us leave Europe," Père Bruno was saying. "Yet here we are."

The day after tomorrow they would dock first on the quarantine pier, and then at pier eight on Staten Island. Everything she and Heinrich owned fit into one suitcase, easily carried in one hand. They had twenty-five dollars. On deck, Jentje cried silently and the other adults continued to airily debate and discuss, as if the only way to get through was to ask one question followed by another, without the possibility of meeting an answer.

When Hannah was a child her mother used to play a game, pretending that she was a stranger. Her mother would claim not to know her, laugh that she had changed, that some aberration had taken over face and soul. One day the game went on and on, never-ending. At last, distraught, wild, she'd gripped her mother's two hands, crying over and over: "But I am your child, I am your Hannah!" She repeated this over and over, even after her mother ended the game.

Now Heinrich was looking at the sea and she was looking past all the other passengers towards Heinrich. Everyone would scatter when the SS *Guiné* arrived at harbour. A decade ago, she had written to the Lecturer, *My path is wide and it runs through the world* . . . but she had not really believed these words. Back then, they had been a way to take the smallest step, and then the next, away from him. Evening was arriving, merging sea and sky. This instant felt like the shell of an infinite memory, of two mirrors facing one another and surprising themselves into an endless labyrinth. She went to sit beside Jentje. The sea slowly rocked them on its breathing.

"I left everyone behind," he told her. "I'm alone."

Yes, she told him, and no. Yes and no. Like the tide against the shore. And she held him.

Lulled by her voice, the child fell asleep under the gaze of the sky.

∞∞∞

My father left a few minutes before midnight. I felt some part of my own self leaving to make the journey with him.

Until late the next morning I sat beside him, and the neighbours took care of us. They made arrangements while I let hours and minutes fall away. Don't look back, I told him. Don't grieve. You did everything you could to prepare me for the voyage.

The neighbours lit offerings. They brought me food to eat and tea to soothe me. If not for the others, what would I have done? They continued so that I could hold still.

Days later, from the window, I saw a ship appear on the horizon. Around me were the table, bed, five chairs, the bookshelf, the red curtains. Starlight came in from the north and west, and met where I stood in the middle of the floor.

I went down the stairs past the hot water room. There was no line, only a boy and his mother on a bench outside the door.

I'd seen the boy before, in the rooms around West Gate. I recognized him as one of the children who foraged on the beach, towing in logs and whole trees, all kinds of species which couldn't always be identified.

The mother noticed the three books in my hand. "*The Great Lives of Voyagers*," she said, bursting into a smile. "I haven't seen those in years."

I paused. There was a hat on the woman's knee, decorated with feathers which shivered when she moved.

"We had them in our school library," she continued. "Number 1 is Zheng He, and number 23 is Ibn Battuta."

"Ibn who?" said the boy.

I held up the covers for him to see. "It was a series of adventure books." A bag lay open beside the boy, and I said, "A ship has arrived. Are you also leaving?"

"Not yet. We need more time to prepare."

Starlight in the passageway curved around us. I already knew the answer but still I asked, "Where did you come from?"

"Foshan."

The books sat in my hands. "Here. Take these."

"No, no, no," she said. "Those things are rare. I haven't seen that series in a decade."

We could hear the boiler of the hot water room coming to life, a giant churning.

"It's okay," I said. "I don't need them anymore."

The mother's touch on my wrist was soft. "Let me give you something in return."

I knew there was nothing they owned which they didn't need, so I refused. But she lifted the hat from her knees. "Take this. No, really. I gathered these feathers on the road during our journey. This one comes from a night egret and this one from a baitouweng—"

"A baitouweng," I repeated, savouring the sound. Those birds had been common in Foshan but I had forgotten.

"One morning, near the beginning, all the birds seemed to go north, do you remember? My son was still small when Daybreak happened and we were forced to leave. On the ships it's important to have a hat. Just remember to tie it under your chin. I sewed a ribbon here, see? You're moving on, aren't you? Do you have a voucher already . . ."

We talked about the ships, about rumours we'd heard and maps we'd seen. I told them there was a comfortable room upstairs with kind neighbours where they could live until they were ready to continue. We said goodbye.

I continued down the stairs, the hat in my hands.

Lina, Lina, I heard, but it was only the wind through the building. My wrist ached as if someone were holding it fast. I was certain I would see bruises all along my arm, but when I looked there was nothing, only the hat and the feathers, endlessly moving.

I know now that however far I travel, no matter how I wait, I will not see my mother, my aunt and Wei again. All these years, I have not accepted this truth. Now, as I put these pages together, as the sound of the tide rises and falls, something comes to rest in me, like a circle drawn once and forever in the sand.

Sometimes we travel centuries in the hope that we might return. After grief, my mother tells me, after acceptance, time comes together once more.

I waited with dozens of others on the shore. The sun slipped below the horizon and a silver moon climbed the sky. The night thickened and dissolved. Little by little, morning came. Behind me the Sea emerged like a thousand pieces of coloured glass. I searched for our building and the red curtains of our windows. When figures appeared on the roof, I thought it was the neighbours looking for me one last time. They were too far away to be clearly seen, but I lifted my hand and felt the breeze against it. A small boat came, nearly full. Two sisters, who had slept beside me on the beach, called to me. The grip of their hands on my wrists unlocked my memories. They pulled me into the boat and made a space between them. The vessel scratched against the shallows, and it pulled away. I didn't look towards the horizon, but kept my eyes on the buildings, unable to believe they were growing smaller. We passed the cottage of Gao Lisheng, who siphoned electricity from the ships. We passed a man in a cloak sitting in a barge, which drifted near to us. There was a teenaged boy with him, holding down the old man's hat, which would otherwise have blown away, and they sat talking. The boy recited something, a poem or a prayer, but I was already too far away to hear.

Time has filled these pages. Now I must create the words that memory could not retain.

I looked up and saw the path curving into the cemetery. It was high up, the highest point of the Sea, and the road was lined with tall pines that had been planted long ago. I could see a parade moving through the mist, a long procession with blue and yellow banners, whose music I couldn't hear but which I knew created the path and set the course. At the very front of the procession I saw a girl wearing a hat with feathers. I saw the path fold and fall towards me, and I knew that on the other side of the buildings, boats were arriving from the north, and the newly arrived would search for a room in which to recover and begin again. Most would stay only a few days or at most a week, trading for what they needed, and leaving other things behind. I knew that everywhere people were being carried to lives they couldn't imagine. The hat on my knees, decorated with such care, gave me comfort.

When I had said goodbye to Jupiter, he had asked me, out of the blue, "Lina, what year is it now?" I had searched for an answer. Finally I told him, "I wrote it down somewhere. If we can find that piece of paper, we'll know." Then the neighbours and I sat at the window and waited, watching the tide go out. It grew late and one by one they fell asleep. When the time for my departure came, I chose not to wake them from their dreams.

"There aren't enough days," Jupiter had said earlier that evening, "to finish the story." How, for instance, Du Fu had been captured by a rebel army. How the great poet had re-entered Chang'an, a prisoner among a thousand prisoners, and seen the imperial city in a horrific state of siege. How his family, hearing no word for two years, thought him dead. How all Du Fu's hair turned pure white, as if he were taking up a new disguise, and how on a moonless night he escaped the rebel garrison. He shuffled out, leaning on a cane. *No one knew anything of the old man, only that he came from the frontier.* He walked for two months, through abandoned villages and unimaginable battlefields. He was carried in farmer's carts, and slept in ruined villas, beneath stone horses and torn paintings. One day, he arrived at the emperor's court-in-exile and, upon his arrival, the emperor himself put his hands on Du Fu's elbows. He raised the poet up from the ground.

Is it really true?

It's true. The emperor rewarded him with a place at court. It was everything Du Fu had ever wanted. He became a Reminder in the Chancellery Division.

What's a Reminder?

A person whose role is to correct breaches in statecraft. Once upon a time it meant something, but by Du Fu's time, and without his realizing it, the role had become an artifact. No more than a symbol.

The sky is such a crisp metallic gold. Jupiter thinks that if he were to knock on the sky with his hand, it might crack like a plate.

So then what happened?

He wants to tell her everything, but her boat has already come loose from the shore. Already it is headed for open sea.

Jupiter said, Du Fu stumbled, of course. It was wartime and the world was in disarray. He was imprisoned. He barely survived with his life intact.

And then what?

Jupiter didn't want to tell her that Du Fu buried another child. That he quit the court, grew poorer and poorer, and wandered further and further from home, and his poems, which had seemed so much about the present, about the war, family and the everyday, began to escape. They slipped free from the loop of time.

Only the faintest outline of her boat is still visible. The cargo ship in the distance waits as a line of vessels approaches it.

Years have folded together but Jupiter remembers the evening Wui Shin and Lina arrived. The girl had put so many questions to her father. He had heard them talking late into the night, weaving things together as if each moment had the ability to summon another moment, past or future, even if people themselves must forget. Hearing their voices had reminded him of his own past. He remembered, or perhaps foretold, a boat swaying on the river between cliffs that rose like a giant staircase, in a channel that was overflowing and disappearing.

It is morning now. He remembers his wife and the two children he lost. Soon my home will appear on the bend of the river, he thinks, and I'll finally disembark. Any day now, I'll touch land. His eyes are heavy. Slowly they close. Tall pines wave above him and he follows the voice of his child. Sleep comes. He feels it take his hand.

ACKNOWLEDGEMENTS

The Book of Records, guided by histories, letters, philosophies, poetry, mathematics and physics, is a work of the imagination. I am indebted to the library, and to librarians, archivists and translators, for their companionship and light—they are the steadfast keepers of the building made of time.

On Du Fu, I'm grateful for the countless hours spent in the company of David Hinton's *The Selected Poems of Tu Fu*; Wong May's *In the Same Light: 200 Poems for Our Century from the Migrants and Exiles of the Tang Dynasty*; William Hung's *Tu Fu: China's Greatest Poet*; and *The Complete Poetry of Du Fu*, translated and edited by Stephen Owen. The typewritten pages which Hannah pockets in Lisbon are inspired by William Hung's wonderful prose translations of "The Autumn Gale Tears off My Thatched Roof" and "Drunk."

On Benedict Spinoza, I am indebted to *The Collected Works of Spinoza*, Volumes 1 and 2, edited and translated by Edwin Curley, as well as Curley's *Behind the Geometrical Method: A Reading of Spinoza's Ethics*; *Spinoza's Ethics—Translated by George Eliot*, edited by Clare Carlisle; Steven Nadler's *Spinoza: A Life*; Jonathan I. Israel's *Spinoza, Life and Legacy*; Karl Jaspers's *From the Great Philosophers, Volume II: Spinoza*, edited by Hannah Arendt; and, relatedly, René Descartes's *Discourse on the Method*, translated by Laurence J. Lafleur. The deeply moving catalogue of 391 books owned by Spinoza, which were sold at auction upon his death at the age of forty-four, can be found at Museum Het Spinozahaus in Rijnsburg.

On Hannah Arendt, I cherish Elisabeth Young-Bruehl's *Hannah Arendt: For Love of the World*, a biography I have lived with for over two decades. I turned often to Arendt's *Love and Saint Augustine*;

Rahel Varnhagen: The Life of a Jewish Woman; *The Origins of Totalitarianism*; *The Human Condition*; *Men in Dark Times*; *Between Past and Future*; and the writings collected in *Essays in Understanding: 1930–1954*; Marion Kaplan's *Hitler's Jewish Refugees: Hope and Anxiety in Portugal*; Hannah Arendt and Martin Heidegger, *Letters: 1925–1975*, edited by Ursula Ludz and translated by Andrew Shields; *Within Four Walls: The Correspondence Between Hannah Arendt and Heinrich Blücher, 1936–1968*, edited by Lotte Kohler and translated by Peter Constantine; Karl Jaspers and Hannah Arendt, *Correspondence 1926–1969*, edited by Lotte Kohler and Hans Saner, and translated by Robert and Rita Kimber. The letter attributed to Hannah's first husband is translated by Samantha Rose Hill, and can be found in her excellent critical biography, *Hannah Arendt*. Contemplating the light of the south, Hannah thinks of Vincent van Gogh's August 18, 1888, letter to his brother, Theo. While in the Pyrenees, she recalls lines of poetry from *Hyperion* by Friedrich Höderlin, here translated by Ross Benjamin. The reference to the stranger from the frontier—in a fragment floating loose from time—is from "Tlön, Uqbar, Orbis Tertius" by Jorge Luis Borges, published in *Labyrinths* and translated by James E. Irby. Immanuel Kant's warning on Spinoza appears in his *Prolegomena to Any Future Metaphysics*, translated by Gary Hatfield. I hope that Lisa Fittko's extraordinary testament, *Escape Through the Pyrenees*, translated by David Koblick, will one day come back into print; it belongs in our collective memory. Hannah's recounting of a stone thrown in the air is drawn from Spinoza's October 1674 letter to G.H. Schuller. The essay Hannah begins on the Lisbon typewriter will become, "Franz Kafka: A Revaluation," published in *Partisan Review* in 1944; her correspondence with Salomon Adler-Rudel is available at HannahArendt.net in the original German. In the Chiado, she picks up Fernando Pessoa's *The Book of Disquiet*, here translated by Richard Zenith. I have made a seismic deviation from history which cannot go unnoted: Hannah Arendt was able to obtain an emergency visa valid not only for herself and Heinrich, but also—although it was agonizingly delayed—for her mother. Martha Arendt-Beerwald fled Königsberg in 1939, carrying gold coins she had camouflaged as buttons, joining Hannah and Heinrich briefly in Paris and, later on, in Montauban; the sale of the coins helped all three survive for a brief time. When her visa was finally processed, Martha escaped France via a different route, and sailed separately from Lisbon to New York in June 1941.

The epigraph that opens each volume of *The Great Lives of Voyagers* is from Book XV of *The Annals,* when Tacitus recounts the death of Seneca. Hannah, meditating on friendship, thinks of Seneca's *Moral Letters to Lucilius,* specifically Letter IX; the first instance is translated by Richard M. Gummere, and the second by Robin Campbell; Baruch, twice eavesdropping on Clara Maria's Latin class, hears Letters II and XXVIII, translated here by Gummere. The song, "Fidanico de Yasimin," which Esther sings and Baruch recalls, can be heard on the beautiful album *Sephardic Folk Songs,* sung by Gloria Levy, with notes and translation by M.M. Benardete. Clara Maria sings from the Song of Solomon 4:6. The true name of Jan Rieuwertsz's bookshop was in't Martelaarsboek (In the Martyrs' Book), and wonderful descriptions of this and other bookstores in the Netherlands, and of Amsterdam in Spinoza's time, can be found in Andrew Pettegree and Arthur der Weduwen's *The Bookshop of the World: Making and Trading Books in the Dutch Golden Age* and Simon Schama's wondrous *Rembrandt's Eyes.* I am indebted to Huib Modderkolk's *There's a War Going On But No One Can See It,* translated by Elizabeth Manton. The book stall in which Du Fu does not find himself is named in honour of Bei Dao's book of poetry, *The Rose of Time,* translated by Eliot Weinberger. Baruch is comforted by Maimonides, *The Guide for the Perplexed,* translated here by M. Friedländer.

I am indebted to Brook Ziporyn's two immaculate and soulful translations, *Zhuangzi: The Complete Writings* and *Laozi: Daodejing;*

to Gia-Fu Feng and Jane English's translation of the Tao Te Ching; and to Burton Watson's *The Complete Works of Chuang Tzu*. Bertolt Brecht's "Legend of the origin of the book *Tao Te Ching* on Lao-tze's road into exile" can be found in *The Collected Poems of Bertolt Brecht*, translated and edited by Tom Kuhn and David Constantine. The neighbours, when discussing the frame in art and literature, refer to lines written by Italo Calvino in the days before his passing. These lines are quoted by Esther Calvino in *Under the Jaguar Sun*; Bee chances upon these lines on the website Calvino Chinese Station, which collects works by Italo Calvino translated into Chinese. I have drawn Hannah's reflections on "hopeless hope" from *Hope and Despair: A Writer's Journey in Israel and Palestine* by the remarkable poet and scholar David Shulman. The lines from Marcel Proust's *Time Regained* are from the 1981 translation by Andreas Mayor and Terence Kilmartin, later revised by D.J. Enright. The neighbours—who say that "we are to God as waves are to the ocean"—quote Clare Carlisle's brilliant introduction to George Eliot's 1856 translation of Spinoza's *Ethics*. A guiding light throughout the writing of this novel has been the work of Walter Benjamin, in particular: writings collected in *Illuminations*, edited by Hannah Arendt, and *Reflections*, edited by Peter Demetz; and *The Correspondence of Walter Benjamin 1910–1940*, edited and annotated by Gershom Scholem and Theodor W. Adorno, and translated by Manfred R. Jacobson and Evelyn M. Jacobson. Benjamin's postcard to Hannah Arendt dates to July 8, 1940; his dream of the letter *d* appears in an April 15, 1939, letter to Gretel Adorno. On November 2, 1939, he wrote to Gisèle Freund: "And under these circumstances, happiness equals hope for me." Words from his final letter can be found on the Walter Benjamin memorial in Portbou, Spain. I am grateful to Ian Fowler, Maps Curator and Geospatial Librarian at The New York Public Library, who showed me not only maps of lighthouses on the Chinese coast, but also the Cheonhado, the *Map of All Under Heaven*. In this Korean circular map, the place names of the inner continent, drawn from history, are considered known and real; the place names of the outer continent, drawn from myths and stories, are considered unknown and fictional; and the whole is surrounded by an unnamed outer sea, which bears no names.

The Book of Records, although bound by history, dwells in the moments when biographical certainties surrounding Du Fu, Spinoza and Arendt are non-existent, scarce or blurred. In this way, I wished to explore not only individual lives—but the times themselves, timelessness, and namelessness.

The words that lodge in Hannah's mind and memory, "In order to extend life and preserve civilization, we are obliged to rescue one another," are from Yu Qiuyu's *The Book of Mountains and Rivers*, translated by Jeremy Tiang.

ooooo

My gratitude and love to Jill Bialosky, Charles Buchan, Sarah Chalfant, David Wright Faladé, Julia Foulkes, Rawi Hage, Lynn Henry, Samantha Hill, Karolina Hübner, Jonas Hassen Khemiri, Jacqueline Ko, Bella Lacey, Catherine Leroux, Melanie Little, Nara Milanich, Angelica Nuzzo, Irene Flunser Pimentel, Moriel Rothman-Zecher, Josephine Rowe, Philippe Sands, Justin Steinberg, and Eliot Weinberger who read these pages or who spoke tirelessly with me about Arendt, Spinoza, Du Fu, and buildings made of time; to my students and fellow writers at Brooklyn College at The City University of New York; to my beloved friends at The Cullman Center at The New York Public Library. Thank you for all the conversations we have shared, which have given me a home in days of sorrow and joy. In memory of my mother and my father. *All real living is meeting.*

And to my beloved Rawi, the storyteller. Always.

CREDITS AND PERMISSIONS

ABOUT THE AUTHOR

Madeleine Thien is the author of the story collection *Simple Recipes* (2001) and three previous novels: *Certainty* (2006), *Dogs at the Perimeter* (2011) and *Do Not Say We Have Nothing* (2016). *Do Not Say We Have Nothing* was shortlisted for the Booker Prize, the Women's Prize for Fiction and the Folio Prize, and won the Governor General's Literary Award for Fiction, among other honours. Her books have been translated into twenty-five languages, and her stories and essays have appeared in *The New Yorker*, *Granta*, *Times Literary Supplement*, *The New York Review of Books* and elsewhere. As a librettist, she created *Chinatown*, a full-length opera by Alice Ping Yee Ho and Paul Yee, and collaborates on a range of chamber works. In 2024, she received the Writers' Trust Engel Findley Award, honouring a writer in mid-career. Born in Vancouver, Madeleine lives in Montreal and teaches part-time at Brooklyn College at The City University of New York.